"You can do  because I don't kn_____. _____ me." Gemma pulled on the reins and struggled to lead her over. "Swim the other way!" She pressed her face against Lolly's soggy cheek, not knowing how else to help. Surrendering to wild fright would only take them under. She closed her eyes, listening. *"Panic is never useful,"* she heard Nani say. *"Stay calm. Slow your thoughts. Focus."*

Newfound grit spurred Gemma's words. "Get us back to the bank, sweet girl. That's all there is to it."

Like a miracle, Lolly pulled forward—finally swimming in the right direction. But as soon as safety appeared, it vanished. The river opened wide and snatched Gemma away, as if a sea monster had grabbed hold and yanked her from below. She flailed in darkness, lunging for Lolly, whirling in all directions. She pushed upward, desperate to climb toward light. Desperate for air.

Everything went black before the crown of Gemma's head ruptured the surface, her lungs bursting open. A bloom of brilliance filtered through her eyelids—the sun, ageless as truth, beckoning her return. *Am I dead or alive?* Head bobbing, Gemma eked out a pitiful cry for help. She couldn't take in enough air to do any better than that.

And then she plunged under again, the water churning and twisting like Mama's old clothes washer. She thought about the branches and logs lurking below—anyone pinned under would never see light again. *I'm a goner.* When stars shot across her eyes, she figured that was it. *My secret is sinking with me. But please, Creator, don't let Lolly die.*

Praise for *A RIVER FOR GEMMA*

"*A RIVER FOR GEMMA* is a poignant and heartfelt story with a propulsive mystery flowing just underneath its surface. The beauty of its relationships makes you want to hold this family, and the people they love, close forever. Alexander created a world I did not want to leave. I couldn't put this book down..."

~ *Audrey Burges, award-winning author and humorist*

".... rich, rewarding and deliciously raucous, exploring the themes of mental health, faith and how loss is, indeed, the cost of love. Good books convince us of such deep truths, and Alexander succeeds in doing just that."

~*Bob Welch, award-winning journalist and author*

"*A RIVER FOR GEMMA* brings us an unconventionally bright and daring heroine to challenge our ingrained perspectives on disability and capability. A much-needed story for our times, compassionate and well told."

~*Ellen Notbohm, award-winning author*

"...Full of engaging characters, and beautiful descriptive Oregon scenery vividly capturing the changes in seasons, *A RIVER FOR GEMMA* is an uplifting, hopeful, and a delightfully escapist read."

~*Lainey Cameron, best-selling author*

"*A RIVER FOR GEMMA* offers a hefty dose of drama and tension with a superb conclusion. With a thread of mystery, this story keeps readers turning pages."

~*Carmen Peone, award-winning author*

A River for Gemma

a novel

by

Debra Whiting Alexander

A River for Gemma

Cover Art by *Kim Mendoza*

The Wild Rose Press, Inc.
PO Box 708
Adams Basin, NY 14410-0708
Visit us at www.thewildrosepress.com

Publishing History
First Edition, 2021
Trade Paperback ISBN 978-1-5092-3406-6
Digital ISBN 978-1-5092-3407-3

Published in the United States of America

Dedication

For Eliza,
love you more

Acknowledgments

So many people help spark a story into being.

My thanks go first to Maureen Thrash, who prompted the beginning of this novel after we shared a heart-stopping encounter, not unlike Gemma's.

To Katelyn Kelley for early inspiration, to Nicole Skinner, Carmen Peone, Melissa Lind, and Deb Holm Ritchey for cowgirl wisdom and feedback. To my husband Bob, for believing in this story, and to Audrey Burges, Lainey Cameron, Janice Carr, Shane Hawks, Lisa Montanaro, Ellen Notbohm, Maureen Thrash, Carlton Whiting, and Kathryn Wilson. Every revision grew stronger because of you. Any errors in known facts or misrepresentations are mine alone.

I also want to acknowledge The Cow Creek Band of Umpqua Tribe of Indians, who Gemma draws precious strength and wisdom from.

I've had the privilege of working with a wide-range of individuals with disabilities, all of whom helped inspire this story. However, as with any group or culture, there are as many differences as there are people. The fictional characters of Gemma and Walter by no means represent all.

Special thanks to editor, Ally Robertson, cover designer, Kim Mendoza, and their colleagues at The Wild Rose Press.

Finally, to my granddaughter, Eliza, who inspired Nani's heart for Gemma. This novel would be a far dimmer shade of itself without her.

The last word of gratitude belongs to you, the reader. Thank you for creating the time and space in your life for this story.

Chapter One

The Holding Tree

"We live, we die, and like the grass and trees, renew ourselves from the soft earth of the grave. Stones crumble and decay, faiths grow old and they are forgotten, but new beliefs are born. The faith of the villages is dust now...but it will grow again...like the trees."
~Chief Joseph, Nez Perce (1840-1904)

She nestled on the ground with her knees pressed to the grave, the warm earth like balm to her wild-eyed worry. There would be a reckoning for what she had done, but she didn't care. Sometimes a dream was worth chasing.

Lowering her face, she steadied her eyes on the timeworn marker when *poof!* She pitched back, her whole body quailing. A little soul awakened from the grave and touched her flesh. She swore it did. The moment prickled down her spine like a tiny pinecone.

But she knew such a claim would only be jabber for gossip—or worse. Because the world would not accept the truth about Gemma Porter—even though it radiated from her like Creator's flaming medallion in the sky.

Yet the truth was simple. Gemma had different

abilities, not "disabilities."

And it was Gemma who sparked a chain of miracles that year.

But most people living in the small town of Sugar Creek, Oregon, didn't believe in other worldly dimensions, or in supernatural events, and certainly not in ghosts. It was 2018 after all. Gemma and her mother even had doubts about the afterlife—though Nani seemed to doubt that less.

So, at age twenty-six, when something ghostlike happened to Gemma in Luper Pioneer Cemetery, she knew it was anything but ordinary. Because when it happened, her mind expanded at dizzying speed. And she knew it wasn't because she grew up in special education, or because they had measured her brain and said it was different. It happened, she believed, because she cherished the pioneer babies buried beneath her feet, because since age five she had tended their graves with love.

And that's what Nani thought too.

The air lay stagnant over Sugar Creek; thick as mud that morning. The humidity so oppressive, Gemma's thick ebony waves, flashing streaks of periwinkle on the ends, all but coiled up to her ears.

When Gemma and Nani climbed into the hollowed center of a deep-rooted Oregon maple and sat, the sturdy, muscular limbs encircled them in a craggy bowl. Sweat poured off their brows, but Gemma didn't mind—her face sunny with joy no matter what the weather. Through the portly branches, pennies of sunshine spattered the rows of gravestones surrounding them. A living tree among the dead. Its roots most certainly wrapped the deceased with its energy—or

2

perhaps the lost souls sustained it with theirs.

The massive leaves formed a dramatic, towering canopy over them. A glorious umbrella of green. And the view, out of this world. Lush emerald fields of rye grass and acres of Oregon hazelnut orchards surrounded them like a symphony. It was the perfect place for a picnic.

The old maple smelled good too. Gemma didn't know what to call it, except to say it was a cheery smell. From the first day Nani took Gemma to Luper, she had enjoyed herself.

"Is there room for everything?" Gemma had asked at five years old.

"Of course," Nani said, hoisting her up. "Our tree can hold everything."

"Did cowgirls ever sit here? Cowgirls like us?"

"I like to imagine they did, yes."

"This tree is old like you, Nani."

"Older, Tink. Everything in Luper Cemetery is way older than your Graham Cracker."

Even now as an adult, Gemma took delight in being called "Tink"—the nickname she earned learning how to knit. The idea that she need only tink back a row of stitches to correct a mistake filled her with endless optimism. "Anything can be fixed as long as you're a good tinker," she liked to say.

The desire to wear princess tiaras on top her long bouncing waves sprouted then too, a fashion statement that made her the target for more bullies as she grew older. She pretended the teasing didn't matter anymore. But it wasn't true.

"You try to protect Gemma too much," Mama told Nani once.

"I teach her how to protect herself, Maggie. From the bullies. It can be taught, you know."

"Maybe. But you can't be with her every minute. She'll always be a person with an intellectual disability; her IQ is never going to change, and—"

"Who wants it to change?"

"I'm only saying—"

"Whoever did her intelligence test sure didn't compare her to the people slinging insults her way, now did they? Let's measure *their* integrity and compassion next to Gemma's and see who's 'low' on that scale now!"

Mama's words were calmer than Nani's. "I'm simply saying you can't make Gemma your only mission in life."

"I can't imagine a more important one."

"You can't save her from the world, Mom."

"No. Not from the world—just from a few people in it."

Nani moved fast as a cat for a grandmother in her sixties. She had no trouble climbing trees, riding horses, or hauling bales of hay around the barn. She held the kind of strength the women in town gossiped about.

"Olivia Porter shouldn't have the right to look so good," Gemma overheard someone say in the beauty shop. "But her type *has* to look good... If you get my drift," another woman smirked.

Personally, Gemma didn't think Nani cared how the gossip ran. But she did agree Nani's remarkably fit body resembled her own.

In one corner of Luper, a rusty wheelbarrow sat half hidden in tall grass and a battered, sagging fence weaved through a few scraggly apple trees along the backside. Sitting in the old maple with Nani, Gemma's thoughts often untangled themselves, and sometimes they spilled out without permission.

She scaled down the rugged grayish trunk, trying to avoid the temptation to confess things she wasn't yet ready to. For a long time, Gemma wondered if her ghostly experience would have happened at all had she not scrambled off the tree at that moment. The truth is, the whole happening had served as a helpful diversion. Without it, the real bombshell she was hiding may have launched.

A luscious waft of honeysuckle passed under Gemma's nose, and the secret she carried followed under her feet. She stepped clumsily over rocks and rabbit-eaten twigs to her favorite marker—the one that had French fleur designs engraved on the corners. Her boot swept aside the bristly pinecones covering the small grave. "I don't remember how to figure out baby Harriet's age," she said.

Nani peered between leaves as big as supper plates, her white hair clipped up in a messy bun, Katharine Hepburn style. It was the one movie star Gemma liked to compare her to. "Okay, read me the first numbers."

"One, eight, six, two."

"And the next?"

"One, eight, six, five."

"Only three years old when she passed. Died 153 years ago."

"Poor, sweet, little baby Harriet." Gemma dropped to her knees, lowered her face to the ground where the baby lay buried, and turned her cheek sideways. She couldn't say why she did it, only that when she did, something in the air stirred. In a matter of seconds, the memory of what happened next etched in her mind forever.

"Nani?" Gemma's voice quivered. "Come here, please." She tried to slow the beating of her heart.

Nani had her eyes closed, the way she always did when she relaxed in the arms of nature.

Gemma was often told not to shout at people, but just as often she forgot. "Graham Cracker!"

Nani shot to attention. "What is it?!" She scrambled down the tree, hurrying to Gemma's side.

"Here." Gemma touched the soft velvety spot in the center of her cheek. "I felt it right here."

Nani ran a finger lightly over Gemma's skin. "I don't feel anything. It looks fine."

"My face was next to the gravestone. Close to the ground." Gemma's eyes bloomed. "There's someone here."

"What do you mean, Tink? There's no one here but us. I mean, there is. But they're all six feet under. Or more. Actually maybe less, I don't know, but—"

"Graham Cracker! It hit my cheek!"

Nani dropped and knelt close to Gemma. "What hit your cheek?"

"Someone's living air! A strong blast of it. Like this…" Gemma blew a deliberate gust against Nani's face. "It came out of nowhere. *Poof!* Right up from the grave. I'm telling you—someone's here."

Chapter Two

A Harbored Dream

Gemma's heart knocked so hard she laid a hand over her chest to muffle the noise.

Her voice hushed. "It happened right over baby Harriet's grave." Maybe talking about her had brought her spirit back to life if such a thing were possible. Or maybe death wasn't permanent after all. Wouldn't that be nice.

"Well," Nani said. "Maybe baby Harriet felt your presence and caring. Maybe she wanted you to know."

Or maybe she knows my secret. It could be a sign. Gemma held fast to the well-guarded dream she carried. A secret even Nani might not like.

Nani lowered her timeworn, silky, lined face sideways to the ground. Snowy wisps of hair fell across her cheek. Gemma leaned in against her head and the sharp edge of her peacock-blue jeweled tiara poked into her skull. Nani must have felt it too. She shifted a little before she gazed at Gemma's face. And then she said the same thing she had a million times before. "You have such bright eyes—brown as the freshly turned earth in my garden."

Gemma knew this already. Right then, she only wanted her to feel what she had. "Someone blew against my cheek," she whispered. "It was perfectly still

like it is now. We have to wait for it to happen again."
Gemma focused on the familiar web of wrinkles under
Nani's clear blue eyes—eyes so blue, they reminded
her of the solitary pools in the river.

Gemma knew a poof of air like that didn't come
from nowhere. There wasn't any wind—not even a
breeze to break apart the heat.

Nani angled her ear to the ground and waited. Her
eyes focused on the numbers and letters once sharply
chiseled into clean, bright granite. All of it worn and
weary now from over a hundred years of sun and dirt—
ground down by the wind and unrelenting rain that
pelted the Willamette Valley more days than not.

"Right there," Gemma directed. "That's where I
felt it." Their heads pressed together, hovering, their
breathing in perfect rhythm. Gemma strained to feel the
life beneath her again. But nothing came.

"Fascinating," Nani finally said.

Gemma noticed she didn't say, *Nonsense!* or,
you're sounding like a child, or, *it's only your
overcharged imagination,* or, *your brain is different—
don't talk that way.* No. Nothing like that. Instead, Nani
was as interested in what happened as Gemma.

She believed her.

Even though Gemma was a grown woman, there
were still those in her family who spoke to her like "the
slow child." Doctors had deemed her intellectual
disability to be in the "mild to moderate" range, and
predicted she'd only need minimal to moderate
assistance, but her relatives came to their own
conclusions. "Gemma's special," her aunt had touted at
a family reunion. "She can only do so much."

"She's only as limited as you make her!" Nani shot

8

back.

The dusty earth under Gemma's nose made her sneeze. She sprang upright and stretched her back. "Well, I guess dead people can't breathe," she said. "I know that. But can their souls? Because something did. Trust me. I felt it."

"Fascinating," Nani said again. "Let's go eat."

"I felt it!" Gemma snapped. "No one will believe me, will they?"

"I believe you. But it doesn't matter if you're believed or not. If you tell the truth, it overrides everything. Whatever happened was meant only for you. These things happen sometimes, especially to children." Nani's left knee cracked when she pushed up and trod back to the tree.

"I'm twenty-six and a half years old. I live in my own apartment, I know how to drive, and I have a job." Gemma wiped off the seat of her pants and followed. "I'm not a child."

"Of course not. I only meant your heart is pure like a child's—and more open to the unseen. That's all." Nani settled into the tree and reached in the basket for strawberries. "To have the heart of a child is a great compliment. A gift, really."

Gemma remembered what a counselor once told Mama. "What your daughter lacks in cognitive reasoning, she makes up for in emotional intelligence. Especially empathy." Gemma hadn't fully understood her words, until Nani explained it like this: "You often feel emotions the way a person without sight hears— like an extra sense. Everyone's original, Gemma," she told her. "Especially you."

She settled back against the tree, studying Nani's

face. "I do feel things sometimes. Things others don't. Even Mama says I do. Maybe it comes from Creator."

"I have no doubt you're right."

Creator became a part of Gemma's worldview in the third grade. She attended her first powwow and learned the ways Indigenous Nations honored their ancestors, elders, and most of all—Creator. "Dancing shows honor and respect," a Native woman explained to her class. "We dance to pray." It made perfect sense to Gemma—especially the way they prayed.

The community-wide gathering was filled with laughter and music—the intertribal celebrations vivid, bold, and colorful. Gemma adored the women's regalia, especially the jingle dress dancers wearing handmade shimmering dresses with small metal cones attached. The women dipped and swayed gracefully to the rhythm of the drum, floating along the ground, one foot always connected to the earth. They raised their fans, releasing prayers from the small tinkling cones attached to their flickering dresses. At eight years old, Gemma stood spellbound.

To her complete surprise, they offered her a Dance Shawl, inviting her to participate in the ceremonial circle. Streaming with a rainbow of long ribbons, the Dance Shawl was so beautiful, so vibrant, it sent her eyebrows shooting heavenward. Gemma wore it with pride, knowing it was sacred. She twirled and skipped and jumped and hopped, ribbons blowing like the quiet swaying of grass over the fields. Encircled by jingling sounds, the dancing filled her with perfect pleasure.

Gemma formed life-long friendships that day with members of the Cow Creek Band of Umpqua Tribe of Indians. She attended powwows every year thereafter—

not only for the beauty of the circles, but for the way the circles made her feel. For Gemma, they became a place of acceptance and belonging—a place where she was an equal. And her spirit felt whole.

For a few hours, the weight of Gemma's secret had lifted. She was grateful for the reprieve. But it returned and played heavily on her mind on the trail ride home—needling her like a dug-in tick. Nani should know the truth, and yet the words refused to leave her lips.

"Hey, Tink." Nani glanced over her shoulder. "I'll be gone the rest of the day. If you take Lolly out for another ride, stay on the property. Not beyond."

"I know. I will." At least she meant it when she said it.

When Nani's winter-white farmhouse came into view, waves of heat rose off the barn roof like flames, the midday sun roasting everything. Gemma already longed for a cool breeze against her face. She couldn't help it. The briny scent of the river was always sharp in her nose—she imagined the frothing tide, tumbling and twisting, spraying her flesh with an icy mist. *Lolly and I could accidentally nose our way down there—couldn't we? It's not that far off the property—is it?*

All was quiet on the farm. Nani had left, the horses were watered, and Gemma had eaten lunch. The river was waiting.

But first, the sway of Nani's porch swing lulled her into a nap, even as the memory of what happened that morning replayed in her mind. Whether she had an encounter with the spirit of the dead, or the spirit of the living—she wasn't sure. But from then on, she would always wonder if souls mingled in secret places, whispering among themselves at Luper.

Chapter Three

Strength of a River

As soon as Lolly's hooves hit the river rock, Gemma knew it was a bad idea.

First of all, the water was deeper than it looked. When they stepped into the river, the mare's black legs disappeared. And then the muscle of the current strong-armed Lolly forward so fast, she lost balance and tipped sideways. The idea was to take an easy ride straight across. No one would ever know. But now they were off and sailing.

"Whoa! Hang on, Lolly!" Gemma slid off her back into the invigorating rush of the McKenzie River and wrapped her arms around the neck of her beloved mare. "Holy catfish. I didn't know *this* was going to happen."

At least she had Nani's strength. "Gemma's long brown legs are strong as a horse," Mama always said. Although Gemma liked to imagine she had her father's strength too. She had no way of knowing of course, because she had never met the man. She only knew he was strong, handsome, and fifteen years old like Mama when they fell in love.

The rhythm of the river, a full-throated clatter of charging energy—was as familiar to Gemma as her horse's back. But the strength of its power and control that day made her feel as big as an ant. Her boots filled rapidly, pulling her down. Gemma stretched her neck until it ached. *Don't go under!* Her legs swung heavy, groping to find land, but there was nothing but rolling current. Until now, she had never been at the river's complete and utter mercy. Not like this.

Gemma resigned herself to taking a foolhardy ride down the McKenzie, clinging to Lolly's chocolate brown coat. "Lolly-pop," she muttered. "Where in the world are we headed?" *Toward a waterfall?* In the movies, a giant one always appeared and dropped off the edge of the earth.

Lolly fought to remain upright. She battled the current with a fierce, wild force—an intractable instinct to survive. Gemma yanked at her beloved mare's mane, grabbed the rein, and gripped with all her might. She planted pressure against her, hoping Lolly would lean into the current. But instead, she fought harder against it.

"Come on, baby. Swim over there." Gemma didn't dare point. She might lose her grip. "You can do this. You have to be brave because I don't know how. Come on, girl. For me." Gemma pulled on the reins and struggled to lead her over. "Swim the other way!" She pressed her face against Lolly's soggy cheek, not knowing how else to help. Surrendering to wild fright would only take them under. She closed her eyes, listening. *"Panic is never useful,"* she heard Nani say. *"Stay calm. Slow your thoughts. Focus."*

Newfound grit spurred Gemma's words. "Get us back to the bank, sweet girl. That's all there is to it."

Like a miracle, Lolly pulled forward—finally swimming in the right direction. But as soon as safety appeared, it vanished. The river opened wide and snatched Gemma away, as if a sea monster had grabbed hold and yanked her from below. She flailed in darkness, lunging for Lolly, whirling in all directions. She pushed upward, desperate to climb toward light. Desperate for air.

Everything went black before the crown of Gemma's head ruptured the surface, her lungs bursting open. A bloom of brilliance filtered through her eyelids—the sun, ageless as truth, beckoning her return. *Am I dead or alive?* Head bobbing, Gemma eked out a pitiful cry for help. She couldn't take in enough air to do any better than that.

And then she plunged under again, the water churning and twisting like Mama's old clothes washer. She thought about the branches and logs lurking below—anyone pinned under would never see light again. *I'm a goner.* When stars shot across her eyes, she figured that was it.

My secret is sinking with me. But please, Creator, don't let Lolly die.

Chapter Four

The Scenic Route

Seconds after she pleaded, something solid pushed under her ribs.

Lolly?

The mare's head nudged Gemma to the surface. She broke through white suds gasping, frantic to grab on to Lolly. But the mare reeled ahead, leaving only her coal-black tail within Gemma's reach. She seized hold, Lolly dragging her forward, their heads bobbing over the raging current trying to kill them. Dapples of twilight green shone on the water and slammed into Gemma's face, rushing up her nose and mouth, her mind flittering like bees. She held tight—it was all she could do. *At least we're together. At least we're still alive.*

A sudden bend in the river came into view, charging forward with speed. *Could be our last chance...* Thick weeping willows sagged overhead, so close she could touch them. Gemma freed herself of Lolly's tail, grabbed handfuls of leafy branches and pulled.

Lolly lurched forward and hit the shore first. Gemma drifted until her boots sank into sludge. "I've landed!" she squealed. A musty smell rose from the swirl in front of her steps, snaking up her nose. She almost lost her footing from the slippery slime but struggled to shore. She pressed her face lovingly against Lolly's but felt guilt cutting to the bone. "I'm so, sorry, girl. This is all my fault. If I had lost you—" She tried to swallow, but the air went solid in her throat. "We're joined at the heart... I can never lose you... *Right?*" When the sun glistened off Lolly's back, the mare's flanks sparkled the way the river did.

Gemma led Lolly farther up the bank and collapsed in a heap, her feet drowning in her boots. She rolled over, almost tasting the warmth of light covering her face like a layer of butterscotch. When the scent of pitch filled her lungs, the tangy sweetness triggered a trail of memories. Since age three, she had been hiking these woods with Nani.

Gemma's denim work shirt clung to her chest, her squelchy faded blue jeans rubbing skin raw every time her legs scraped together. But she gave thanks for every sharp pebble stabbing her back and for every grain of dirt grating against her flesh. *I'm one with Mother Earth again.* The rise and fall of her chest proved her heart had strength, still beating like a wild stallion.

She stared into space and thought of ways she could explain this whole mess to Mama and Nani.

For instance, "A couple of yahoos came out of nowhere, chased us off Nani's property, and shoved us right into the river." But that didn't feel right.

Or the truth: "I know, I *know*. I wasn't supposed to leave your property. Or ride without a helmet. But I did it anyway. Lolly and I rode straight into the river, got dragged out by the crazy-strong current, and my soon-to-be-dead body almost floated belly-up all the way to the Pacific Ocean—without a helmet on."

Gemma saw no point in stirring up a hornet's nest.

"Nope," she told Lolly. "Sometimes you have to leave the truth out of things."

Maybe it was the way Lolly's ears swiveled that warned Gemma of looming danger, or maybe it was the slight change in wind that signaled something wasn't quite right. Whatever the reason, when ice snaked through her veins, she knew it meant trouble. And then she knew why.

She wasn't alone.

Gemma did a sit-up and rotated backward. Two heavy-bodied strangers, their eyes black as iron, towered in the brush behind her.

Her pulse thundered.

"*Yeshche net!*" One with bushy brows yelled to the other wearing a knit cap, his whole face scalded with fury. More hard-flying words tore through the air.

Why would he wear a knit hat in this beastly heat?

Something twisted in her when she gave them a weedy half smile. "Excuse me. What did you say?" she asked.

The roar of the river must have drowned her voice. The men argued with one another in a funny language. But when no one returned her smile, she knew they weren't the friendly type. *The same kind of bullies I've had to escape my whole life. Only with accents.*

Two seconds didn't pass before Gemma pushed off the ground and scrambled to Lolly, blood pounding in her head. She sprang into the saddle and lurched forward in the opposite direction from the men. Their paltry eyes fixated on her face and maybe on the shirt clinging to her wet chest too.

She pushed Lolly hard to move deep into the black-fingered trees, cranking her neck back. "They aren't coming for us, sweet girl. Just a couple of yahoos." She leaned in, stroking Lolly, a tender feeling settling in her chest. "You saved us again."

Gemma and Lolly took it slow on a steep incline, everything quieting in the trees out of earshot of the river. The only sounds arose from the black-capped chickadees, coasting from limb to limb, and Lolly's hooves—her trotters clomping against the hard dirt like a soothing, steady, drumbeat.

Gemma's underwear remained unpleasantly soggy, but she breathed in the scent of river muck glued to her clothes with gratitude—it meant she had survived.

She picked up her helmet from behind the old tire at the edge of the creek, examining the trickling of water over rocks. *It sounds like any other day.*

Gemma groped the top of her head, feeling for her tiara. *Gone with the river.* She fastened the helmet under her chin and road home—as if nothing out of the ordinary had happened at all.

"Never left the property," she rehearsed with Lolly. "We took the scenic route. That's all we have to say."

Gemma owned two secrets now. But the first one carried the weight of a hundred.

Chapter Five

Summer in the Cemetery

They say being different is a natural part of the human experience. Olivia believed it. She considered her granddaughter everything a blessed gift could be. In her eyes Gemma held proof of the goodness of God, the miracle of love, and the uniqueness of every person. These sentiments had not escaped the keen observations of Olivia's own daughter, Magnolia, who told Gemma once in her most convincing attorney voice, "According to your grandmother, you walk on water. You have the humility of a saint, the heart of a celestial angel, and the conscience of Jesus. I'm sure she expects you to tell us all the meaning of life someday." Magnolia had a reputation for sarcasm in the courtroom too.

Gemma flushed with shyness when her mother had said it—maybe from embarrassment, or maybe from shame, though Olivia guessed Gemma didn't know why. Gemma's whole life, it seemed, became prattle for debate. Especially between Olivia and her daughter.

The lingering scent of freshly baked croissants wafted from Olivia's kitchen into the living room where columns of golden sun streamed through the windows. "Sorry I missed you yesterday," Olivia told Magnolia that morning. "I went for supplies and was gone all afternoon."

"I wondered where everyone went. Gemma and Lolly weren't around either."

"They couldn't have gone far. Gemma doesn't leave the property when I'm gone."

"Are you sure?"

"Yes. She knows the rule."

"Really?" Magnolia swept back her curly tresses, a deep shade of roasted coffee, and kicked off pointy heels. "I wouldn't be so sure."

"Oh, Maggie," Olivia sighed.

"Oh, Maggie, nothing." She set her briefcase against the restored mahogany stair banister, skillfully refurbished along with the entire farmhouse. "Rules are never constant in Gemma's mind. And the truth is, the child doesn't have a lick of sense." She plopped into the recliner. "Almost none."

A noise from upstairs drew Olivia's attention. She glanced up in time to see Gemma duck around the wall, eavesdropping. But Magnolia's words had already been launched, the damage done.

Such clumsy remarks stung Olivia the same way they hurt Gemma. First a sharp, jarring stab to the chest and then a dull ache that never left. The weight of shame on Gemma's spirit wrapped around both their hearts and didn't let go.

"You're wrong," Olivia shot back. "She's as clever as a jack rabbit. You should get to know her."

"Oh, please. I'm her mother."

"Yes, Maggie, you are. So take some time off and come with us to Luper for a picnic today. It's always cooler in the shade of our tree."

"Seriously?" she gasped. "You're still having picnics in the cemetery?"

"Of course," Olivia said, unmoved. "It's summer."

Magnolia's face soured. "You surround the poor girl with buried corpses and then expect her to eat? Who can eat chicken legs on top of the limbs of dead people? Honestly, Mother, it can't be good for her."

"I don't see it that way."

"Of course you don't."

"You know, Maggie, for a highly educated woman, you surprise me sometimes. She 'doesn't have a lick of sense?' It's enough she has to hear that from the bullies, but why from her own mother? Give Gemma some credit. And me too for that matter."

It sparked another hullabaloo.

Magnolia bolted from the big leather chair and scooped up her heels by the straps. "I have to be in court." The door banged open and she took off in her bare feet, stepping gingerly over small, sharp stones littering the brick walkway.

Olivia followed with her briefcase. "You forgot something!" The two of them had more words on the pebble-strewn driveway. Both of them could talk endlessly.

"You're teaching her to be morbid, Mother."

"Gemma loves the cemetery. We have fun there." Olivia spotted Gemma at the open window upstairs standing still as a statue. *Poor Tink.*

"You're completely obsessed with those graves." Magnolia plonked down into the seat of her car. "It's not healthy."

"Nonsense."

Truth be told, Olivia only obsessed about the historic, antique roses in the cemetery. Some over a hundred years old. Nothing you could ever find in

21

today's nurseries. She took small cuttings and grew them at home—the same roses the pioneer women in Oregon likely planted themselves. She and Gemma always made a point to arrange them with sprigs of Queen Anne's lace and lay the small bouquets on the graves during blooming season.

After the din died down, Magnolia backed her car out. She cranked her neck and waved goodbye to Gemma—still standing like a frozen ice sculpture at the upper window, nose glued to the screen.

Olivia stepped into the entry and flung open the coat closet. She pulled out a wide-brim cowgirl hat, the worn gray dingy one she wouldn't let go of. "Your mother won't be joining us!" she hollered.

"I know! She thinks it's creepy."

Olivia paused. *What if she's right? Maybe I'm not seeing how truly disturbing it is to have picnics in a graveyard.* "Nah," she said. "Come on down, Gem! Zork already saddled Buster and Lolly."

"He's flying his plane!" she yelled back.

"Nope, he fertilized the crops at the crack of dawn. Lunch is almost packed."

Zork ran a crop-dusting business on Olivia's property and trained horses across the field from her home. He had a reputation for being gruff, in a burly-bear kind of way and preferred being by himself. Even though he didn't socialize much, he made it his job to watch out for all the Porter women, even though he technically only worked for Olivia.

Or at least that's what they told people.

Long before Zork's hair turned a grizzled white, he became best friends with Olivia's husband. When a devastating hunting accident took Sam's life, Zork stayed with him to his last breath.

Or at least that's what they said happened.

Gemma leaned over the upstairs rail, and they smiled at one another with sudden cheerfulness. Gemma's childish voice, the one always ready to break away from the mechanical adult one, piped up, "Yippee ki yay!" She tore down the stairs three at a time. Excursions through the orchards always made her heart soar and in turn made Olivia's heart soar too. "But Nani," Gemma commanded. "*No* chicken bones."

Olivia's horselaugh rang through the kitchen. "Knew you were listening." And then, to no one in particular, she muttered, "Honestly. You'd think I was forcing her to drink blood."

Gemma poked her delicate fingers through the lunch basket and, with the unpredictable bluntness that frequently followed her thoughts, she asked, "Why don't you marry Zorro, Nani?"

Olivia froze, her hand ready to yank off a paper towel. "Marry him?" She ripped. "Will you ever call him Zork? It always throws me." She wiped at her hands.

"*You* can call him Zork," Gemma said. "I like calling him Zorro. It's more exciting." She inspected the sandwiches. "Why not marry him? I think marrying a pilot would be romantic."

"Zork?" She laughed with her mouth wide open. "Honey, he's about as romantic as a buzz saw."

"Your friend Bertie Lou calls him a moldy old man." A guilty grin crept across Gemma's face. "I hope Bertie isn't making fun of Zorro in a bad way—the way others make fun of me."

"He's not her type. That's all."

23

"Okay, because I don't think he's moldy. He's different, like me. Well, not exactly like me, but you know, he's different."

"He's a little rough around the edges, yes." Olivia pulled out napkins from the drawer. "Well, okay, not a little. He's just plain rough. But he's a good man. Reliable as rain and sturdy as a mountain. Works hard."

Gemma rearranged the sandwiches to lay on top of two small cartons of ice-cold chocolate milk. "I think he loves you, Nani."

"Oh, hon, no," she promptly corrected. "Not in a marrying kind of way. Your Grandpa Sam is gone, but I'll always be married to him—and only him. And Zork knows that."

"Well then, I wish my Grandpa Sam stayed alive for you." Gemma opened her arms wide and enfolded Nani in a tight embrace. "And for me," she added.

"I do too. But the timing of life is never ours…" Olivia closed her eyes. "Sam never planned on leaving us. That's for sure."

"My mom barely remembers him."

"She was too young for many memories." Olivia released Gemma, who always had the habit of hugging longer than anyone else she knew. She tucked the napkins in the basket.

And then Olivia detected something off. A sickly shade of gray washed over Gemma's face.

"Tink, are you okay?"

Chapter Six

Worry Kills the Soul

"I'm fine." Gemma spun away from Nani.

"You don't look fine. You look like you need to sit."

"No! I have once-a-month cramps but barely any now." Gemma pushed her bangs off her face. "I want us to go," she said ardently. "I got hot, but now I'm not. *I want to go.*"

"Okay." Nani sounded cautious. "Have some water and let's get our boots on. But take it easy. It's another hot one today. Don't want you to have a heat stroke."

In the mudroom, Gemma pulled out an old, weathered pair of leather riding boots, her own still sopping wet and drying at home. A layer of pale dust covered the toes. She swiped at the dirt with a sleeve and remembered the secret she protected. She hadn't figured out yet if others would consider it a "good" secret or a "bad" secret, which made it a problem. She only knew when she thought about it her gut tightened and a queasy sensation pranced around her insides. She wondered if the time had finally come to expose the truth to Nani. She thought if she did, it might help her sleep better at night. It wasn't easy, all the worry it caused.

"Worry kills the soul, you know," Nani always

said. "No use in worrying."

Gemma tucked the bottom of her jeans into her boots. "I'm ready."

Gemma was taught how to exercise authority over the mare she rode, but Zorro chose Lolly to be Gemma's for a reason. Bomb-proof, Lolly had "heart." She handled with ease, gentle and calm. Not only the right temperament, but to Gemma's delight, her supple coat gleamed like a dark brown seal, casting a glowing light under the sun. Lolly had a soft eye, especially with children. Nani's horse, a buckskin palomino named Buster, behaved for her, but he could be a stubborn one and never let you forget it.

The blistering heat of summer continued, and the queasiness Gemma had downplayed earlier came back. *Stay hydrated*, she remembered hearing. *Don't have a heat stroke*. Gemma reached into her saddle bag for a water bottle and chugged.

Buster and Lolly knew the trail to Luper without any need for coaxing. They halted outside the cemetery gate, where the lacy green leaves on the willow trees hung motionless—the stillness so quiet it made Gemma's ears ache. She dismounted, waving away the heat from her face and traipsed to baby Harriet's grave, reenacting the exact same steps she had taken the week before. For months after, Gemma performed the ritual every time she visited Luper in hopes of another encounter with the baby's spirit. But soon enough, she would bear witness to something far more miraculous.

After Nani had secured the horses in a shady spot, she joined Gemma in the bowl of their tree. "My mom was mad at you today." Gemma plucked off a broad leaf and waved it as a fan over both of them. Nani's face was full of pleasure when she closed her eyes and dropped a burgundy grape in her mouth.

"She wants to protect you from ghosts and goblins, that's all."

Gemma forced a fake smile. What she said next was real. "She thinks I don't have sense. Not a lick of it."

Nani's face turned serious. She didn't say a thing. And then she did. "Your mom makes mistakes like everyone else. And what she said was a mistake. She was wrong to say it and wrong to think it because it isn't the truth. You have more than enough sense to do just fine in this world. You are a highly capable, able-bodied young woman. All the things you're capable of doing are important. They matter, Gem."

"What if I want to do surgery on brains?"

"Do you want to do surgery on brains?"

"No."

"Then it's not a problem."

"Okay," she said. "I guess that's true, but I thought you'd say I could do anything I wanted, if I wanted something bad enough."

"Well, that would be a lie. Because you won't be able to do everything you want. The same way I'm not able to do everything I want. We can only do what we're capable of."

And just like that, Gemma felt better. Her appetite returned.

Every spring, the branches of the old maple hung laden with sweet-smelling bouquets of creamy yellow flowers. Even at the end of August, one small cluster still hung above them, the evening grosbeaks still eating the seeds. Nani inhaled deeply. "I've always prayed the world would be made beautiful to you," she said. "Even the smells are heavenly."

Nani considered nature more important than anything, even more important than the ancient scrolls written by dead men. "God is in the here and now," she always said. "This is where our focus should be." Nani turned to watch a junco dancing from limb to limb and they heard a warbler buzz.

"I do see the world as beautiful." Gemma stopped fanning, took a whopping bite out of her sandwich, and swiped a napkin across her face.

"I'm glad, Tink." She smiled. "I think nature is proof of God's motherly instinct—kind and gentle. I find such peace here."

"Nature *is* God. Cow Creek believe it, and so do I." Gemma recited what she had learned: "Creator is good. And only good, beautiful things come from Creator. Nasty, unkind things do not." She pulled a pinecone from under her hip and flung it into space. "This day came from Creator, Nani-pie." She squeezed her napkin into a ball. "But tell me the truth," she said in a new voice. "And I mean it."

Nani lowered a glossy Honeycrisp under her nose, breathing it in. "Okay."

"Do you think there's really a heaven?"

"Well, I sure can't see the universe and doubt God exists."

"But is there a heaven? Because if there is, why did someone blow on me on the ground? Shouldn't they be up there?" She pointed to the sky.

"Maybe it's meant to be a surprise—I don't know." Nani shrugged. "But I trust some kind of an afterlife exists. And I have to believe I'll be with Sam again."

"Why?"

"Because our lives together weren't finished."

"How do you know?" Gemma cracked her knuckles and wiggled her arms.

"Well. I guess I don't. But it's always felt unfinished to me." Nani squeezed the back of her neck.

Gemma could tell when the spark of joy that usually shone in her eyes had taken flight. Nani noticed when it did too.

"Gemma, is something else bothering you?"

Of course there was. Gemma wrestled with herself over whether to tell Nani the most important thing she had yet to own up to. She decided to recount the recent wound she had suffered instead. Because that needed telling too.

"It happened again last night." Gemma heard the sadness around her own words when she said it.

"What do you mean?" Nani stiffened. "What happened again?"

"I asked two boys at the hardware store where I could find the monkey catch. I told them my landlord said they come in handy."

"A monkey wrench?"

"Yeah. So I told them I thought it would be a good idea to have one in case I ever needed to unclog a sink pipe. But I didn't know where to find it. The monkey tool, I mean."

"And?"

"They laughed at me. And that was the nice part." Gemma frowned. "They spit out poison words too. But don't worry, Nani. I won't repeat them. I never say them out loud anymore. I do what you taught me. I watch the poison words bounce off me and go right back where they came from." Gemma shielded her chest with both hands. "I didn't let them come inside."

"Good. Those words are not yours to hold. They don't belong to anyone but those boys." The agony on Nani's face was obvious. Hearing such cruelty made her fume. Especially when it came to Gemma. But Nani never stopped listening. She simply sat as a witness to Gemma's experiences. It seemed to be the only way toward healing.

Tears oozed down Gemma's cheeks like melting wax. "I didn't know how to find it. Because I've never seen one. That's all. Do you know what a monkey thing is?"

"Yes. But there was a time I didn't. There was a time when those boys didn't either."

"They figured out fast that I'm a slow thinker."

"You process information more slowly than others—that's all."

"I know! I even told them that. But they still said mean things and ran. No help at all."

"We aren't born knowing what a monkey wrench is, Gem. We have to learn this stuff. Most people understand that. Most would've stayed and helped you."

Gemma shifted from one side of her fanny to the other. "I just have to say, even my father ran away from me."

Nani's face went blank as the summer sky. But then her eyes turned to seawater. "He didn't run from you. He moved away with his family. Remember? He had no choice, and—"

"I know, I *know,*" Gemma groaned. "And Mama's letters all came back and she never heard from him again." Gemma's words thickened with sadness. "He probably doesn't even know I exist. I've heard it all before."

Nani tugged at a leaf and gently pulled on the whole branch it clung to, arching it over their heads. "Your father was a good, kind person. Just too young. Your mom was too, of course, but she learned to be brave because she wanted you more than anything." She let the leaf slip from her hand, and the branch bounded back into place.

But Nani's words did nothing more than hang in the branches. Stuck like the ball in Gemma's throat. For a moment, the whole maple blurred and shut out the sky. She smeared wet streaks across her cheekbones, but the fear ran as fast as she could wipe. More emotions swelled like waves and swiftly crashed into physical distress.

"Gemma, what is it?"

She couldn't answer. Her breathing sped to a pace she couldn't catch—the force of anxiety knocked the wind right out of her. Gemma knew Nani recognized the mask of terror she wore. It wasn't the first time.

"Sweetie, you're having a panic attack. That's all this is," she said calmly. "Remember what to do? Take my hand."

Gemma's sweaty palms latched on tight to hers. She squeezed every time she had a crazy bird-like urge to chuck herself out of the tree and free fall to the ground. But Nani's eyes kept her pinned down.

She peeled back Gemma's grip and flipped her hand over. "Now, focus on the inside of my palm. Use one finger and trace the lines you see. Focus on them like little roads to follow. One road at a time. Trace them slowly. Notice everything about them while you take a slow, deep breath—in your nose and out your mouth." Nani waited for her to complete the instruction. "This will pass. It's passing now, even as I speak. It won't hurt you."

Gemma nodded, confident in Nani's words even as a storm filled both eyes.

"Take your own hand and do the same thing with your palm. Accept the feelings and breathe right alongside them. They won't harm you. It's okay to feel them. They're important to listen to."

Gemma's hands softened. She let Nani set the pace as they inhaled in and out together.

She listened to the wings of a jolly, red-breasted nuthatch swoop through the air above them. The rustle of leaves crackled when a squirrel skittered across the dirt below. The clicks and chatter disturbed the hush of the cemetery, but it was a soothing noise. She inhaled, exhaled, and listened to a bald eagle screeching in the distance until her breathing flowed easy again.

"Okay," Gemma finally said. "I was stiff as a whisk broom. I'm better now." Her shoulders lifted and then rested.

Nani's palms cradled Gemma's wet cheeks. "I'm so sorry about what happened in the store, Gemmy. Do you think that's what set this one off?"

"I guess," she said weakly. But she knew it was more than that.

"You have nothing you need to change about yourself. *Nothing*," Nani told her.

"I'm tired of being different."

"I know."

"I want to be like everyone else."

"I understand."

"Smart, like those boys are."

"Those boys aren't smart, Gem. They may know how to do things. But so do you. You didn't know the name of the monkey wrench, but you surefire could use one, couldn't you?"

"Yes. You and Zorro have taught me how to use lots of tools."

"Right. And if they had seen you use one, it may have shut them up. But here's the thing. You have something those boys don't. You hold compassion and the understanding of what it means to be human." Nani's hands wrapped around Gemma's. "You have the heart of a genius. Something I'm afraid those boys will never understand. Not without a lot of help anyway. They were being cruel at your expense. That kind of behavior is unconscionable." She wiped at the corners of her eyes.

Gemma stared blankly. She didn't understand all the words Nani used sometimes.

"What I mean is," Nani explained, "I know what they said cut into you like a sword. It does the same to me."

Gemma's forehead crinkled with empathy. "I'm sorry I made you cry."

"Those boys made me cry, *not you*. Some people have understood something one way all their lives and refuse to see it any other way."

Gemma wiped at her face again and drew a long, troublesome breath. "Like the way they see me?"

"Yes. Like that. But when others see weakness in you, I see strength. And I'm right. I'd take your abilities over theirs any day."

Gemma's frown tugged upward. "At least my heart is a genius."

"It's the truth."

"I want to be brave, though. Like you and Mama."

"What makes you think you aren't?"

"Because. You and Mama aren't afraid of anything. Nothing stops you guys from doing what you want. Everything stops me."

Nani shook her head. "Not everything, Tink. But sometimes people have to take risks to learn to be brave."

Yeah. Like going down river with Lolly...

"But s*afe* risks," Nani added, her liquid gaze straining into hers. "You know the difference."

Gemma nodded. She knew the difference all right. The river ride had taught her that much. But she wasn't about to share why she was so smart about that.

Gemma's eyes grew moist again. Troubled thoughts crept in sometimes. "Promise you won't die," she said, gazing at her palm. "It scares me."

"Oh, Tink." Her voice softened. "I'd live forever if I could—just for the love of you."

Gemma pressed her sun-warmed head against Nani's breast, relishing the familiar stroke of fingers along her hair as little fiery splotches of sunlight broke through the leaves, cascading over them.

"Your Grandpa Sam and I promised each other whoever died first would come back to help the other if we could."

"Has he?"

"I don't know. Maybe. But I promise to do the same for you." She tightened an arm around Gemma. "Like your mom, Gem, from the first moment you screamed out at the top of your lungs, I loved you with my whole heart."

So many things Nani told her sitting in that tree.

And so many things Gemma had yet to confess. But it wouldn't be long before she'd have to. When secrets escape, everything changes.

Chapter Seven

The Music of Nature

At the end of the week, the long hot spell broke
and a light breeze finally crept through the thick wall of
air, shifting the leaves bowed over Nani's picnic table.
The field of tall grass shimmered in the sunlight,
swishing melodiously like silk. Gemma sat on the
weathered bench next to the cucumbers, zucchini, and
tomatoes flourishing in Nani's tidy garden, bountiful
because she weeded and watered it daily.

A gentle waft fanned a tang of basil under
Gemma's nose like smelling salts. But it wasn't enough
to keep her awake. The hum of running water through
the garden hose put her in a stupor. She laid her
forehead against her knees and dozed.

Gemma had worried herself awake most of the
night. Her thoughts had grown as invasive and eager as
chickweeds. She couldn't wrestle the fears down. The
truth grew more unwieldly every day.

The screen door clamored shut, and Nani clumped
through the garden in thick boots. "Let's go somewhere
different today."

Nani's words brought her fully back. She shook off
the trance and sprang off the bench in a jig. "I'm
ready," she said in a fever of impatience. "Let's ride,
Nani-pie!" She needed another distraction—avoidance

had become a habit.

Gemma removed the rainbow-colored tiara pinned to her hair and fumbled with her black riding helmet. She pulled it over the bruised skin on her forehead where a black and blue bump still remained. She had charged outside when she heard Zorro's plane in the air and smacked her head on the corner of the door. Gemma was always needing to sort herself out from one mishap or another. "Such a little spitfire," her mother would say. "Always busy as a bird dog and always getting hurt."

She was right in a way. Things always seemed to happen to Gemma. Not because she was a person with a "disability"—at least she didn't think so. She preferred Nani's explanation: "Gemma's exuberance for life makes her impulsive sometimes, and her thoughts simply can't compete with her energy."

It was the reason she loved to run. Every morning she sailed through town, across the fields, and through the orchards. "Let her off the leash," Zork crowed. "Gemma needs to run." The truth is she had the bullies to thank for being so good at it. They were the reason she ran so well.

That morning, when she shifted in the saddle and squeezed Lolly a little too hard, the mare obeyed. She lurched and took off into a hasty trot. The jouncing at first made Gemma bite her tongue. "Ow!" she hollered. "Easy girl." They came alongside Nani and Buster.

"Horse feathers. That hurt." Gemma pressed a gloved hand to her mouth and inspected it. "Help. I'm swallowing blood."

"Tongues heal fast. Spit a few times and you'll be fine."

"Okay." Gemma bent to the side and spit at least ten times. And then spit more.

"I said a *few* times."

"Oh. Okay." She laughed for the pure pleasure of it. "Which trail should we take?"

"Bear right," Nani said, pulling Buster's reins to take the lead. "We'll make a loop back through the orchards after I show you something at the river."

Gemma nodded, not disappointed in the least. She swung about and plodded up a small rocky incline behind Buster.

When the trail narrowed, Nani pulled Buster to a stop. "Go ahead and dismount. We'll hike the rest of the way in."

To see if she could do it, Gemma lifted a leg over the bay's withers, slipping off frontwise, her boots blasting to the ground with a loud thud. She tied Lolly to a tree and swiftly fell into step beside Nani. As a child, she had to skip to keep up with her, but as an adult, her stride had grown long like Nani's. In all ways, Gemma appeared like any woman her age. Until people had a longer conversation with her, they didn't know anything was different.

The midday sun wrapped around them in a heavy cloak of heat. Gemma enjoyed the sound of their thick-toed boots against the rocks, the clamor and screech of birds, and the cow bawling somewhere in the distance. The smell of dust and rosemary streamed in the air. It pleased her as much as cotton candy and popcorn cooking at the Oregon State Fair.

Nani jerked to a stop and pointed. "Look! It's a scarlet tanager." The excitement in her voice was contagious. "It's like a red flame lighting the tree."

Next, she directed Gemma's attention to a cobweb hidden from the sun. "See that? On the blueberry bush. Like crocheted lace sprinkled with diamonds."

Gemma fumbled for her phone, sat cross-legged on the dirt, elbows on knees, and leaned into the camera. "That's so cool."

"Nature is a miracle," Nani said. Her deep azure eyes never missed anything—unless she didn't want to see somebody.

"Oh, dear," Nani warned. "Here comes Bertie." She heaved a sigh. "Imagine that."

The first thing Gemma observed when Bertie came scuttling toward them was her hair—it practically glowed. *A berry-red mop at her age?* She noticed the flimsy silver sandals and polka-dotted capris too. *She's a wild one.*

Bertie Lou happened to be one of those friends who talked too much. Something Gemma had frequently been accused of as well. But Nani also described Bertie once as "Terribly meek and sort of sat-upon."

"She sat upon what?" Gemma had asked.

Nani tried to explain, but it didn't sink in. Gemma only knew Bertie required all of Nani's attention whenever she came around.

Bertie waved, trotting full speed ahead.

"I have no right to berate poor Bertie," Nani groaned. "It's just that she carries on something awful. About *everything*."

"Should we turn around and run?"

"No, we can't do that. She means well. I'll give her that."

"I have a plan then. I'll say, 'Hurry, Nani! We have

to go!' And I'll pull you away before she starts yacking too much." Gemma hooted. She turned the opposite direction and in a hushed voice rehearsed. "Hurry, Nani. We have to go."

Bertie was puffing when she reached them. "Whew!" she gasped. "Well, hello!" she chimed. "Zork told me you'd be here."

"Did he? Well, of course he did. Hello, Bertie," Nani said.

"Yeah," Gemma broke in, "and *Bertie* has to go! Whoops. I mean, Nani *wants* to go! Wait. I mean…" Gemma tried to sort through the flustered thoughts ganging up on her. "Hurry, Nani!"

Nani arched her brows and shrugged. "Gotta go, Bertie. We have big plans today."

"Oh." Bertie slumped. And then with a step in her voice added, "Well, I'd love to join you." She waited in the silence with the face of a droopy-eyed hound.

"Oh, we would too," Nani fibbed. "But not this time. This is Gemma's day." Which was not a lie.

Bertie leaned into Nani's ear with a secret, but Gemma heard just fine. "We have to get together and talk about my 'you-know-what' life." She made rabbit ears with two fingers around the "you-know-what" part.

"Bertie, honestly, what decade do you live in?" Nani asked.

"Well, Gemma's here!" she snapped. "I'm being careful. It's practically X-rated. But listen, I have a big decision to make. Big. And I don't know if—"

"Come on, Nani!" Gemma didn't always catch social cues, but that time she did. "We need to hurry!" Gemma tugged on her sleeve and pulled her away.

Nani shrugged again. "Another time, Bertie."

Gemma kept hold of Nani's sleeve and pelted along the dusty trail hooting like a young cow all the way to the river. One arm flagged a sweeping goodbye to Bertie nearly planting them both on their faces.

Bertie watched them disappear into the distance, drooping like a wilted flower before she slunk away.

"Does she talk to you about sex stuff?" Gemma asked.

Nani's boots kicked alive the dust when she braked and locked eyes with Gemma.

"It kinda-sorta sounded like it."

"You picked up on that. Good for you," Nani grinned. "And yes, sometimes she does. Okay, not sometimes," she corrected. "Every time. It's all very tiring, actually." Nani trodded forward again.

"Why?"

"I guess I'm not as patient as I used to be. And I sure don't want to be a sex therapist for Bertie Lou, hearing all the sordid details about—"

"No, I meant why does Bertie talk to *you* about it?"

"Oh! Well, for some idiotic reason she seems to think that's what I'm here for."

"What's a sex therapy?"

"A sex *therapist*. It's someone who helps people with problems, or..." She stopped to think how to explain it to Gemma. "People need help sometimes to understand how, or what, or when, or maybe need some advice or something. About sex."

"Huh?" Gemma frowned.

"I don't know what the hell they do. Never been to one. No idea why she thinks I'm such an expert."

"Don't you know a lot about sex? Being old and everything you must know a lot about it. Unless you can't remember."

Nani flashed a lopsided grin. "Entirely possible. Let's just say I get tired of explaining things to a grown woman. She should know these things. It makes me crazy."

"Know what things?"

"Things about sex. That's all. Believe me, I have to tune out half of what she says. It bores me."

"It bores you? I wouldn't think *that* would bore you. Not that I know or anything."

Nani glanced sideways at Gemma. "No. You wouldn't think so, would you? And yet, for me, it is. So I give her books to read and names of people to call— professionals who can at least make a few bucks while she drones on."

Gemma tried not to jitter, but her arms wiggled before she could stop it sometimes.

A hefty, flat rock hung over the river's edge at the end of the path. White ripples somersaulted below, churning over themselves in a mad rush westward. "*The music of nature,*" Nani liked to say.

"There, under those bushes." Nani pointed. "That's what I wanted to show you today."

"It's a family of ducklings!" Gemma yelled. "Look at them all!" She slipped on the stone ledge and landed hard on her tailbone, but it didn't faze her. "So many cute little babies!" she cried. "Can we get closer?"

"Probably not. The mother wants to protect them from the likes of us. Or at least from the likes of me," she added, lowering herself down to sit.

Gemma inched toward the water, laid her hand on the surface, and reached out her palm. Children and animals came to her as they would to no one else. It had always been that way. "They trust you," Nani explained once. "Their instincts tell them you're safe. Your kindness is like a beacon to them." Sure enough, a baby duckling swam right into Gemma's hand.

"You have to see it to believe it," Nani marveled.

Human or not, Gemma loved caring for babies.

"You know," Nani remarked, "your face is all rosy today, but I can tell when something's bothering you. Even when you're happy."

Gemma's spirits plummeted. "You can?" She pulled away from the ducklings.

"Yes."

"You know?"

"Well, I don't know what. But yes, I can tell something has been stuck in that craw of yours. And today your arms are wiggling a lot."

A boulder lifted off Gemma's shoulders, far heavier than she realized. The truth poured out. "It's something bad, and people won't be happy." She sucked in a tank of air. "I'm sorry, but I did—I did something I wasn't supposed to and I know you'll all be mad, but I did it anyway and—"

"Tinker," Nani said, gently holding a finger to Gemma's lips. "Take a deep breath and slow your thoughts. Then tell me what you think you did wrong."

Gemma forced a swallow over a bone-dry throat.

"Take a breath with me," Nani said again. "Reset your clock."

They took a long breath in together, and slowly let it out.

"Okay," Nani said. "Now, explain. Nice and easy."

Gemma sat in silence until she judged herself ready. "I had—" Her mouth slammed shut.

"Yes? Speak your mind, Gemma. Remember, always express what goes through you."

"Okay," she said bravely. "What I want to say is…" Her mouth opened, but nothing came out.

Nani lifted Gemma's chin and nodded her on.

"I had in-ter-course," Gemma announced.

"Oh," Nani said casually. "Okay. With Walter?"

"No. Not Walter."

"Oh! Okay then, with who?"

"With Walt. He changed his name to be like a famous poem writer…" She stopped to think. "He's some dead guy."

"Walt Whitman?"

"Yeah! That's it! He thinks it sounds more important."

"I see. So you and Walter, I mean Walt, both consented? You both wanted to have sex?"

"Yes."

"Okay, well, Gemma—"

"That's not all."

"Okay. Go on."

Gemma zeroed in on Nani's face. "Is it okay to tell you? I don't want to bore you with sex talk like Bertie does."

"It's okay, Gemma. I promise. Tell me anything."

"Okay, because no one knows I tried to make a baby. On purpose. Walt had to help me because he has the sperm seeds in his penis. See, more than anything I want a baby of my own. I do, Nani." Gemma glanced her way to see if she should stop.

"Go on."

"You know I love children. And I'm good with them. There's nothing I want more than to be a mama.

Nothing. Every visit to Santa, every falling star, every birthday cake, every penny I find… That's what I've wished for my whole life. It's my dream. Even if it's not supposed to be. And if Creator wasn't okay with it I'm sure I wouldn't want one so bad."

"Well, I wouldn't—"

"I know what people think! I'm not supposed to because I won't know how. But I will. I can learn like I've learned other things. Including babysitting!"

Nani listened and waited. Her face unwrapped, open to receive whatever needed to be said.

Gemma took a deep breath, exhaled with her lower lip jutted out, and felt the curl in her bangs dance. "It's the only thing I want. It's my dream, Nani."

"I know it is. And you *are* wonderful with kids. And animals too. Everyone knows that." Nani shifted, her legs dangling over the river. "So. Let's think about your dream and talk about all the pros and cons. First, the pros—"

"I did that already."

Nani's eyebrows squished together. "Okay…"

"And it only takes once."

"To do what?"

"To make a baby."

"True. It can, but honey, you're wearing a patch. It prevents pregnancy. You're not saying you think you're pregnant, are you?"

"Oh, no," Gemma said. "I'm not saying that at all."

"Okay, good."

"I'm saying I *am* pregnant."

Chapter Eight

Through the Blackberry Vines

"But your patch, Gemma. You can't be pregnant. I'm sorry, but that's why you wear it. Remember?"

"Yeah. I remember."

"You still have it on, right?"

"Nope. I peeled it off."

Nani's eyebrows zipped up to her scalp.

"I had to!" Gemma explained. "So I could make a baby. You can't keep it on to do that. And you know what?"

Nani sounded unwell when she answered. "What?"

"I didn't know it was so easy." Gemma was full of wonder.

"Trust me," Nani said. "That's the *only* easy part." Then her face relaxed, and she seemed better. "You haven't been to a doctor for a test, have you?"

"No. But I had in-ter-course with Walter, I mean Walt, when the app on my phone told me to. Here, let me show you." Her finger flew around the phone screen until Nani stopped her.

"It's okay, I know what you're talking about."

"Plus, I lied. I never had my once-a-month cramps. They never happened."

"Yes, but that doesn't mean—"

"And I bought testing at the dollar store. It's almost

one-hundred percent right which seems close enough."

"The dollar store has *pregnancy* tests?"

"Yes. For only a dollar!"

"Well, I don't think one test—"

"I bought three. I paid a total of four dollars. I mean three. See? I'm getting better at counting my money."

"You read the test results yourself?"

"Three times." Her face caught fire, and she had no idea why. Gemma noticed she flushed hot one minute and went lily white cold the next. "All three said 'positive' after I dipped it in my pee. Walter, I mean Walt and I figured it out together. So I know I am. And my nurse agrees. I called her. Plus I pee more, barf sometimes, my boobs hurt, and I'm already bloated. Even though the nurse thinks I'm only two weeks pregnant."

"*Two weeks*?"

Gemma's chin bobbed like a bouncing spring. "Well, maybe more."

"Holy-Saint-Mary." Nani drew in air and released it slowly the way she had instructed Gemma to. She inhaled again. "Let me untighten my insides." Her face turned peaked like Gemma's did sometimes.

"It'll be okay, Nani. Don't worry," Gemma consoled. "Worry kills the soul. No use in worrying."

Nani's lips squished up to the left. "Well." She finally spoke. "This is some news."

"I know. I thought it would be awful to tell you, but guess what?"

Nani waited.

"I'm excited!" Gemma beamed. "You finally know. I didn't have the guts to tell you right away." A spark of hope kindled her confidence. "But now I'm so happy I did!"

Nani nodded, as if she understood. "Gemma, what about Walt? What does he think?"

"I don't know."

"Well, does he want a baby too?"

"He doesn't care. He wants me to be happy."

"I see, so he did this for you?" Nani scooped up a handful of small rocks, pitched a flat one, and watched it skip across the rolling river of light.

"Yup. All my idea. I told him he didn't have to do a thing except shoot the seeds out."

"But a father has responsibilities too. And Walt has his own limitations—in some ways more than you."

"No, that's not true. Besides, we help each other figure things out. But anyway, I told him he doesn't have to take care of the baby. I can do that like you and Mama did."

Nani's head dropped into the palm of her hand for a split second and then bounced up again. "I've always wanted you to have everything in life you wanted, Tink, but this won't be easy. It'll be the hardest thing you've ever done. And it will be the hardest thing you do for the rest of your life."

"Yes, but this baby girl is who I want."

"Girl?"

"Yes, she's a girl. Don't ask me how I know. I just do."

"I don't doubt it," she said. "And honestly, I care about your happiness. I do. But—"

"I knew you'd understand!" Gemma folded into Nani's arms and clung tight. "I can do it. And just think. Next year, on our first summertime picnic to

Luper, my baby will be with us."

"Imagine that." Nani relaxed as if she would hold Gemma as long as she wanted. "You do have the right to make your own decisions. You're a grown woman, but I want you to hear what I'm saying. This decision carries responsibility like you've never known. If you want to keep this baby, you'll have to work hard."

Gemma plugged backward from Nani's arms. "Of course I want to keep my baby! That's why I made her! Well, Walt and I made her. And I *will* work hard. I promise."

"People will tell you what to do, and how to do it. You'll have a lot more rules to follow. You'll have to listen and do exactly as they say. It won't be easy, Tink."

"I know. I *will*. I'm even dying the ends of my hair with all natural periwinkle because it washes out without chemicals. The nurse approved of it."

Nani's shoulders slumped. "Have you told your mother?"

A jolt charged up Gemma's spine. "No! Don't you tell her either."

"Of course I won't." Nani launched another pebble into the current. "Because you're going to."

"How am I gonna tell Mama this?!"

"The same way you told me. You'll figure it out."

Gemma fished out a small insect tangled in her periwinkle strands. "Maybe she won't notice."

"Honey, everyone will notice."

"I know." Gemma sighed.

"You made the decision to do this. And grown women take responsibility for their actions and their decisions. Right?"

"Right," she said weakly, twisting a lock around a dirt stained finger.

"So take responsibility now. That means being honest with people. Especially your mom. This is a baby's life we're talking about."

"True. I guess I can't exactly hide it."

"No, you can't."

"But I can wait *a little*—"

"Gemma. Tell your mother. Don't wait any longer."

"But why?"

Something cracked through the blackberry vines with a rowdy force.

Gemma flinched. "It's a nutrient rat!" she yelled. "It came up from the river!"

Nani threw her arms around Gemma—her back as a shield. "You saw nutria down there?"

"I think I did, but maybe not." She whispered into the soft fold of Nani's ear, "But they're super snarly and they attack."

An even louder snap broke through the scrub on the other side. Before another word was said, Gemma knew by Nani's face exactly who was standing behind her.

"Not a nutrient," they heard Mama say.

Chapter Nine

Long Ride Home

When she stood, Gemma's chest hammered stronger than her worst panic attack. The sun slammed its heat against her head. And then the sky seemed to suddenly slip backward as if moving away from them. And then it occurred to her she might faint.

"Mama," Gemma uttered, feeling sick again. She moved toward the water and squatted close to the stream. She reached in, cupped an icy-cold handful to her lips and wet her face. The cooling was instant.

"So. You need to tell me *what*, Gemma Jane?" Mama's eyes spit sparks. "What's going on?" She tossed a nasty look at Nani too.

Gemma struggled to think.

"It's okay," Nani urged her. "You have the words."

Chin held high, Gemma pushed up her sleeves and swallowed back fear. "I'm a twenty-six-and-a-half-year-old woman. *Not a child*. And I can handle it. A baby, Mama—I'm getting one of my own." Gemma felt her eyes radiating something wild and free when she said it.

"What are you talking about?"

"A baby is growing because I want it to."

Mama's eyes narrowed, her lips unmoving.

"She's pregnant, Maggie."

Mama's face lost all color. She turned to Nani. "But she's on birth control."

"She was," Nani confirmed. "Until she wasn't."

Mama's eyes darted to Gemma, her words piercing. "You stopped it?"

"I ripped it off and threw it away. So that means, yes. I stopped it."

"Oh my god. Seriously?"

No one answered.

"Tell me you're joking."

"It's no joke, Maggie," Nani said.

Mama dropped on the edge of the big flat rock next to them. All they heard, for what seemed like an eternity was thundering white water rushing away into another world.

Gemma waited for a sign. A hopeful one. She waited for a smile, or a hug, maybe a "congratulations." Something to signal it would be fine. A sign that her mother would be eager and full of joy to have her first grandchild.

Nani stood, staring at the bristling river. "I'll let the two of you talk. Buster and I will head for home. Maggie, I trust you have Banjo?"

"Yes. Rode the blue roan today," Mama confirmed, her voice flat as a cowpie. "We'll see you later."

Nani kissed Gemma on the head, squeezed her shoulder, and left.

"How could you let this happen?" Mama asked. "Why would you ever stop your birth control?"

Not the happy moment Gemma knew better than to expect.

"I mean seriously," Mama continued, "you know you have to stay on birth control for it to work. Don't you?"

"Stop! I know that. You don't have to say it."

"Yes, evidently I do. Look what happened!" Mama's words churned like butter, gaining speed. "From now on, I guess you get shots, or we get your tubes tied, or *something*. But right now we need to deal with this. And then it needs to never happen again."

"What tubes? I don't understand."

"Exactly! That's why you're in this mess. I hope you haven't told Walter. Walter did this to you, right?"

Gemma stared at her feet.

"Did he hurt you? Or did someone else?"

"No! Nobody hurt me." Gemma's cheeks felt like one of Nani's sun-scorched garden tomatoes. "It's Walt. And he does not hurt me. Ever! And he doesn't care I have a baby in me." Spittle shot out with her words. "He knew what I wanted to do. I did it on purpose! He wants me to be happy. He understands."

"Oh my god. We need to get home." When Mama raised she slipped and took a skid. "Shit!" She caught her balance. "This can't happen, Gem. Surely you know that. We need to get you to a doctor. I'll make an appointment, and we'll take care of it." She pushed her hair back and heaved a sigh. "And then we'll move on as if it never happened."

"I already have a doctor," Gemma told her.

"Okay, good. We'll tell Walter you had a miscarriage—while riding Lolly."

Do not make Lolly part of your bitchy-faced lie. Gemma thought better than to say it.

"From here on, you never take that patch off again. Otherwise, we do something else. Understood? This has got to be the most irresponsible thing you've ever done." Her words stung.

Gemma's thoughts tangled like vines on a trellis, her boots heavier on the path back. She stomped on the puddles of sun in front of her, flinging her arm wide, whacking her hand against pine boughs and sword ferns fanning the trail. If it had been any other day, the hint of apple blossoms trailing in the dust would have filled her with happiness.

"Nani says I'm a grown woman, which I am. And she says I can make my own decisions, which I can. And that sometimes we have to take risks, which I do." Her jaw clenched.

"Of course she says that. Because she's not your mother. Let's get home." Mama untied Banjo's lead from the tree.

Gemma did manage to admire the way Banjo's coat gleamed a stunning bluish gray tint. Streaks of his copper mane popped against it, providing a welcome distraction from the otherwise ugly moment she found herself in.

"Sorry I got so mad..." Mama sounded like she begged the words to leave her maw. "We'll both feel better once this is all over." She reached toward Gemma. "It'll be okay."

Gemma recoiled like a snake and moved away from her. "You can't stop me. I'm having my baby, and—"

"Gemma." Mama's voice grew stern again. "There's no way you can have a baby. I'm sorry—I am. I wish things were different."

"You wish *I* was different."

"I did not say that. But trust me, you can't handle it. If things were different..." Mama tried again. "If you had the ability to raise a child, then, yes. But you don't. I'll help you get through this, honey. I promise." She stepped over the stones between them and held Gemma's shoulders. "Hey," she said. But Gemma's eyes remained on the Oregon holly trampled flat around her boots. "We'll get through this. Together. I do love you."

Mama's words clung to the air like a dirty haze. They were good for nothing. Gemma raised her head and met her gaze without blinking. "You mean you'd take away the only thing I've ever wanted. That's what you mean." A tear escaped her left eye. Everything blurred as she mounted Lolly. "I may not be able to do a lot of things, Mama. And some things I may never get right. But I can love. I *can* do that."

Waves of fury rolled through her. The anger steered her home.

****

By evening, Gemma didn't feel right. She tried to sort through her thoughts, pacing through her apartment, rambling from room to room, arms wiggling. But her ideas skittered off like flies. She couldn't get close to one. And then she stopped breathing. She swore she did. Until she started pumping air.

Gemma went straight to the kitchen sink and splashed water in her face. *I need air… It won't go in!* Her limbs tingled and buzzed. She stumbled to the sofa, dropped, and wiggled her fingers and toes. Everything went numb. Sweat formed on her brow, her heart beating out of control. *I'll be dead soon!* She flailed for a phone that must have vanished.

Winded and panting, she pretended to talk to Nani.

"I'm having that buzzy thing again."

"Another panic attack?" Nani asked.

"Yup. A real corker."

"You know what to do, Gemma."

She stared at the lines on her palm and followed them with one finger. She knew what else Nani would say too.

"Listen to your music. Singing will clear the stress away, remember?"

She did remember. Nani also said people who sang every day extended their lives by at least four years. She scrolled through her music and went to a beautiful song she learned from the Cow Creek Tribe. She closed her eyes and sang along to the traditional Ojibwa Lullaby, "Hey, Hey, Watenay." Gemma's breathing felt effortless again. The lyrics, both haunting and comforting, flowed as easy as a freshwater stream—untangled and free.

"It's okay, little one. I'm here," she said slowly. "We'll be okay. We won't die without knowing each other. I'm not going to leave you. I promise."

Gemma took a stroll outside with newfound strength, her energy bolstered by the ritual of the Native people. *The ritual of* my *people*, she told herself. She wished it to be true so many times, part of herself believed it was.

"We're okay, baby girl," she repeated. "Somehow we'll be okay."

Chapter Ten

A Woman's Independence

If there was one thing living with Magnolia taught you, it was how to pack and unpack boxes. The woman moved around more than a tomcat. Eleven times in sixteen years to be exact. She always said if she hadn't become a lawyer, she would've been a real estate agent or interior designer. She relished staging homes and the adrenaline rush of buying and selling. "That sounds like a problem," her mother told her.

"It's my hobby," Magnolia said in her own defense.

Olivia blamed Magnolia's moving obsession on HGTV. Specifically to that show, *Fixer Upper*. And when inconvenient to move, Magnolia simply rearranged furniture and redecorated a room. One makeover at a time. Olivia and Gemma found the whole thing terribly exhausting.

But Magnolia did become a lawyer, and still Olivia heard the same announcement she had heard eleven times before: "We're moving, Mother."

Two days earlier they learned of Gemma's pregnancy. Now this.

"Oh?" she responded nonchalantly. "Along the river this time, or the lake?"

"No," she said.

Olivia sliced into another oversized perfectly ripe peach picked that morning and tossed the pieces into a clear bowl.

"I was offered the position. I'm joining the prestigious law firm I told you about."

"The immigration and family law group?! The one in Seattle?"

"Yes! With a terrific offer. Gemma and I will be set." Magnolia bowed over the glistening yellow and red clingstones and breathed in. "I'm so ready for the city."

"I'm proud of you, Mag. Honestly, you never cease to amaze me, but—"

"Of course we want you to come with us!" Brightness spilled out of Magnolia's eyes when she said it.

"Well, no, I wasn't thinking about me. I'm wondering if you've told Gemma yet." Olivia ran the faucet, rinsing the sweet juiciness off her hands.

"I thought I'd wait til after this whole pregnancy thing is over."

"This whole pregnancy thing?"

"Yes. Once she gets through this, I think the move will be good for her. Perfect timing, really."

"You'd wait eight months to start your new job?

"What? No. The position is waiting for me now. We'll leave in a few weeks. Didn't Gemma tell you the plan?"

"What plan?"

"She didn't come running to you about it? I'm *shocked.*" Her words bristled. "I scheduled her an appointment with a doctor this week. There's no way she can have this baby. You do see that, don't you?"

"Gemma agreed to this appointment?"

"Not exactly. But I'm sure she knows I'm right. She'll come around I think, with your help."

"With *my* help?"

"Well, yes. She listens to you. She can't be a mother. Surely you agree."

"It's not a question of whether I agree or not." Olivia began whipping the air with a large steel spoon, the atmosphere charged with electricity. "It doesn't matter what I think. This is a question for Gemma. And I think you know the answer."

"Mom!" Magnolia squawked. "She has the mind of a child. What—*maybe* a twelve-year-old?"

"Older than that. And they said she'd never be able to ride a bike, Maggie, remember that? Not only did she learn to ride a bike, she learned to knit, drive a car, ride a horse, and could probably learn to fly if she wanted."

"Don't be ridiculous."

"And she lives in her own apartment, and has a job—"

"All thanks to her caseworker," Magnolia said. "She only has those things because of disability services."

"So what." Olivia swirled the peaches, ready to beat them to a pulp. "She's learned to live quite independently for the most part. And been promoted twice in five years. Her boss told me she's the best worker they have. She does learn. She knows how to take care of every animal that comes in."

"Yes, she works two days a week in an animal shelter. We're talking about a baby here. A child whose life will depend on Gemma's ability to care for it." She stretched for the flour sitting on the top shelf.

"You think I don't understand that? We were single parents. She's older than either of us were when we became mothers. You did it without a man. I nearly did too."

"Yes. One father disappeared, one died. We both struggled. I did it alone because I had to. So did you."

Olivia stopped stirring, pulled out a rolling pin, and skated it across the island toward Magnolia. "I'm simply saying Gem has a right to that struggle too, if she wants it."

"Mother, her mental capacity will always be immature. You can't honestly think Gemma can make that decision. Do you?"

"She already has! She planned this pregnancy." Even from a distance, Olivia felt the slow burn of Magnolia's petulance. "Maggie, like it or not, Gemma is a grown woman with a mind of her own. *Newsflash*! She has dreams too. And this is one of them. You can't take that from her. You of all people know she has a legal right to that decision."

"Of course, I know that." She finger-painted the rolling pin with flour. "I'm all for the right to choose— if someone is capable of making such a choice."

Olivia flashed a scowl at Magnolia but backed up the words that almost sailed out.

"I'm sorry if that sounds cruel, but it's true. And you can help her see this is wrong. I know you can! She'll listen to you. Please help her see reason."

"*Whose* reason?" Olivia tossed the spoon from five feet away and sent it clattering into the sink. "I will do no such thing." Her jaw tensed as she pushed aside the peaches, tossing things right and left into another mixing bowl for the crust.

60

"Oh, please. Here you go again. Whatever Gemma wants, Gemma should get, right?"

There it is. Resentment.

"You coddle her, Mom. Always have. Gemma can do no wrong. You've put her on a pedestal."

"I only—"

"You *only* do everything for her. She fully depends on you. Always has."

"I do not do everything for Gemma. She's clever. She can problem solve so many things." She added butter to the bowl and turned on the food processor.

Magnolia's voice raised over the clatter. "Yes, she can. And the very next moment she can be alarmingly clueless."

"Exactly." Olivia was almost shouting. "That's exactly what her doctors and therapists have told us to expect. These discrepancies are normal for Gemma."

"But they're not normal for a mother."

"Are you kidding me?" Olivia switched the processor off. "Who of us is not alarmingly clueless at times?"

"That's not what I mean." Magnolia poked at the dough. "What'd you forget to put in this? It feels funny."

Olivia peered into the bowl. "Who knows." She poured in more cream and sent everything whirling again. "How many of us always get it right, always have sound judgment? How many mothers are capable of doing everything without any help? I'll tell you how many—*zero!*"

Maggie leaned against a drawer and sighed. "You don't get it."

"Look," Olivia said. "It scares me too. It does! But

61

I also think Gemma can learn to be a mom. In fact, she could be a better mother than most women. Would she need help? Of course she would. With the appropriate social support, she could be successful. Many people with intellectual disabilities are. Especially with parent training and help in the home. And Gemma loves to learn. And she loves children, and children love her! At least she has that going for her. Gemma has a kindness lost to most of us."

"I know having a disability doesn't mean you can't be a wonderful parent. I know that. But in Gemma's case, her love of children is not enough. My god, she dyed her hair periwinkle because she watches *Frozen* every night. Every night!"

"Great movie, strong women." Olivia switched off the processor and lifted the bowl to the island.

"You're in denial, Mother."

"At least a maternal instinct comes naturally to her—"

"A maternal instinct for animals and babysitting is not the same. I played with dolls when I was little, and then I developed out of it. That's where she's stuck, but you aren't seeing it."

"I *am* seeing it. As clear as anything I see it."

With one heavy thunk, Magnolia dumped the dough out. "She is developmentally delayed. Don't mistake her love for babies and animals as someone ready for motherhood or someone who can adapt to it."

"I don't."

"Really? You don't? You still call each other Tink and Graham Cracker. This is a woman who can care for a baby?" She started punching the blob, sending puffs of white into the air.

"That's where we differ, Tink," Olivia slipped. "Or Gemma—I mean, *Maggie*! It makes no difference. She can and does adapt. If we show her how! She wants to learn."

"Of course she does. She wants to be normal."

"Being different *is* normal, Maggie. It's called neurodiversity. That's the part *you're* not seeing. Wonderful parents exist in every group. You're not accepting the wide range of abilities that are in all of us. Including Gemma!" Olivia folded her arms. "You still see her as a child—someone who hasn't grown and developed. And while I'm at it, why shouldn't we parents and grandparents put our children on pedestals? That's what love does."

"And yet you were so busy jetting around the world with your business, you hardly noticed when I grew up."

"You know it killed me every day I was away from you." She took the mixing bowl to the sink and started scrubbing. "My job had to be finished before I could leave. You know all this! But tell me, in all those years, did you ever feel unloved? *Ever?*"

"No."

"That's right—because you've always been loved. So deeply loved. And did you ever lack for fun?"

"No. But that's the thing. We weren't together enough. I missed you."

Olivia's eyes watered. "And I missed you." She stopped scrubbing and squeezed out the wash rag. "Every trip I took I missed you like crazy. You know I did. Whether it's true or not, I told myself we had more fun when we were together because we were apart so much."

Magnolia seemed to consider the possibility that maybe her mother was right. But then said, "Nah. More time together would've meant more fun." She kept kneading.

"Okay. Probably right. But that's not what we had. I did my best."

"I know you did."

"Nobody gets everything easy. There are always challenges. But do children always grow up with memories of love and fun? No."

"You're right. I have both. And I'm grateful for that."

"Gemma is part of you, but she is her own person."

Magnolia shoved the dough across the island to her mother, handed her the rolling pin, and sighed. "She's actually a lot like both of us, isn't she?"

"Yes. And that's a compliment."

"I know. You're right. I simply can't, I mean I don't know—"

"Stop, honey. No matter what, Gemma has to do what's right for her." Olivia pressed the wooden pin into the dough, but couldn't make it roll. "Feels like rawhide." *Why did I think I could make a pie?*

Magnolia's voice grew firm again. "You know Walter has more challenges than she does. At least about some things."

"Gemma doesn't think so."

"Oh, I realize that. Trust me. But he's on the spectrum, and—"

"Do you know what Gemma told me?" Olivia stopped tussling with the dough and let out an avalanche of thoughts. "For many Native American Tribes the concept of 'disabilities' doesn't even exist.

Only 'being different' does. They actually make room for differences in their culture. I think that's why Gemma feels so much acceptance from the Cow Creek Tribal Community." Olivia's eyes settled on her daughter's. "Many also believe the altered mental states of people like Gemma and Walter bring better connections to the spirit world. I believe it. I think Gemma does have a spark of the divine." She cast another scoop of flour over the counter. "Imagine living in a culture that actually strives to learn from the abilities of people like Gemma and Walter. How beautiful is that?" She tried again to roll out the thing in front of her—she couldn't say if it was dough or not. "Anyway. They're right. It's a good way to think about it."

"It is a good way to think about it. But it doesn't change a thing for Gemma." The dough was sticking everywhere like gum. "I'm not asking you to tell her what to do, but will you at least talk to her more about having this baby? Help her think it through? To be sure?"

"Yes. I can do that. But I guarantee it won't change a thing."

"Maybe not. But thank you." She started plucking clumps of dough off the back of her mother's hands. "So, about the move. How do you feel about Seattle, Mom?"

"I love Seattle. Always have. And if this is what you want, I think you should go for it."

"Well, I am. I've already accepted the position. But I meant for you. I want you to come with us."

"Oh, Maggie. I have no desire to move. Oregon is my home. I finally have this one-hundred-year-old farmhouse." She stood rooted against the counter. "I've been all around the world, and this is where I belong. Better prepare yourself for Gemma wanting to stay too. She loves having her own apartment, and she loves Lolly so much, she loves her job, and—"

"And she loves you."

"Yes, she does. But I was going to say, 'and Walter's here.' "

"Walter? They're having sex—that's all."

"Honey, I'm sure it's more than that. They're practically living together." She brushed her forehead with the back of one hand. "They genuinely care about each other. There's a bond there. Maybe could even marry one day."

"*Marry?!* Please, don't put that idea in her head."

"She has her own ideas, Mag. Like I said."

"Well, she won't leave if you don't. So I guess you decided it for her."

"Not true. Gemma will do what's right for her. The same way you and I do." Olivia sprinkled water over the lump in front of her. *Is this ever going to turn into crust?*

"I'm no expert, but doesn't dough have to be refrigerated before you roll it out?" Magnolia asked.

Olivia contemplated the idea for several seconds before curse words flew like the flour dust

"Look. I agree your farmhouse is awesome, Mom. I don't blame you for not wanting to leave. I only hoped…"

"I know. You want us all to stay together." Olivia pushed everything aside and sat.

"I do. And I don't want to leave Gemma."

"Of course not."

"I have to try and convince her to come with me. No matter what happens with this baby, she's going to need me."

"Well, you're right about that. She'll need you more than anyone."

Magnolia groaned. "But if she keeps this baby, I cannot be one of those women who ends up raising their grandchild. That has never been my plan."

"Hah! You think that's anyone's plan? Sometimes there's no choice."

"I know."

"You'll do what every loving grandparent does. You'll do everything in your power to do what's best for your child and that baby."

"Like you did for me and Gemma."

"Yes, and you know why? Because that baby will steal your heart so fast you won't know what hit you."

Magnolia grinned. "You speak from experience. But, for me, I'm not so sure."

"I do speak from experience." Olivia stood and lobbed the wad of dough straight into the trash. It landed like a bomb. "Should've made cobbler to begin with." She reached for the oatmeal and brown sugar. "Gemma's not going to move, Maggie. And she is having this baby. Not unlike the decision you made yourself twenty-seven years ago."

Magnolia rubbed her ear as if she didn't want to hear it.

"I think it's time you listen to your daughter." As fast as Olivia opened the refrigerator, she closed it, facing Magnolia, square on. "And another thing. If you're going to be an immigration attorney and work compassionately with stressed-out families, you better practice with your own first."

This time when Olivia pulled open the refrigerator, she extracted a bottle of pinot gris. "Time for lunch."

Chapter Eleven

Into the Orchards

On the last day of September, the lingering heat of summer finally rolled away. In every direction, scarlet trees blazed against the fall firmament—their twisted boughs scattering leaves like sun-flame gold and crimson glitter.

The juicy aroma of a crusty brown, crackling-crisp prime rib permeated Olivia's kitchen, swirling in the air and plunging her at once into comfort. Who knew a smell could be so intoxicating. "Now *this* is Sunday supper in a farmhouse," Olivia crooned

It was a farewell dinner for Magnolia because Olivia had predicted right. Gemma wouldn't budge. She was adamant her baby would be born in Sugar Creek—not Seattle.

The more Gemma discussed the prospect of becoming a mother, the more enthused she sounded. Needless to say, Olivia knew it wasn't the upshot Magnolia had hoped for.

As soon as she had finished her last bite, Gemma stood and whacked her knife repeatedly against the edge of her dinner plate. "I have an announcement! I am telling everyone this at once." She plunked the knife down. "Mama, Nani, Zorro, Walt, and everyone else." Even though there was no one else.

"Excuse me, Gemma," Walter interrupted. "The name Walt no longer suits me." He tugged at his pine green sweater vest. "Please resume calling me Walter," he instructed, spreading his sandy brown hair over his scalp with a splayed hand. At thirty-one years old, Walter complained it was too thin, blaming it on chromosome 20 and heredity. His ball cap went back on as soon as he finished his meal.

"That will confuse me again, Walt!" Gemma huffed. "I mean *Walter.* See?!"

"I've come to the conclusion the name Walt isn't appropriate as I'm not actually the poetic type. I'd rather identify myself with Walter Cronkite." He burst into raucous laughter.

"You're too young to know who he is!" Olivia quipped.

"I do know who he is. And the name of a highly esteemed news anchor clearly suits me better. My real name is Walter, and I'm sticking to it."

"Well, stick to it for good," Gemma barked. "What I have to say is, everyone can stop trying to change my mind about my baby. *Our* baby, I mean. Not all of you. But some of you. Including the ladies I told at the beauty shop. So…" She took a swig of milk. "Stop telling me all these things you keep saying. Because I can be a great mother. I can learn how. Like you guys did. Well, like the mothers here did. Maybe even better than they did!" she howled.

Walter let out a snort. "Now that's funny!"

"So," Gemma continued, "stop talking me out of it, or I mean trying to, because you can't. And, Nani, I'm going to do that thing you taught me sitting in our tree." Gemma stuck her thumb on the end of her nose and wiggled her fingers. "Remember?" She leaned over her mother's face, wiggling madly.

Magnolia pitched backward. "What on earth are you doing?"

"It's for all the critics and naysayers. Did I say that right, Nani?"

"Perfect, Gem."

"I thumb my nose at them in my mind."

Olivia crowed, "I taught Gemma that a long time ago. Wonderful advice, wouldn't you agree?"

"Wonderful advice, Mother." Magnolia raised to clear the table. "But she didn't exactly do it in her mind now, did she?"

"Sometimes I do it for real too," Gemma added.

"I say Gemma's right. No more naysaying from any of us," Zork said.

"Hear, hear," Olivia chimed. "And you stop clearing the table, Maggie. Sit," she ordered. "This is your farewell dinner. No chores for you. Walter and Gemma will help."

"And so will I," Zork told them.

Walter raised his tall, lanky body out of his seat like a wooden soldier. He saluted first and then organized the dirty silverware into a pile. After that he stacked the plates and bowls according to color and size.

Everyone stood, and with one glance, Zork signaled Olivia to the garage. He pulled the door shut. "Any more emails?"

"No. Nothing."

"The one you forwarded kept me up all night."

Olivia smirked. "Welcome to my world."

"The devil certainly has a way with words."

"Doesn't he? Look, I know it's not all about the intel I have, but trust me Zork, it has more to do with intel than his dead brother."

"Probably. But he gets off on revenge…"

"This time I may too. I haven't forgotten who they took from me either."

Zork stared at his boots. "Nor have I." He met Olivia's gaze. "I look forward to what comes next."

"Me too. And I won't tell them, Zork. Not one word of what I know."

"I know that."

"Sam died for this, and I will too if necessary."

"It's not going to come to that." He squeezed her forearm. "Not this time."

The dishwasher was full when they stepped back into the kitchen. Gemma and Walter playfully nudged each other in the hip as they wiped down the counters, launching a chase around the island.

In the living room, Magnolia hit the television remote, the screen going from "Breaking News" to black. "Boy, have we lost our way," she said. "All respect for truth and integrity is gone in this country—I simply can't stomach it."

"Is it any surprise?" Olivia tossed a newspaper in the recycle basket. "Think about it. There have been bad seeds all through history. Some of them rise to power. It's not the first time, and it won't be the last."

Magnolia grimaced. "Let's go wander through the orchards. Come on, everyone." She stood, stretching side to side. "It's my last chance to roam among the trees." A twinge of gloom spread around her words, but only her mother seemed to notice.

Olivia tightened an arm around her shoulders.

"You'll come home a lot, won't you? To visit us and the orchards?"

"Definitely."

Zork grabbed his black leather jacket, while everyone else pulled on wool coats, hats, and gloves. Olivia swaddled her neck in one of Gemma's luxurious hand-knit scarves, the color as rich as plum jelly. It instantly took the bite out of the air.

Most of the hazelnuts had already separated from their husks and dropped in the orchard. Crops of them were swept into rows awaiting pickup by the harvester. Walter and Gemma ambled ahead with Zork who listened to their stories about riding the roller coaster at the fair and barfing on the whirly-cups—goliath-sized strawberries. According to Walter, they spun faster than a centrifuge.

Olivia and Magnolia sauntered behind. All their lives they had rambled through the orchard in every direction, their chatter bubbling through the unbroken, endless rows of foliage. Countless secrets lay cradled there—twisted love, mangled grief, and sometimes great peace, all memorized in the raw earth between the trees.

"We were standing right here," Olivia recalled. "Right here in the heart of the orchard where the air tastes so sweet and aromatic." A few nuts thunked around them when she inhaled. "This is the spot where I learned I was going to be a grandmother."

"And where I fell in love with Gemma's father." Magnolia sighed.

Olivia couldn't be certain, but she thought she heard a twinge of regret in Magnolia's voice that night. Perhaps it was harder to leave than she expected. After all, she would be leaving alone.

The next morning would be Magnolia's last shot at persuading Gemma to change her mind. And Olivia had a feeling she would give it her all.

****

It was an adrenaline-charged, fast and furious, wild-eyed dream. Galloping across the field in a daring escape, Gemma's long black gown streamed in the wind, flapping over Lolly's tail. They were dodging a spray of bullets, whizzing right and left, when Gemma's phone alarm chimed and everything vaporized. A slow and steady stream of bells were ding-donging at five thirty in the morning. *Phooey. Now I don't know how it ends.*

She silenced the bells and stared at the cracks of muted gray streaming between the cracks of the curtain. "Oh," she muttered. "Mama leaves today."

"Shhh!" Walter said, tossing himself over.

Bleary-eyed, Gemma untangled her twisted sheet and tiptoed to the bathroom, the doorknob squeaking in her hand when she shut it slowly behind her. She hurriedly pulled on leggings and a sweatshirt, inspecting herself sideways in the bathroom mirror. "Nothing yet," she grumbled. "Barely a pooch." She sounded disgusted even to herself.

Headlights lit up the parking lot when Gemma peered out the window.

—I'm here— Mama texted with a smiley emoji.

—I'm here too— Gemma replied. —I'll be down soon. Maybe a few seconds. Or way less— When she stepped outside, the blackness closed around her like midnight. She loped down the stairs with an envelope in hand.

"Hi, sweetie." Mama had her window down. "Thanks for getting up so early to see me off."

"You're welcome." Gemma wagged the envelope at her. "I made you a card. For your new house."

"That's so nice. Thank you."

"Promise not to read it until you get there."

"All right." Mama placed the card on top her purse.

"It says I want my baby to have what I do—a mama who loves her and a nani who is always on her side. And also that I hope you'll be with me when she's born. If you want to."

"Of course I want to. I'd love that." Mama got out and slumped against the car door. "Remember, if you ever change your mind about Seattle, you're always welcome."

"I know."

"You'd have a wonderful room with an incredible view of the city. I can't wait for you to see it. There's room for a nursery too."

Gemma glanced away and then to the half-moon winking in the sky. "Hey! A falling star!" Gemma sealed her eyes shut and raised her face to the sky. *This time I wish to be brave.*

Mama's arms folded. "You know, if you did move, it could be a fresh start. I'd hire help for the baby, and I promise, you could travel home and see Nani whenever you'd like, and—"

"Mama—"

"And Walter," she hurriedly added.

"No. You keep asking. Every time I say no, because I do not want to leave." Gemma made her words sound strong. And brave.

"Just think about it," Mama urged. "If you and

Walter don't stay together, you may feel differently."

"We will stay together! But if he can't be a dad, it's okay. I can do it alone. You and Nani did."

Mama sighed. "Yes, but—"

"I am not leaving! That's my final answer." She giggled. "I sounded like that game show on TV."

Mama didn't finish her sentence. She sniffed the air like Gemma did when the scent of baked bread wafted past from a nearby bakery. "Okay." She sighed. "Had to try. The thing is, I already feel the ache of missing you."

"I'll miss you too."

"And I'm sorry I haven't been happier about you having this baby."

Gemma glanced at her toes, admiring the aqua nail polish. Even in the dark light of morning it sparkled a little.

"I am sorry for that," Mama said weakly. "But I see things you can't sometimes."

"You aren't always right."

"I know I'm not."

"I deserve happiness, and I can be a good mom."

"Of course you do. But motherhood is more complicated than you realize."

"They say it is for everyone until they do it."

"I know. And I realize I've been hard on you, but that's my job."

"No it's not." Gemma felt the prick of flesh under her fingernails when she gripped her upper arms. "That is *not* your job."

"But most mistakes can be prevented if—"

"My baby is not a mistake." Gemma stepped back.

"I didn't mean that. I meant—"

"I'm going to prove you wrong!"

"I hope you will. But I'd be lying if I told you I wasn't worried." Mama slumped.

"This baby is a part of me. You should already love her the way you say you love me."

Mama tenderly took hold of Gemma's shoulders. "Okay, look. I'll say this once and then never again. I promise."

Gemma rolled her eyes, arms crossed over her chest.

"This won't be easy. I won't be here. And your nan can't do it. She shouldn't have to. You'll have to listen to your caseworker and everyone she connects you to. And you'll have classes, and—"

"Nani and I already talked about all this! And I *want* to attend classes!"

"Shhh. Hear me out. Please." Mama pressed on. "If you don't do everything right, you could lose this baby. That could happen too."

A splash of fear tightened around Gemma's ribcage.

"It'll be hard," Mama continued. "And it will challenge you in ways you've never been challenged before. You have the most important and the most difficult job ahead of you that you've ever faced."

"Gee whiz." Gemma breathed noisily. "I'm not going on a mission to Mars."

Mama drooped.

"I will not lose this baby, Mama. I won't."

"It's more than a supervised babysitting job. You won't know what to do half the time. I sure didn't."

"You didn't?"

"Of course not."

"Well, then, see? It's okay if I don't either. Remember what my teacher told us, Mama? Mistakes make our brains grow. That's how we learn. Our brain muscle gets stronger with practice." Gemma's arms timidly unfolded. She reached for Mama, and they embraced.

"That's true. And I'm not trying to scare you. The truth is… *I'm* scared." She squeezed Gemma tight.

"Don't be scared, Mama."

They caught each other's gaze.

"I do love you, Gem. I'll call when I get to Seattle. And you can call me anytime."

"I know."

"I'm sending a check each month. To help with anything you need."

"Wow." Gemma almost didn't know what to say. And then she remembered. "Thank you."

"And I want you to take the train and come see me. Will you?"

"Yeah, that'd be fun."

Mama flashed a satisfied grin and opened the car door. "What are you doing the rest of your day?"

"Going on my run, flying with Zorro, and then seeing Nani. It's okay if I fly pregnant. And I can jog too, since I've always been a runner. But I can't ride Lolly. The doctor said, no."

"Lolly will have to wait then. How far are you running?"

"Same as always. Nani says I go four miles each way. So six total."

Mama wrestled with the seatbelt. "Eight total," she corrected. "Well, have fun."

"I do. Especially when I fly the plane."

"When *you* fly the plane?"

"With Zorro right next to me!" Gemma squealed. "Duh, Mama!"

"All right. I'll call you and Nani later."

Gemma bent down through the open window for one last peck on the cheek. "I hope you'll love my baby."

"Of course I'll love it."

"*Her.*"

"Whatever." The car rumbled awake. "Love you." Mama swung back around the crowded parking lot and drove past one last time, blowing kisses.

Gemma had barely turned when she heard the squeal of brakes. Mama's car door flew open and out she came.

"What in the world?" Gemma scampered toward her. "What happened, Mama?!"

She grabbed Gemma's hands. "I can't leave with any regrets, and I have a whopper of one I can't take with me."

"What do you mean?"

"You overheard me say something at Nani's that was wrong. And untrue. There was no excuse for it."

"Oh…" Gemma pretended to barely remember. "What did you say?" Her face wrinkled up.

Mama glanced down when her ankle boot squashed a teensy pinecone with a satisfying crunch. "That you had no sense."

"Not a lick of it," Gemma added. "Almost none."

Mama's head shot up, her eyes glossy. "Right. I'm so sorry. It's not the truth, and you didn't deserve that."

"Why did you say it then?"

"Because I'm scared to let you go. And accept the

fact that your choices belong to you now—not me. You have every right to make your own decisions, right or wrong. The truth is, I'm the one without a lick of sense. Will you ever forgive me?" She enfolded Gemma in another long embrace.

But Mama didn't need to ask. Gemma forgave everyone. She waved until Mama's car disappeared on the horizon, right as the sun rose and brightened the sky.

****

The dry leaves of autumn chattered under Gemma's boots on the brick walkway leading to Nani's front door. She followed her nose to the kitchen where the air was spiced with cinnamon and ginger. When Gemma breathed in, a warm, pleasurable sensation rushed through her. She slipped back into her childhood self. All the seasons in Nani's home held memories—stored like gold inside her.

A shiny copper tea kettle whistled on the stove.

"Graham Cracker!" she bellowed all the way up to the second floor. "Where are you?"

"In the bathroom!"

"Whatcha doin?" Gemma scampered up the stairs.

"On the pot."

"*You* smoke weed?"

"No, I don't smoke weed."

Gemma pressed her mouth against the crack of the bathroom door. "Walter does. It's okay though, it's legal. But I don't let him do it in my apartment because of my baby. Well, I should say *our* baby. He did shoot out the seed. But anyway, he's very careful. I have strong rules."

"Good! And I said I'm on the pot. Meaning the

toilet, not weed."

"Have you ever smoked weed, Nani?"

"Yes."

"Whoa! You did?"

"A long time ago."

Gemma gasped. "I bet it wasn't legal!"

"No, technically it wasn't."

"Wow. You broke the law."

"No, I didn't. Long story."

"But you smoked it un-legally. That's against the law. You could have gone to jail for doing that."

"Well, I didn't. And I don't break the law."

"Thankfully you didn't get caught. Almost done?" Gemma rolled her head to the center of the door.

"Well, I'm having a little trouble."

Uh oh... Not enough fiber. Gemma barged in like a bull. "I can help! Lift your feet up. This works."

"I appreciate your help, but—"

"Here." Gemma bent over and held both of Nani's feet off the ground. "Bend your knees and lift up like this. It works for me."

"What?! Honey, I ran out of toilet paper. That's all."

"Oh!" Gemma snorted, dropping Nani's feet with a thud. She reached in the cupboard, chuckling. "Here ya go." She tossed a roll to Nani and watched as it bounced off her legs, flew into the bathtub and unraveled. "Oh my gosh!" Gemma giggled chasing after it. "Sorry! I crack myself up."

"You crack everyone up," Nani chortled. "And that's a compliment by the way. We could all use more of what you have."

Gemma liked the way Nani pointed out good

things about her all the time. It made her feel special—in the right way. It made her want to help Nani more.

"After Mama left, I went on my run and then Zorro and I went flying. I can't ride Lolly for a long time, but I can be in a plane and drive a car. That's okay. But no horses. Not till after the baby comes out."

"Well then, shall we hike to Luper today? I have roses for the graves."

"With food?"

"Of course. You up to it?"

"I think so. I only get sick a little sometimes. My food goes down when I swallow and then it moves right back up, but if you don't bring tuna fish, I probably won't barf."

"Good to know. Put something warm on and we'll leave when you're ready."

But when Gemma was ready, Nani wasn't. A couple of knuckled raps against the rustic wood door of her farmhouse startled them both.

Nani had a few secrets of her own that came knocking.

Chapter Twelve

Men in Suits

A face appeared at the window beside the front door when Nani flung it open. "Yes?"

"Olivia Porter?"

"Yes." Two men in swanky suits reached for papers out of their breast pockets. "Save your breath," Nani said. "I'm a believer, and no, it's not with your religion." She pointed to the NO SOLICITORS sign. "That's for everyone."

One had deep-set eyes darting everywhere—the other a bald stocky man who immediately stepped forward. "Sorry to bother you. We're not solicitors."

Nani frowned. "What is it then?"

"We're with the FBI. May we come in?"

Gemma's mouth dropped for a second. "My mom's driving to Seattle," she blurted. "Is she okay?"

Nani wrapped an arm around Gemma's shoulders.

"This is only concerning Olivia Porter, ma'am."

Gemma's pounding heart lost some of its urgency.

"Do I know what this is about?" Nani asked.

"Like I said we're with the FBI. Special agents. This is about an investigation." He straightened his tie. The other man shifted his weight and seemed irked. "May we come inside now, please? You really don't have a choice."

Gemma's ticker sped up again like a turbo jet. Even the calming scent of Nani's shampoo, the smell of a coconut smoothie, didn't help when a whiff of it coasted by.

Nani blew out a hefty puff of air, fiddling with her messy chignon. "Your badges, please."

They slapped them open by the time she said "please."

Nani scanned them and stepped back. "Come in," she said, pushing the door all the way open. "Gemma, please tell Zork I need him right away."

"Oh no," Gemma gasped. She raced from the entry, through the kitchen, and slipped on the rug. She scrambled to her feet, opened the door, and screamed. "Zorro!" Her voice boomed across the back porch. "This is serious! Nani got caught!" The screen door clacked to and fro, making a racket behind her.

Chapter Thirteen

The Warrant

The FBI agent with the deep-set eyes raised his eyebrows.

Olivia tried to explain. "My granddaughter likes to broadcast it when she thinks someone's been 'caught.'"

His face pinched up, while the other glanced down the hall with a steely mug.

Gloomy looking gentlemen. "Let me clarify." Olivia offered a sheepish grin. "My granddaughter thinks you're arresting me because I smoked pot a few decades ago." She glanced at her phone. "But I'm betting you did too."

One sported an off-kilter smile. The other paid no attention.

Cranky bastard. "May I see your badges again, please? With your written I.D. cards this time."

Olivia lowered her glasses and peered at the papers. She tilted each identification card until the light gleamed right and then studied their faces. "Okay." She closed the door behind them. "What can I do for you?"

"We'll be confiscating all your electronics."

"What? That seems a bit rash. Why?"

"Here's the warrant, ma'am."

"Warrant? What's this about?"

"All computers, laptops, phones, tablets, all devices in the home. We'll be taking them with us."

"Taking them? Because?"

"We're not authorized to disclose that."

"And what investigation is this exactly?"

"Like we said, you need to direct us to your computers and bring us what we've asked for."

Olivia examined the warrant. "This doesn't explain—"

"Hang on, men," Zork stepped in. "Let me see your identification please."

Olivia handed him the warrant first, with a little backhand flick.

Zork unfolded his glasses and calmly adjusted them over his nose. He shuffled through the documents, scanning everything front to back. He finally handed them back. "Okay." He dropped his spectacles into his shirt pocket. "Have at 'em."

Olivia's face jerked. She shot Zork a not-so-fast expression.

"It's legit, Olivia. You have no choice."

She accepted his response and used the arm of her glasses to point them to her office. "Second door to your left," she said, and turned back to the kitchen where Zork was pouring coffee—as if it were any lazy, carefree, Sunday morning.

He lifted his mug. "Want some?"

"No." She pulled out a bar stool and sat. "You certainly seem relaxed enough. Must be what I think it is."

"Yep."

"Not FBI?"

"Oh, they're FBI." He took a sip. "But they don't

know who we are or who sent them. I'll help get things collected. I need your phone." Zork lowered his voice. "Got your backup cell?"

"But of course." She slid her other phone across the island to him.

He sipped his coffee and stood to leave. "We'll talk more later."

****

After practically everything plugged into a socket left the house, Olivia stood at the front window, hands on her hips. "Well. I hope they left the blow dryer at least. And a blender for my extra-large margarita tonight."

Gemma stomped through the hallway talking on her phone and abruptly handed it to Olivia.

"Who's this?"

"Mama. I called and told her you need help."

"Oh, Gemma. I wish you hadn't."

Gemma shoved the phone up to Olivia's ear.

"Hello, honey!" she forced out. "Did you make it there all right?"

"I'm pulled over on the road. What's happening? Gemma said you're in trouble and getting arrested for drugs. What is she talking about?"

"Oh, well, no. I'm fine. Not in handcuffs yet!" she quipped. "I've done nothing wrong. And nothing I feel the least bit guilty about, either."

"She said men came inside and took things."

"Well, yes, they did. All my electronics. The FBI had a warrant so I had to let them, but it's obviously all a big mistake."

"What?! The FBI does not come in and take things or get a warrant without good cause."

"They make mistakes, Mag. Happens all the time."

"No, Mom, not *all the time*. Look, you need to take this seriously. You need a good lawyer. Should I turn around and come back?"

"No! Of course not, don't be silly. I'm sure it's nothing. Probably something I barked about on social media. You know how I get. I probably said something that caught their attention. I do figure things out sometimes; maybe I let the cat out of the bag and didn't even know it. Top secret information. Hah! Or said a little something they took wrong. That's all."

"Mother, please. If you've said anything that sounds bad it could be a mess. It could be in the news tomorrow."

"Oh for heaven's sake, Maggie. That's a bit dramatic. No one cares about my opinions. If they did, this country would be right back on track. They probably have to follow some silly protocol with any little thing that's said. Even something remotely suspicious."

"Remotely suspicious? What little things have you been saying? Seriously. This is not good. Get off social media if this is what you do on it. Grab a pen and paper and call this guy right now. He knows me well and can help you. Hang up and promise you'll call."

"Okay. Ready." Olivia raised a finger and drew scallops in the air while Magnolia rattled numbers off. "Thank you and I appreciate it."

"Let me know what happens."

"Will do. Need to run."

Olivia tapped "off" and tossed the cell back to Gemma. "Bundle up and meet me outside for our hike, Tink. I'll be there in a minute."

Gemma bounced off the sofa, paused *Frozen* with the remote, and clapped animatedly. She scurried to the screen door, belting out the movie's theme song all the way out.

Olivia motioned Zork back to the kitchen. "So?"

"Everything's taken care of," he said. "It's a whole new game now."

Olivia studied Zork's eyes. "Okay." She nodded. "Time to get on with it then."

Chapter Fourteen

In the Tiny Sparkles of Light

Nani was right. The brisk air required bundling up. Pleased for another trek to Luper, she gently covered her small periwinkle tiara with an ivory fur-lined hat— *Doctor Zhivago* style, and twirled a matching scarf around her neck. Her chin instantly warmed.

It was the first of October, and the orchards were already cold and empty. Cold enough that frosty grass crackled beneath Gemma's copper-toed boots.

"Two more days until my baby picture thingy. What is it called?" She yanked up her deerskin suede fringed gloves, a bucket of apricot roses on her arm.

"An ultrasound?"

"Yeah. That's it."

"Already?"

"They can see things even if she's only five weeks old, but they think I might be *a lot* more pregnant than that. Or a lot less. We don't know. The picture will tell us."

"I see."

"I want everyone there. Well, first Walter. And then you, Mama, and Zorro. If that's okay."

"Of course. It's your choice every step of the way."

"I know. Okay. And I told Walter he better not faint if it's twins, or triplets or six babies! It happens."

Nani chuckled. "If there's more than one, I'm going down right with him."

"Yeah! And then I'll faint." Gemma chortled. "But I'll be lying down, so hopefully I can't if I'm flat already. Unless fainting happens lying down too…"

Nani's white teeth filled her wide smile. "It'll be fine. And I must say, you look all glowy. You're practically bouncing with joy."

"Good. Because you can tell who has strong muscles down there by the bounce in their step." Gemma pointed to her crotch. "Did you know that, Nani?"

"Wait, what?"

"Yeah, women who spring and bounce when they walk have good muscles that help you push the baby out. Well, not you, but me." She giggled. "And"—she grinned a little shamefacedly—"the nurse also said strong muscles down there help other good things happen too." Gemma winked.

"You mean, orgasms?"

"Yeah. So we have to spring and bounce."

"Is that so?"

"Yeah. Like this." Gemma demonstrated exaggerating the move by lifting her heel and pushing up on her toes. She halted for the pure drama of it.

Nani mirrored her movements. "We look ridiculous."

Gemma howled. "Well, it's what we have to do if we want sparks and fireworks to explode."

"Well, then by all means bounce away." Nani lifted the cemetery gate and pushed in. "Our tree is warmer than the log bench. Think you can get up there all right?"

"Sure." After Gemma rested three roses on baby Harriet's grave and a single stem on the others, she set her boot into a notch in the tree trunk and pushed. But nothing happened. "Whoa! I must weigh a ton. And the baby is only the size of a jellybean. We think anyway."

Nani lifted her rear end. "Heave ho! And you're up."

"How can you be so strong?" Gemma asked.

"Because I work at it. You'll be strong at my age too if you do the same. It is a choice. Heart, mind, body, and soul. They all need our attention."

"Running keeps me strong."

"Yes, it does."

"I did win gold for long-distance running in the Special Olympics. Four times!"

"You sure did, Tink." Nani brought both sides of Gemma's coat together over her belly and zipped it up. She wasn't sure if the warmth of the coat comforted her, or if Nani's doting over her had. It reminded her of being tucked into bed at night—and feeling loved.

"Why didn't you bury Grandpa Sam here?" Gemma placed a peanut butter sandwich in Nani's hand.

"They don't allow it. Luper is a historical site."

"So no new dead people can come here?"

"Nope. Only the pioneers who came before us. They're preserving their history, and rightfully so. Maybe someday you'll have picnics here with *your* grandchild. Wouldn't that be something?"

"Sure. As long as you still come. But that's a lot of people. How many of us do you think could fit in our tree?"

"I guess we'll find out."

"Where did the rest of Grandpa Sam go after you put him in your necklace?"

Nani set the sandwich in her lap and broke off a loose piece of bark. "Well." She peeled back a layer. I'll tell you something no one else knows."

"A secret?"

"Yes. A good one."

"Okay. Why doesn't anyone know?"

"Because I'm not sure what I did is allowed."

"Uh oh. Another un-legal thing? Like the drugs?"

Nani's face opened with a wide grin. "I've never done anything *illegal,* not knowingly anyway."

"If you say so," Gemma said.

"I did something on impulse. Afterward I wondered if I had broken some rule, but anyway, after your Grandpa Sam was cremated, I carried him around with me for a long time."

"Is that against the rules?"

"No. People keep ashes of their loved ones all the time. I simply carried Sam's with me everywhere I went."

"How'd you do that?"

"He was in a bag. His ashes, I mean."

Gemma's lips squished up. "Ewww."

"I know." Olivia's lips mirrored hers. "It's sealed of course, and nobody knew I took him places, but it was a comfort having him with me. Heavy as an ox, but a comfort. I wasn't ready to accept he was gone."

"You carried him around like a bag of groceries?"

"Pretty much. I put him in the front seat of my truck and off we went."

"I don't like the idea—being in a bag. It's weird burning up into nothing."

"I know it sounds dreadful, but lots of people accept the idea, and even prefer it. I know I did."

Gemma's forehead wrinkled the way it always did when she was trying to figure things out.

Nani continued. "All through history people have seen the value of cremation. It can be a sacred way for the body to return to the earth where all life begins."

"Burying people sounds a lot less painful than burning up, though."

"There's no pain. Not once you die."

"How do you know? If you've never been dead, how do you know that? I don't understand how you can stop feeling."

A soft groan escaped before Nani answered. "You ask me all the hard questions."

"You're the only one I can."

Nani wagged her head knowingly. "Look, lots of people have questions. I don't know how it happens, but I'm confident we move on in some form. And I know when the brain is gone, feelings and pain are gone too."

"But I don't get how a body can stop breathing. I've tried it and it doesn't work. There's no way I can hold my breath forever. Maybe by the time I'm super, super old, people won't die anymore."

"By then you might want to."

"Huh?"

"Never mind. What I meant to say was people have been dying since the beginning of time."

"True. That's a super long time." Gemma tapped her chin a few times and stared at Nani. "I'm scared of being a ghost."

"You won't be a ghost, Gemma. Maybe an angel,

but not a ghost."

"Okay… *Good*. But Mama's not sure she believes in Creator. Not the way we do."

"I know."

"I wish everyone believed the same thing so I knew for sure what was happening."

"Maybe we're not supposed to know." Nani stretched her arms behind her head. "People make it much harder than they need to."

"But it is hard."

"Maybe it doesn't have to be. Maybe if you know love, you know God—your Creator. Simple as that."

"That would be nice."

"If you think about it, where else would love come from? It has to be from God."

"Yeah," Gemma said. "And I think I felt baby Harriet's soul. That must be proof of something too."

"Exactly. Sometimes we forget to pay attention to what's right in front of us."

Gemma snuggled into Nani's arm the way she always did for comfort. "Well, then, Creator, must be in everyone."

"Well, not everyone." The look on Nani's face raised the hair on Gemma's arms. "It's a malevolent world."

"What does that mean?"

"It means there's a lot of evil mixed into some people. Evil and deception."

"Well, that's not good." Gemma tipped her head all the way back and stared upside down at the branches, one hand grasping the top of her hat. "It looks cool when you do this. Try it."

Nani always played along. She tipped backward

until their cheeks touched side by side.

An old familiar sensation awakened when Nani's skin pressed against hers. Love rose in Gemma's chest and coursed through her, the feeling as big as the sky. So strong, she felt her soul float all the way up to where heaven might be. Gemma rotated and planted a big smacker on Nani's cheek. It made her glow.

"This *is* cool," Nani marveled. "Like a piece of art seeing everything this way." She pulled out her phone and took a photo.

"You didn't tell me the rule you broke."

They pulled themselves upright.

"Okay, so—Sam was a little heavier in that bag than I expected. Hence, I made the decision to take some of him out. First for this custom-made necklace." She gave the silver drop a quick polish with her scarf.

"That sure didn't help much."

"No. It didn't." She snickered. "But I liked having him with me. Still do. But that gave me the next idea."

Gemma reached for the necklace at Nani's neck, caressing the smooth surface the way she had so many times before.

"I decided to bring him here with me," she continued.

"You carried his heavy bag here? To Luper?"

"I did. I put him in my saddlebag. A perfect fit. Sam and I, well, Sam's ashes and I, rode together on Buster. The Buster before mine, that is. Buster Senior."

Gemma sat straight. "Not to be rude, but that's kind of funny, Nani."

"It is, actually."

"Grandpa in a bag on Buster Senior?"

"Yup. Sam would have gotten a big kick out of it."

"I thought you couldn't bury him here."

"I didn't bury him here. But it helped carrying him with me. All I know is it helped." Nani paused. "Until it didn't."

"Why?"

"I don't know. One day it did, and then one day it didn't. And yet, I still couldn't let him go. So I unsealed his bag, reached in with both hands, and held a scoop of him against my heart. And then I poured him right into the big crack of this old maple."

Gemma felt her eyes swell as big as blimps. "*Here*?" She bolted up. "We're *sitting* on him?"

"It's okay! Look," Nani pointed at the largest crevice in the bowl encircling them. "This is where he is. We're not on him—we're sitting *by* him. He surrounds us here."

"Whoa." The idea made Gemma squeamish. "Do you think he knows it?"

"I don't know." She loosened her scarf. "Then I waited for a warm evening and let the rest of him float away on the river. I told him to rest on the current and take his journey toward the setting sun, toward the warmth of light, and into the arms of God."

"Did he hear you?"

"Maybe."

"Is that the secret? That you poured him inside our tree and then into the river?"

"It's not really a secret, but I'd like it to stay between us. I don't know why. For some reason it feels important for you to know."

"It's good you told me then, Nani." Gemma fidgeted. "You believe me, don't you?"

"About what?"

"That my baby's a girl."

"Yes, I do." Nani spread both hands around Gemma's tummy and beamed. "In a matter of months, I'll feel the warm motion of life under these hands. And then I'll say, 'Yes! This baby girl is a strong one. That feels like the foot or an elbow.' "

Gemma's forehead wrinkled. "Will she have a brain like mine or yours?"

"No idea."

Gemma glanced away wondering what the future held for her daughter.

"What are you worried about, Gem?"

"I hope she's a regular thinker. Not like me."

Nani's eyes, blue as deep water, caught the light when she turned and studied Gemma's face. "Honey, no matter what—your baby will be who she's supposed to be. Exactly like you are. If this baby is even half the person you are, she'll be lucky."

"Okay." Gemma grinned with shyness but didn't know why. She circled her stomach with her fingertips. "She could have Walter's brain too, you know. And that'd be just fine. But I hope he doesn't faint when she comes out."

"Me too," Nani said. "Let's head out, Tink. It's getting colder."

Gemma didn't move at first. She breathed in and smelled rain coming, the oil of the earth releasing its scent. The raindrops began slow and easy, landing in gentle thunks above them, pattering casually atop the leaves as if they were tapping velvet. "Nature's piano is playing, Nani. Let's stay one more minute."

"Make it two," Nani said.

Twenty minutes later the showers passed and

Gemma pushed the cemetery gate open to leave. Her eyes lifted to the hills. "Hey! There's those two weird cowboys again. See them up there on horses?"

"What do you mean *again*?" Nani reached for the compact binoculars folded in her pocket. "You've seen them before?"

"Yeah. Twice. This time is number two."

Nani focused in. "Not our kind of cowboys." She lowered the field glasses, inspecting Gemma's face. "Where have you seen them before?"

After a few spiked heartbeats, she answered. "Lolly and I did *not* body-surf down the river, or anything like that. We took a scenic route, and that's when I saw them."

Nani cut a narrow look at Gemma. "At the river?"

Her heart pumped harder. "Not *in* the river. Just very *near* the river," she fibbed. Gemma busied herself with the top button of her coat so her arms wouldn't wiggle. "One had a sweater cap on, not a cowboy hat. I thought that was awfully odd, Nani." She cleared her throat. "Especially when one of them yelled strange things. Like different words or something."

Nani peered at the men again. "So you heard them talking."

"Well, yelling. Only a little. Like they screamed gobbely-gook at each other. I couldn't understand it."

Nani dropped the binoculars in her pocket again. "I don't like the looks of those two."

"Me either," Gemma said with a snarl. She shut the gate extra tight. "Why don't we like the looks of those two, Nani?"

"Doesn't matter why. Always trust your gut, Gem. Always. When something doesn't feel right, trust that feeling." They tottered along the gravel road at a fast pace toward the orchards.

"It's critical that I know about anyone you see. Next time, tell me."

"Okay."

"Let's review everything again. Never leave my property with Lolly when you're by yourself. I don't want you anywhere near the river." Nani peered at Gemma, her eyes penetrating. "And. Don't talk to anyone you don't know, unless you're with Zork or me. I mean it."

"Okay." *Already did both...*

Sharp as laser beams, Nani's eyes pierced Gemma's. "The rule is, you're not to be alone at the river," she repeated.

Gemma's face turned tight as wire. *At least she didn't say* in *the river.*

"Not *anywhere* out here, alone," Nani said again. "Those are the rules. Got it?"

A bird flew past them, bright as a lemon, flitting through sunless branches, sending a shiver through the turning leaves.

"Got it. And I know what to do if someone messes with me," Gemma said. "I dig my thumbs into their eyeballs and I kick em' in the cubes."

"Show me how. Now don't hurt me, but let's practice again."

"Okay, like this!" Gemma performed the moves the way she had learned.

"Nice. When you can't get away, you fight like hell."

"And dig my nails into their skin."

"Excellent. And sometimes you lie like hell. If it

gets you out of danger, you lie. You do and say whatever you must in order to survive. Understood?"

"Yes," she said proudly. "I'm good at that. If I *have* to lie, I mean." Gemma balanced herself atop a fallen trunk, pretending to walk a tight rope. "Yesterday at work, a girl yelled some poison words at me. I remembered what to do. I made her mean words bounce off me, but ohhh, I wanted to fight her right then! But I didn't. I controlled my anger." She leapt off the trunk and caught up to Nani again. "But if she had put one finger on me I would've flipped my lid."

"Of course you would have. No one has the right to touch you without permission. But good job, you didn't hit her for making a comment. Even a nasty one. Shame on her."

"I know."

"And what's our emergency code word?" Nani asked. "Do you remember?"

"Squirrel."

"Right. If you said, 'This lime is so sour it could set a squirrel's teeth on edge,' I'd know you were in danger or ready for a fight."

"What if I don't have a lime?"

"Then you make something else up. Anything you want. You can be brave, Gemma. Don't forget it."

"I know. But I'm still not sure I am."

"Sometimes feelings take longer to catch up to the truth. And the truth is you can do anything you must to protect yourself. And I'll say this again—do not go anywhere off the property by yourself. Not ever again."

"Okay." Gemma's boot had a pebble rolling around inside. She sat on the old tractor tire at the edge of the creek and fished it out.

"I know why the water does that," Gemma said, watching the stream shimmer.

Nani waited for Gemma to say more.

"Haven't you seen the way the river sparkles?"

"I have, and I love it."

"You should."

"Why's that?"

"It's Grandpa Sam showing us he's okay. Like a sign."

"What a lovely thought, Gem."

"I've felt him there before in the tiny sparkles of light. Honest."

Nani's face brightened. "Really..."

"Yeah, and now I know why." Gemma zeroed in on her eyes. "It's because you sprinkled him there."

"I love that you told me this... And I love that you feel him too." Her voice thickened when she brushed a tuft of hair away from Gemma's eyes. "I can hardly wait to see Sam sparkle again."

They linked arms, playfully pulling each other sideways as they slow-poked down the trail. "Can I eat something before I leave? I'm starving."

Nani yanked her the opposite way. "I have *four* horses to feed now, don't I?" She spun around, held up her binoculars, and studied the men on horses two more times. She texted something on her cell, and then tucked it away. She blew out a long stream of air and muttered something.

Gemma paid it no attention; she was too busy bouncing heel to toe. "Don't forget, Nani. Put a nice, bouncy spring in your step."

"Springing all I can, Tink."

****

The rest of the way home, Gemma sang the soundtrack of *Frozen*. Olivia could hardly fathom where the years had gone, struck again by the childhood innocence that remained in Gemma's sense of wonder. Early on, a physician had pronounced that Gemma would remain childlike and "be incapable of forming deep connections with others and within herself." Olivia never believed it. Too many times, she had witnessed the depth and emotionality Gemma held even as a young child. *We need only listen to find a person's wisdom. Any person. Everyone is original*, she reminded herself. *Especially my Gemma.*

The black shutters on the farmhouse came into view as they rounded the last curve, Gemma dancing over every dimple in the road.

"Nani." Gemma pointed, her voice rattling. "That same secret agent car is in front of your house again. They're back for you."

She was right—the FBI had returned.

"They aren't back for me. I've done nothing wrong."

"Well then, why are the bad guys back?"

"They aren't bad guys, sweetie. They're returning my stuff. That's all. Zork is helping them set everything up again."

"So it's all okay?"

"Yup. All a big mistake. Just like we thought."

"Oh, good! Congrats on it being a big, fat mistake. I'm also glad they didn't put you in jail for smoking un-legal weed."

"Yes, at least I won't be a jailbird for that."

Zork sauntered down the front porch stairs, checking his watch. "Pretty quick, huh?"

"I'll say," she said. "And?"

"All set."

Olivia reached into her pocket. "Gemma, would you mind taking my cell inside and charging it for me?"

She grabbed it from Olivia's hand, scrambled up the steps, and through the front door.

Zork gave Olivia his full attention.

"We could have interference on the property any day now," she told him.

Both hands rested in his back pockets, waiting for her to continue.

"I sent you photos a little while ago. I spotted a very familiar Russian tattoo."

"And I bet it climbed right up his neck." Zork spat into a bush. "Hoped we'd never have to set eyes on that thing again."

"Well, now that we know we do, I'm rather looking forward to it. I will happily take a good long look at it for as long as I have to. For Sam."

Zork's face reset itself with rugged resolve. "Me too, Olivia."

"And it seems only fair that he should get the same send-off I gave his brother. Don't you think?"

"I do," Zork said.

"Revenge seems to be the only thing he and I have in common."

"I reckon you're right about that." He sniggered. "Think this will ever end?"

"Oh, it'll end." Olivia kicked up a wild mushroom out of the grass with the toe of her boot. "Hopefully before we're both dead."

Chapter Fifteen

A Flicker of Joy

The truck powered down the highway, Olivia glancing longingly at the empty passenger seat next to her. *Wish you were with me today.* Even Sam's ashes sitting there would have been better than nothing.

She took her eyes off the road long enough to scan the sky. It was Gemma's first ultrasound, and she swore the clouds embodied the sublime that day.

Zork pulled into the parking lot the same time she did.

"Excited?" he asked, stepping toward her.

"More than I expected." Olivia pressed her remote until it beeped and tilted her head back, squinting at the sky. The storm clouds seemed chock-full of new life, plump with the budding expectation of birth—the sun still bright behind them.

"What aftershave do you have on?" Olivia tipped her nose to the air.

"Don't use aftershave."

"Well then, I swear I just smelled Sam. After all these years, his scent still floats around me from time to time. Wish he were here."

"Maybe he is," Zork said. "It is a special day."

Olivia tried to smile but mostly felt like crying. "I know it's too soon to know yet, but I believe Gemma when she says she's having a girl."

"Oh—I believe her too. She knows."

Olivia braked before she entered the building. She swung around, aiming the remote at her truck, listening for a beep.

"You already did that," Zork told her.

"Did I? I don't remember hearing the beep."

"It beeped."

Olivia rolled her eyes, critical of her own memory.

"Your head's in another place. That's all," he told her.

"I know. I don't like it when I'm not on top of things. Not with everything happening."

"It's okay. I got your back."

"I know. And I'm grateful you do."

Olivia found Walter sitting by a fish tank in the middle of the waiting room. His knees bounced recklessly. "When will they call me?" he asked. "Oh, I mean hello. How are you, Nani?"

"I'm fine, Walter. How are you?"

"When will they call me? I'm fine, thank you."

"Soon, I'm sure. Is Gemma here?"

"Yes. She got here forty-three minutes early. On purpose. They called her name but not mine."

"They'll let you know when it's time."

"I hope it won't hurt her. I can't watch if it hurts. It will scare me and—"

"No, Walter," Olivia stopped him. "This is a test that doesn't hurt at all. Remember? Gemma explained everything last night. It'll be fine, I promise." Olivia patted his arm.

"But what if—"

"No *what-if's*," Olivia said. "Stay in the moment.

Right now, everything's fine. You have nothing to worry about." *Hmmm. If only that were entirely true...*

"Olivia's right, Walter," Zork added. "I want you to study those fish. Count only the blue ones, and report back to me how many you find."

Walter promptly followed Zork's instructions, his head bobbing as he counted. He didn't stop.

Magnolia burst through the front doors, heels clipping across the tile, her thick curls pulled up into a chic up-do. She never faltered in heels the way Olivia did. Even in her career days, Olivia made it known she would only dress casually. And that's why.

That afternoon, Magnolia's shiny black heels matched her snug knee-length skirt and form-fitting designer suit coat. Olivia marveled at her sense of style. *Clearly didn't get it from me.* She dusted off her favorite worn boot-cut blue jeans and riding kicks.

"Hey, Zork. Hi, Mom." Magnolia gave them each a hurried hug. "Hello, Walter," she added a little out of breath.

It took concentrated effort for him to stop counting fish. "Hi. Nice to meet you. *See you*, I mean. My nerves are an enormous problem today." Walter raised up like an arrow, reached out, and shook Magnolia's hand. "May I hug you?" He opened both arms.

"Thank you, Walter," she said, embracing him. "Can't believe I got out of court in time. Hardly ever happens." She sounded like the air was being squeezed out of her. She peered at her mother over Walter's shoulder.

"Gemma told me I need to lengthen my hugs," Walter announced. "Is this long enough?"

"I think you..." Magnolia huffed. "...only need to

lengthen them when hugging Gemma." He released his grasp, and Magnolia exhaled, taking a seat.

A loud metal bar on a heavy door clunked open. "Walter West?"

His hand raised. "Present."

"Come on down," the nurse said. Walter grabbed at his raincoat, but it slipped off the chair. Flustered, he tripped over the hood when he snatched it up. Walter's cheeks reddened as he stalked off dragging the slicker on one arm. But before he reached the nurse he braked and loped single-mindedly back to Zork. "Seven, sir. Two large, one medium-sized, and exactly four infant fish. One asleep or dead, three appeared to be eating, two hiding in rocks, and one actively swimming the whole time. All blue, sir."

"Nice work, Walter. Now go take care of Gem."

"I will, sir." He turned on his heel and moved swiftly toward the nurse.

"Now we wait." Magnolia crossed her arms. "How was Gemma today?"

"Terrified this morning, but excited," Olivia said. "She's convinced she's having sextuplets."

"*Why*?" Magnolia sounded perturbed.

Zork cracked up. "Cuz, that's what our Gemma does! Runs that imagination into the ground until it becomes the truth. To her anyway."

"So," Magnolia said cautiously, "no one is telling her they may have detected more than one heartbeat?"

Zork gave Olivia a light whack on the arm. "Look at her. She's as bad as Gemma."

Magnolia rolled her eyes. "Well, don't scare me. Please. Don't even think it." She tucked her purse against her hip and snatched up a home-decorating magazine.

"Glad you came, Maggie," Olivia said.

"Just because this is difficult for me doesn't mean I don't care."

"I know that. And I know how much it means to Gemma to have you here. That's all I meant."

"Well, I'm full of dread to be perfectly honest."

Olivia sighed.

"Get used to it, sis," Zork spat out. "Best accept it. Won't do any good to keep fighting it."

"I'm not 'fighting it', Zork. I'm only—"

"*Fighting* it cuz you're scared of all the *what-if's*— just like Walter. Take some advice—roll with it, Maggie. Don't let it steal your joy. Things rarely happen the way we imagine they will anyway."

Olivia raised her eyebrows. "Quite a speech there, ol' dad."

"You gotta let things unfold the way they will in life," he continued. "Things happen the way they're supposed to."

"Except when they don't," Magnolia groaned. She flipped through the magazine at high-speed.

"Well," Olivia offered, "I do agree it steals joy when we fight against what is."

Magnolia tossed the magazine back. "Look. Things happen that we make happen. And we all screw up a helluva lot."

"Geesh." Olivia's lips curdled. "Your lack of faith is disturbing, though I can't say I completely disagree with your assessment of mankind's stupidity."

"So, Mom." Magnolia's tone switched. "I heard all your stuff came back. What happened with the FBI raid?"

"*Not* a raid, dear. As Gemma said, it was simply a big fat mistake."

"Fine, but you never explained how such a big, fat mistake happened and if you contacted my attorney friend."

The same metal door handle clunked open and everyone's head bounced in that direction.

"Magnolia, Nani, and… *Zorro*?" the nurse called.

They grabbed their belongings and hustled toward her.

"Time for you to meet your new grandbabies!" she said.

"Plural?!" Magnolia snapped.

"Just a joke." The nurse grinned, and ushered them into a small, dark room. "That line never gets old, though."

Gemma twisted her neck around. "There's a real baby in there, everybody! Only one, but Walter can't figure it out."

"I don't get it, but I believe it," Walter said. "If you say that blob in the picture is a baby, okay, I guess it is!" he roared.

Olivia watched the glowing black and white image on the screen in front of them. In the center of the picture there was a faint flutter, a wee bit of movement.

Magnolia sat next to Gemma and stared at the screen—her eyes shining water.

"Okay." The technician signaled. "Everybody ready?" Olivia and Zork watched from behind the table.

"There's the heart," the technician pointed. "Do you see that little flicker? I told Gemma that means she's about eight weeks along."

Magnolia gasped. "It *is* a she?"

"Well, Gemma's sure of it," the technician said. "She could be right, but since it's only the size of a gummy bear there's no telling."

"See, Mama?" Gemma blurted. "I know she's only a gummy bear, but that's her. I'd say more of a lima bean than a bear though. You see her?"

The technician handed Magnolia a tissue. "At the moment I can't see a thing." She dabbed her eyes and tried to focus. It reminded Olivia of the first time Magnolia had observed Gemma inside herself. She had saturated her tissue then too.

Olivia tilted her head, studying the screen. "Another Porter woman is on the way…"

Gemma's zeal for her pregnancy kept the wild green life of summer alive that fall, but no one knew if Magnolia's tearstained cheeks spelled joy, fear, or a sense of doom. No one knew for certain, least of all Magnolia. Olivia knew her daughter well enough to know that.

****

That evening, Magnolia pulled out the hide-a-bed in her mother's guest room and changed into sweatpants and an oversized T-shirt. Olivia watched her push into fur-lined slippers before they schlepped down the stairs, phones in hand, checking messages.

"Nice you're staying the night, hon. Like old times. Wish you didn't have to leave at the crack of dawn, though." Olivia plopped across the sofa. "Oh!" She bounded right back up. "Want popcorn?"

Magnolia nodded feverishly. Her voice went up a notch as Olivia strolled into the kitchen. "Hey, there's something I've been wanting to ask you about."

Olivia slammed the microwave door and poked her

head from around the kitchen. "What is it?"

"I don't mean to open old wounds…"

Olivia rambled back to the sofa. "About what?" She sat with empty bowls and napkins on her lap.

"About the past. About my dad to be specific."

Olivia's chin jutted back. "What is it, Mag? You sound so serious."

"Just wondering." She hesitated as if she might not ask after all.

"Yes?"

"Well, I guess I want to know more. Have you told me everything you know about the way he died?"

Olivia handed Magnolia a napkin and gently set the bowls on the table. "As much as I can, yes. Why?"

"Because I remember something as a kid. Maybe Gemma having this baby got me thinking about things again. I don't know."

"Got you thinking about what?"

"Something I never told you."

"Really? What?"

"I picked up a paper, something from your safe. And I read it."

"Our safe? When?"

"I must've been nine or ten. You were right there, sorting through a stack of files. Something dropped and I picked it up and read it while you rearranged things."

"What was it?"

"Part of your will, I think. Or insurance papers. I'm not sure."

The popping grew louder, and the smell of buttery roasted corn permeated the room.

"Okay, so what did you read?"

Magnolia set her napkin aside. "Dad wasn't killed

in a hunting accident, was he?"

The microwave buzzed, and Olivia bolted up. "Why would you question that?" She swooped into the kitchen, knowing full well she was fleeing the question.

"I always felt there was a secret around this," Magnolia said. "What I read indicated his death may not have been due to a hunting accident."

Olivia returned with a large bowl of steaming popcorn even though her appetite for it had vanished. She placed it between them on the sofa.

"And I'm more convinced than ever I'm right. I think I know what happened."

"Maggie, please, know what?"

"Did my father commit suicide?"

"Suicide?! No." She shook her head. "Honey, no, he didn't."

"Look…" Magnolia paused as if to collect her thoughts. "Have you ever considered he may have?"

"Why would I? Zork was right there. With him to his last breath…" She halted, suddenly bending forward. Grief trundled over her like a steamroller, squeezing all the air out of her.

"Mom, I'm so sorry. I didn't mean to—"

Olivia promptly raised a hand. "It's okay. Give me a sec…" She took in a shaky drag and blew it out. "I'm okay. This isn't the first time. Won't be the last."

"I know, but still."

"The truth is, you never finish grieving the loss of someone who was your whole heart." Olivia leaned back. "Your father was and still is the love of my life. Always will be."

Sadness swept across Magnolia's face. "I'm sorry it still hurts so much."

"Don't be. I never forget how lucky I am to have had your father with me while I did. But you know, in some ways it's like he's never left. I've made a new life for myself, but strange as it sounds, he's still in it. Always will be."

"Which is why Zork, isn't?"

"What do you mean?"

"I don't know. It just seems—has *always* seemed, that you and Zork... I mean the bond you two have is undeniable. Everyone can see it. Isn't there any part of you that has been curious about falling in love again? With him, I mean?"

"No." Olivia's head shuddered. "Not one bit curious." She clawed at the popcorn and dropped it in her bowl. "Zork and I are like family. You know that. That will never change. Your dad is the only man I'll ever be in love with. It's the way it is. And I'm fine with that. More than fine with that."

"But is Zork?"

"Of course."

"I think he'd be with you in a heartbeat."

"You're wrong. Zork is not pining away for me, Maggie. Your Dad and Zork were best friends."

"I know—if anything, that strengthens my case."

"Your case?"

Magnolia smirked, pushing the bowl of popcorn toward her mother. "I'm sorry. I wondered about dad because..." She plunked another fingerful in her mouth. "Oh, never mind. I'm being overly suspicious. Been in too many trials. Seen too many things."

"It's okay. Not knowing him, you could think and imagine all kinds of things. But I can tell you this. Your father loved life, and he never held back from living it.

He didn't show any signs of depression. Always a natural optimist. And positively over the moon about you. And oh, how he wanted to hunt geese with you someday." She knew the light of such a gentle memory had to be shining in her eyes.

It appeared Magnolia was weighing the evidence. Her head sank backward. "It's just such a mystery how that could've happened. I mean, with so much hunting experience... How could he be so careless with a gun?"

"He wasn't careless." Olivia's words grew strong. "Like I've told you before, a manufacturer's defect was to blame. He was *never* reckless when it came to guns. Never."

Magnolia moseyed to the window and drew the curtains. "I know, but then why didn't you pursue a lawsuit against the manufacturer?"

Olivia shifted her legs.

"I'm just curious, Mom. I don't mean to—"

"It's okay." Olivia wiped her hands on a napkin. "Of course we tried. Zork made it his mission in life. Believe me, we didn't want anyone else going through the same thing. But the law firm concluded we didn't have enough evidence. Interestingly enough, the problem disappeared soon after. As I recall, the manufacturer knew about the design flaw, even though they didn't admit it."

"Which law firm?"

"Blimey... After all these years? You expect me to remember *that*? I honestly have no idea."

Olivia hoped Magnolia had heard enough truth in her words to leave it at that.

Chapter Sixteen

The Ladies of Sugar Creek

Bertie Louise. The name flashed on Olivia's phone
screen. Tired from staying up late with Magnolia the
night before, she couldn't bear to hold an afternoon
"therapy" session with Bertie. Not today.

"Yes, Bertie. How are you?" Olivia regretted the
question the moment she asked. She knew from
experience that within a short time she would know
more than she wanted to.

"I'm so sorry I never got back to you," Bertie
gushed.

"For what?"

"For our get-together. Remember? Girl talk? I had
questions about my love life? I promised I'd be over for
tea? When I ran into you and Gemma at the river that
day?"

Her questions never stopped. Sometimes
everything came out that way. "So odd," Olivia told
Magnolia once. To which she replied, "The woman is
unsure of everything, Mother. And she's speaking to
someone who is unsure of nothing. So of course she
comes to you with questions." She supposed Magnolia
might be right.

Olivia lowered the volume on her phone. "Yes, I
remember, Bertie," she said flatly. *Here it comes…*

"The good news is—I figured it all out."

"Yeehaw!" Olivia gasped. "That *is* good news." *A flat-out miracle.* She didn't dare ask Bertie what she had figured out. She wanted nothing more than to hang up.

"Yes! The realization struck me like a two-ton tractor that I'm in love. Positively in love."

"You don't say. Well. I'm delighted for you, Bertie. I mean it. That's wonderful."

"But that's not why I called."

"Oh." *Too good to be true.*

"We need an extra person for bunco. We're short. And of course, we'd *love* you to join us."

"That's why you called?"

"Yes. Why?"

"You know I hate games. And no one would love me to join in. You know it and I know it. In fact, we know you're asking because you're desperate."

"Oh now, Olivia. Did I say that?" she spluttered. "No! Of course I didn't say that."

"You didn't have to."

"You are the most popular woman in town. Of course everyone wants you there. And hopefully no one will ask you about…"

"What? My unwed pregnant, incapable-of-having-a-baby granddaughter?"

"No! I mean yes, but no. Even her mother is worried, you know. The ladies are thinking of the baby, that's all. That's the only reason they're all gabbling about it."

"Right." Olivia stroked her throat. "Maybe it's high time for the ladies to be thinking a little bit about Gemma, too."

"I hear ya. You're preaching to the choir, sister."

"Am I?"

"Of course you are! I know Gemma is the sweetest thing. I know she is. Now listen, we'd love you to come," she continued. "Forget about all this unwed mother, granddaughter stress, and come have some fun. We sure need that extra person to fill out the tables. Please?" she whined. "It'll ruin the whole evening if we're short."

"For the record, I am not experiencing *any* stress about my granddaughter, Bertie. None at all."

"Good. You're a lot more fun when you're not so serious."

Olivia groaned. "What time?"

"My house, six thirty. Tonight."

"*Tonight*?!"

"Potluck first. Bring something for eight, maybe twenty. Anything you'd like at all. Brownies would be best—the ones you made once with walnuts and chocolate chips. But anything you'd like, if you can. Oh, and be sure you don't overcook them this time. You know, so the corners don't come out like cement. Broke a tooth on your last batch."

****

There was nothing Olivia hated more than sitting in a room full of twenty screeching women, all of them behaving as if their lives depended on the little rolling dice tumbling across the table into the artichoke dip.

And yet, that's exactly what she found herself doing at six thirty that evening.

Olivia overheard the real reason for her invitation; one of the group's favorite players was absent because she had surgery on her big toe.

"I surely hope Iris is back next month," someone bemoaned.

"Yes, poor thing won't be able to walk without that heavy boot for weeks," another lamented.

"It's sure not the same without Iris!" every table bewailed.

Olivia finally blurted, "Well, so glad I could be here to help! Where's the welcome committee?" But the response was colder than ice so didn't bear repeating.

I'm filling in for the gal with a bunion. Not one person has greeted me, thanked me, or even noticed I'm standing here with a plate full of brownies. Not one square edge of them with a rock-hard edge.

Olivia tossed the brownies on the counter, painfully aware of the reason she swore off games with the ladies of Sugar Creek. *I'm beginning to sound like them.* She checked her phone incessantly in hopes of an emergency that would give some earth-shattering reason to flee. It seemed the evening would drone on forever, the room booming with ear-piercing noise.

"Bunco!" someone screamed again.

"Change tables everyone!" Bertie ordered for the tenth time. She held up a wine glass and a spoon. *Ting, ting, ting.* "Attention everyone! Your attention, please. After you're seated again, listen up." She raised her voice. "That means you, Mary, Janet, and Connie." The giggling subsided.

"I have a very important announcement before we continue the next round."

"I hope it's an extra traveling prize. I'm still waiting to win one," someone grumbled.

"No, no, no. Ladies, this is not about the game.

119

This is about *me*," she said proudly drumming her shoulders with all ten fingertips. "I have a personal announcement. One I think all of you will find, well, I almost said *arousing*." She giggled. "But I meant thrilling." All twenty women except one sour puss, burst into a naughty giggle. Bertie's face scrunched up like a little pig, practically squealing with excitement.

Not the least bit amused, Olivia slunk back to the kitchen. She opened the cupboard above the oven, reached around the cheap stuff in front, and helped herself to a bottle of expensive bourbon. She poured a shot and heard Bertie Lou in a honey-sweet tone, pleading, "Olivia, will you please be so kind as to join me?"

"Hang on. I need a shot or two before I do that." But no one seemed to hear.

"Olivia?" Bertie sang again. "Where are you? Come quick! You can bring the wine with you. Is that wine you have? Oh dear, did you get into my hard stuff?"

"Why, yes, I did."

Several women gasped. The extra prissy ones gasped twice.

"Oh, well, never mind." Bertie remained lighthearted. "Nothing will bother me tonight. Hurry and get yourself up here. Right next to me. That's an order!" she cackled.

Olivia dreaded Bertie's silly announcements. The whimsical way she sing-songed her words rankled her. She shot the last bit of whiskey down her throat. She hated whimsical.

Why do I have to be up here? She stood alongside Bertie with a tight smile. The ache of her cheeks threatened to give her away.

Bertie brightened, her face glowing with purpose. "I am *electrified* to tell you all, my dear, wonderful friends that something special has happened. Finally, yes." Bertie spread open her arms so wide, Olivia had to back up. "I…" She paused as if performing a stage show. "Have found…" She gazed at the ceiling, filling her chest with air. "*Love*," she exhaled.

Wow. Olivia smacked her lips, tasting some leftover bourbon on the upper one.

The room sang a chorus of aahs—romance dancing in everyone's eyes. "And girls," Bertie added, "I'm officially engaged!"

The room exploded. The uproar so full of hot-blooded hysteria, it knocked Olivia off her feet and into the chair behind her. Mary yelped, Janet hopped in the air, and Connie blubbered. One by one the ladies of Sugar Creek made their way to Bertie and practically squeezed the living life out of her.

Dumbfounded by the clatter and commotion, Olivia hoped this meant the night was over. She pressed her way past the mob of prepubescent boomers hoping for another shot of whiskey. But she wasn't fast enough.

"There's more, girls!" Bertie shouted above the ruckus. "You come back here, Olivia! That's an order," she bellowed again.

Olivia turned and waited.

But questions kept flying. "When is the wedding? Where are you getting married? Have you chosen your colors?" They sounded like teenagers leafing through their first bride's magazine. "We have to do a bridal shower!" someone swooned. "We can do a *bunco* theme!" They all gasped.

Oh, come on. As if all the divorces, crummy marriages, custody battles, alimony fights, and cheating husbands this group had suffered through had never happened.

"Girls!" Bertie hollered. "Don't you want to know who in the world I'm marrying?"

The room hushed.

"Well," she delivered melodramatically, "my husband-to-be is none other than the incredible, wonderful, romantically strong and handsome, Mr. Canby himself. *Zork* Canby!"

The room spun—Olivia's ears buzzed. She grabbed for a chair before she landed on the floor. *I didn't just hear that.*

The shrieks and squeals were deafening. "What?" Olivia mouthed to Bertie. "Who?" Shouts from the crowd drowned her out.

"Yes, Olivia, it's true!" Bertie beamed over the squalling. "Zork and I have found love. He's the most wonderful man in the world. In *every* way, I might add." Bertie's cheeks flushed with a devilish tee-hee. "And I guess this is as good a time as any to announce my next bit of exciting news. Olivia..." She stopped to poof up her hair. "I want you to have the privilege of serving as my matron of honor."

The noise level in the room took a sudden, hard thud. Olivia's eyes said, *you're crazy*, but her mouth said, "Matron of honor?" A whisper echoed from behind. "Why would she ask *her*?" But Olivia hardly noticed. Or cared.

"It was Olivia's wise counsel that helped me rediscover, or shall I say, reignite my love life."

More deep breaths from her audience.

"Hold on a second," Olivia said, hand held high. "Back up. Did you actually say you're marrying *my* Zork? Who works for me, I mean?"

Bertie burst into laughter. "I know it's a shock, dear. But it was you who helped me take the risk again. And if it hadn't been for you, and the tea we shared, and all the talk about *you-know-what...*" She giggled. "This might not even be happening. Whoo-hoo!" she shouted.

And up from the tables they came. A stampede of ladies, latching on to Bertie as if she had risen from the dead. In some ways, maybe she had.

Still numb, Olivia slumped back in the chair. She had only explained to Bertie that many women in their sixties and seventies, herself not included, still enjoyed sex. Nothing more. Well, perhaps a little more. But everything she told her, she assumed, was in the public domain and not worth all this. And now, because of that, Olivia was being appointed the matron of honor to the blushing bride and groom. *Wait*, she thought. *What groom? Zork is no groom.*

"Sign me up for a tea date, Olivia." Connie giggled.

"Me too," Janet joked.

Oh, no, you don't. Olivia slunk down the hall to the back room. She dug her purse out from under a pile of coats, slipped out the back door, and prayed to God, begging the Almighty, that she be released from any further dice games with tables of shrieking women for the rest of her life.

She hurried to her truck, imagining how to break the news to Zork—the gossip this time involved *him*.

Olivia stared into the beams of light cast on the asphalt racing ahead of her, the accelerator pushing hard in the chase.

Poor Bertie has the wrong idea. It has to be a mistake. "Of course it's a mistake," she said out loud.

She pulled into an old, deserted gas station and put Zork on speaker phone.

"What the hell is going on?!" she asked. "Are you aware of what Bertie is telling the whole town?"

"Nope. But that's a fine howdy-doo. What are you talking about?"

"She announced she's marrying you."

"Say what?" The laughter rolled right out of him.

"Yes! At the bunco game tonight with half the community there."

"You been drinkin?"

"Not near enough."

"She said that to the whole bunch of those women? During bunco?"

"Yes, can you imagine?"

"Damn. Isn't that exactly like her?"

Relief washed over her. "Well, yes. I guess it is. What are you going to do?"

"What can I do?"

"Listen, she's certain it's the truth, Zork. I don't know how she got this in her head, but she believes it. You've got to let her down gently because this will kill the poor woman. And the whole lot of them! You should have heard them when she announced it."

Zork guffawed. "She's only having some fun. That's all."

"She was serious! Somewhere in her fantasy world, she's convinced herself it's the truth. And *I'm* her

124

matron of honor."

"Why not?" Zork snickered. "You'd be a great matron of honor. For the both of us!"

"Oh, Zork, please. Be serious. She's planning a wedding. *Your* wedding."

"All those women went wild, huh?" He gave a snort. "I guess I'm quite the stud!"

"You don't get it. Bertie may drive me nuts, but she'll take it hard when you confront her. I can't help but feel sorry for the woman. The sooner you put a stop to this the better. Just be nice about it."

"I'm not confronting anyone!"

"Well, *I'm* not doing it for you! But please—let her down easy."

"You keep saying that as if I don't have a heart for these kinds of things."

"Well, it's me who will have to pick up the pieces when she crashes. So whatever you can do upfront to minimize the damage would be greatly appreciated."

"We don't have to do a thing."

"Why?"

"Because Bertie-boo announced the truth. That's why."

"The truth?"

"Yup."

"*Bertie-Boo*?!"

"It's my pet name for her."

"What are you talking about? I can't be hearing you right."

"You're hearing me right. Everything she said is the gospel truth. I'm off the market, babe."

****

The road rolled on forever. Black and narrow, like

125

a tunnel of doom. *Maybe it's tunnel vision from the shock.* Olivia wasn't sure.

First Bertie's announcement. And then Zork's startling response. Olivia went numb.

She pulled off the road again. This time at a rusty old raspberry stand, closed for years. She put her phone back on speaker.

"Maggie, it's me."

"Mother? It's almost midnight. Are you okay? Is Gemma okay?"

"Yes. We're fine, but—"

"What is it?"

"I'm gobsmacked. In complete shock."

"What happened? It's not the FBI again, is it?"

"No. Nothing like that. Bertie Lou announced tonight at bunco that she's getting married."

"*You* play bunco?!"

"Only as a favor. It was a dreadful night."

"Wait. *Bertie*, you said? Getting *married*?"

"Yes."

"Weird."

"It gets weirder."

"Who in the world is marrying Bertie?"

"Zork didn't tell you?"

"No. He doesn't talk about Bertie. But who wants to marry her? Who would even be Bertie's type?"

"Are you sitting?"

"Lying. You woke me up, remember?"

"Even better. Stay flat. It appears the man who is Bertie's type is none other than Zork. Unbeknownst to any of us, Zork is the man who wants to marry Bertie."

"Excuse me?"

"You heard right."

"Are you drunk?"

"Sober as a judge. Almost."

"You've got to be kidding."

"Wish I was." Olivia played with the window control, leaving a crack for air. Then double checked her locks.

"How? I mean, how did this happen?"

"I have no idea. None! He calls her Bertie-Boo."

"*Bertie-Boo*?"

"Yes! Can you believe it?" Olivia fiddled with the foil-wrapped brownie rejects she left on the floor of her car. "So ridiculous." She grabbed a rock-hard one.

"I think I'm seasick," Magnolia said. "Popping an antacid as we speak." Olivia heard the bottle rattle.

"Zork kept this from me. How could I not have known?" Olivia gnawed at the burnt edge, careful not to chip a tooth. "That's the worst part. He kept this from me."

"Yeah. Thought you two were so close."

"I thought so too!"

"Well, to be fair," Magnolia offered, "we aren't exactly jumping for joy in support of the man. Maybe that's why he didn't tell us. He probably knows how we feel about her."

"And why would we be supportive? How could we? This is not right!"

"Mom, are you okay?"

"I'm in shock!"

"I get that. I am too. But—"

"It's Bertie, Magnolia! Of all people, it's Bertie."

"Yeah. It's Bertie. I get it." Magnolia blew out a loud mouthful of air.

"I gave her a class—S*ex 101*. Taught her

everything she knows. Truly, you'd think the woman lived in a convent. Little did I know she used my lessons on Zork!"

"Mom?"

"What?"

"You sound jealous."

"Don't be ridiculous," Olivia scoffed. The suggestion she might be jealous was preposterous, and yet, she couldn't get away from the idea fast enough. "I'm going home to sleep. This whole night has been a nightmare. Sorry I woke you, hon. Talk more soon."

"Hang on! Now be honest with me. Is there any part of you that might be a little, *tiny* bit afraid of losing Zork?"

"Where would you get an idea like that? Of course not. It's just..." Olivia exhaled.

"Just what, Mom?"

"Well, everything will change."

"That's what I mean. I know you said you'd never be more than friends, but, well, you and Zork. It's always been you and Zork. That's all."

Olivia sighed again. Her head in both hands.

"Mom?"

"Yes, well, I'm flummoxed. Of all the women in the world. And how did I miss it? I've been blindsided."

"Well, sometimes people find each other and it works. For whatever reason. I don't know, Mom. I guess if they're happy, why not?"

"Oh, Bertie is over-the-moon happy. That's for sure. Bursting at the seams with happiness. One big happy-float."

"And Zork wouldn't propose to just anyone. You

128

know that. He's sensible."

"*Do* I know that? I thought I did."

"Yeah. You sure you're okay?"

"I'm fine. Had to give you the shocking news. That's all." Olivia tucked up the back of her hair, sat tall, and readjusted her seatbelt. "Gotta run. Good night, sweetie."

Olivia shut her phone off before Magnolia could continue grilling. She tossed it in the cup holder, unfastened her seat belt, and slumped. She didn't have to run. She didn't have to go anywhere. She wanted to be alone to think.

She stared out into the blackness and remembered exactly how it felt to be with Sam. So many of her memories were over-handled and worn to dullness. But not this one. She remembered precisely the weight of his hands against her back, the hot burst of breath that caressed her neck when they made love. And the way he leaned in and murmured something so sexy in her ear she could hardly stay standing. She remembered Sam's arm wrapped around her waist, his feet curled around her own in bed each night, and the way his big toe always massaged the sore part of her sole just right.

And their first kiss. She would never forget that either.

Sam had suggested they take a stroll. They left the stuffy, old barn holding a mutual friend's party. Sam led Olivia to the bottom of a hill under a canopy of willow trees, a starry sky flickered behind the long branches swaying in a fresh, invigorating breeze. Whiffs of Mexican orange scattered on the air—a comforting scent still brimming with remembrance. When Sam took her hand, they climbed to the top of a weather-beaten picnic table. A Neil Young song blasted from the barn, streaming loud and clear. Under the full light of moon, Sam wrapped her in his arms and they slow danced to "Harvest Moon"—their song from that night forward.

And she would never forget the way the pond reflected the full expanse of the night sky, the water shining dapples of light, the breeze soft against her face. Love held such strength and brilliance. When Sam kissed her for the first time, her heart burst open like a shooting star.

She shut her eyes from the ache of remembrance. *Maybe being alone* isn't *healthy. Maybe there's nothing good about it at all. Maybe deciding never to share love with another man again isn't right, period. In fact— maybe it's just plain wrong.*

Until that moment, Olivia had never doubted being alone. Now she needed air, her head spinning again. She pressed the button, watching the window roll away, and a painful awareness crept in with the night breeze.

The truth was, she had never been alone. Zork had ensured she wasn't. From the day Sam died, he had been there for her.

And she hated it. She hated thinking she had used him in some way—perhaps avoiding her own life and preventing him from finding his.

The peepers chirped against the backdrop of a distant freeway, humming like a serenade. The sounds slowed her thoughts but not her sorrow.

****

She couldn't say how long she sat there. Only that she was wrung out when she finally stopped crying. Like a robot, Olivia drove the rest of the way home.

She pushed the remote, opening the garage door. When the car rolled inside, she glimpsed something in the side mirror. *Something moved.* A shadow—hooded maybe. The wind picked up, and she watched the tree branches swinging violently in the mirror. *My observations are clearly weak and unreliable at present. It was the tree.*

Olivia turned off the ignition and watched the garage door close. After she dropped her purse and keys in the mudroom, she headed for the shower. As if washing her hair a second time that day would help change everything.

In the months following Sam's death, Olivia was consumed by a bottomless pit of sorrow. She experienced vivid reunion dreams that shattered her heart repeatedly and intrusive, unyielding regrets. The unwelcome weariness that accompanied those days rolled through her again.

She dropped her clothes on the floor and stepped under the hottest water she could tolerate. She rubbed her face with lavender-infused soap which she hoped would make everything all better.

"I miss you, Sam," she told him. "Why aren't you here? Why did you travel to the one place I begged you not to go? If you had listened, you'd still be here. And none of this would matter."

An outdoor motion detector flickered on and flashed through the window blinds. Olivia cranked the faucet off, pressing her ear to the wall. She heard a rustling outside beneath the window. *Not a raccoon.* They were footsteps—fast moving footsteps crunching gravel. *The hooded shadow.*

Zork tried to convince her to let him install security

cameras. "Absolutely not," she told him. "This is my home. Not San Quentin." *If only I had let him install the cameras.*

She switched off the light, covered herself in a robe, and reached under the sink. She unlocked the small safe, removing her Glock 19 and emergency phone. Pushing numbers into the cell, she crept back to the window and peered out a small slit in the blinds. She heard more movement—someone traveling toward the rear of the house.

I didn't trust my gut. What was I thinking?

Olivia hurriedly wrapped the belt around her robe, one brown naked ankle cracking when she crept across the hallway. She descended the stairs in blackness, moving weightlessly, creeping along the wall that led to the kitchen. Ear pressed against the back screen door, she repositioned her pistol. Movement on the porch reactivated everything inside her—the heavy, leaden steps of a savage always made her blood boil.

Olivia took one deep breath and barreled through the door into the cold, vast black of night with a rage so strong, she hardly felt a part of it.

Chapter Seventeen

Under the Ivory Moon

Two white headlamps pierced the darkness and flickered across the lawn, flooding everything with light. Zork hit the high beams and drove his truck as far back as he could, trampling the purple azaleas in his path. Olivia caught sight of someone. A dark figure zipped through the garden and into the grassland. She took off in a chase.

"Stop or I shoot!" She didn't care how thorny of a shot it was. She wanted to pull the trigger.

"Olivia!" Zork bellowed from his truck. "Stop!"

The hooded figure receded farther into the field, past the blackberry bushes and across the creek.

"Ollie, stop!" The ferocity in Zork's voice made her brake. "It's a set-up!"

Olivia bent over and held both knees, her feet soaked in dew. "Damn it." she cursed. *He's probably right.*

"The sheriff's checking the fields. You okay?"

"Yes. What if we head out together?"

"Too big a risk. I have a bad feeling about it."

Olivia straightened, one hand on her hip. "Okay," she said, puffing. She trusted Zork's intuition. She had witnessed it right too many times. "But they'll never get him now."

"It's okay. Get a look at him?"

"No. But it's him, and I'm sure he wasn't alone. I didn't catch on soon enough. I was too distracted when I drove into the garage tonight. I missed it."

"You didn't know."

When Zork followed Olivia inside, the back door opened so fast it banged into the opposite wall.

"I did know. Someone passed the garage when I came in. A shadow went by, maybe two, and I chose to ignore it." She flicked on lights and inspected her muddied heels.

"You didn't know."

"Zork, please. You know as well as I do that we can never let our guard down. Not for a moment. I knew better. I'm damn lucky I didn't get blindsided *twice* tonight." She grabbed a towel and wiped the soles of her feet.

"What do you mean, twice?"

"Oh, please..." She slapped the air. "Forget it." Olivia tossed the towel in the washing machine, secured her pistol, and hurried up the stairs.

"Forget it?" Zork followed, pulling off his ball cap, rubbing his head. "You saying *I* blindsided you?"

"You have to ask?"

"Hold on there! I wasn't aware I needed your authorization to make marriage plans. Since when was I required to check in with you first?"

"Really, Zork? You're asking me that? And saying it that way?"

"Damn straight I am. What'd you expect?"

Olivia turned the bathroom fan on instead of the light, fumbling for the switch. "Look. I don't have time for this. We need to focus on our job. They're planning an attack and they're getting close to acting on it." She placed the pistol in the safe, double checked the lock, and skirted past him.

"Nothing more we can do right now," he said, trailing her. "They won't act tonight."

"I realize that." She retightened the belt on her bathrobe and ushered Zork toward the front door. A halo of light from the lantern in the entryway fell in a circle around them. "Holy crap." She waved her hand in front of her face. "What is that? Foo-foo in Paris?"

He lifted the shoulder of his shirt and sniffed. "Just a little of Boo's perfume."

"You smell like a damn petunia." She pulled the front door back as far as it would go.

"Before you show me the way out, answer me this. What was I supposed to do? Get your permission before I proposed? Or maybe I'm not supposed to marry. Is that what's going on here?" His words were sharp as glass.

Olivia rubbed her neck. The sting of cut skin smarted. "Give me a break."

"Then what's wrong?"

"We've never kept secrets from one another. Never. Why now, Zork?"

"No secret. You just never asked."

"Why on earth would I ask? What reason would I ever have to think you even *liked* Bertie?"

"I don't know. It never came up!"

"No, it didn't. And of all people, why Bertie?"

"Well, why the hell *not* Bertie?"

Olivia yanked on the belt around her robe again. "If you have to ask, I'm done with this conversation." She felt all of sixteen years old when she said it.

"So be it." Zork charged toward his truck.

A gust of bitter cold air swooped in when he stormed out. "Goodnight!" She shivered when she yelled it. "Thank you for coming over, and my congratulations to the happy couple!" She sounded more foreign to herself than she thought possible.

Without turning, he raised his hand and swatted her away like an annoying fly. It's entirely possible his middle finger extended too.

Olivia shut the door louder than usual and stomped into the bedroom. She grabbed the book off her end table that gave her hope for the future of the country. The importance, the necessity, the absolute obligation for ethical leadership and integrity in a democracy. *A big topic for a sixteen-year-old.* She tried reading, but couldn't concentrate.

She blamed it on Magnolia.

It had been Magnolia, after all, who had sparked such troubling thoughts—the annoying ones that kept intruding.

Zork and Bertie? It's always been Zork and me. We're a team. Not them. Us.

All these years, she thought, *Zork's been there for me.*

Olivia closed the book and tossed it to the foot of the bed. She heard the selfishness and sense of entitlement in her thinking. It made her queasy. But it continued unabashed.

Olivia swept back the curtains and let the moonlight, bright as diamond flames, pour its pool of light over her bed. Somehow, the crushing loneliness felt less unkind under it. As if a faithful companion remained near.

Chapter Eighteen

The Child Whisperer

Gemma arrived early to her first parenting class. Already overcrowded, the dingy office painted in shades of desert sand, smelled of wet coats and wool socks. The odors yanked on Gemma's gag reflex.

Pregnant women in all shapes and sizes shifted their weight in small plastic chairs, squirming for comfortable positions. Many had snotty-faced children hanging on them, all of them whining they were hungry and bored—refusing to listen, sit still, or be quiet.

Why should they be statues? Gemma wondered. *They aren't made of ice.*

Gemma admitted that over the years, Mama had been right about most things she had lectured her about. Fiercely loved, she never doubted her devotion to her. But the children in the waiting room that morning ignored their mothers for good reason.

Their never-ending fussing, cries, and screams amped up to a deafening level until Gemma couldn't take it anymore. She clapped both hands over her ears, eyes flaring. "Listen to them!" she burst. "They're talking to you! Stop yelling at them!" She tried not to yell when she said it. "I just have to say it's mean. And they don't need to be swatted like flies. They aren't bad! See, they can't sit and do nothing. They wanna play and talk to you." Her voice relaxed. "And they might be starving. That's a very big problem sometimes. You should always carry snacks. Honest. It'll help."

Every eyeball in the room spooled back. The woman next to her grabbed a diaper bag, the wrists of two toddlers, and dragged them off as if Gemma had something catching. The sharp bite of disapproval would have disturbed most people, but Gemma paid more attention to the children, even as her cheeks throbbed with hot red blotches. So hot, she thought she might go up in smoke. She used the backs of her hands to put the fire out.

The stench of stale cigarettes clung to the coats around her; she tried not to retch when she caught a whiff. She moved across the room to a child-sized coloring table positioned below a cracked window. *Aah, I can breathe again.* Something refreshing drifted in. She peered through the open slats in the window and spotted a *Daphne odora* in full bloom, the magenta flowers filtering the air with its fragrance. Gemma inhaled with pleasure, grateful to cleanse her nose of the tobacco and weed clinging to her insides.

She watched a girl with curly black pigtails whimpering on her mother's knees. When they exchanged smiles, she slipped off her mother's lap and made her way to the table where Gemma had spread out paper and crayons.

"Get back here!" the mother snapped.

"I don't mind playing with her." Gemma pulled out a small chair. "Want to color?" Gemma's head lowered to the level of the pigtailed girl. "You can let your mommy rest while we play if you want." When Gemma checked for approval, the girl's mother was gathering her belongings.

"Taking a smoke. Be right back," she said, darting out the door. *Maybe she'll never come back and I can keep her.*

The pigtailed girl remained fixated on Gemma. Two more children wrangled out of their mother's laps and joined in, and then another. Gemma made room and introduced herself to each one.

None of them obeyed their mother's orders to, "Stay right here, or else…" Which did not help Gemma win any popularity contests. Not at first anyway.

The women conversed among themselves, as if Gemma couldn't hear them.

"Who does she think she is?"

"She's never been a mom."

"Obviously."

"Just one of the babysitter's."

"Well, they better not tell me how to raise my kid like she did, or I'm leaving. I don't need that bull."

"Nope. And they better not tell me I can't take a paddle to my kid either."

"Tell me about it! I'll whoop my kid's ass if I damn well please."

"Listen. We can't trust this place. They'll take our babies if they can."

"Like hell they will. I've already had two taken; they're not getting their hands on this one." The woman flung her head in Gemma's direction. "What's with her? Look at the way she plays with them. Something's not right."

"No. She's not all there. But at least the kids like her."

"Right? Let her babysit. I can't afford one. I never get a break. *Never*."

"Hell, no. Me either. Mine hangs on me constantly."

"Yeah. It's like having a god-damned leech stuck to you all day." They all tittered. "We should take the break while we can."

Suddenly, the mothers relaxed. One buried her face in a gossip magazine while another closed her eyes. The others stared at their phones and disappeared. And just like that, Gemma wasn't so bad after all.

"Ten-fifteen Nurturing Parenting Class," a young woman announced. "This way, please." She directed them to a room off the hall. "If you have children with you this morning, the babysitters are next door on your right."

One by one, Gemma embraced the children, giving each one a small leaf from her pocket. They waited eagerly, eyes full of wonder when they received their gift. Gemma grabbed her purse and raincoat but before she could wave goodbye, the girl with pigtails wrapped around Gemma, smooching her arm. Gemma kneeled, holding her eyes steady on hers, lightly stroking her black ringlets. "Never forget how good you are, okay?"

Gemma blew the children kisses and inched down the hall with the other adults. But the same mean voices followed, talking behind her back.

"*What?* Are you kidding me?"

"Thought she was the babysitter!"

"Oh my god. She's in this class too? With *us*?"

"We're in a damn class for—"

Gemma pressed her coat to her ear to block out the last word they said. Nani was right. Poison words weren't good for anyone.

"They want to take her baby away. That's why she's here."

"In her case, they should."

Gemma heard them this time too. She stared at her toddling feet and found a chair in the back row. *They want to take my baby away? And she thinks they should?* Her lower lip started to shake.

Gemma didn't say one thing through the entire class. She only sat there remembering the truth of how different she felt.

What did I do wrong?

Chapter Nineteen

Apologies Mean Nothing Without Change

Two days had passed since Bertie's bombshell announcement on game night. But Olivia didn't awaken in the black of morning because of that. She awakened to the cries of babies—a pack of howling coyotes punctuating the darkness, their wails echoing across the field. Naturally, they quieted when she was wide-awake. *May as well get up.*

The barn was opaque inside when she dragged open the metal door and heard Zork on his cell. She tugged at a string attached to a pale bulb hanging from the hayloft and raised a hand to greet him.

A whiff of tatty damp blankets smacked her in the face when she nearly stumbled into three of them flopped over the first stall.

Zork continued talking in the semi-darkness, his woolen voice deep and resonant. He gave up cigarettes years ago, but you could hear the change in his throat that only happened from decades of smoking.

"Don't underestimate Olivia Porter," she heard him say. "That woman could whip the ass of a raging pit bull."

Zork turned when he heard Olivia throw Buster's gate open.

"We're on it," he said, and hung up.

She turned, examining his face.

"What?!" Zork snapped.

"Did I say something?"

"You have that look."

"Oh, please, let's not bicker like an old married couple," she said. "What was that about?"

"Warning us to stay alert," Zork scoffed. "That's all. Told them there was no need to worry. Assured him you could hold your own."

"They have a right to be concerned after last night. I wasn't focused. But I am now. I won't let myself be distracted again."

"You still mad?"

Olivia didn't answer at first. And then she did. "Yes, Zork. I am. We're not just friends and business partners. We're a team. Not disclosing this put us at risk—all of us."

"Hold on right there. My not disclosing upcoming wedding nuptials put no one at risk. No one."

"It's information I should have known."

"Why? What difference would it make? Why would that rattle you?"

"It created a sudden distraction. I wasn't on my game. I could've missed more than I did."

"But you didn't. You did all the right things."

"I was *not* on top of things. You know it, and I know it. But it won't happen again."

Zork flicked the air with his hand, moved through the gloomy shadows to the next stall, and left the barn with Banjo.

When Olivia reached for the curry comb and dandy brush, Buster nuzzled his shiny cheek against her waist. "I love you too, boy," she told him. "What would I do without you? You're my favorite guy, you know that? The best ever." She kissed him between his eyes and then again on his soft, velvety nose.

When the blackness of morning evaporated, cracks of light streamed through the old wood beams and a rooster crowed somewhere in the distance. Olivia inhaled the pleasing scent of Buster's velvety equine ears as she cleaned him. But even then, the gloominess of something inside lingered. Like wearing the dark glasses of depression, distorting her view of things. She kept brushing Buster's white mane, wishing she could brush away her gloom with it. But the pang of loss wasn't so easily erased.

Zork leaned in. "I'm saddled and ready to go."

Olivia flinched.

"Let's take a quick look around on the hill," he added.

"I'll handle things today," she said.

"What's that supposed to mean?"

"I mean, you don't need to be here. It's okay. I've got this."

"I know you're on edge. You have good cause. All the more reason for us to take a ride, Olivia. Together." He sauntered back inside.

"Gemma's coming over. Go ahead without me. Call if you need anything."

"What? You're making no sense. Gemma's not coming. She told me she and Walter drove south to his parents yesterday."

"Oh, you're right. They went after her class. I forgot."

"You forgot?"

"I did." Olivia shuffled to the other end of Buster.

She wanted physical distance from Zork, though she didn't know why.

"You're not yourself, Olivia. You haven't been for weeks. Not since Gemma's baby news."

"I suppose that's true. I'm sorry. Too many things cropping up at once."

Zork flopped his arms over Buster's gate. "How do you think it'll go with his parents?"

"About as well as it went here, I suppose."

"Mag-pie will come around, but I can't say I blame her. I wouldn't want to be any of their parents. They have a right being worried for this baby."

"Oh, please," she said crisply. "You too? Talking to Bertie, no doubt." She felt resentment wrap tight around her words.

"Yes, I talk to Bertie." Zork threw off his hat with a sudden surge, his once inky-black hair now flour-white and thick as the wool on a lamb's back. "But that's beside the point. Gemma's baby won't be easy for us either. You know that. We have more to worry about."

"Yes I know that. Don't remind me of all the responsibility we shoulder for everyone!" Olivia dropped the brush and tripped over a bucket.

"What in blue-blazes is eating you? You're wound tighter than a tourniquet."

She searched herself for an answer. Any answer. "It's Maggie, I guess." *Partly true.*

"Because this baby has her all out of sorts?"

"No. But that doesn't help."

"What then?"

"She's been asking a lot of questions about the past."

145

Zork's head tilted. "Sam questions?"

"Yes. How'd you know?"

"She's asked me too."

Olivia turned. "About how he died?"

"Yes."

"And?"

"And I told her the same thing you did. We agreed what to say, right? There's been no change in that."

"No. Of course not. But I hate lying. I'm lousy at it when it comes to Maggie. She deserves the truth."

"I hate it too, but we have no choice."

"She feels something's off. Knows it in her gut."

"Smart like you." Zork entered the stall and gave Buster's hooves a quick look over.

"She's smarter than me. Maybe not about Gemma and this baby, but about a lot of other things." She paused. "You know, maybe she knows better about Gemma and the baby too. She might be right about all of it. Including you." The moment the words cleared her lips she wished for a way to suck them back in.

Zork jerked around. "What about me?"

"I didn't mean you," she lied.

"Like hell, you didn't."

"Okay, all right. Just things she said about you and this whole Bertie thing."

"This whole Bertie *thing*? Look. I know you don't like her. You've made that abundantly clear."

"It's a shock, all right? As I told you, I don't get it. I mean, *Bertie*? *Marriage?*"

"You know something?" Zork's boot whacked the bucket between them and sent it hurtling. "I'm sick of hearing that line. Wipe that sheepish *I'm-better-than-her* expression right off your face. I need to say a few things."

For a moment, Olivia thought he was about to confess that the whole idea of marrying had been a joke, or a cover for something else. But that moment left as soon as it came.

"First off, who the hell do you think you are talking smack about Bertie? What gives you the god-damned right to do that?"

Stunned, Olivia waited for him to continue ranting. And he did.

"Over and over again, you've done nothin' but make wisecracks about her, and what makes you think that's okay? When people talk smack about Gemma, you wanna kick their ass, and yet you think it's okay to rip apart Bertie the same way? You see what I'm saying here?"

If she hadn't known better, Olivia would've sworn Buster had kicked her in the gut. The truth of what Zork said became clear as glass. "I see what you're saying—and you're right." She tugged at her scarf, wishing to be less visible.

"She may not be the career woman you are," he continued, "or as educated. Maybe not as witty, either. And I admit she has some pretty damn weird ideas about you too. But her heart compares to no other. Just like Gemma's. And guess what, hotshot?" Zork shook the dust off his hat and placed it on his head again. "Bertie gives me peace. She cares about making a mean ol' son of a bitch like me happy. And I'm the happiest I've been in a long time. And I'm enjoying it. I consider myself the luckiest old man this side of the Mississippi. I only wish you could see it for yourself. It's a shame you can't." He steamed out of the barn.

Olivia felt herself shrinking. So small she could have been mistaken for the heap of dust beside her boot. When she left the barn with Buster in tow, a gust of cold air splashed her cheeks. She climbed on top Buster and shifted her weight, facing Zork. "Thanks for pointing out my hypocritical flaws so proficiently. Because of course you're right. And I mean that," she said, her breath hitching. "And I'm sorry. I truly am."

Zork bounded on top Banjo, let the reins fall against the horse's neck, and trotted up beside her. "Apologies mean nothing, and I mean *nothing* unless you change the behavior you're sorry about."

"Agreed." She turned away but kept talking. "I'll say it again. You're right. I've been far too critical and disparaging." And then she stared straight at him. "It was wrong of me. Unforgiveable, really. I hate anyone doing the same toward Gemma. You're right—I wouldn't stand for it. It won't happen again."

"Okay, then. You're forgiven." Zork clicked his tongue repeatedly, urging Buster up the path.

When she came alongside him, Olivia swung the reins over her hand and slowed. "And listen," she said. "I have no business being her matron of honor. Tell Bertie you forbid me from being in that role. Tell her why. I deserve it."

"Oh, no, you don't. You're not getting off that easy. You'll be in our wedding. You'll be there for both of us."

"No, Zork. It's not a good idea."

"Listen. I know she's not your favorite BFF chum and you hate weddings and—"

"I do not hate weddings."

"Well, being in them and all the hoopla around

them—"

"I do not hate being in them, either. Although, honestly, don't you think we're all a little too old for bridesmaids? And bridal showers? And a registry? You must agree it's a little silly."

"What registry?"

"I'm sure she'll get one." Olivia stepped into something she shouldn't again and backed up her words. "Its fine of course, if that's what Bertie needs, or wants. It's just not the way I'd do it.... Not that this has a thing to do with me." Olivia was exhausted. Her rattling on had been tiring, even to herself. She took a deep breath. "Whatever. It's all good." She made her voice lighthearted. "It'll be fun, won't it? Especially bride bingo."

"Olivia?" Zork hesitated. "If I didn't know better, I'd have to wonder a little..." He halted when she reached for her phone and answered it.

Only she didn't answer it. She pretended to and rode away.

Chapter Twenty

Dancing Women

The next morning Olivia's age glared rudely back at her in the bathroom mirror. She attempted yet again to smooth out the fine lines on her cheeks with sunscreen. The kind that guarantees to deactivate, or at least minimize, all wrinkles in a week. Nothing had happened in a week, or a month. Not even three months. Except more wrinkles perhaps.

At least I don't have a sunburn.

"Death happens to all of us," she told her reflection. "When I'm dead, I'll certainly look the part."

She unlocked the front door in anticipation of Gemma's arrival, lumbered into the kitchen, and hit the button on the Bluetooth. *If anything can boost my energy, this song will.* She blasted it—elated at how young it made her feel.

The front door slammed, booming over the music. "Nani! Whatcha doin?"

"In the kitchen, Tink! Lock the door behind you, please."

"Nani?" Gemma dropped her coat and keys, staring. "You're rappin'."

"Is that what I'm doing?" Olivia laughed. "I had no idea." She moved around the island wiping the counter, dancing.

"You're kickin' it, Graham Cracker!" Gemma slipped out of her shoes and joined in. "Here we go, Nani-pie." Gemma sang, "Wickey whack, slap my back, can't go back, get the cheery-oh-hole out of this sack."

"What?" Olivia asked.

"Oh, I don't know what they're saying. It just sounds like that. Keep dancing. This is fun. I never knew you could rap."

"How can anyone not like this?" she asked.

"I know!" And then Gemma set loose and performed some new hip, neck, and arm moves for her grandmother. A yellow tiara bounced twice before it flung off her head and landed on the floor in front of them. Gemma carefully swept it aside with her purple sock, but it snagged on her big toe. She stopped to untangle it, crashed into Olivia, and the two of them landed, barely missing the open dishwasher.

Olivia cackled.

"Nani! You okay?!" Gemma pulled herself up and then her grandmother too. "Do your Mick Jagger imitation!" she pleaded. "Please? It's so funny when you dance like him."

Olivia selected a Rolling Stones song, slid across the open floor, and showed off another hidden talent: a halfway-decent imitation of Mick Jagger performing on stage.

Gemma howled.

Olivia punched the volume down. "Your trip must have gone well, Tink. You look good. Your cheeks are rosy and smiling."

"It's because I'm here. Home with you and having fun. I didn't like his mom. Can I have a turkey sandwich for breakfast? I'm starving."

"Coming up. Tell me what happened." Olivia went to the refrigerator.

"She didn't like our baby news. She wasn't very nice. I had a stomachache the whole time we were there."

Nani made a face. "I am so sorry."

"And Walter got super nervous and ran away."

"*Ran away?*"

"Yup. His dad found him hiding behind the gas station at the end of the street. I wanted to go with him, but his mom told me not to."

"So what did you do?"

"Told her I was sorry and not to blame Walter. I confessed he had nothing to do with it. I mean, I know he did, you know, have a lot to do with it. And he liked doing it too. So did I!" Gemma's cheeks warmed to a red-apple glow. "But the baby was my idea. Not his."

"Then what?" Olivia pulled a sharp knife out of the drawer.

"Then she gave me a paper to sign. I think saying it's my fault." Gemma repositioned the tiara over her forehead.

"Did you sign the paper?" Olivia halted.

"I didn't want to because I didn't understand it. But she told me if I did, everything would be okay."

"So you did sign it? Where is it?" Olivia held the knife perfectly still.

"I don't have it."

"So you did or didn't sign it?" Olivia's heart rate shot up.

"Walter had me all mixed up about it. I told her I would, but I hurried and ran to the bathroom."

"And then what?"

"I had the trots. From the stress. When I came out, I told her I'd sign it after I felt better."

"And did you?" Olivia still waited to slice the sandwich as if Gemma's answer depended on it.

"We left and drove all the way home."

"Okay. So you didn't sign it?"

Gemma paused. "I don't think so."

"You're not sure?" *Just cut the damn thing.* Olivia carved the sandwich in half like she was sawing timber.

"There were a ton of pages. I wrote my initials on one of them. Maybe more. But then I stopped. I didn't finish because it didn't make sense."

"Okay. Well, you did the right thing not continuing something you didn't understand."

"I know. But Walter thought it was okay since it was his mom making us do it. He said we should obey."

"You have the right to understand everything, Gem. No matter who is telling you something—a stranger, his mom, me, anyone." Olivia reached for Gemma's favorite flo-blue plate and arranged the sandwich.

"She told me it wouldn't be good for us to be parents because we aren't smart enough. Especially me." Gemma's lips pressed into a grim line. "I didn't want her to know I didn't understand the papers. I didn't want to prove her right." She twisted her ring.

"You only would've proven that like all people, you needed to fully understand what you were signing! Next time say, 'I need more time. I'm taking this home to read, and I'll let you know what I decide.' "

"Yeah, I should've said that!" Gemma bounced a curled knuckle against her mouth.

"Don't let anyone rush your decisions. You deserve whatever time you need."

"I know. Mama told me that too." Gemma checked her phone for messages. "But guess what? I knew all the answers in the parenting class. All of them!" She chomped into the bread, her mouth full of lettuce.

"Wow! You like the class then?" Olivia yanked open a bag of tortilla chips.

"No." Gemma shoved a dangling piece of red lettuce back into her mouth. "I mean I do, but I can't say anything."

"What do you mean?" She handed her a napkin and poured chips into a colorful hand-painted floral bowl. "You said you knew all the answers."

"I did. I just didn't tell anyone I did."

"Why not?"

"Some people in the class made me feel bad. I was too afraid to say anything aloud. But I knew the right answer every time." Gemma took another sloppy bite and licked avocado off her finger.

"They made you feel bad?"

"Yes. Stuff they said. Including poison words. Not everyone, only a couple of them. Maybe more."

"I see." Olivia peeled the lid off a new container of salsa. "Normally I'd tell you to ignore them, but you know what? Screw that! Speak your mind. Tell them their hatefulness won't be tolerated. *It's against the law*. You have the right to feel safe no matter where you are! Next class you raise your hand, Gemma Jane, and thumb your nose at the naysayers. Maybe not in your mind this time! And report them."

"Yeah!" she sneered.

"You're there to learn. Speak up for yourself and

for your baby."

"Yeah!"

"Do your best, Gemma. That's good enough."

"I will!"

Olivia plunked two small cartons of chocolate milk down and sat beside her.

"I *could* sit in the front row so I only see the teachers when I say an answer."

"Yes, you could. Good problem solving." Olivia dipped a chip into the salsa and crunched.

"They said the teachers want to take away my baby. And that in my case they should."

"What?!" Nani cheeks puffed out when she grimaced. "That is not going to happen. The teachers are there to help you, not hurt you."

"I thought so too. But when they said that it punched my insides—the same way talking to Walter's mother did. By the way, I decided I'm not talking to her ever again." She opened both cartons and started gulping.

"Pretty sure you'll have to, hon."

"Remember you told me to trust my gut? That my feelings can help tell me what to do?"

"Yes."

"Well, my feelings are telling me that his mother is not nice. She's the one who gave me the stomachache."

"Give her time," Olivia said, sighing. "Or not."

Gemma opened the refrigerator and grabbed another milk. "But my gut sure worked then, didn't it? The runs got me right out of there. Just in time."

Chapter Twenty-One

Born to be Wild

The rest of the afternoon wore on Gemma, and she couldn't explain why. She only knew that when she got home from Nani's, something changed.

She climbed the stairs to her apartment with care. She had to. Scattered showers made everything slick and when she focused on the open space between the steps, she got dizzy, imagining herself falling through one of them. She felt her knees sag.

But the cracks between the stairs were the least of it. Gemma blubbered all the way up to the front door. And when she got inside, she sat and bawled. Then she called Mama.

"What's wrong, Gemma? The other day you bragged about how easy you were having it. Your jeans even still fit! What happened?"

"I don't want to fall and drop the baby," she told her.

"No one wants accidents to happen. But you can't worry about that or you'll never relax."

"It's kinda a lot, Mama."

"What's a lot?"

"It's a lot to worry about." The truth is, worry was whittling away at Gemma. "I know you warned me, and I think I can do it, but what if I do things wrong? Like *really* wrong?"

"You will do things wrong, hon. Count on it." Mama took a sip of something. "I don't mean only you. All mothers make mistakes."

Gemma swallowed hard, at battle with no one but herself. "I guess no one can know everything."

"That's right."

"But it's putting a lot of stress on me. Walter, his mom, my work, doctor visits, and the classes. I'm almost tardy to everything. And I don't want to get fired. I need my apartment, and—" Gemma covered her eyes, a wave of sensation breaking over her.

"Gem?" Mama paused. "You okay?" She sounded scared too.

"Yes…" She caught her breath.

"You sure?"

"No."

"Honey, what is it?"

"I'm scared. All of a sudden I'm crying a lot."

"Pregnancy can do that—it's normal to be a little moody. Nerves get brittle sometimes when your hormones are all over the place. Not to worry. It'll pass."

Mama's being nice.

"And remember… This is what you wanted. This was your dream… I warned you it wouldn't be easy, but as I recall you weren't interested in what I had to say."

Well, that wasn't so nice. "I know that. And I know this baby only grows, it doesn't shrink."

"I don't mean to be unsupportive." Mama sounded like she was trying to change, but slipping up a little. "You have to think positive, honey. Now, keep your chin up and everything will be fine! Okay?" Her voice sounded cheery, but it was phony.

"Okay, well, I'm cooking dinner now so I have to go." Gemma positioned her finger over the off button. "Walter just got here. Bye."

Only Walter was at work. And she wasn't cooking anything.

Gemma didn't feel one bit guilty about the lie. She curled up on the sofa and found a lighthearted show with two funny brothers remodeling a dump. When the nice couple on the show learned their dream home was full of mold—*black mold!*—she burst into tears, which was not like her. She knew the mold always got fixed because the brothers were nice.

"I'll never be happy again," Gemma said to no one. She jammed a heavy pillow over her face and screamed, "What have I done? I can't do it! I'll never get it out of me. I just called her an *it,* and I don't even care!" Gemma bawled until she couldn't anymore.

Everyone was right. Why, oh why, did I think this was a good idea?

****

Gemma had been asleep forty-five minutes and missed two phone messages when the doorbell rang. She lay there trying to rouse from a dream. She opened her eyes, not knowing for sure if she heard the television show or the bell on her own apartment.

"Dagnabbit!" she said, staring at the television screen. "I didn't see the moldy house get fixed."

And then the doorbell rang again.

Gemma peered through the peephole, squealed, and fumbled to unlock the door. "Zorro!" she cried, and leapt into his arms.

"Now, that right there is what I call a welcome!" He beamed. "How you doin', sweetheart?"

"Not good. But now I am, cuz you're here. Why are you here?"

"Mr. Harley pointed me right in this direction and straight to you. Want to take a ride?"

"On your motor-sickle?"

"It's right down there." He pointed to a slick black V-Rod. "How about a drive out to Lone Pine Farms for a sody pop while we're between storms?"

"Sure!"

"Grab your leather jacket."

"Whoa. Me and you on your Harley." Gemma grinned. "Like Hell's Angels!"

"Born to be wild, babe. Let's ride."

"Hang on." She ran down the hall.

Gemma sat on the toilet trying to remember what she was upset about before she fell asleep. *Was it really the moldy house? No.* It was a lot more than that. And still the worries festered even as she tried to flush them away. The truth was, Gemma reckoned all the naysayers were right—every one of them. She didn't have the courage to be a mother.

When she zipped up her black leather jacket, Zorro handed her a bright red helmet. "Tiara off. Brain bucket on," he ordered.

"Do I have to?" She peeked at his face and knew the answer. "Okay."

Zorro checked the fit and refastened the strap under Gemma's chin. She climbed on and wrapped her arms around his waist. "Blast off! Go fast, Zorro."

When he revved the motor and sailed out of the parking lot, a spark of freedom lifted Gemma's spirits.

They rolled along their favorite country road, weaving in and out of the shadows singing, "Hell, yeah! Speed it up! Right on!"

They rode for miles under beams of sun that balanced a colossal rainbow that only the skies in Oregon could paint.

****

"The baby shouldn't have soda pop, Zorro. I'll have a strawberry milkshake."

But maybe soda pop would make me miscarry. Guilt pressed heavy on Gemma. *That's not nice.* The thought racked her heart.

"One root beer float, and one strawberry milkshake, please," Zorro ordered. He pulled his wallet out of his back pocket and handed the waitress a twenty. "Keep the change," he told her.

Gemma took in a long drag of the enticing sweet kettle corn popping in a huge pot over an open flame. She stared, mesmerized by the large steel paddle stirring and scooping it up hot into bags.

Zorro led her outdoors and turned two chairs around. "Air's got a bite, but this sun sure feels toasty. You warm enough, Gem?"

"I'm good." She drew on the straw, satisfied with the creamy thickness. Jovial children scampered alongside wheelbarrows full of pumpkins, all of them thumping along as if rolling over an old-fashioned washboard. She tipped her head back listening. The sounds so pleasing, and the sun so brilliant, it made her eyes shut.

"So. You heard the news about my proposal?"

When Gemma's head snapped up, she choked on the sip of shake in her mouth. "Your what?" She coughed, wiping pink dribble from her chin.

"My marriage proposal."

"You asked her?"

"I did."

"She said yes?!"

"She did."

"Zorro! I knew it!" Gemma's chair rocked, and she nearly fell over. "I knew it. Some things are meant to be."

Zorro put out a hand to steady her.

"I feel happy again! When is the wedding?" The news was brain-rattling. *Like another miracle.*

"Soon. We want a barn dance."

"I knew you loved her! I knew it, and I love barn dances!" *I even feel happy about my baby again.*

"We'd like you to be in the ceremony, Gem. Your nan wants you there too."

"Well, you can't have a wedding without me! What do I get to do?"

"Well, I'm not sure how you women decide all that. Up to the bride I guess."

"Okay, well, I'll do whatever she wants. I'm all keyed up, Zorro! I'm super happy now."

"Well, so are we. I'm a little old for this, but it's never too late to fall in love and get hitched, is it?"

"Of course not! Not when it's meant to be! Not like it is for you and Nani."

Zorro froze. "Wait. Didn't your nan tell you?"

"No! You did, silly."

"I know I did, but I thought you knew—"

"No one told me! I saw Nani yesterday. Did all this happen last night?"

"I proposed a couple weeks ago. But—"

"A couple *weeks* ago?! Why didn't anyone tell me?"

"Gemma." Zorro blew out a weighty puff. "I proposed to Bertie. I asked Bertie to marry me. Not your nan."

His words gutted her. Gemma's face wouldn't move.

"I thought you knew about Bertie and me. I assumed—"

"Wait." She pushed the milkshake away. "*Bertie?* What do you mean you re-posed to Bertie?"

"Proposed," he corrected. "It means I asked her to marry me and—"

"I know what it means!" Gemma's voice ruptured. "I understand that! But what are you thinking?"

"You said you understood."

"I do! I understand perfectly. Why *Bertie?*"

"You have a problem with Bertie, too?"

"Of course I do! She's not Nani! How could you?" Gemma crumpled her napkin single-fisted, tossing it across the table and grabbed the cold, wet milkshake, certain her face was burning bonfire red. She pushed away from the table with such force her chair tipped backward and clattered against the gravel. She scuttled, stiff legged across the parking lot, through the playground, slammed her milkshake into the garbage can and sprinted past the chicken coup and horses, straight into the maze of corn fields.

She ran and didn't stop.

Potholes were everywhere. She didn't dodge one fast enough, fell hard, and skinned her knee right through her jeans. She wobbled to her feet, surrounded by corn stalks that she guessed to be at least a hundred feet tall. Gemma was lost.

Who would want a mama like me anyway? Always getting hurt, always getting lost, and never figuring things out. I don't know diddly-squat about being a mama.

Sad and hollow, Gemma dropped, doubling over in heartache.

Poor little baby. I don't want to run away from you, but I'm a mess.

****

As abruptly as the sun had broken through the clouds, great, gloppy drops of rain returned. It didn't take long before sheets of it rippled over the corn fields. Somewhere deep inside the maze, Gemma rested— huddling beneath a wooden sign of black skulls. It read: "HUNGRY ZOMBIES AND CHAINSAWS AHEAD. CONTINUE AT YOUR OWN RISK!" Halloween was still over two weeks away, but the farm was already prepared for spooky madness.

"Gem?" Zorro approached her cautiously. "Is that you waiting for a zombie?"

"Not funny." Gemma huddled on the ground, face buried in her knees.

"Hey. Come on, Ace. You're getting a seat full of mud and getting wet to the bone."

"I'm not leaving with you. I don't want you anymore."

Zorro took longer than usual to say something. "You've never talked that way to me before."

"You never said you were marrying *Bertie* before." Spit flew out when she said her name. "I don't get it."

"Why are all you Porter women so dead set against Bertie? And suddenly so dead set against me?"

163

Gemma didn't have an answer.

Zorro checked his watch, pulled his hood up and stepped closer to Gemma. "I'm not leaving you here. Get up and let's head back." He swatted her arm and held out a hand.

"You *are* leaving me." Gemma raised her head and glared at him.

Zorro didn't move. He kept his hand extended until she finally pulled up. "Why are you so fired up?" he asked, wiping away the rain pounding his face.

Gemma marched ahead, staying silent. The winding paths were already beaten down by the pitter patter of children's feet, all of them screaming and crashing into one another, practicing for the big night.

She didn't mind that she was drenched and muddy. Or that her hair was coiled in a state of shock from the storm. She would be mad at Zorro for the rest of her life, no matter what the weather was doing.

"Don't you want me to be happy?" he finally asked.

She stopped, hands in her jacket pockets, and then turned and faced him. "I thought you were happy."

"I am! I have no complaints. But what's wrong with more? You can never have too much of it."

"What about us?"

"I wouldn't trade you all for anything. And now, I have another person to share life with. Bertie is an addition to you, not a replacement."

The rain came in torrents. Their voices grew louder over the downpour.

"She's not Nani. It should be Nani, and you should be my grandpops and my baby's grandpops, too." Gemma sniffed back the rain that had swept up her nose. "I always wanted a grandpops. I'll never have one now. I thought you loved us." Gemma's hurt spilled from her eyes and ran full force under the sting of marble-sized hail spattering her face.

"Whoa, Gemma. Hold on. You've got this all wrong."

"No, I don't. And I'm not stupid! I don't get everything wrong."

"You know I don't think that. Never have. But this time you're wrong."

"I'm not wrong. Why didn't you choose Nani? How could you cheat on her?"

"Cheat?"

"Yes! You're cheating on her!"

"Hey, stop right there. I am not cheating on your nan. You have to be with someone to cheat on them."

"You have been with her. And me, Zorro. I mean, *Zork!*" Gemma turned on her heel grinding down rage with one boot, searching for the exit. She twirled right, left, and then right again—desperate to escape the rows of corn and desperate to escape Zorro's words.

"Your nan and I have never been together the way you and Walter are." Zorro followed close behind. "Never. We don't love each other that way. We're like family, and you know that. It's the way it is."

"That can change! It can. Did you even try and marry her? Nani loves you. You didn't try hard enough."

"Gemma, listen to me." His hand cradled her shoulder, and they both stopped. "I do love you, and I love your mom and your nani. I love you all very much. And I loved your real grandpops, too. I never had a chance to have a family, and you all gave me one. I'm

165

honored to be your second grandpops. And honored to have that role with your baby. I wouldn't miss out on that for anything. But Bertie won't take away a thing from our family. She'll only add more love to it. Do you understand?"

"I wanted to be Nani's maid of honor."

"Well, I'm sorry. Your nan's agreed to be Bertie's matron lady, and we both hope you and your mom will be in the wedding too.

"Nani's going to be *Bertie's* maid of honor?"

"Matron," he corrected.

"*Sick!*" she sputtered. "That's just plain wrong."

"It won't be. You'll see."

Gemma didn't know why, but the tension eased up around her eyes. Both shoulders drooped as her pace slowed. "I thought you were marrying, Nani. I was so happy. And now I'm not. Now I only feel sick again."

"I'm sorry, Gem. I didn't realize—"

"And all those talks!" Gemma blurted. "Nani had big talks with Bertie about sex. For hours!"

"What?"

"Nani taught Bertie about who knows what. She was her sex doctor."

First, Gemma thought Zorro had stepped in cow dung, and then she thought he might be losing it. He turned into a ball of hysteria. "No wonder Olivia reacted the way she did!" he cackled. He laughed until he couldn't anymore.

Gemma stared. "What's so funny about that?"

"Explains a few things. That's all."

"Wow," Gemma uttered.

"What?" Zorro reached back and gave his hood a shake.

"This means Bertie was doing sex with *you*."

It was as if a plug had been yanked out of Zorro's throat. His mood soured. "You know what?" he said all crabby like. "Talk to your nan about this. Wait. You better not. She'll get mad again. But here's the thing— this conversation about Bertie and me is now over."

"Nani would only get mad at you if she loved you. I mean truly loved you. Not like family. See what I mean?"

Zorro inspected the cornstalks as if measuring them against his six foot, one inch frame. But said nothing.

"Some things I get right, Zorro."

"Oh, I know, darlin'. That's what I'm afraid of."

Gemma spun around. "We're lost."

"No, we're not. Take two more turns to the left and we're out."

"How do you know that?"

"I pay attention, sweetheart. I never forget the steps I've taken. Not one."

"You know everything."

"Not by a long shot. Especially when it comes to women. I can tell you that."

"Promise you'll never leave?"

"That's the last thing I'd ever want to do."

But Zorro made a promise he couldn't keep. Not that day anyway. When they took cover under the roof of the outdoor market, Gemma saw him on his phone. He strode past the fruits and vegetables and made two calls out of Gemma's earshot.

Gemma had a warm bag of kettle corn when he wandered back. "Your nan is on her way for you. Stay right here. I have a work emergency. But don't you move. You understand me?"

Gemma stiffened, her eyes swiveling. "Can I sit?"

"Yes. But do not leave this market. Understood?" His tone was full of force.

"Yes. Okay." She plopped on a bench. "But it's not raining anymore. See?" She pointed. "There's blue sky again. Can't I just ride home with you?"

"Sorry, sweetheart. I'm headed somewhere else. I may be gone for a few days. A work thing." Zorro kissed the top of her head. "Gotta run, but I love you."

"I know things, Zorro," she said again. "I know a lot more than people see."

Zorro squatted, planting his glossy eyes squarely on hers, his calloused hand cupping her chin. "You know more than all of us combined when it comes to heart. Right in here," he said, tapping his chest. "Exactly like your nan says."

Gemma's face flushed, her mouth quivered in a way that showed her pleasure and embarrassment, though she didn't know why.

Zorro fastened his helmet, hurrying across the dirt lot.

"I love you, Zorro!" she hollered.

He turned, skipping backward. A wide smile swooped across his face.

The Harley took a long slide when he revved it against the gravel; for a few seconds, it tipped sideways, nearly parallel to the ground. Gemma knew he did it on purpose for her. He balanced it out and roared south on River Road, traveling between fields of pumpkins and apple orchards.

She's confused, Zorro. Don't get married yet. Gemma listened until she couldn't hear him anymore. *You just wait.*

****

As soon as Olivia pulled into the Lone Pine Farm parking lot, she turned off the engine and watched her in silence. Gemma—sitting on top a picnic table, no surprise, surrounded by a flock of starlings. Their black oily feathers slicked back and shining. One by one they swooped in for a kernel of kettle corn, plucking it straight from Gemma's hand. She looked achingly innocent.

Full of sparkling magic—with birds, animals, and babies... It seemed like magic, anyway. But Olivia also thought about Gemma's clear, intentional, spirited love of life—the easy joy that flowed from raw, uncensored passion. It seemed she recognized others' emotions like a super-power. That distinct area of Gemma's brain, in Olivia's opinion, was nothing short of brilliant.

It's been said a grandmother's love is biased, and of course why shouldn't it be. But Olivia's love for Gemma reached beyond that. In all her years, she had never met someone with a soul like Gemma's. And she had decided a long time ago she would do anything to save it.

When she approached Gemma, the starlings rose into formation and glided in unison, unspooling like a waving flag.

"He left *again*, Nani. I wanted a ride home on the Harley, dang it." Gemma pushed off the ground and shook off the crumbs of sticky corn stuck on her jacket and jeans.

"He'll be back. He always comes back."

"I know. But who knows when. He's here and then he's gone. I like him around."

"I know you do."

"Well, don't you too?"

"Hon, he runs a business. He leaves when he has to. He still trains people, even when it's not crop-dusting season."

Gemma peered in another direction, absently following her grandmother. "That's not what I asked," she muttered.

"You okay?" Olivia asked. "Your mom said she was worried about you. And Zork is too." She reached the truck first. "Climb in and tell me what's going on."

Gemma slumped in her seat. "I don't know. If I can get over it, I won't be upset."

"Get over what?"

"I'm tired of talking about it."

"Okay. Let's get home. I smell wet animal." Olivia made a stink-face.

"It's my woolie scarf. We got drenched in the downpour." Gemma undid the knot and tossed it to the back.

As soon as Olivia pulled onto River Road, she opened all the windows and moon roof and let the sun pour in like holy light. The clear, crisp air swept out the inside of the truck. With any luck, she hoped it would cleanse their psyches as well.

Gemma laid her head on the window opening letting the wind hit her in the face. But she lurched back when the air shot up her nostrils. With a decided look, she turned to her grandmother and said, "Because."

"Because what?"

"I was mad because he's getting married," Gemma confessed. "And it's not to you."

"Ah. He told you."

"Yes."

"Look, I know Bertie isn't exactly our type. Sometimes the woman drives me bonkers, but—"

"She doesn't drive *me* bonkers. I don't think anyway. I don't even know what that means, but I don't care, because she's never mean to me."

"No. You're right. She's never been mean to either of us." The unwelcome tug of guilt pulled at Olivia again. "Why are you so mad then?"

"He won't be ours anymore."

"He's not ours now, Tink. Never has been. People don't own each other."

"I know." Gemma cupped her hands over her breasts, watching rows of orchards flip by before the scenery opened. Sheep, cows, and horses passed her window in a fast-moving parade, the meadow grass turning brown again. "You said she called him moldy because he wasn't her type."

"Did I? Shows you how much I know." Olivia glanced at Gemma's hands spread over her bosoms. "Time for a maternity bra."

"They're getting huge. Walter loves them."

A closed-lip grin canted up on one side of Olivia's face. She noticed Gemma gently squeezing. "They hurt?"

"No." She kept squeezing.

"Then, what on earth are you doing?"

"Feeling my bazoombas."

Olivia braked for a yellow light.

"And wondering why they turn Walter on. He wants to have sex when he touches them. They're blobs of fat, Nani. Why do guys care so much about blobs of fat?"

"I've wondered the same." The light turned green,

171

and she gunned the engine a little too fast.

"You don't know?" Gemma's head jerked up. "You're the sex doctor."

"I am *not* the sex-doctor. Men like soft, bare skin. That's all. No matter where it is."

"But cantaloupes aren't soft."

"Why do you say that?"

"Sometimes when Walter sees one in the grocery store he says it makes him think of me. Like a turn-on. So I don't let him shop for melons. I don't want things to happen around the cantaloupes. Can you imagine, Nani?"

"Yes, I'm afraid I can. You'd be wise to steer him to the cereal aisle."

"That's what I do! But the whole shopping trip he tells me he's going to find the melons."

"Remind me not to grocery shop with you two. Am I the only one who hears these stories?"

"Uh…" Gemma tapped a finger over her mouth. "Well?" She gawked at the sunroof. "Yes. You are."

"Good. Keep it that way."

Gemma yanked on the visor and popped the mirror open, fishing for something stuck in her eye. "Tell me something," she said. "Do you love him?"

"Walter?"

"No, silly! Zorro."

"Zorro? Oh Gem, please. Enough about Zork."

"No. Listen to me. It's a very important question." Gemma snapped the mirror closed.

"I'm sorry. Okay," Olivia said. "Yes, of course I love him. Like family."

"Then why does your face change when you're around him? It changes. And when you talk about him too."

"Oh, Gem. I don't know what you're talking about. I mean I'm sure you see something, but what you're seeing isn't a face struck by romance. More likely it's struck by a bad burrito."

"You ate a bad burrito?"

"No. It's an expression, honey. But listen, this won't change. We need, I mean, you need to accept that Zork is marrying Bertie. Like it or not, they will be a couple. Zork and Bertie Canby." As soon as she said it, the awareness swept over Olivia in a different way, in a new sick wave of regret.

"There. That's the face on you right now." Gemma said.

"Yeah. Only a little indigestion. That's all. Definitely not romantic love. I am not pining away for Zork. Trust me. You can trust me on that."

Gemma smirked. "There's something else I figured out."

"What's that?"

"I'm afraid Mama and all the naysayers are right about me and this baby."

The truck held a new silence, even as the engine droned on. Olivia warily turned her head toward Gemma, waiting to hear more.

"I'm afraid they're right about why I shouldn't have a baby." Gemma's voice grew stern. "But I'm serious. That's all I'm going to say right now, so do *not* ask any more about it." Gemma turned away from her grandmother's gaze and peered out the window, rows of orchards whisking by again.

"Tell me when you're ready," Olivia said. "And remember, Tink. I'm on your side... No matter what."

Debra Whiting Alexander

Chapter Twenty-Two

Spiritual Practice

The following Sunday, Olivia felt compelled to sit in a church that was listed in the historical registry. Preferably one with an old-fashioned wedding-dress-white steeple—her real reason for going.

It wasn't that Olivia was against church, she simply didn't believe in attending unless she felt like it. This one, she recently learned, had a history tied to Luper Cemetery and, so naturally, she was intrigued. She hoped to learn more about the families of the pioneers buried there. After all, they were like family—she had been cleaning their headstones and weeding their plots for half her life.

"This morning's reading is from Hebrews 13:21," the man boomed from the pulpit. His voice strong and distinct. Olivia liked that he was in a plaid flannel shirt and not all gussied up for church like a lot of men.

"God has given us everything we need," he continued, "to do everything we're meant to do."

Then why do so many of us do nothing?

She stood and sang "Amazing Grace," the sun spangling through the stained glass windows with luminous colors of lavender, red, and aureate, flickering over the rafters.

When the congregation sat, the preacher switched

places with the reader.

The opening to his sermon was all right. She didn't object to anything read from the Psalms. And his message wasn't bad either. But then his words took a detour. Suddenly, he was talking politics. *Politics!* she screamed inside.

She could have left; she considered marching out twice. And when she considered it she imagined the scene she could make getting her point across. But she had read somewhere that exercising civility was a spiritual practice. She decided to stay and practice it. *I'll be civil when I tell him exactly what I think about it too.*

"May the Lord, bless you and keep you. May His light shine upon you and be gracious unto you. May He give you peace."

Yes, please. She joined the congregation speaking in unison. "Amen."

Outdoors, the preacher extended his hand at the top of the stairs, the front of the church half-swallowed in the shadows. "Welcome. And you are?" he asked.

"Olivia Porter." She grabbed hold of his handshake and noted a firm, solid grip, his dry skin enwrapping her own. His face reminded her of a sculpture—strong but kind.

"Oh, yes. The Porters from the farm near the creek. Is that right?" He stepped to the side where a small patch of sun fell between them.

"Yes." Olivia was distracted by his appearance. He looked different up close—the corners of his eyes wrinkled and thinning. He had a full head of thick hair, all of it smoky except for the white swans floating gracefully at his temples.

"Nice to have you with us this morning. Did you fill out a visitor card?" He pulled one from his pocket and offered it to her. "We'd love to stop by with a welcome gift."

"Let me guess. Homemade pie?" She grudgingly accepted the card.

"How'd you know?" His eyes sparked a little gold on top of dark brown.

"I'd be lying if I said I hated pie, but a visit isn't necessary. I love the bones of this church; sitting inside it is such a comfort. For me, the ritual of your worship is too. I only didn't care for the politics that, in my opinion, were incongruent with your message." Her throat clamped shut before she could say more.

"I see. Sorry you received it that way. Would you be up for a meeting when I have more time to discuss it?"

"Yes, I would. But honestly, I'm more interested in learning about the history of the church building. Especially its connection to Luper Cemetery."

"Oh, of course! I'd be happy to discuss it. Are you a historian? Writer?"

"No. Just curious."

"I'm a bit of a history buff myself. And I love talking about Luper. Way more than politics. Would tomorrow morning work? Say, eleven at Luper?"

"That would be great. Thank you, Reverend. You have a long line forming, so I won't keep you. See you in the morning."

"I look forward to it, Olivia."

She moved through the crowd and promptly set the visitor information card on the stack of others near the door. When she descended the steps, she feared their meeting could be a long one if she didn't keep the reverend focused on the topic of the cemetery. She had no patience for a theological debate. Especially if politics became a part of it.

She left the church and ambled through the orchards, in awe of the tiny buds clinging to twigs, all of them prepared to hold tight for the winter. Proof that the resilience of life is strong. *At least something is.*

The leaves crackled like potato chips underfoot— her eyes watering the way they always did when the temperature dropped. Slits of light pierced through the orchard. She chose whatever direction kept her under the brief spotlights of breaking sun the longest.

Olivia had never been a woman in need of company. Quite the opposite. She refueled on the rare days she had time alone. And yet the new sting of loneliness since Zork and Bertie's announcement had troubled her. She feared isolation and seclusion might not be healthy. But she only feared it a little. That day there was no sign of it. Maybe, she concluded, a fleeting reaction held no weight at all. *A false alarm.* After all, she had been remembering Sam when she succumbed to the loneliness. Being content in the company of no one that day seemed like a good sign.

The branches of the walnut tree spread black and tangled against the silver tin sky. Large walnuts, like lumps of coal, lay scattered around the old, battered tree. Olivia found the bag tucked in her front pocket and collected the pitch black, scaly ones. She lifted, inhaled, and crushed the leaves in one hand, dragging the spiced citrus scent deep into her lungs, the aroma strong enough to enjoy from her fingertips the entire way home.

She made one last stop at the wild plum tree that had filled so many of her bowls with the juicy, sweet yellow and purple fruit. The plums had been plentiful for years, but the tree wouldn't make it another season. The shovel and bucket she left there stood waiting. Olivia set the bag of walnuts next to the tree and dug out the seedling growing closest to it. She dumped everything into the five-gallon bucket and hauled it home praying it would take root. "You have to stay alive," she told it. "You've witnessed too much history."

And then the familiar hum of a drone buzzed in the air around her.

She had observed it earlier in the week too. It flew in close—far too close this time. A wormy unease circled her insides.

Olivia set everything down and fiddled with the scarf wrapped around her neck. She yanked it over her head, gathered her things, and changed directions. It would be a longer way back, but the safest thing to do.

The trail carried her home just before noon, the smells of crabapple trees and wild onions rising in the gentle headwind.

The walnuts needed drying. When Olivia reached her back porch, she pulled on garden gloves, peeled back the black layers of oily shell, and spread them over newspaper in a warm corner of the mudroom. All the while, she replayed the drone's appearance in her mind—knowing better than to dismiss it. *Zork needs to know.*

Olivia was in the mood for something lively. Music that would break up any foreboding thoughts. As soon as she powered on the B-52's singing, "Love Shack," she felt young again. A favorite in her twenties, the song coursed through her—as if everything would be all right. Overall, it had been a pleasurable day and she remained grateful for it.

When she spotted Magnolia's name flashing on her phone screen, she lowered the music, sat in her favorite chair, and tossed the throw blanket over her lap. "Hi, Maggie. How are you?"

"Mother—where have you been?!"

"A lot of places. What…" She decided a peevish response was justified. "I'm not allowed to have a Sunday to myself?"

"It's Gemma. She's been in a terrible accident."

"Oh dear God." Olivia bolted from the chair. "What happened? Is she okay?" She scrambled for her purse and truck keys.

"I'm fifteen minutes from the hospital now. They called while I was driving into town. Thank goodness I was already on my way. I've been trying to reach you. Even Zork isn't answering."

"Is she okay?" she asked again. The poison of regret surged through her. *I didn't turn my phone back on after church.*

"I don't know yet."

"And the baby?"

"I don't know anything. Just that some asshole blew through a red light and hit her in an intersection. The witnesses said the guy was going fast. Super-fast."

"I'm on my way."

My dear, sweet Gemma. The truck burned rubber when she ripped out of the garage. *I'm on my way.*

Chapter Twenty-Three

Holding on to a Heartbeat

Gemma's eyes fluttered open to the crescendos of noise traveling the halls of the emergency room. She strained to lift her lids, even to a slit, when she spotted Walter peering through a crack in the curtain surrounding her. He pierced through the folds of buttery cloth, stood close, and stared. Gemma watched as one hand slid along the backside of his hip, and then the other. They were sweaty as usual. The wet beads of worry lined his brow too.

Walter flinched when the curtain flounced open behind him. A man hustled into the room covered from head to foot in blue.

"I'm Doctor Moore. Are you the husband?" He rolled a computer stand next to a tall chair.

"She doesn't have one."

"Are you a relative?" he scrolled the screen.

Everyone awaited Walter's answer.

Eyes blinking, he finally sputtered, "I, well..."

"Do you know this woman?"

"Yes!" He jerked to attention.

"How do you know her?"

"We met in the first grade at Spring Creek Elementary School, sir."

"Where's her family?" The doctor typed a few

words, searching the screen.

"I don't know."

"Are they here?"

"I don't know." A shaky panic enveloped his words. "Gemma?"

"I hear you, Walter." Her eyes swiveled around the room. "I guess I'm not dead."

"No," Walter answered. "I expected to see you dead. Or see you die a calamitous death in front of me." He wiped his brow while the doctor peered into her pupils with a light.

"Nope," the doctor quipped. "She's alive to see another day."

"What about my baby?"

"How far along are you? In weeks?" He typed something into the computer.

"Week nine. Almost. Or more. But I'm not sure. She's alive, right?"

"You know it's a girl?"

"I do."

"From a blood test?"

"No."

"Have you had an ultrasound?"

"Yes."

"Okay." He scrolled through the computer again. "Here it is," he said, peering at the screen. "That was way too soon for a gender reveal."

"I know that," Gemma said. "But she's a she. Did you hear her heartbeat? It thumps super loud and fast. She *always* has one."

"We'll check in a minute. Have any pain anywhere since this happened?"

"Since what happened?"

"The car crash. You were hit pretty hard."

"I know. Why didn't he stop on red? He drove like a maniac! Like he had the green. But he didn't. I had the green. The police told me I was right."

"Any pain when I do this?" He pushed around her tummy in different spots.

"My bones hurt." Gemma winced, stretching a little. "Do I have bruises?"

"You will," he said. "Let's take a listen to you first, then we'll find this little guy."

"Gal," she reminded. "Not a guy."

The doctor gently opened her gown and stamped the stethoscope on her chest.

"Yikes! That's cold!"

He stared to the right and listened.

"How did you get here, Walter?" Gemma asked.

"I took three buses."

"Did you see it happen?"

"Quiet, please," the doctor said. He moved the metal disc over her bare belly to different spots, listening with his full attention.

"Sorry," Gemma apologized. "Oh my gosh, this tickles." Her lips sealed shut in a tight line, trying not to laugh.

Walter forgot and continued. "I couldn't see it happen from work!"

"Shhh!" Gemma told him.

"They let me leave work to come here," he added.

"Walter." Gemma held a finger over pursed lips. "Quiet. He's listening to her."

The doctor cocked his head, pushed back, and typed on the keyboard again.

"Did you hear it thumping?" Gemma asked.

183

"Very faint if I did. The OB needs to evaluate."

Gemma only heard what she needed to. "Okay. At least it's working. Even if it's faint. How did you know I got crashed into, Walter?"

"Your mom called me."

"*She* called you? From Seattle?"

"No. From the freeway. She was driving here to bring you stuff."

"Ohhh." Gemma wrinkled her nose. "Why do I have this big thing around my neck?"

The doctor finished typing. "It's a cervical collar. And I know having an x-ray isn't ideal, but we need to check your neck and spine."

"Oh. Okay."

"Have you had any pain since I've been in the room?"

"No. But you heard a *little* heartbeat, right?"

"Possibly. The OB has a far better way of listening than I do. After—"

"The who?"

"The obstetrician. A pregnancy doctor… After that exam and x-rays, we'll see if you can go home." He rinsed his hands haphazardly at the sink, tossed a paper towel in the trash, and left.

"Bye, Dr. Moore!" Gemma called out.

The top of the curtain slid noisily open again. "We're here," Mama said, pushing through with Nani behind her. "The nurse told us you should be fine. Thank God. I don't know how you survived it." Mama tenderly laid her face against Gemma's.

"But we did," Gemma said. "Thank Creator."

Mama kissed her on the forehead and Nani squeezed Gemma's hand. Then they both fired off a round of questions: "How do you feel?" "Is the baby okay?" "Any pain anywhere?" "What did the doctor say?"

"Gee-whiz," Gemma said. "Slow down everybody. This is fifty questions!"

Walter hooted.

Gemma breathed deeply, calming herself. "I feel okay, you guys. Except for all my bones and skin because I'm getting bruises. A baby doctor has to check me, and I'm getting a test or something. Then I can go home. And the baby is fine," she assured.

"Oh good," Nani sighed. "What test?"

"I forget. But one is to find a heartbeat. Not mine. Hers. But it's okay—she's not going anywhere."

"He didn't check for the baby's heartbeat yet?" Mama asked.

"He listened," Gemma told her.

"Did he hear one?" Mama peeked at Walter when she asked.

"All these questions are confusing," Gemma said. "I'm not sure."

"He said maybe he did, maybe he didn't," Walter piped in.

Gemma blew out a noisy breath. "But Walter, as her mother, I would know if she wasn't breathing."

"How would you know that?" he asked.

"She'd tell me, and I would feel it! She's *fine*."

"She can't talk yet," he argued. "And you said you can't feel it move yet either!"

Mama and Nani stayed out of the tussle. They were used to letting Gemma and Walter work things out in their own way.

"Walter, she's not an *it*. She's a *she*. And I would

know. Just like I know she's a she. And she's fine." When Gemma stared at the ceiling, she spotted it. One tiny seed of doubt planted right there in her own brain. It was only the size of a poppy seed, but still. Her eyes closed. "She *better* be fine."

As soon as she said it, Gemma suffered another breathing malfunction. A flood rose up when she opened her eyes. "She has to be okay!" she gasped. "I didn't mean it." She practically gulped the oxygen out of the room. "I thought I didn't want her. I was thinking crazy, because I was scared," she panted. "I want her more than anything."

Gemma wondered if the crash had bruised her heart too. It didn't feel so good.

Nani stepped in, lightly stroking the hair off Gemma's face. "It's okay, Tink. Everyone gets scared."

"But if they can't find her heartbeat it will be my fault." She glowered at the shiny metal cart next to her bed, smooth as a sheet of unscored ice. Two dark puddles of fear reflected back at her. "She knew I changed my mind and wanted to run away from her. What if she leaves me?"

"Uh…" Walter paused. "I don't think a little blob can think that much. Or get up and go anywhere. You don't have to worry."

"I do have to worry, Walter. You don't get it."

"I saw the blob. I get it."

"Don't call her a 'blob'!"

"Sheesh," Nani exhaled. "You guys are exhausting." She pushed off her knees and stood. "Stick to the facts, Gem. The baby knows you aren't running away from her, because you didn't. And you aren't going to—right?"

"Right." Gemma wiped her face with the sheet.

"Okay. So there you go. It's all good." Nani sat again.

"I'm sorry if our last phone call stirred up all this worry," Mama said.

"It was stirred up before that," Gemma said limply.

An orderly in the same blue get-up with a paper hat and mask around his neck, came through the curtain. "Can you tell me your name and date of birth?"

"It would appear you're having surgery, Gemma," Walter warned.

"I'm not having surgery, Walter." Gemma's eyes concentrated on the orderly's face and didn't move when she asked him, "Right?" He took forever to answer.

"Right." He stared at her and Gemma stared right back. "Name, please?" he asked again.

"Oh! Okay," Gemma reset a full-size grin on her face. "Gemma Jane Porter."

"Spell your last name please and tell me your date of birth."

Gemma asked Mama to check her spelling and numbers. But his questions kept coming. And then she signed things. Maybe she was confused, or maybe she was woozy, but she was done. "I need help."

Mama reviewed the form. "It's all correct."

"Okay, we're ready for you. Next stop, X-rays."

"Hold on." Nani raised a hand and stopped everything. "She's pregnant. What X-rays?"

He rifled through a chart. "Pictures of the neck and spine." He closed the file. "Doctor's orders."

"We need a few minutes to discuss this."

It took Mama aback. "We do? But Mom—"

"If you don't mind." Nani opened the curtain and directed the orderly out. He wasted no time leaving.

Mama's eyes spooled to the back of her head.

"Okay, look," Nani said. "I'll check Gemma over and see if this is necessary."

"What?!" Mama erupted. "How would you know, and it's only an X-ray for god's sake! The doctor ordered it."

"Maybe she needs one, maybe she doesn't. It should be avoided if possible."

"You think they don't know that? We have to worry about Gemma at this point! Not the baby."

"Mama!" Gemma lit up. "Maybe you don't care about my baby, but Nani and I do."

"I never said that! Don't put words in my mouth."

"Technically the baby is mine also," Walter said. "Although at this point in time I suppose in principle it's more yours than mine."

"Stop everyone!" Nani ordered. "Let me check a few things, and if there's any doubt, she'll have the X-ray." Nani moved around the gurney and pulled back the sheet. She took hold of both Gemma's feet, examining them as if she knew exactly what she was doing. "Do you feel this?"

"Yes."

"Any pain when I do this, Gemma?"

"No."

"Mother," Mama groaned. "Seriously? Should we call you Dr. Porter?" She sounded bothered.

Nani ignored her and continued. "Any pain when I do this?"

"No."

"Always good to have a doctor in the family,"

Walter said.

Nani moved to the other end and placed both hands under Gemma's head. She focused on the ceiling, nudging gently behind her neck and along her spine, fingers pressing in. "Anything here?"

"No."

"My mother is not a doctor, Walter. And this is ridiculous," Mama fumed.

"I trust Nani. Let her check me."

"Oh, I know you trust her, but—"

"She might know, Mama! She knows a lot."

Mama folded her arms. "Yes, she must have been an ancient healer in a past life."

If words had been posted on Nani's face they would have read, *don't be a smart ass*.

Nani adjusted Gemma's sheet. "She's fine," she pronounced. "There's no need for an X-ray. Trust me."

"The doctor says she needs one! Please don't—"

"Well, I don't want one if it hurts my baby," Gemma snapped.

"Great," Mama blew out a lung full of air. "So you're defying doctor's orders. *Real* doctors with degrees and training. Just great, Mom."

"No, she's not, Mama. I am. It's my baby and my decision." She squinted at Walter. "Our baby, I mean."

"Okay, look." Mama turned for her purse. "You both will have this conversation with the doctor. Maybe they can talk some sense into you. I will not be a part of it. Walter, do you want to stay and talk with the doctor, too, or go for coffee?"

"I don't think it's a good idea for me to stay on account I'm not particularly good at talking to doctors. Especially about Gemma and our baby. It's extremely nerve-wracking for me."

"I agree," Gemma said. "You should go, Walter." She glanced at Mama and Nani. "He might cry."

"That's true," he said, turning to Mama. "I'd be happy to get you coffee. What would you like?"

"I meant for you to join me. Do you want coffee too?"

"Not unless you want to see me on crack."

"He's right," Gemma confirmed. "He acts like a tweaker on it."

"Well, have you tried de-caf?" Mama asked.

Walter squinted. "No."

"Okay, then. Come with me. If you'd like a break."

"I would like a break."

"*Me* too." Mama slung her purse over a shoulder, "Can I get you something, Mom?"

"Double shot please."

"This way Walter," Mama directed. "I need fresh air."

****

Nani paced around Gemma's bed. Then she poked her head out between the curtains. "Honestly. It'll take an act of congress to get you out of here." She shut them again.

"The baby doctor has to come first," Gemma said.

"I know."

"And they're short staffed," Gemma explained.

"They are." Nani sighed.

"The nurses have a harder job than the doctors. We should be nice to them."

"Yes, we should."

"At least you got coffee."

"True, but—"

"Practice patience, Nani. It's essential to living in peace."

Nani's head shot up. "You remembered."

"Sometimes I remember things I didn't even know I remembered." She giggled.

"Well, you're right. I did tell you that, and it's true. You must be tired, though."

"I am. So was Walter. It's good Mama drove him home. He rode three busses getting here. Sometimes it takes him six to go to work."

"*Six*?"

"Yeah. When he messes up."

"Oh." Nani sat. "He went through a lot to be with you today, didn't he?"

"Yes. He cried at work when Mama called him, so they told him he could leave."

"He does love you, doesn't he?"

"He says he does. I believe him because Walter never lies."

"No. I'm sure he doesn't."

"My daughter has a good daddy."

"Yes, she does," Nani said.

A split second later, Gemma's eyes screwed shut. She felt her forehead crumple up like the sheet her clammy paws were gripping. Her brain flipped to another place without permission.

"Gem, what is it?"

"I was in my car. Right this instant!"

"You're white as a ghost." Nani went to the sink and wet a paper towel.

"I felt him hit me again! I saw everything all over! And the sounds... Stuff exploding everywhere. It was so real, Nani," Gemma panted. "What is wrong with me?"

"Nothing. You had a flashback." Nani patted cool moisture along her forehead. Then placed it at the back of her neck. "It happens for a while but lessens with time. It's intense, but a natural reaction, honey."

"I don't like it."

"No. But you survived this—you'll survive the memory too. You need more time to come to grips with what happened; it's a difficult experience to take in. Your counselor can help you learn how to settle it down."

"Have you had backflashes, Nani?"

"Flashbacks. And yes, I have. Way too many in fact."

"You had car accidents?"

"Yes," she lied. "A long time ago."

"Okay. But Nani, I need a bathroom. Bad."

Nani unstrapped the neck brace and used the length of her arms as a brace against her back. "1-2-3, up," she said. "How do you feel?"

"Fine, I think. Except for all the bruises I'm getting."

The corridors were full of patients in wheelchairs, on gurneys, and those staggering with IV drip bags, holding tight to the back of their gowns. No one was available to assist Gemma, so Nani handled everything. "Take it slow and veer left. I'll wait here outside the door."

When Gemma stepped inside, she left the door cracked so she could see Nani. She didn't want to be alone. Nani stood in front on her phone, protecting Gemma's privacy. "Zork. Olivia here," she said. "Pick up if you're there. Tried calling earlier. At the hospital.

Gemma is okay, but she was broadsided. Not sure about the baby yet."

"My baby is fine, Zorro!" Gemma called out.

"Anyway, Gemma was lucky. Still in the E.R. Maggie and Walter left. I'll keep you posted."

"Nani?" Gemma asked.

"Yes?" She dropped the phone into her pocket.

"Can you come in and see this?"

Nani slipped inside. "What is it, sweetpea?"

"Look at what's in my underwear. Something gooey and bloody."

"Okay." She inspected her panties. "Let's head back so you can lie down."

"What is it?"

"Probably nothing. But the doctor needs to weigh in. Any cramping?"

"It's not my baby coming out, is it? She can't leave me, Nani. She's not ready! And I want her! I swear I do!"

"Gemma, I know that. I believe you."

"I screamed awful things about her into my pillow, and she could hear everything. But I didn't mean any of it. Honest! I love her, Nani."

"I don't doubt it for a minute. And neither will she."

"My whole life I've been waiting for her. And *only* her."

You know that's the truth, Creator. Please don't take her back.

Chapter Twenty-Four

Something Looming

"Zork, me again. I'm helping Gemma get dressed, and we'll be out of here soon. Her cervical plug needs to heal, but they found the baby's heartbeat and Gemma is fine. Everyone's in one piece. No worries. Oh. One more thing." Olivia stepped out of earshot of Gemma. "Second time now that same drone has been on my property. Happened again earlier today."

The phone dropped into her pocket again. "Need any help, Gem?"

"Not yet. So my plug repairs itself?"

"Yup. That's what they said. Bedrest for three days and no sex for a while. I thought you could stay with me if you'd like."

Delight swept across Gemma's face. "Movies and popcorn three nights in a row!" She slipped off her gown.

Olivia arched her brows. "You have *got* to get a maternity bra. It's the only place you definitely look pregnant."

"Mama brought me some. But Walter likes this cleavage, you know."

"Yes, I know."

Gemma buttoned up the rest of her shirt and screeched, "Zorro's here!"

Olivia turned, startled to see Gemma was right. "Good thing you weren't Walter."

Gemma giggled.

He eyed them both but didn't ask why. "I leave for a few days and see what happens? Nothing but trouble." He gave Gemma a hug.

"No trouble for me," Olivia said. As soon as it rolled off her tongue, a bitter taste filled her mouth. He turned as if he had gotten a smack of it too. "By the way..." she said, hoping to reset the conversation. "Something important came up on the property today."

Zork nodded. "Heard your message on my way to check out Gemma's car. Thanks for letting me know. The car is pretty banged up, but nothing I can't fix."

"Really?" Gemma's mouth dropped in awe. "You can fix anything, Zorro. You're always here for us."

She's right. "I'll meet you two out front," Olivia said. "The wheelchair should be here soon."

"Okay, Nani."

Olivia shimmied through the curtains and slipped away. She wanted to thank Zork. Not only for fixing the car and dealing with the drone, but for always being there for them. She wanted to thank him but didn't. She rushed away instead—as if fleeing something bigger. If she had been honest with herself, she would have admitted there was something bigger. Something looming now in every room she and Zork occupied together. The thing is, while she had an inkling of what she was avoiding, she still didn't fully understand why.

But Zork did.

Chapter Twenty-Five

From Past to Present

The next morning, Olivia checked the clock in the barn, pleased to see her ride to Luper could be a leisurely one. She saddled up Buster, breathing in a moment of serenity. Gemma was safe with Zork; she could relax. She only hoped she could relax with the reverend. *Please God, no theological debates today.*

The shining sun revealed a clear, scrubbed, cerulean October sky, even as a cold spell dropped the temperature again. Olivia needed an extra layer under her apple green cable knit sweater and matching scarf. She didn't mind. She had become adept at layering the right way decades ago.

She clicked her tongue, urging Buster ahead. They took the picturesque trail near the thundering white water—the vibrancy of the river surging against the rocks and bounding over the trunks of fallen trees. The smell of old timber always warmed her insides. Olivia sensed Sam nearby when she passed—his lively, bustling energy still moving alongside her.

"Don't ever leave me," she used to tell him. "Promise me you won't die first."

When Buster reached Luper, he stopped at the tree in the precise spot where Olivia always tied his lead. "Good boy, Buster."

The reverend approached the gate, both hands resting behind his back, "Good morning." His smile rolled out like a welcome mat.

"Good of you to meet me, Reverend."

"My pleasure. But first, let me ask how your granddaughter is. I heard she was in a terrible accident yesterday. And is expecting."

"Yes, gave us quite a fright."

"I assume she's well or you wouldn't be here. And the baby too, I hope."

"Yes. Both should be fine, thank you."

Olivia noticed his jeans, as faded and worn as her own, his chest muscle-bound through the shoulders. Long underwear peeked out beneath a gunmetal-gray flannel shirt, untucked with the sleeves rolled up, his arms exposing a laborer's tan. *Odd for a preacher.* "She's with me for a few days. Zork and I are taking care of her while she's on bedrest."

"Ah. She's in good hands, then. I just met with Zork and Bertie about a week or so ago."

"Oh?" Olivia's breath caught. "Of course. For the upcoming nuptials, I assume." The seconds seemed to move in slow motion.

"Had a wonderful visit. Couldn't be happier for them."

"I didn't realize they selected your church to be married in."

"Bertie and I go way back. I knew her family before I moved here. She's a character. Perfect for Zork if you ask me."

"Is she? I mean, she really is. And the wedding... I think Zork said it's happening in the spring? Or is it sooner?"

"Much sooner! They aren't wasting any time."

"No, I'm sure she's not. *They're* not," Olivia corrected. "So you'll be marrying them..." They strolled along the path between rows of graves.

"Yes. Looking forward to it. Bertie's been alone for as long as I've known her. It's always nice to see people happy, isn't it? When they finally find someone they want to share life with?"

"Yes, it is. If marriage is what you want."

"Well, right. It's not for everyone. To each his own—or her own. Which is my stance on politics too, by the way. I'm sorry you found it otherwise in my sermon yesterday. I think I owe you an apology."

"Well, I know it's hard to keep a civil tongue these days. For either side. I do understand that. It's... Well, you know what? Maybe it doesn't matter. I accept your apology."

"No. Please, say what's on your mind." He held a patient, calculating gaze.

"Well, in my humble opinion, there's no quicker way to corrupt the church than to put politics into it." Olivia bent down and plucked a weed from the dank soil, the sweet, fresh fragrance of earth percolating under her nose.

"I'm afraid I—"

"Freedom of religion is a promise this country makes and it wasn't founded on just one." Olivia felt the slow simmer of righteousness rising in her chest. "I think the country is far too mixed up about that right now. I'm sure what you said yesterday seemed harmless enough, but it's a slippery slope. There's good reason for the separation of church and state."

"Actually, I—"

"When the two are intertwined, it's not a healthy thing in my view. Not for anyone. I think it corrupts our understanding of God." *Stop cutting the poor guy off! And I thought Bertie talked too much.*

Olivia knew it didn't matter, not that much, what she had to say about his sermon. And yet, it seemed to matter to him. He listened, appearing open to what she had to say.

The reverend nodded thoughtfully and waited. Anyone could see she hadn't finished.

"That being said," she added, "the music was lovely and I enjoyed the singing. And I loved watching the way the sun nudged its way through the stained glass windows at that time of morning. Seeing the kaleidoscope of colors dance on the ceiling and walls filled me with sheer pleasure."

"Well. At least we gave you a light show," he snickered. "I plan to discuss this Sunday. I apologize again."

"No need. But thank you."

Sometimes Olivia regretted making her opinions known. But not for long. The older she got, the less likely she was to stifle her sentiments about anything.

"What a beautiful job they've done in the restoration of your church," she told him. "I've enjoyed watching it transform—practically raised it from the dead. Who took that on?"

"I did. Not alone, of course. I had plenty of help. But thank you. It's been worth every bit of sweat I poured into it. Gave me the opportunity to use my contractor skills again."

This took Olivia aback. "I had no idea." *There's more to him than religion.* "You have multiple talents, then. I may not agree with all your positions, Reverend, but you seem like a good man. Just misinformed," she added with a sly grin. "And thank you for your commitment to restoring such a historic church. We can't let these structures be forgotten or destroyed. They matter. They hold the past."

"On that we completely agree." He snickered. "Actually, we agree on more than you think. And I value an honest perspective. Glad you shared yours with me."

"Thank you." *He seems like a good man.*

The same two men on horses traversed the hill and caught Olivia's attention. She gazed their direction, a hand shielding her eyes. "Know anything about those two?"

"No," the reverend said. "I'm out here fairly often... Don't think I've seen them around before. You know anything?"

"No," she lied. "But I worry about Gemma. She comes here a lot."

"Yes, I see her sometimes."

"She's usually with me, but comes on her own more often now."

He moved into the open and watched the two men disappear. "Nope. They don't look familiar. But I haven't seen you here before either." His eyes followed the panoramic view around the countryside—a spattering of blue and yellow wildflowers dotted the verdant hills.

"I've been coming to Luper forever. With Gemma since she was five years old."

He swiveled around, visibly dumbstruck. "I've been here a few years now. How odd that we've never met. I'll be sure to keep an eye out for Gemma."

"Thank you. She's a strong, capable young woman, but—"

"I understand. She's a person with an intellectual disability, isn't she?"

"Technically, yes. But I never think of her that way. She's so much more than a label or medical conclusion." Olivia sat on the massive, curved log made into a bench not far from the maple and shook a pebble out of her boot. "To me, she's always been exactly who she's supposed to be. Like any of us."

His eyes narrowed. "She's lucky to have you."

Olivia discerned the sincerity of his words. "Well, I'm luckier to have her. I mean that."

"I'm sure it hasn't been easy for her mother or you."

"Parenting is never easy. Do you have children?"

"No. So I don't know what I'm talking about, I know."

"It's not that. I've come to realize that it's not raising a child with a disability that's difficult. It's raising the children who are cruel to them that's much harder."

"I'm sure you're right." He plopped on the bench.

Olivia leaned forward, admiring the subtle shades of color in the rain-drizzled pebbles at her feet. "The scent of damp rock has always been like perfume to my nose."

He tipped forward too and breathed in. "There's really nothing else like it, is there? Ready for a history lesson?" he asked.

"Please. Starting with baby Harriet."

****

On the way home, Olivia plodded Buster up the hill where the men on horses had been. She dismounted and detected fresh finger marks in the dust. Someone had been sitting on the matted grass near the edge of the hill. She pulled out her binoculars, scoping the valley floor when she realized she didn't even know his name. Reverend was all she had called him.

She checked her phone for messages, relieved to see none. *Good. I can take my time.*

The familiar whine of a drone lanced the air, suspending her thoughts. She inspected with binoculars, confirming it was the same unmanned aircraft swooping around her as before. This time she didn't turn away and leave; she sat and watched. *Definitely not someone's toy.*

Olivia pulled her Sig Sauer P228 pistol from the saddle bag. It was time to take the thing down.

"Let's find out what you're doing, shall we?" Olivia steadied her hand, slowly taking aim. "Come to Mama."

****

The kitchen was toasty warm when she stepped inside, Zork and Gemma playing cards in front of a crackling fire in the living room. A delectable bouquet of earthy spiced cider drew Olivia to the stove. Allspice, nutmeg, and cloves mollified the air like sweet bark. She grabbed a hefty mug.

"Gee whiz, Nan. You've been out with the reverend a long time. We're hungry!"

"Well, then why didn't you eat?" She dipped the ladle in the red, cast-iron pot and poured herself a steaming cup.

"Zorro said to wait for you."

"Why do that? Feed that baby." Olivia set the mug on a coaster, unwrapped her scarf, and flung it toward the stairs. A flash of lime shrouded the bannister.

"Out with the *reverend*?" Zork piped up.

"Yeah, she was," Gemma answered. "From Bertie's church."

"You mean, Samuel?" he asked.

Olivia was taken aback when she sat. "His name is *Samuel*?"

Gemma's head lifted. "You spent all day on a date and didn't even know the guy's name?"

Zork's head lifted too. "A date?" He set aside a handful of cards. "What are you talking about?"

"Stop. Both of you. It wasn't a date. But funny. I had no idea his name was Sam." She smirked. "Go figure."

"Go figure what? Why you talkin' to him?" Zork asked. "Or is it personal?"

Gemma's eyes opened up like tickweed. Olivia knew exactly what she was thinking: *Zorro sounds jealous.*

"We share a love of history. That's all. Especially around Luper Cemetery, and I learned all kinds of things about the families there. Including baby Harriet's."

Gemma perked up. "What about baby Harriett?"

"Talk about that after I leave," Zork said. "I'm taking off." He pushed back his chair from the table. "You take it easy, Gem, you hear me? And I'll beat you at cards next time. You watch." He gave her a smooch on the side of the head when they embraced.

"I don't know, Zorro," Gemma said. "Maybe you need a new loaf of cards. You're not so lucky." Gemma grabbed the TV remote, clicked on *Frozen*, and stretched out on the sofa, cuddling a new fluffy polar bear. "Thanks for my get well present." She squeezed it under her chin. "And thank Bertie, too. I love him."

"You're welcome, darlin'."

"And I want to go flying again! As soon as I can."

"You got it, Ace. See ya both—"

"Hang on, Zork." Olivia's mug clunked on the table. "Have something out back for you."

When the screen door rattled to a close behind them, Zork stomped around the porch smashing stink bugs. A sour and fermenting odor saturated the air around them. "What's up?"

"I'll show you in the barn." Olivia plowed into thick rubber boots. "Gad, I hate that smell."

Her lungs cleared when the pleasing scent of compost and cedar chips freshened the air on the way to the barn. She went directly to the drone, hidden underneath Buster's navy blanket liner. "Here. See what you can find on it." She handed it to him. "I took it down on the hill. It's the third time this drone has been on me."

"Whoa," he said. "Okay. Glad you sequestered it." He searched it over with a sharp eye. "Not too banged up. Nice shot."

"Surveillance I'm guessing."

Zork raised his brows. "Yep. Getting a lay of the land. We know how it works."

"Yes, we do." She sighed. "Let me know what you find."

He tossed a gunny sack around it and tucked it under his arm. His stride, long and nimble traipsing back through the mire. He reached his truck and ran a finger through the dampened dirt along the side of it. "Olivia? When do you plan on telling me what's going on with you?"

The question stopped her but not for long. "Let's stay focused on what we need to right now."

"Never mind." He hopped inside. "You don't fool me, though."

"I wouldn't dream of trying. Except for that drone, there's nothing else we need to worry about."

"Yeah. Well, we'll get back to this." Zork cranked the engine over. "Count on it."

Olivia turned her back to him and waved him off. "Like hell we will," she said to no one. But she knew holding back truth was the very thing she had accused him of. She had been right; it put them all at greater risk. Being a team required complete honesty.

But it's hard to be honest when you don't know what the truth is…

Chapter Twenty-Six

Somewhere in the Shadows

After a bowl of chicken stew, Nani and Gemma ambled to the game table wearing king-sized knee length look alike T-shirts with wild horses on the front.

"How about this one?" Nani held up a game board and waved a clear bag in the air, multicolored marbles chinking against each other inside it.

"Sure." Gemma sat. "So you said baby Harriet is actually related to Bertie Lou?"

"She is. A distant relative, but yes. Isn't that something?"

"Does Bertie know?"

"The reverend showed her the documents proving it."

"Wow. I know someone related to her." An unruly belch exploded from Gemma and rendered her speechless.

Nani's brows lifted. "You feeling all right?"

"Am now!"

"Have you felt okay all day?"

"Yeah."

"Pain anywhere?"

"No. Nothing in my underwear either."

"Good."

Gemma sorted through the marbles. "I'm green.

You're blue."

Nani eyeballed the dice as if she didn't trust them.

"Who's your favorite movie star, Nani-pie?"

"I don't have one."

"No, I mean, like who makes you swoon? Or used to when you still swooned?"

"I can still swoon, Gemma." She tipped her head. "I think, anyway."

"You can?"

"Probably."

"Over who?"

"Oh, I don't know. Maybe I'm lying."

"Well, then who did you swoon over when you were young? In the movies, I mean."

"Well, if I had to pick…"

"Yes. You have to."

"Okay, Paul Newman."

"Who?" Gemma slapped the marbles down and put her phone screen up. "Spell it for me." She tapped in the letters Nani dictated, and then enlarged a photo with two slender fingers. "Wow. You picked a cute one."

"Yup."

Gemma ogled. "I can even swoon over him. And he's a cowboy in this one. Our favorite."

"Well, of course. I'd only want a cowboy."

"Me too! Except Walter sure isn't one."

"Well, no, but you don't want to grow old with someone you don't genuinely love, or who doesn't genuinely love you. That's the most important thing."

"Walter loves me in his own way. It's real."

"That's what counts."

"And I don't want to grow old without him. You know what?" Gemma raised the phone and put an eye

207

closer to the screen. "He looks a lot like Reverend Samuel."

"Who?"

"Paul Newman."

"What?"

"Look!" She handed it to her.

"Oh, my goodness." She lifted her glasses and glanced at Gemma. "He does. At least in this picture."

"No wonder you like him."

"Not the way we like Paul Newman. Besides, Paul's eyes are blue, not brown like the reverend's."

"Oh. Okay." She scooped up the dice and studied them the way Nani had. "But you have to admit Reverend Samuel is cute." She smiled.

"He's a man of the church for heaven's sakes. Probably married."

"Nope. He's not. My friend's mom had the hots for him. She went to his church to try and get a date."

"How did that work out?"

"Not so good. She hated church, and he didn't want a date." Gemma slapped the dice down, pushing them toward Nani. "I counted the dots on these and I think they're all there. When will we know for sure my plug is fixed? I'm bored staying home all day."

"Two more days of rest." She pushed the dice back. "Go ahead and roll."

Gemma plunked them into a plastic cup, shook like mad for at least ten earsplitting seconds, and spilled the dice over the table. "I miss riding Lolly. I took a nap with her today and we snuggled. She likes my company."

"She loves your company."

"Zorro was jealous, I think."

Nani squinted, but didn't say anything.

"Yup... Of Reverend Samuel."

"Move your marble."

"He *was*! I'm good at noticing things, you know."

"Yes, you are, but sometimes you notice what you want to."

"Well, I feel it too."

"Okay, well, you're feeling it wrong this time. Move your marble."

"I'm not wrong. And it's not what I want to see anyway, so that's not why."

"What do you mean?"

"I think it's okay for Zorro to be with Bertie." Gemma counted six spaces and rolled again.

"You do?"

"Yeah. I think they make a cute couple. Like Walter and me. Only different. And Bertie likes me."

"Yes, she does. I'm delighted you're okay with it."

But are you okay with it? Gemma had to wonder. "I'm also not afraid anymore. I mean I am, but it's okay." She moved a marble and gave Nani the dice.

"You're not afraid of having the baby, you mean? Or of being a mother?"

"Both." Gemma made a sour face. "I'm still scared of the whole thing, but it scared me more to think of losing her. The crash made me see it right."

"Harrowing events can do that. The thought of losing you scared me too," Nani said.

"I know. I don't want to lose anybody."

"Well, right now, no one's losing anyone. We're all okay."

"I'll never forget how much I love her again." Gemma's head drooped. "I want her more than anything. And I've decided to be brave when I have to get her out. Will it feel like pushing cement, Nani?"

"Being that she's not cement, probably not. But you won't know until you're in that moment. Right now stay in this one."

"True. Some women say it's as easy as squeezing out a bad stinker. That'd be nice! But whatever, I'll do anything for her. I've decided to be brave."

"Then brave you shall be." Nani's face softened when she sat back. "She's a lucky baby to have you. You know that?"

"I'll do my best to make that be true."

"It's true now, Gem. It's one hundred percent true."

Gemma rolled the cup against both cheeks, certain they were the color of cherry blossoms. "Thank you. I'll never feel those awful things again. I promise."

"You don't have to promise that."

"But that's why all this happened."

"No, honey. That's not why. Saying you're scared doesn't make bad things happen. You admitted what every mother feels sometimes. No need to hide that."

"But people expect me to panic and not know how to handle things. If I say I'm scared, it'll prove them right."

"Then explain you can handle it and you're scared too. You can be both."

"Okay. Let's play."

"Gem, the first time is scary for every woman. It's nothing to be ashamed of. Promise me you'll tell us if you ever feel that way again. Do you promise?"

"I promise."

****

The night wind picked up over the fields around three in the morning. The sound, like heavy blankets batting the backside of Nani's home. And then, with one solid gust, it tightened and shook the old farmhouse, walls creaking everywhere. Gemma couldn't sleep.

She threw the bedroom window up—a soothing rush of cool air spread over her sticky skin, the black sky dotted with so many stars it made Gemma's brain spin. *How do we know all those speckles of light are even real?*

She climbed back into bed, but the branches outside scoured her bedroom window nonstop. The shrill constant screech against glass was as unnerving as a high pitched dentist drill. *Make it stop.*

She shot up again with a flashlight and examined the tree. Chill bumps rippled across the back of her neck. She trampled across the hall to Nani's bedroom.

"Nani," she said, in a hushed, pressing voice. And then louder. "Graham Cracker!"

Nani bounded up. "What is it?"

"Can I sleep with you?"

"Of course. What's wrong?"

"Something gave me the heebie-jeebies. The noises scare me in this house. Everything creaks and squeaks."

"It's only the wind, honey. A heavy one tonight."

"And I don't like the shadows either."

"Of the trees?"

"Yes. And of the monster behind the biggest tree. As big as Bigfoot!"

"Huh?"

"Out my window."

"You spotted something out your window?" Nani

bolted up, pulling on the jeans and boots that remained like fixtures next to her bed.

"Yes. Like a big monster ape."

"Show me where." Nani slipped something down her boot and tromped across the hall.

"I think he's gone now." Gemma linked her arm to Nani's, stumbling to the window. "There." She pointed. "He was right over there behind the big tree that's between those two trees. He ran away fast."

"You keep saying *he*."

"I know. I shined a flashlight on him. Maybe it was Bigfoot. Or a zombie. Oh my gosh, Nani. Like the scary movie I saw!"

"Okay, time to—"

"He was stiff and dead and huge!" She shivered, breathing fast and heavy. "Like he was chasing someone! I think he—"

"Slow your thoughts, Tink. Panic is never useful."

Gemma took a deep breath and exhaled slowly.

"Okay…" Nani said. "First of all, zombies aren't real. And second of all, there isn't a Bigfoot. At least not in Sugar Creek. Maybe you were dreaming. Show me the flashlight you think you used."

"I *did* use." Gemma grabbed it off the bed and gave it to Nani. "I wasn't dreaming because my eyes were wide open! This is where I was standing when I saw his gun."

"His *gun*?"

"A big one. Maybe he was an elk hunter!"

"No elk around here."

"Well, he was like a big shadow, so I don't know."

"I need to go out and take a look around—you stay here."

"No! I'm coming with. Don't leave me."

"Look at me, Tink." Nani waited for eye contact. "You have to stay inside. Do *not* leave this house. Take my phone and push the emergency number if you need it. I want you to—"

"Wait! How will I know?"

"I want you to crouch right here and listen through the crack of the window. If you hear a gun, or if I yell, then you push this button and hide in our secret place. Exactly the way I taught you."

"Nani, no..." She tugged at her sleeve. "What if you get shot?"

"Gemma. This is only if there's an emergency. These are the rules for safety. The same rules we've practiced your whole life."

"I know. But hurry."

"I will. Now follow me and lock everything on the front door when I step out. Don't open it for anyone unless it's Zork or me."

"I know." Gemma followed orders. She latched, chained, and secured all six locks and then did a ballerina dance. "I'm ready to pee my pants," she said to no one. She held her crotch and scuttled to the bathroom.

But Gemma never made it back to the window.

Chapter Twenty-Seven

Night of Angst

When the back door banged shut, Gemma heard the ferocious clomping of boots downstairs.

Just what I need. Bigfoot attacking me on the toilet.

"The beastly creature you spied in the trees has departed," Nani announced, her voice booming up the stairs. "So glad Zork convinced me to add a garage on to this farmhouse. You remember where the key's hidden out there?"

Gemma didn't answer.

"You can come out now!" Nani called. "Gemma?"

Only a few words squeaked out before she heard Nani's strong steps tromping up the stairs.

"Hey, you okay in there?" She tapped on the door.

"No. I feel sick."

Nani stepped in and found Gemma hunched over on the toilet. "Sweetie, what is it?" She flicked on the light.

"Something hurts. And it won't stop." She took a deep breath and blew it out with force. "It hurts bad."

Nani touched her forehead. "You have a fever." She crouched, holding Gemma's gaze, her eyes as calming as a blue sea. "Gemma, does it hurt anywhere in your tummy? Like cramping?"

"No," she grunted. "Only where I pee."

"When you start or when you finish?" she asked.

"Both. Worse at the end. Like peeing out pine needles."

"Lean over, sweetie." Nani stared in the bowl. Then she inspected Gemma's underwear. "Okay."

"What?"

"I'll call the doctor."

"Is the baby coming out?!"

"No, no—"

"Is this labor?!"

"No, honey. This is not labor. I think it's a bladder infection."

"Oh no." Gemma whacked her temple with the palm of her hand. "Not a bladder infection." She screwed her lips to the left. "What's that?"

"An infection where you pee from. It happens, hon. Common for women. You'll need antibiotics." Nani grabbed her phone and dialed in Gemma's ob/gyn. "Here," she said. "Tell them what's happening. I'll be right back."

Gemma described her symptoms to the on-call nurse.

"Make sure she knows you're recovering from the car wreck, Gem!" Nani hollered from the bedroom.

"She knows, Nani! I told her about my plug!"

Nani returned with a black bag and took out a sealed package and ripped it open. "Tell her I'm getting a clean-catch specimen and bringing it over to the 24-hour lab."

"She heard you, Nani." Gemma said good-bye and set the phone aside. "Is that a real doctor's bag?"

"Yup."

"How'd you get that?"

"Long story."

"Are you a secret doctor?"

"Not exactly. Just had a little on-the-job-training." Nani handed Gemma a shiny metal water bottle. "Here, drink."

"But it'll make me have to pee more. It hurts too bad." Gemma's face tightened. She drew in air and held it.

"I know. But it's what you have to do. And we need a sample."

Gemma expelled a lungful. She gulped the water until she had to come up for air, gasping. "They trained you to be a doctor because you traveled around the world selling stuff?" She puffed more wind out.

"I traveled to dangerous places sometimes. Had to be prepared for anything."

"Ow." Gemma's face squeezed into a knot.

Nani wrung out a fiery-hot washcloth over the sink, the steam clinging to the mirror above. "Here, honey. Press this against yourself. It'll help a little. After we get a sample you can sit in a hot tub."

"Nani." Gemma panted. "This is killing me." She positioned the washcloth, wincing. Misery trundled down her rigid cheeks to her chin.

"I know it hurts. I've had a few in my day too." She turned on the tub faucet full force.

"You have?" Gemma grunted.

"Yes."

"And it got better?"

"*Yes*. It will get better fast with the prescription. Can you get anything into the cup now? Doesn't have to be full."

"Okay." Gemma did as she was told, but the torture

continued. "How did this happen?" Gemma met her reflection in the water bottle, her face blazing red with pain. She clutched the washcloth against herself.

"Hard to say. Maybe honeymoon cystitis."

"That's crazy! I haven't had a honeymoon."

"A lot of sex, hon. It means a lot of sex over a short amount of time."

Gemma wanted to tink back another mistake. "Uh oh," she mumbled.

Nani smirked, ushering the cup away. "That should be plenty." She twisted the cap on tight. "I know it hurts like the dickens, but you'll be fine. So will the baby." She pushed the faucet off. "Let's get you in the water. Trust me. It helps."

Gemma took everything off and lowered herself into the tub with Nani's help. "Aah... That feels so much better already. You always know what to do."

"Pee in the tub while I'm gone."

"*What?*"

"Yes. In the tub. And add more hot water if it cools—"

"Wait. You want me to go number one in the bathtub? Are you sure?"

"Yes—"

"*Whoa.* That's crazy."

"It'll be a lot less painful. Now, I'll be back as soon as I can. I'm giving you a walkie-talkie if you need it. It won't harm you if it gets wet, and here's a towel if you need that."

"Did you find Bigfoot?"

"No Bigfoot. But there was a print out there. A man's size twelve work boot. But no sign of him."

"I don't want to be alone."

"You're not, hon. Zork's right outside with the other walkie-talkie. Speak to him whenever you want."

"Thank goodness. But Nani?"

She fished her truck keys out of her pocket. "What is it, hon?"

"I didn't know how many times were allowed. We did it a lot before the car wreck."

"Sex?

Gemma nodded, covering a breaking smile with her hand. "*A lot* of it."

"Oh, sweetie. You're happy and in love. It's fine."

"It's not fine anymore," Gemma said sure of herself. "He's never touching me again. *Ever.*"

Nani topped off the water bottle, grinning as if she knew a secret that she'd never tell.

"I mean it! I never want one of these bladder attacks again!"

"I understand." She handed her the full bottle. "And you can do anything you want."

"Yeah. And I will."

"I believe it." Nani trampled down the stairs. "Drink all that water by the time I get back!"

Chapter Twenty-Eight

Truth and Lies

Four days later, milky strips of light zigzagged across the ground on the trail in front of Buster. Winter was approaching, but the air was still warm enough to make the branches drip with sweat. Swollen dewdrops dove from the trees and smacked Olivia intermittently in the face.

She wiped the splatter off her brow, shut her eyes, and inhaled. The scent of hay and cow manure had always given her pleasure. She blew out, bringing the day back into view. Black scraps of clouds littered the sky, a bald eagle stroked the breeze, and then a moment of peace enfolded her. A moment of forgetting everything. "What a perfect day to fly," she told Zork.

Smoke curled from a nearby chimney as Olivia and Zork rode past Luper, the ground sloppy wet with thick sludge.

"Called operations," he said. "We've got great weather."

"Terrific," Olivia said, determined to get past any awkwardness. She couldn't let it continue. She had only accepted his invitation to go flying to prove to herself, and to him, that she was over it. Whatever it was.

"You sure Gemma's okay?" he asked, scanning for movement behind the trees. Forever vigilant, Zork had learned to expect the unexpected.

"Yes. Her medication helped right away. Thank goodness."

"And the plug's good?"

"Her doctor checked her yesterday. Everything's fine."

"Thrilled to hear it. That car wreck shook Bertie up too. She asks about her every day. Has a soft spot for Gemma. Like we all do."

Olivia squirmed in her saddle hearing Bertie's name. "I wish everyone had a soft spot for her."

The canary yellow biplane sat like a beacon in the middle of a stark, open landscape. This part of the field made an ideal landing strip, one of the selling points of the property.

"Was that medication dangerous for the baby? Bertie's worried about that too."

"Of course it wasn't dangerous for the baby!" she barked. *That's enough—now be nice.* They untacked the horses and led them into the corral Zork had built for flying days.

Olivia tucked her wool scarf inside her jacket and jogged to the plane. After they completed the preflight walk-around inspection, Zork lifted the hood and checked the oil. Olivia climbed into the cockpit noticing the ground below, pops of shaggy yellow dandelions poking through patches of frost. "There's still life blooming out here."

"Yes, indeed—it's a great day to fly." Zork dropped in the other seat.

"Is there any day for you that's not?" She chuckled.

"Oh, there's been one or two."

"I remember them," she said.

"You're driving today, Olivia. Don't want you to get rusty."

"Seatbelts secured," she said without any hesitation. "Checking fuel... Can you believe no one still knows?"

"Knows what?"

"That I can fly."

"I believe it," he said.

"I'm so used to secrets."

"You don't need any more questions. It's for the best. Still can't get Bertie in this thing, though." Zork snickered.

"Why on earth not?" Olivia flipped the engine switch on.

"Fear of flying."

"Oh, Zork. You've gotta be kidding. How will that ever work? You're in this plane all the time!"

"And I still will be. She accepts that."

"*Just wait...*" she muttered. "For now she does..." Olivia turned her attention back to the business of flying. She taxied out, ran the engine up, and checked the mags. Their heads swiveled in a constant check of everything surrounding them.

"Checking for traffic, birds, and drones," Zork said. "You heard the message I forwarded about the drone, right?"

"Every last word of it."

"Hate it when we're right."

Zork smirked but his eyes never left the skies. "All clear," he confirmed.

"Ready to roll." Olivia put power to the engine. The plane raced across the field and took off. Olivia's heart pounded with happiness. The weight of every bad thing in her life was left on the ground—the experience of a smooth lift-off never got old.

"You're as happy as a bird dog! Beautiful take off," Zork told her. "Get your coordination and get used to things with some S-turns. Five or six should do it."

Olivia performed the S-turns with no trouble.

"Great job," Zork told her. "Let's climb and do some stalls and practice some spins."

Olivia climbed to 7,000 feet and executed the procedures without any trouble.

"That's the way—you got it," Zork said. "Come on down a little and let's cruise. Finish what you were saying about Bertie—I need to *just wait* for what?"

Olivia decided to be blunt. "It won't be long and Bertie will be complaining that all you want to do is fly. Then she'll be after you to spend more time with her and insist that you break-up with your airplane. I can hear it now."

"Hah! That won't stop me. I'll always be flying."

"You better hope so, Zork. Don't let her run your life." Olivia paused. "I mean, it happens in relationships all the time."

"Oh, that's right. You're the expert. About all kinds of things."

"Hardly."

"I hear you're the local sex doctor of Sugar Creek."

The plane took a nosedive, and Olivia sharply corrected it.

"Nice recovery." He simpered.

"Is that what Bertie told you? That I'm the local sex doctor?"

"No, Bertie did not," he said, smugly. "Gemma

did."

"Gemma?! Oh…" Olivia's head bobbed. "Right. Gemma."

"You meddle too much, Olivia."

"You did not just say that."

"Well," he sputtered. "It's obvious you give everyone advice."

"I give advice when asked! And only when asked. But no worries. I am *done* with that." Olivia busily scanned the horizon and everything around her.

"You're right. I know you don't meddle. But there is more you want to say isn't there? To me at least."

"No. Actually there isn't."

"Oh? Well, I say there is. So start talking. Give me all the advice you want. Right now."

"What?"

"I'm asking. And I'm serious. Tell me what you think I need to hear about marrying Bertie. I do trust you, and I value what you think."

The reverberating of the engine was the only sound they heard for an expanded moment or two.

"Go on! I want to hear it."

"Up here?!"

"Yes, up here! No one can hear us. Get it off your chest. I know it's sittin' there like lead."

He was right, of course. Except it was more like dynamite. "Okay. Here's what I think and why," she said, sure of herself. "You need to be positive Bertie is the right woman for you. I've known her far longer than you have and I know you, Zork. And I know you need a companion you can share everything with. You need someone who is your equal in every way."

With a pointed squint, Zork stared right through

her. "You mean someone like you?"

For a moment Olivia thought she had executed a barrel roll. She double checked the control panel.

"Nowhere to run up here, Olivia. You can't run this time." Zork leaned to the right, searching the valley below.

"You planned this," she said.

"So what if I did. Answer the question."

"Well, yes." She swallowed. "I do mean you should be with someone like me. Only not me, of course. Just *like* me."

"I see," Zork said. "Set her down when you're ready."

They let the silence rest between them without further need to cut into it. Olivia made the touch down and loosened the scarf around her neck.

"Perfect landing." Zork nodded. "A real greaser."

"Wasn't it?" She beamed. They rolled in near the horses.

"Switch it off, and let's get out of here," he said.

Banjo neighed under the shade of an old fir while Olivia went to Buster and stroked his face.

"Thanks for the flight, Zork."

"Didn't know if you'd come today or not." He bowed over the rail of the corral, one boot resting on the bottom rung. "You've been avoiding me." He spat into a bush near the tree.

Olivia inspected Buster's eye. "I know I have."

"You know, Ollie, sometimes I have to wonder—"

"Oh, I know." She sighed weakly. "I've wondered the same thing." Buster leaned in and nuzzled her waist.

"And what's that?"

"If I'm jealous."

"Well—"

"And the honest truth is, yes, I am."

His brows turned into twin Arc de Triomphes.

"Yes. There you have it," Olivia said. "I've said it. And now that I have, I know it's true." She rubbed Buster's face.

"It's true?"

"Yes. And I feel much better now that I've told you."

"Well, what the hell are you saying? This almost sounds like—"

"I've been selfish," Olivia explained. "About everything. Your time, your help, your companionship. But especially about you finding happiness—with someone who wasn't me. That's the truth of it."

Zork wiped the sweat off his brow. "Well, isn't this the way it always goes." He slumped against the tree sheltering them.

"The way what goes?"

"The way relationships go. I'm wondering if you've finally fallen for me. By accident, of course. And at a most inopportune time. And yet, isn't this the way it always goes…"

"Oh, Zork. I don't know." Olivia glanced away. "I'm sorry—I feel like an absolute idiot. Like I'm in seventh grade again and I don't know anything."

Olivia kept her distance from Zork as if one of them might get zapped with a live wire if she didn't. He followed her inside the corral.

"If you've grown some kind of love interest in me, I need to know," he finally said. "I've assumed it would never be right—you and me together. Never. I moved on from the idea a long time ago."

"I'm sorry, Zork."

"Why? Nothin' to be sorry for."

"Have I been wrong all these years?" she asked. "I'm having doubts."

"What kind of doubts?"

"Doubts about my feelings for you."

"And what exactly might those be, Olivia?"

"I think I've taken you for granted. Taken us for granted. I assumed I'd always have you here." For a moment the desire to kiss Zork grew alarmingly strong. She jerked around and tied Buster to the fence to keep her hands occupied.

"I'm not goin anywhere."

"If you marry Bertie, you'll have to. I mean, *when* you marry her."

"Who says I have to leave because of that?"

"Look, I know we have this interminable link to our past. But it doesn't mean you can't leave. Your life has been on hold long enough. I can take care of things. Whatever happens."

"I know you can, but I've spent my life doing what I want. Wouldn't change a thing."

"It wouldn't be right to stay on here. Not if you're married." She adjusted the saddle pad and swung it over Buster's back, rocking it back and forth into position.

"It only wouldn't be right if you're in love with me and haven't been truthful about it."

No one moved, yet the physical relationship between them shifted.

"You're right. And I'm not certain."

Zork studied her face with unwavering attention.

Olivia positioned herself so Buster stood between them. "Clearly, I haven't even been honest with myself about it." She stroked Buster's mane as a pool of emotion moved up her throat. She struggled to hold it back.

And then as a person might behave when acting on impulse—as if entirely absent of all reasoning—Olivia stepped around Buster, reached for Zork's arm, pulled herself in, and kissed him—with heart-slamming intensity. The way she remembered kissing Sam.

Because she wanted to know.

And as soon as she did, it all came back. Memories of the past swooshed in, every nerve crackling with remembrance of a time when all was well.

"This is crazy," she said, kissing him again—his eyes black and bright, possibly aroused. Olivia realized Zork wasn't a buzz saw, after all.

It was all there. Passion, comfort, tenderness, respect, love.

Everything I could ever want.

Everything she could ever want except what mattered most.

It was all there, except Sam.

And Olivia knew without him, it meant nothing. She pulled away first.

"There," Zork said. "You see? It will never happen. It can't. You know it and I know it."

Olivia couldn't hold back any longer. Her eyes clamped shut.

Zork leaned in and embraced her, his arms steadfast and healing. Grief for Sam swept over her again—she had lost count of how many times.

"It's okay, Olivia," he consoled.

Every ounce of resentment toward Bertie evaporated like steam. This wasn't about Bertie. It was about Sam. For a moment, her insides softened.

She took a deep breath, but another spasm of grief overtook her like a wave. As if it had to bring her down before she could rise again. And then, for the second time that day, a moment of peace fell over her. A deep, relieving, welcome sense of peace. "I'm so sorry about this. I don't know what to say."

"I do," he said. They rested their arms on top the fence, a gaggle of Oregon cacklers sailing over them in a high-pitched frenzy. "And I understand. What you had with Sam…" He held steepled fingers to his lips for a few seconds. "No one can hold a light to it. I know that. Always have. I love you. And in the years after Sam left us, I fell in love with you. That much is true. But I knew you wouldn't leave him. And I understand that. Hell, I respect you for it. I never gave it a second thought. So don't be sorry. But I'm sure glad you made sure. Because as crazy as it seems, I *have* fallen in love with Bertie. Like no one else before."

Olivia met his gaze and smiled. "I'm overjoyed for you. I truly am."

"It means a lot to finally hear you say that. And mean it."

Olivia raised her face to the open sky, clean and never-ending. What she and Sam had still existed. Kissing Zork had proven it. The joy between them was still alive and well. And that was enough.

"Bertie is a lucky woman." The words left her lips as easy as air. "But I mean it, Zork. You've been bound by a promise long enough. You've stayed close to us for Sam. And it's not fair. So much time wasted—you could've been finding your own life."

"I have found my own life. I don't waste my time

for anyone. Not even you."

"What I meant was—"

"I've found my life," he repeated. "And it's with Bertie. I never would've met her had it not been for you and the girls."

Olivia paused, considering what he said. "I suppose that's true."

"It is true! And I love all *five* of you now. You can't get rid of me. Or Bertie," he sneered. "And you never know, Olivia. There could be a time when someone comes along who *can* shine a light to Sam. A different, but equal light. Lord knows, Bertie was a surprise to me. Don't shut down the idea. That's all I'm saying."

"I appreciate the thought, Zork, but I'm fine."

"I know you are." He saddled up Banjo.

More out of habit than anything, she pulled out binoculars and peered at the hills around them, slowly scanning.

"There's something else, Olivia. May as well tell you now."

"What?" she said, her gaze still on the hills.

"Sam said something else. Right before he died."

Her eyes shifted to his, her face unmoving. "More than what you've told me?"

"Yes."

The binoculars dropped. "More than him wanting you to help Maggie and me?"

"Yes. Sam told me something else."

Chapter Twenty-Nine

Unspoken Words

The sting of hot rage surged up Olivia's neck, a snapping combustive charge igniting from the inside. "What else? What did he say?!" The urgency in her breath was palpable; she struggled to steady herself. Zork's words leaked out abnormally slow—like a protracted, laboriously long speech. "Tell me!" she retorted.

"Years before he was killed, he shared something with me. At the end, he reminded me of it again."

"What are you talking about? Shared what?"

"He didn't want you to be alone—if something were to happen to him. Not in the life we live. And he said it should be me who was with you. He said he wanted us to marry, if that's what we wanted."

"What? I can't believe you never told me this." *More deception.*

"Why would I?"

"Because—" Olivia's eyes locked on his. "They were *Sam's* words. I had a right to know each and every last one of them."

"Not telling you prevented unnecessary complications between us. If things had been different, I would've told you. I wanted to know it wouldn't be Sam's influence that brought you to me. That's all."

"What?! You know I have a mind of my own. *Nobody* influences me. Not even Sam." Her words trembled no matter how steady she tried to make them.

"Believe me—I know. And I apologize. That's why I'm telling you now. I wasn't intentionally withholding."

"But you were! And you *did*. I don't know what to say or think right now." Olivia climbed on top Buster and looked down her nose at Zork. "You deliberately withheld his words from me. You blindsided me again. It's getting harder to trust you."

"I haven't withheld anything!" Zork's jaw tightened, his eyes ready to burst into flames. "Those words were to *me*, Olivia." He fist bumped his chest. "Not for you—for *me*. I told you what he wanted me to tell you. *This was meant for me*." He moved briskly around Banjo, tightening his cinch. "It's the way Sam wanted it."

Olivia heard the truth in what he said, but didn't concede at first. She held on to her anger like a flaming torch—a wild light of truth exposing everything. As if it doing so might undo everything. Or at least change something. Her breath turned heavy and full of grief.

"I'm sorry." Olivia sighed. "I know Sam would agree." She resigned herself to this truth too. "It's just like him to have said such a thing."

"I promise there's no more. So be angry and chew me out, but get over it. Please. You haven't been blindsided. Not intentionally." He mounted Banjo.

"It's difficult information to hold at the moment," she said.

"I understand that…" Zork shifted in his saddle. "He did not leave you easily, Olivia."

"I know that." She swept away her heartache with a gloved finger across her cheek. "And Sam was right."

"About what?"

"You *are* the only other man who would measure up to him. If I were looking."

"Not true. But I'm honored you think so."

"I'm grateful for our friendship, Zork, and the strength of it."

"Likewise."

"We're good then?" she asked.

"Always have been. No more doubts for you?"

"None," she said. And meant it.

"Can't blame you, though." He puffed out his chest. "Hell, a catch like me? Women will be boo-hooing in the streets now that the most eligible bachelor in town is taken."

Olivia howled, walking Buster in closer to him. She reached out her hand to Zork's and squeezed. "I hope Bertie knows how lucky she is."

"I don't let her forget it," he said. "Glad we cleared the air. And now if we could clear up everything else in our lives this easily."

"Don't I know it," she said, leading them out of the corral. "Oh, and Zork? Remember that thing you said back in the barn about me being able to whip the ass of a pit bull?"

"A raging pit bull," he corrected.

"I sure hope I can still do what I used to."

"I've seen what you can do. Keep Gemma's face in front of you, and you can do anything."

Olivia stroked Buster's neck, hoping it was the truth. "We could take them down now and end this today. I've had plenty of opportunities. Seriously, we could—"

"Patience, Olivia. We always stick to the plan." Zork picked up Banjo's pace again. "We let them come to us. Then we end this for Sam."

Clucking Buster on, Olivia charged past Zork and Banjo, knowing he was right. And he was right about another thing too. Keeping Gemma's face in front of her was more than enough to kick up all the strength she ever needed. The way she used to when Maggie was young."

Before long, Olivia would visualize a great-granddaughter's face in her mind too. Gemma said so.

Chapter Thirty

Pregnant in Seattle

The back of Gemma's hand pressed against cold glass, her cheek resting against her palm. The train jangled and vibrated as it threaded through Portland, inching its way past people she would never lay eyes on again.

A barrage of hail-thickened wind battered the windows and dropped the temperature inside the train car by at least ten degrees. She zipped up her fleece jacket, pulled a turquoise knit hat down to her periwinkle strands, and watched the terrain roll by like a movie. One day, she imagined she'd have her baby daughter traveling this route to visit her own Graham Cracker in Seattle.

With care, Gemma pulled out the "Certificate of Completion" tucked proudly away in her back-pack. It read, "Congratulations! Gemma Jane Porter has successfully completed the NURTURING PARENT COURSE equaling ten hours of education." Instructor comments followed:

It was a pleasure having you in our class. We appreciated your enthusiasm and the many contributions you made to our discussions. Great job! Your greatest strengths are empathy and compassion. These are critical to forming a healthy, loving bond with your child. You are well on your way to becoming a nurturing parent! As discussed, we are recommending assistance in implementing a routine and structure for infant care, as well as appropriate safety measures and procedures. While ongoing supervision is seen as necessary, the department will continue to assess your needs over time. You are welcome to take this class as many times as you'd like. And please, don't forget to introduce us to your baby! We wish you all the best. Sincerely, Kelly and Tammy, Instructors

Gemma slipped the certificate back into her backpack, feeling proud. *I can't wait for Mama to read it.*

Gemma shifted her weight, struggling to stay awake. "Common in the first trimester," the nurse had told her. She gave in, letting herself go under into a calming sea of dreams.

Two and a half hours slipped away like magic. It seemed like no time at all when the squeal of brakes and bells pulled her from a deep slumber. "Next stop, Seattle," she heard from somewhere in outer space. "Seattle is our next stop."

Gemma didn't move until she had to. When the hot acid of her last meal lurched up her throat, she had to. "Ohhh," she groaned. "Too much tuna. I hope I don't get sick."

When the man sitting on the other side of the aisle took notice, Gemma flashed him a full-lipped smile. "I'm ten weeks pregnant, and some things don't agree with my baby," she said. "But I don't usually barf anymore. Only sometimes."

He ignored what she said and resumed reading a newspaper. But Gemma knew he heard. She always knew when people were uncomfortable around her. She popped two fruity chewable antacids, grabbed her backpack, and moved toward the exit as the trained lurched to a stop. The door opened with a bang. By the time she stepped down to the rain-soaked asphalt, she already felt better. The fresh air made her forget everything else but the excitement of being in a new city with Mama.

She stood motionless, staring straight ahead. "No sign of her," she announced.

"I'm right behind you."

Gemma swung around. "Mama!" She wrapped her arms around tight. "I'm so happy to see you."

"Me too, sweetie."

"I'm here in Seattle!"

"You are! Finally. I got here an hour early I was so excited. I can't wait to show you everything."

Gemma kept hugging and wouldn't stop. "I missed you, Mama. Do I look any different?"

"I don't know. When you let go of me I'll take a look."

"Oh! Okay." Gemma backed up, smoothing her jacket over her belly.

"Well…" Mama squinted. "Is there a baby bump there yet?"

"There is when I'm naked."

"Exciting! We'll inspect later."

They linked arms and strolled to the car.

"I earned gold stars in my parenting class. Next week is my childbirth class. They want me to take that one now and again later. So three times. Or two, I mean."

"Great idea. Will Walter join you?"

"I think so, but he might faint."

"Hop in." Mama threw her bags in the back seat of her car. "The class will help prepare him so he won't faint."

"No. You don't understand. He faints talking about it. I think he sees it in his brain, and then he hits the floor."

"Oh, dear." Mama and Gemma fastened their seatbelts at the same time. "Well, he may not want to be at the birth then." She punched the gas and left the train station.

"Yeah. That's what I'm thinking. You still want to be there with me though, right?"

"Of course I do."

"And Nani, too. She'll be another doctor in the room."

"Hah. Well, I'm not sure how the real doctors will feel about that, but yes, she likes to act like one."

"She helped with me being born, didn't she?"

"Yes." Mama hesitated. "She did in fact. It was impressive, and oddly weird at the same time."

"She's good, Mama. She always knows what to do."

"She seems to, yes."

"I hope you can get there in time."

"I'll fly there the minute I hear something is happening."

"Okay. I'll call you. Or Nani will. Or Zorro. Or Walter. Maybe the nurse?"

"Yes. Someone will call me."

When Mama turned into a long driveway and stopped, Gemma's jaw dropped. "Whoa." It's all she could say.

"Here it is… My new place."

"Whoa," Gemma said again. "This is hip! So modern. Like Nani would say, "I'm diggin' it!""

"Wait till you see the views. I love this city. I'm taking you out on the ferry for a tour. And then to Pikes Market for dinner."

"A boat ride?! Wait till I tell Walter and Nani!"

Mama grinned, and when she did, Gemma knew her response sounded like a goofy little kid tickled for a boat ride—a young, enthused, mostly bewildered child with a baby inside her.

Chapter Thirty-One

The Wedding Planner

Stepping into Bertie's kitchen was like entering a giant egg yolk. A dense, impenetrable shade of yellow covered the walls, matching the ruffled gingham curtains over the sink. Collections of vintage cookie jars sat in every open space on the same eggy-colored Formica counters.

Everywhere Olivia turned she viewed shelves showcasing tea sets, sugar bowls, hand painted miniature bunnies, and Russian nesting dolls. The sunny walls sagged with kitsch. Bertie remained bent over her stove, scrubbing, when Olivia joined her.

"Okay, you two, I'm off." Zork saluted.

"Oh, Zork, do you have to go? I hoped you'd stay and help with the planning," Bertie crooned, still scouring the burners.

"Nope. It's all yours, darlin'."

"Oh, all right. Have fun."

Zork flew out the door.

Bertie stood back, examining her work. "I spilled spaghetti sauce all over the range last night. What a pain. But listen, I'll stop so we can get to the fun stuff."

"The fun stuff?" Olivia plunked down at a small dinette table with matching yellow and chrome chairs.

"Yes, wedding planning. *Fun stuff.*" Bertie glanced

out the window. "Good. He's gone."

"Why so relieved?"

"I only asked him to stay so he wouldn't feel bad. The truth is I don't want him involved at all. I like doing things my own way. You know how I am."

Olivia's eyebrows flared.

"So. Listen up," Bertie rattled. "We don't have long. We moved everything up. The new date is November second."

"Ah… November second. Wait—of *this* year?"

Bertie slipped into the chair opposite Olivia. "Yes. I know." She hid her face behind two fists. "Only two weeks away."

"Hey, it's not my wedding. Do whatever you want."

"I knew you'd understand."

"So what do you need me to do? Tell me and I'm on it." Olivia propped her elbows on the table, chin in both hands.

"Well, the church is reserved."

"Okay."

"The barn next door is too. For a barn dance slash reception."

"Fab-u-loso." Olivia checked her watch.

"Have somewhere to go, dear?"

Oops. "Nope, only here with you."

"Terrific. We can take our time then."

"Right." Olivia's fingers drummed the table. "Well, not too much time though, right?"

Bertie gave her a stony stare.

"But as much time as you need, of course," Olivia added.

"Very good. So… Do you like my save-the-date

cards? They match the invitations." She scooted them across the table.

"Why do you need these? It's in two weeks. I'll help call people."

"They've already been called. But people need these things in writing. Trust me. Save-the-dates go out tomorrow, invites the day after that. People need more than one reminder, Olivia."

"Okay, then!" Olivia raised her hand in a high five. "Way to go." She dropped it when Bertie sat stock-still, and gawped at her jacked-up hand. *Well... Aren't we haughty.*

"So"—Bertie pushed on—"I also have the programs finished."

"Programs?"

"Yes. Of the ceremony. Zork helped with that part. And here's what I'm thinking for colors." She pulled out shiny swatches of pink, gold, and raspberry fabrics. "I'm in linen-white and gold, of course. You and the girls will be in carnation-pink. And raspberry is the accent color for flowers and other décor."

"Ah. So pink for me? Are you sure?"

"Something wrong with pink?" Her chin jutted back.

"Well..." Olivia considered. "I'm sure without any poofy ruffles and bows it'll be fine."

"Oh, no. Your dress will be nothing like that. Only one *big* bow in the back and a few layers of lacy ruffles around the hem and neckline. No big deal. Oh, and around the sleeves. Not huge ruffles. Medium-sized."

Olivia winced.

"And the dress has a built-in plume of netting already." Bertie raced on. "So no slip required! We want a little poof, Olivia. Just a teeny bit. Trust me."

"Trust you? It sounds like Little Bo Peep…"

"What?!" Bertie gasped. "It's adorably elegant. Like you. Here's a picture."

Olivia took hold of it between two pinched fingers and tilted it toward light. The image went down about as easy as pickle juice—her lips drew into a sphincter.

She thought about Zork's words and imagined Gemma sitting in front of her instead of Bertie. It worked. "Whatever you want, Bertie." She slid the picture back.

"Darn." Bertie scrunched up her cheek. "Zork warned me you'd hate it. He's right, isn't he?"

"It's fine. This is your wedding, and I will abide by whatever it is you decide. I promise."

"Spoken like a true friend… *I guess.*"

Olivia squinted, detecting a momentary shift in tone.

Bertie's eyes bounced between Olivia and the picture. "You know what?"

Olivia waited, still hearing the way she had said, *I guess*.

"You wear anything you want."

"You mean it?"

"Sure. But make sure it's light pink and more feminine than you usually look."

"I'll do my best."

"Now…" Bertie, checked off something on her list. "I would like help with the favors."

"Let me guess. Bird seed tied up in tulle?"

"That will be for our send off. I'm thinking we could set a little something at the tables too. You know, for a take-home favor."

"I see. And what did you have in mind?"

"These..." Bertie reached under the table, pulled something from a bag, and grinned like a Cheshire cat. She plopped a small pink and yellow birdhouse between them. "Aren't they adorable?" Her face gleamed with delight. "So perfect."

Olivia picked it up, set her glasses on her nose, and grimaced when she read, "With special thanks from the Lovebirds—Mr. and Mrs. Zork Canby—November 2, 2018."

"What's wrong?!" Bertie snatched it back. "Did I misspell something?"

"No, but are you sure you don't want your name on it too?"

"It's there. What do you mean?"

"I mean, shouldn't it say Bertie and Zork?"

"Oh, honey, *no*. I love being a 'Mr. and Mrs.' attached to Zork."

"Yes, I guess it does suit you."

"You bet it does." Bertie stood and scurried to the front door.

"Where are you going?"

"Making sure we're alone." She poked her head outside, closed the door, and scanned out the front windows.

"Why?"

Bertie's voice steadied. "Because of the next thing I'm about to say to you."

"Oh my. Sounds serious."

"You bet it is."

Olivia glanced about and waited.

"Let me begin by saying I'm an understanding woman," she said.

243

There's that tone...

"I admit I didn't understand at first. Not at all, in fact. But now I do." Bertie sat again. "At least partially. Zork explained it all. But Olivia, it's my right, and my duty to tell you that it will never happen again."

"Oh, Bertie." Olivia knew what was coming. She uncrossed her legs, leaning forward. "Please, I—"

"Now hold on right there." Bertie's hand flew up. "I like you. You know I do. I always have. But I know your type."

"My *type*?"

"We all know you've led a very—how should I put it—a very *exciting* life. I wasn't born yesterday." Bertie straightened in her chair. "I've seen the way you've snuck away and disappeared. Many, many times over the years. Since I've known you, in fact. I've noticed and so have the other girls."

"The other girls?" Olivia pushed up. "We're not in high school." She opened the cupboard and grabbed a mug and tea bag.

"I imagine that's when this started."

"Oh, for crying out loud, Bertie. When what started? I had a sales job that required regular travel. I didn't sneak away. And the 'other girls'? Give me a break." She set the mug in the microwave, slammed the door, and hit start.

"Well, a few of them think you're a little too sneaky for your own britches. And hon, the truth is, so do I. But your secret's safe with me."

"I am *not* sneaky. What secret?"

"Come now. Do I have to say it?"

"Yes—you do."

"Fine." Bertie's nostril's flared. "*Affairs*. We all

know you have them." She smacked her lips. "There! I said it." She pushed back, drawing herself up to full height. "You're finally hearing what we've known all along."

Olivia's arms flopped over her head when she howled. "Now that's funny, Bertie!"

"And how many of them were married, Olivia? Tell me that!" Bertie packed the birdhouse back in its bag. "We're guessing all of them."

"*All* of them?" Olivia tittered with abandon. "So the whole town has me pegged as a floozy? Wow. No wonder you talk to me about sex!" When the timer dinged, she retrieved the mug and sat again, flinching when she leaned back; the spine of the chair pushed like a double-barreled shotgun against her backbone.

"A lot of women find a sense of exhilaration when they get a married man's attention. I watched a two-part show about it. Bottom line? You need help, Olivia Porter."

"Bertie… This is ridiculous!" she snorted, laughter bubbling up again.

"With all your sexual experience and knowledge?" The back of Bertie's hand slapped the air. "You think I just fell off the turnip truck? How *else* would you know all that stuff?"

"Plenty of other ways!" She wiped the corners of her eyes, sniveling. "This is downright absurd."

Bertie folded her arms, lips curled waiting for her to quiet down. "So. If you ever, and I mean ever, kiss Zork again like the way you did—*yes, he told me everything*—you will never, and I mean *never*, be my friend again. Is that understood? He is off limits, Olivia. *Off limits*."

"Of course he is—"

"You're my matron-of-honor for god's sake!"

"Oh, Bertie, I know. I'm so sorry." Olivia took a deep breath, and again, imagined Gemma in front of her. "You have my word it will never, and I mean never happen again."

"See that it doesn't!" Bertie's face caught fire—red as a cowhorn chili pepper.

"I've never been in love with him, Bertie. Trust me—my husband is who I miss and want. Not your Zork. As silly as it sounds, I acted on impulse, thinking of Sam again. I've never in my life cheated on my husband. Not once." Olivia folded her hands and placed them in her lap. "Honey, I've been celibate since the day he died."

Bertie's cuckoo clock cut through the silence, and by the time the cuckoo bird stopped chiming and the Swiss dancers finished twirling, Bertie sat again.

"Well," Bertie said, her slightly stunned expression fixed on her face, "I still don't like it." She rotated in her chair and checked all the stove knobs. "But I think I believe you."

"Good."

"I told Zork something didn't feel right about the two of you and I needed to know why. I asked him not to tell you that he told me."

"Why?"

"Because. I wanted this between us from here on. Not him."

Olivia swirled the tea bag around, watching the steam. *It's Zork and Bertie now.* "I understand. I don't want you to have any doubts."

Bertie raised up, washing her hands of everything.

"Then we're good. You can run along now."

"What do you mean?"

"I mean we're done."

"What about the plans? And making birdhouses?"

"I lied. Everything's finished. I wanted you to come over so I could tell you off."

"Got it." Olivia sprang up, tossing her keys in the air. "You should be a wedding planner. I mean it. You're on top of everything."

"If you only knew." She hee-hawed. "On top is my favorite pos—"

"Bertie!" Olivia's hand shot up. "From here on, anything to do with sex will only be discussed with Zork, or your primary care physician. I am officially retired as the go-to sex doctor of Sugar Creek. Understood?"

"Completely. Believe you me. I am done sharing that with you."

Olivia gave a nod of approval and fumbled for her dinging phone.

"Nani-pie!" Gemma boomed. "I'm on a ferry boat! We're going around Seattle right now."

"Wonderful! I bet it's beautiful." Olivia waved Bertie off and headed for her truck.

"It's so much fun! The city is so pretty. And mom's condo is so cool. Wait till you see it. Then we were planning on a fancy crab dinner, but not anymore."

"Why not?"

"Because I already hurled right over the edge of the boat, straight into the Pacific Ocean. Even after two acid pills. Don't worry, because my mom's right here— but I wanted to hear your voice. Can you come up? Oh, and we decided you and my mom will be the only ones in the room with me when the baby is in labor, because we're pretty sure Walter will faint."

"Smart. You'll be in labor though, not the baby."

"From what I've learned, she won't have it easy either. So I say she is."

Olivia chuckled. "Good point."

"I want you there when she's born."

"A wild pack of hyenas couldn't stop me." She heard the familiar sound of Gemma's giggles. *Music to my ears.*

"Mama wants to talk now, but what I want to say is, you should come to Seattle. You have to see it! Love you."

"Love you more."

"More than what?" Gemma asked.

"More than the—"

Magnolia's phone went dead.

Olivia finished two loads of laundry, stacked the dishwasher, and rummaged through her closets while waiting for a call back. She clawed through hangers of old clothes, searching for something pink. And slightly feminine. "Please, don't make me shop for a carnation-pink bridesmaid's dress at my age."

Her phone lit up with Magnolia's name.

"Mom, sorry, my cell ran out of juice. Are you coming?" she asked.

"I've gone back and forth about it…"

"We want you here! We have a slumber party planned. Plus you have to see my new office. Gemma is having so much fun."

"It sounds like it. I'm so pleased she's there."

"I am too. She did great on the train. Was right

where she was supposed to be. Finally has the beginnings of a little tummy, but you'd still never know she was pregnant."

"Lucky she's so fit."

"I need to get back to her, but are you coming?"

"I'm going to pass. Unless you need me."

"Well, no, we're fine. I took time off work and we just thought it'd be fun for all of us to be together."

"Gemma needs you, Mag. It's a chance for you to have time alone together. It'll do you both good. But please be sure to come home this weekend."

"Why?"

"I'm hosting Bertie's bridal shower. Everything got moved up. Please, *please*, tell me you'll be there. I need you both."

"We'll be there." She chuckled. "Should be a real hoot. You okay with all this now? With Zork marrying her?"

"More than okay. Zork and I..." Olivia almost said "kissed" but stopped in time. "We had a heart to heart. A genuinely good talk. Cleared up everything and it's all good."

"Great. You sound better."

"I'll tell you about it another time. And listen, if you or Gemma *do* need me for anything, you know Zork will fly me right up. All you have to do is call."

When Olivia finally hung up, the urge to fly to Seattle was so strong she almost couldn't bear it. But something kept pulling her back from the idea. When something tugged on her that way she learned to listen. *This should be their time.*

She put on a pot of tea, scanned the ocean of grass rippling in the breeze, and curled up with a book in front of the fire. Another moment of peace finally filled her lungs again. But she knew it wouldn't last.

And, naturally, it didn't.

Chapter Thirty-Two

A Shower of Love

You would think a woman in her sixties would know a thing or two about throwing a bridal shower. Truth is, Olivia had never been involved in any. Not one. And Bertie knew it.

So, Olivia only suffered a little guilt when Bertie insisted on planning her own. *Can't blame her*, she rationalized. *Some people aren't good at these things.*

Still, she tried to plead a little. Just enough to purge herself of any left-over culpability. "But it's *your* shower, Bertie," Olivia had moaned. "We should be doing all of this for you. At least let me help decorate. At least I can do that."

"It's easier for me to work alone." Bertie told her. "You understand, don't you?"

Yes. And it makes me so *happy.*

The morning of the shower, Olivia put the vacuum away and tried one last time. "Now, what else can I do? I'll do anything. I am the host."

"And a perfect one at that. How 'bout this—you run along and get some milk. Return with a quart at one o'clock sharp. Oh, what the heck—make it a gallon." Bertie waved her off, digits twiddling. "Scoot."

"*Milk?*"

"Well, you never know, Olivia. Someone might

want it. And bring Gemma and Maggie back with you. I'll show you how to be a host then."

Being sent out for milk was nothing but a fool's errand, but Olivia didn't mind. Not in the least.

"Run along," Bertie ordered again. "And while you're at it, take Gemma shopping for some maternity clothes. She's wearing skimpy tops that are way too tight. I think she's starting to show."

"That's how all the girls dress these days."

"When they're P.G.?"

"Especially then. They all show off their baby bumps now. Not like back in the day."

"What next…" Bertie sighed. "Okay, well, be back at one sharp."

"*Sharp*. With a gallon of milk." Olivia climbed into her gleaming cobalt-blue pickup and gazed at the soft lemon-light draped over the fields and orchards. She put Zork on speaker phone. "Bertie kicked me out and doesn't want me back till one."

"Yeah, I figured. And I also heard she had the 'talk' with you."

"Yep, she sure did."

"Promised her I wouldn't tell you. Sorry."

"Don't be. I'm relieved we worked it out. But listen, can you keep an eye on things? I can't leave the property if—"

"Got it covered. Take off. More backup is confirmed when the party starts."

"Thanks." She turned the ignition and bounced slowly down the road. "Oh, and Zork?"

"Yeah?"

"I hear you'll be hanging little ruffled pink umbrellas from the ceiling. At least twenty of the darling things. Have fun with that!" Olivia tapped the phone off and slammed on the accelerator. She watched the dust swirl in her mirror, tittering out loud.

****

"Three hours till the shower, and I get to sit it out. I love it." Olivia collapsed on Gemma's sofa and kicked up her feet.

"Why?" Gemma asked.

"Bertie took over my house and booted me out. Isn't that great?"

"Smart move on her part," Magnolia said.

Gemma tipped her head as if mulling something.

"Thank goodness you'll both be there." Olivia patted Gemma's leg. "Can you run the bride bingo game?"

"I love bingo, yes!"

And will you write the gift list, Maggie? And make the bow thingy?"

"Bow thingy?"

"Yes, some darn bouquet on a paper plate made of all her gift bows."

"Do I have to?"

"We'll do it together then. You know I'm not good at that stuff."

"Yes, I know."

"Gee-whiz, Nani. Don't you want to do anything?"

"I'm bringing milk and hosting the ladies of Sugar Creek. That's enough. Believe me."

"I thought you liked parties. And Bertie."

Olivia took a breath. "You know what? You're right. It's wrong of me to complain. I apologize. I'll be a good sport and embrace this party. For Bertie."

"What did you get her for a present?" Magnolia

253

asked.

"A present?"

"You did get Bertie a shower gift, didn't you?"

Olivia's forehead plunged into the palm of her hand. "Dang!" she said. "I need to buy something fast."

"It's fine." Magnolia cracked up. "I bought something from all three of us. I knew you'd forget."

"Thank goodness! *Thank you,* sweetheart. What'd we get her?"

"A spendy negligee and day at the spa."

"Perfect. I hope it's hot pink and fluffy—full of ruffles and bows. I'd love Zork to see that!" she howled.

"Nope. It's white and classy."

"For Bertie?" Olivia said it as stunned as she felt.

"Well, it does have little pink hearts and tiny satin bows on it. And a dramatic, sweeping ruffle on the hem. Like something off the cover of a steamy romance novel."

"She'll love it!" Olivia erupted.

"I think it sounds cute," Gemma cried.

"It is," Magnolia assured. "Nothing Nani or I would be caught dead in, but Bertie will love it."

****

At one o'clock sharp, the house was already a hive of activity. As soon as Olivia, Magnolia, and Gemma stepped into the living room, the ladies of Sugar Creek took notice. The room hushed.

Why is everyone staring? Olivia checked her watch. *We're right on time.* And then it registered. "The milk! I forgot the damn milk. I'm so sorry, ladies."

Next she scanned her living room. "Wow. Would you look at this…" She clamped her mouth shut. *Holy pink nightmare. I've stepped into a giant barrel of cotton candy.*

Olivia was bemused and only slightly pained by the ruffled umbrellas swinging from the rafters, the shiny sequined hearts circling the plate of veggies and dip, the bouquets of balloons swaying on the end tables, the basket full of fancy ribboned party favors stacked in the entry, the three-tiered cake, shiny tablecloths, paper plates, napkins, and utensils. Everything pink.

Gemma's mouth and eyes grew to the size of small ponds. "Wow-wee," she said, gasping. "It's beauty-full."

Olivia elbowed Magnolia and whispered, "Calls herself *Bebe* now in addition to Boo." She smirked. A string of pink flags hung across the glass picture window and read, Bonjour, Bebe!

"No," Magnolia said. "I don't think so." Before she could say more, the crowd of women shouted, "Surprise!" as if they had burst from a cake.

Gemma stood front and center. "What surprise?" she asked.

"For you, honey!" Bertie told her. "This is all for you!"

"Me?"

"Gemma?" Olivia asked.

"It's a baby shower for Gemma!" Magnolia cried.

"But Bertie…" Gemma shook her head. "You forgot. This is your bridal shower."

"Oh, sweetie. At my age? I don't need a bridal shower. This was my plan all along. I know it's probably too soon, but I hoped it would be the perfect surprise."

"Wait." Gemma uncupped her mouth. "This is for

me?" And my baby girl?"

Magnolia drew Gemma into the crook of her arm.

"Yes, Gemma. For you," Bertie said. "We all want you to know that we love and support you. Some of us, well, let's just say, all of us agree, that you deserve this."

One second didn't tick by before Gemma pounced into Bertie's arms and squeezed without stopping. She didn't let go. When her head finally lifted, she said, "I just want to say, I love you, Bertie. And I hope I don't buzz all over and have a panic attack. I thought this was a bridal shower."

Laughter spun around the room. "Have a seat next to your mom and Nani, hon." Bertie tenderly unwrapped Gemma's arms, still holding snug to her own. She directed Gemma to a chair with a flouncy pink bow attached to the back and ribbons streaming down both sides.

"But your gift, Bertie. We bought you a gift." Gemma turned to her mother. "Can we still give her the nighty you said you guys wouldn't be caught dead in?"

Oops. "Of course," Olivia blurted. "Bertie is the only one who would look so stunning in it."

"Oh, that's sweet," Bertie said. "Let's play the games! I'll get the prizes." She trotted to the kitchen.

Olivia followed, her hand extending to Bertie's back. "Bertie—"

"Or…" Bertie swung around, tipping her head. "I guess she could open presents first, what do you think, Olivia?"

"I think you're an angel."

Bertie did a double-take. "What?"

"Seriously, this is amazing. I am—" The gratitude

swelled, choking back her words.

"Don't you dare puddle up, Olivia! You'll make me start bawling too."

"I can't help it. This was such a loving and kind thing for you to do. I'll never forget it. And neither will Gemma. Thank you." Olivia embraced Bertie and held tight. *Like one of Gemma's hugs.* "I'm proud to call you my friend, Bertie Lou. And I mean that," she said. "No one has ever done anything so special for her. For *all* of us. What a gift."

"I'm so glad. That was the point."

Olivia pulled back and discovered a hint of gray in Bertie's eyes she hadn't noticed before. "I mean it. You'll never know how much this means."

Bertie squeezed Olivia's arm. "I think I do."

"Zork is a lucky man. You're something else."

Bertie winked. "Let's open presents."

There were a mountain of them. By the time Gemma had gotten through half the pile, she asked, "How did you guys all know I'm having a girl?"

"You told us, remember?" Bertie asked.

"Yeah. But you believed me?"

"Of course!" she said. "Zork convinced me you were right. But," she added, "in the unlikely event something unexpected happens, we saved all our receipts!" The room rocked with merriment.

"You won't need to return a thing," Gemma announced. When she tore back wrapping paper covered with gray kittens and opened the lid of a hatbox, a wide and delighted grin swept across her face. Layers of gold tissue poured out like honey. And then she gasped and swallowed all her words.

"What is it?" Magnolia asked.

Gemma reached in, her mouth still gaping, and gently lifted. She held two dried rose floral head wreaths in cupped hands—one for baby, the other for herself.

"Aww," the room sang in unison.

"Look at those!" someone gushed. "Absolutely beautiful!" Utterly smitten, the ladies of Sugar Creek couldn't stop ogling. One of them declared a case of goosebumps.

"See what my baby and I are going to wear?" Gemma finally hollered. "Twin wreaths!" That's when she spotted the tiny tiaras sparkling periwinkle beneath the petals. "There's crowns in them! Like I always wear!"

"Halos for two angels," Bertie cried.

"Who are they from?" Magnolia asked, pen and paper in hand.

Gemma reached in and opened a small envelope. "They're from Bertie!" she cried. "She made them for me and my baby girl!"

The room filled with the wails of love-sick loons.

"They're beautiful, Bertie." Olivia shook her head. "So perfect." If Olivia had told Bertie the whole truth, it would've been this: *I was so wrong about you. What a heel I've been.* The shame fixed itself to her. She prayed for full atonement the next chance she had.

A rumble of thunder shook the windows.

"Oh, my. Look at those thunderheads," someone said, pointing out the window.

As soon as she said it, the skies opened with a flash. Thunder echoed against the ground and the rain roared down. A constant drumroll hammered the horizon. Another loud crack lit up the sky.

"Yikes!" someone yelped. "That sounded like a gunshot. Scared the livin' daylights out of me."

"It's Oregon," Bertie said. "Sunny one minute, blowing up the next." She cackled.

When the power flickered, Olivia grabbed matches and lit four fat pillars, inhaling the aroma of the smoking match with pleasure.

Another clap of thunder gave everyone another jolt. Torrents of rain blew across the field. Gemma tipped her head all the way back and gaped at the ceiling. The room darkened, like a blanket dropping over the entire farmhouse.

"Power's out!" Bertie cried.

"I'll take care of it." Olivia set the candles in the center of the room. "Play a round of baby bingo everyone. Be right back."

Zork already stood at the electrical box in the garage. "Did we blow a fuse?" she asked.

"More than that. Hang on." As soon as he reached in and flipped something, he vaulted backward. "Son of a gun!" he snapped, shaking one hand. "Damn, that hurt."

"Get a shock?"

"Enough to cure a donkey's depression." Zork blew a mighty gust of air.

"Hey." Olivia glanced at something dark on his hand. "You hurt? Let me take a look at that."

"It's not from the shock. Follow me to the barn. We have worse problems."

Olivia reached under the garage steps, grabbed a pistol from a hidden compartment and tucked it behind her waistband. She pulled on rubber boots, hopping toward the door. "Go," she ordered, and pushed her way through. Her nervous system had already activated into fight or flight mode. The way it had for too many years.

"It's not good…" Zork warned. He plunged ahead through a sheet of rain.

Olivia struggled to keep up, slogging through foot-sucking muck. Thunder cracked open again as soon as they reached the barn. Everything darkened.

"Over here!" he shouted.

Olivia hurried in his direction. "*Another* drone?" She moved swiftly one second—and slid to a dead stop the next. "Buster?"

A shockwave hit her like a whip.

"No!"

She bent down and touched his eye, waiting for any sign of life. But he didn't blink. A pool of blood streamed out from under his head and down one side. "Don't leave me boy," she said, knowing full well he had. Olivia lost touch with her body, the trauma like a deadening drug.

And then she remembered Lolly.

She stumbled to her feet as more lightning forked across the sky, the inside of the barn flashing like a strobe light. "Where's Lolly?!" Olivia darted to the other end of the barn where the mare stood, head tossing in her stall. She placed a limp, trembling hand on Lolly's neck. "It's okay, girl. You're okay."

Lolly pawed at the ground, quaking. Olivia rubbed the top of the mare's forehead and stroked her nose—the lather heavy on her neck and chest. "It's okay, baby. I'm here now." Olivia closed her eyes, forehead pressed against her neck. *Thank God you are too. Gemma couldn't take it.*

Olivia returned to Buster—her stomach twisting from the metallic whiffs of his blood. Early that morning she had fed him carrots when he leaned into her with love, laying his clean, golden head against her waist. *He'll never nuzzle me again.*

"I'm sorry," Zork said. "He was gone when I found him. Nothing I could do."

Olivia had lost all sense of time when she remembered the party. "Everyone's inside—" She bolted toward the barn door.

"Whoa," Zork said, his arm going out to calm her.

"It's not safe!" she screeched.

"Everyone's safe! We're secured now."

Olivia's shoulders slumped. With some reservation she circled back to Buster's stall. "I thought we had eyes on everything."

"We did. They took our guys down—but they're okay. Trust me, *no one* can get through now."

"But they got through to my barn. To my horses!" Olivia's legs weakened. She kneeled, placing her hand over Buster's heart. She shook with grief when she pulled back his head. "Someone slashed his throat. They slashed and then they shot. Used a suppressor... A clear warning to me."

With one nod, Zork affirmed what she said.

Olivia fumbled for her phone. "Something came through during the party." She yanked it from her pocket and powered it on, leaving smudges of blood wherever she touched. "Should have known." When the screen glowed, she scrolled until she found it. "They're everywhere, Zork." Her hand went limp. "They have me surrounded digitally."

He lifted it from her palm, wiping away the blood

with his sleeve. "Patience has never been our strong suit," he read aloud. "Cooperate or someone else's lovely neck will be next. You know how to contact us."

A blast of air exploded from Olivia's chest. "I am so done with this," she said through gritted teeth. "He's coming after my family and—"

"Hey," he said, his voice solid as steel. "We're ready. And we have to do it right."

"*But we weren't ready for this…*" She swept hair off her face with the back of her wrist and tenderly rubbed Buster's face, her breathing rickety. I'm so, so sorry, boy." Rain dripped off her hair, trickling over his blood-smeared nose—a crimson stain masking his buttermilk face.

"I'll collect what I can and do a sweep." He shifted away, his sorrow palpable. He had witnessed her grief more times than he could count.

She pinched the bridge of her nose with two trembling fingers. "They've taken away my peace. They've violated my space, my refuge, my very soul."

"Not for long. It's a home game for us this time. We have the advantage."

Olivia wanted to believe him. "You're sure there's enough backup?"

He nodded. "I promise, it's everywhere."

She stayed close to Buster in the dimming light, wishing she could scream him back to life. Zork covered his wounds with a blanket and soaked up the blood with shovels of sawdust and hay.

"I need a minute," she told him. A breeze rustled past but didn't seem to touch her.

"Clean the blood off your face before anyone sees you," Zork told her. And then he let her be, a stiff wind slamming against the barn door as he left.

A current of death rolled through Olivia's veins, the wood stall against her back as hard as reality itself.

And then a hollow pit opened between her ribs. "You were such a good boy, Buster." Rubbing his ears did no good, but she had to do something. "You were the best. And I wasn't here for you... The way you've always been here for me." *I hope you're with him, Sam. Please be with him.*

Olivia folded—the pain tearing at her chest. "Forgive me, sweet boy. Forgive me for not protecting you." She broke, sorrow rolling with such force, she questioned whether or not her heart could take it.

She squeezed out a pittance of air and whispered, "You were my soulmate... There will never be another you. *Never.*"

She couldn't say more than that.

****

The baby shower continued uninterrupted. All the ladies of Sugar Creek, blissfully oblivious to the fact that Olivia's beloved horse had been murdered in their midst.

After the last guest said goodbye, Gemma still had a grin plastered to her face as big as pie. Her joy and excitement beyond measure.

It wasn't the first, or last time the dark elements of Olivia's life had to be hidden, but she had hoped it would grow easier with time. The weight of deception had taken its toll.

After everyone left, she told Zork, "We're still living in splintered pieces. No matter where we are, we lose parts of ourselves—forced to live inauthentic lives. I know it's a sacrifice for something bigger, but I'm having trouble reconciling it again."

"How did you reconcile it in the past, Olivia?" he asked. "Think about that."

His question reminded her of how to keep going. "Can you take care of Buster for me, Zork? Would you mind? I can't…"

"I'll take good care of Buster. Don't you worry. In the meantime, things are taped off. Told everyone we had a fuel leak and to keep their distance."

"Thank you. Gemma mustn't know. Maggie either. Not today."

"I'll handle it."

"What would I do without you?" She massaged her eyes. "Please don't ever make me find out."

****

That evening, Olivia stood longer than usual under a hot shower. The spray of water, shimmering like tinsel, cascaded over her shoulders, the heat slow to reach her bones. Olivia's thoughts were running as steady as the streaming faucet.

Bertie had proven she wasn't the silly, lovesick, fool Olivia had taken her for. *How did I get it so wrong?* The answer came instantly—*I wasn't seeing her.*

That night, Olivia fell into a thin, uncertain sleep. Images of Buster pricked her heart with lightning stealth and wouldn't let go. She heard the sound of his struggle, envisioned his misery, cradled his innocence, and summoned the bond between them, the one reflected in his eyes. She imagined his physical pain too—the suffering he endured alone. She tried to tell herself he died instantly. But she knew there was no way to know for sure.

She flipped on a light and noticed tiny creases of dry blood pooled around her fingernail. She hadn't scrubbed it away—she couldn't bear erasing the only part of him she had left. And this haunted her too: Olivia knew Buster would still be alive if he hadn't been hers. *It's never been safe to be with me.*

But an even more troubling ache began to press against her insides. *What if it had been Gemma?* The thought kept her awake the rest of the night—it kept her vigilant right next to a loaded pistol.

Buster was my horse, but what if it had been my Gemma?

Chapter Thirty-Three

The Smell of Love

"I hope Bertie expects a downpour at the exact moment everyone moves from the church to the barn," Magnolia said. Olivia punched up the volume on her phone to hear her better. "You know it'll happen. Have extra umbrellas for the guests. And boots too. Could be freezing rain. Nothing worse than balancing a wedding cake on top of ice."

November came in wearing the heavy gray cloak of a winter storm. The underbellies of the clouds were growing plump and darkening. The wedding was only a day away, and the threat of more rain was all anyone talked about. And the temperature was dropping fast.

"They already moved it," Olivia assured her. "The whole wedding is in the barn now." She was the only one who knew the truth of it though. For security reasons, Zork had insisted everything be confined to one space. Rain was the least of his worries.

"Smart. Are we still meeting at Gemma's apartment, Mom?"

"Already here. She made dinner for us."

"What gastric disturbance are we in for?"

"A large casserole full of unidentified objects."

"Don't worry," Magnolia said. "I stocked her freezer with pizza for nights like this."

As soon as she heard a rap on the front door, Olivia greeted Magnolia with a hug. "Gemma's in her room sleeping," she whispered. "Let's go in the living room and drink wine."

Magnolia dropped on the sofa, gawping at the two hefty beer steins sitting on the coffee table.

"It's all she had," Olivia said. The tankards glistened crimson as she poured.

Magnolia exhaled with the strength of a horse and said, "I sure hope we survive all this."

"What? The wedding or the baby?"

"Everything." She lifted her stein with both hands. "But I'm thinking more about this baby. I'm afraid I'm not the grandmotherly type." She took a long swig as if guzzling a sudsy lager. "I'll have to leave that to you."

"Oh, no, you don't. You'll do no such thing. And what's the 'grandmotherly type' anyway? But listen, no one will have to twist your arm. Not when you see her. And when you hold her? It's all over." Olivia slurped with a satisfied grin.

"I'm not so sure it'll be that way for me. Gemma was different."

"Of course she was. And this baby will be too."

"I remember how you felt about Gemma when she was born. It meant the world to me that you loved her every bit as much as me." Magnolia paused. "Still does, you know."

"The bond between a child and grandparent can be a powerful one. You'll see." Olivia lifted her stein for a cheers. "Here's to granddaughters and falling in love with them." Their mugs clunked with a clumsy sense of satisfaction.

"Did Walter's mom ever give a reason for not

coming to the shower?" Magnolia asked.

"Didn't Gemma tell you? His parents dragged him away. They all flew back east for a funeral. I'm betting he'll be gone a while."

"Of course he will," Magnolia said, pulling off her boots.

"You think there was a funeral?"

"Not for a minute."

Olivia shook her head, sliding a bowl of walnuts over. "You may be right."

"Such a shame he has to miss the wedding. He was so excited about it."

"He was," Olivia said. "But maybe a part of him wanted to leave too. Gemma says he's a wreck now just talking about the pregnancy. He's scared to death of holding a baby."

"Exactly what I expected."

"He'll come around."

"Maybe. And maybe he won't." Magnolia folded both legs under her. "It might be best if he doesn't." She set the stein on the table with a thud.

"Oh, Maggie. That would be devastating for Gemma."

"Of course it would. But we have no control over that."

"What's wrong?" Gemma's voice echoed from the hallway. She shuffled her slippers into the living room and plopped down next to them.

"We were discussing Walter," Olivia said. "I'm sorry he'll miss the wedding tomorrow."

"He went to a funeral."

"Do you believe that?" Magnolia asked.

"When someone dies, you have funerals, right?"

"Usually."

"Okay. Then, yes, I believe him. Walter doesn't lie. I keep trying to teach him how."

Magnolia and Olivia exchanged a pithy look.

"Only if there's no other choice, I mean," Gemma added, plugging her slippers into the carpet. "But he still won't—not even when we have to!"

"Well, I'm not sure there was a funeral," Magnolia said.

"I told you he doesn't lie."

"No. But do his parents?"

Gemma cast a bewildered face on Olivia.

"Your mom thinks his parents made up the funeral as an excuse to separate him from you and the baby for a while."

"Ohhh…" Gemma's eyes narrowed to slits and then widened again. "But we don't have a baby yet."

"No, but maybe she wants him to distance himself," Olivia explained. "So he's less involved with everything right now."

Gemma's face crabbed up. "His mom would do that. She told him to break up with me." She scooped up walnuts and plopped them in her mouth.

"What did Walter say about that?" Magnolia asked.

"He cried. And he was mad. But he needs to love his mom. Not just me."

"Geeze," Magnolia groaned.

"Now, we can't be certain of anything," Olivia added. "Maybe there *was* a funeral."

"Yeah, people die a lot, Mama. Every day. But it does sound a little fishy," Gemma offered.

"It's fishy, all right." Magnolia flopped a crocheted blanket over her legs. "Regardless, I think being

269

involved with the baby will be difficult for Walter. His mother doesn't want this, and he's scared."

"I know that," Gemma said. "And it's okay. Because I can do everything."

Magnolia and Olivia exchanged another haphazard glance.

"No, you can't do everything," Magnolia said. "I'm hiring someone to help you, remember? You can do a lot but not everything. Even mothers who—"

"I know, I know! You think I need help. You say it all the time."

"Well, Gemma, I—"

"Shhh!" Gemma covered both ears. "All I hear about is how I need help! Well, who doesn't? And I'm the mother, not you. You need to *butt out*." Gemma pushed off the sofa and stubbed her big toe on the leg of the table. "Nuts!" she yelled. "See what you made me do?" She grabbed her toe and plunged backward into the sofa again.

Magnolia threw up her hands, tossing the blanket aside. She pulled on her boots and coat, cinched her scarf, and stomped to the door. "Taking a walk," she announced. "Back in an hour." The front door slammed.

"Your mom is not your enemy, Tink. And you stubbed your own toe."

"But *I'm* the mom. It's my baby! No one else's. My baby needs to know *me*, not some stranger..." Gemma stared out the window.

"She will know you. She'll know you by your voice, your smell, your touch..." Olivia sat forward, leaning toward Gemma. "No matter who else is helping, she'll always know you're her mother."

"My *smell*? I didn't know that." Gemma went quiet, her eyes fixed on a daydream. "Well…" she said in a trance, "this *is* my first daughter."

And hopefully the last. Olivia rubbed her forehead, knowing that some thoughts cannot be reined in.

Gemma's eyes jumped back to her grandmother. "I've never had a baby, so how could I know that, right?"

"Right. So be open and let other people help you. Your mom is right."

Gemma's expression dropped, hangdog style. "I know. Sorry."

"I'm not the one you should be apologizing to."

"I know that too." She picked up her mother's beer stein and sniffed, making a face. "I do want my daughter to be loved by lots of different people. Like I am. I guess it will be okay."

"Sure it will. And you're right—a child can never have too much love. None of us can." Olivia cleared everything away and wiped off the coffee table. "Honey, imagine for a minute you were wrong and this baby *wasn't* a girl. How would you feel?"

"I'd feel fine. I'd have to change the name. That's all. The one I have is only meant for her."

"You have a name already?"

"Yeah. I haven't told anyone because it's personal. But I think you'll love it."

"It doesn't matter if I don't."

"I know."

"Still thinking about it? Is that why it's personal?"

"No. It'll be her name. I'm just nervous telling Mama. She might not like it."

"Everyone's entitled to their opinions. But it's only

yours that matters. Tell her when you're ready."

"I wish I could tell you both now."

"Then tell us."

"When she gets back?"

Olivia shrugged. "If that's what you want."

"Okay! When Mama gets home I'm announcing her name," she bubbled. "I'm doing a name reveal!"

****

Dapples of light streamed through the curtains when Magnolia returned. The sun edged along the earth and sank, but a glint of dusky rose still reflected on the horizon. Magnolia was noticeably happier. As if the brisk clean air had washed away all the hard feelings and restored her optimism.

"What a beautiful sunset." She pulled off her boots again. "The sky does such amazing things. I hiked along the river, and it was absolutely stunning."

"Gemma has some exciting news."

"She does?" Magnolia unknotted her scarf and shimmied it off. "Do I smell pizza?"

Gemma's nose wrinkled. "The casserole didn't bake up so good. Looked like it came out of a horse."

"Well then… Pizza it is. What's your exciting news?"

"I'm doing a name reveal. And I'm sorry, Mama. For yelling at you and everything."

"Thanks, Gem."

"I know I need a helper."

"That's right."

"And it wasn't your fault I stubbed my toe." Gemma enfolded her mother, her nose buried in Magnolia's curls. "Your hair smells like love to me."

Magnolia kissed Gemma's cheek. "Thank you for

apologizing. I only want this to work for you." Magnolia cradled Gemma's chin in a cupped hand. "So you've decided on a name already?"

"Yes." She beamed.

Olivia took a seat, adjusting a throw pillow at the small of her back. "Gemma said she's known for quite a while."

"Wow, let's hear it!" Magnolia burst. "Tell us!"

"Okay. You sit with Nani. I'll be right back." Gemma bounced down the hall, her slippers full of zeal as they slapped against the tile floor. She returned holding the floral head wreaths Bertie had made for her.

Olivia and Magnolia straightened to attention.

"I've been waiting for the perfect name." Gemma's eyes sparked new light. "And then it came to me out of nowhere. Well—not out of nowhere. I'm sure it came from Creator. But anyway, right then I knew. And it's beautiful... Like she is."

"Okay," Magnolia said clutching her hands. "Tell us!"

Gemma's head raised, exposing the length of her neck. She lifted the large wreath and placed it on top her head, the deep red and coral roses popping against her glossy black hair. She cradled the small one on her arm as if holding a baby, angling it so the jewels on the tiara caught the light. In a reading-aloud voice, she launched her words. "Introducing..." She swooped one arm out like a wing. "My baby daughter's name... *River Jane Harriet Porter.*"

No one said a thing.

Gemma inspected their eyes.

And then inspected more.

Still nothing.

"Do you like it?" Gemma's face drooped.

"River?" Magnolia's forehead crinkled. She tipped her head. "Like a *river*-river, where I strolled tonight?"

"You think it's weird." Gemma's lips clamped shut.

"River!" Olivia jumped in. "It's beautiful! And Harriet after baby Harriet at Luper, right?"

"Yes," Gemma confirmed, a sliver of hope humming in her voice.

"I like it," Magnolia blurted.

"You do?" Gemma brightened, as if everything inside her sprang to life again.

"I truly do."

"Great." Gemma's face mellowed. "Because she's already my River. And like all the Porter women, her life will be a force—as strong and free as the McKenzie. She's already been for a swim in it—" Her words skid to a stop. "Never mind about that. It's mostly her name because I was at the river when you both found out she was inside me."

"Oh, Tink," Olivia said with love in her voice. "I adore it. I'm sure it will fit her beautifully. Does Walter know?"

"No. I told you guys first. She's a Porter woman after all. Plus, I wanted to tell Walter at the river tomorrow night. It would've been so romantic after the wedding." She made a face. "Now I'll be alone."

Magnolia raised up and gave Gemma a side hug. "Well. There will be another special time you can tell him. And you won't be alone." Magnolia placed a hand on her small baby bump. "You have a baby with you all the time now. And the more I think about it, the more I love it. River is the perfect name."

"I'm glad you think so too, Mama."

"River Jane," Olivia said affectionately. "The fourth generation of Porter women will be here before we know it."

Magnolia plucked a walnut out of the carpet. "Or..." She closed her eyes and muttered, "A Porter *man* will be here before we know it."

Chapter Thirty-Four

November Second

There was ice on the lilacs in the morning. Olivia stood at the back window and marveled at their hearty nature, closing her eyes recalling the sweet, haunting fragrance of the pale periwinkle petals when it bloomed the previous May. The symbol for lilacs, she once read, was, "The Joy of Youth." She planted it for Gemma.

She swirled blueberries and walnuts around in her yogurt, turned up the heat, and ambled back to the window. Zork was across the field on a new white green-broke filly, kicking her forward when she nickered and threw her mane a little.

Olivia reached him on the phone. "What're you doing out there? You're getting married today." She set her bowl down, staring out at a luminous layer of ghostly fog rising off the horizon.

"I know, I know. Just checking things out again and training this one."

"You nervous or something?"

"Naaaw."

"Zork?"

"Maybe a little."

Olivia guffawed. "Really?" She went to the kitchen and carried back a hot mug of tea.

"I said a little."

"Cold feet?" she teased.

"No. Not cold feet." Zork's tone was somber. "Concerned is all…"

"Sorry. I didn't mean to sound so cheeky. What's wrong?"

"Worried about this happening today."

"You said it yourself—we're ready for anything. And we have an army of backup. I'll manage things, Zork. No need to worry. You're only job is to enjoy this day."

"It's not only today." His tone took a dive.

"I know that," Olivia assured. "But it's a day at a time. That's how it is. That's how it always goes. Remember? You can't stop your life because of—"

"And, we leave tonight for the San Juan Islands."

"I'm well aware of that."

"I have a bad feeling about being gone."

"When don't we have a bad feeling?" she glowered. "It's your honeymoon. Please put everything out of your mind and go have fun. You can't let this dictate how you live your life. We'll be fine. I'll see to it. You need the break, Zork."

"Your backup is out of here after today. There's no more help on the property, unless you issue an SOS. We secured them for the wedding, but after that—"

"I know. They can't be here forever. I'm fully aware of that too. I'm ready."

"And…" Silence followed.

"What else is bothering you?" She listened as Zork expelled a ragged breath.

"Worried about Bertie. I don't want her in the middle of this. If something ever happened…" For a few glum moments no one said a thing. "I've told her what she was getting into. About what we do."

"And…?"

"And she doesn't care—says she's not afraid. But it's eating at me. Something feels wrong."

Olivia said nothing because she knew only too well what he was thinking. The same idea preyed on her too—ever since she gave birth to Magnolia.

"I'm not safe to be around," he said. "Even less safe to live with. You were right. Marrying Bertie is crazy. I should've listened to you."

Olivia spat out her tea. "Right! Like that would've ever happened. And besides, I was wrong. You're a lucky man to be with her."

"I know that. But it's not about my happiness. She's more at risk than ever marrying me."

"Stop. I know how you feel. I do, but—"

"But nothin'. I'm not sure it can work. I'm afraid I haven't seen things clearly."

"This can't go on forever. It *will* end, and then we'll be done. For good this time."

"I'm not so sure," he said. "I'm not sure we'll ever be done with this. I need to call it off."

"What? The *wedding*?!"

"Yes, the wedding."

"No! You're over-reacting—"

"It's the right thing to do."

"Well, this is a fine time to figure *that* out! Hours before the ceremony? Bertie is expecting—" Olivia groaned. "Does she know any of this?"

"Of course not," he said in a grouchy rasp.

"Oh, Zork. Please, don't. This would be a nightmare for her. I can't even imagine."

"You think I don't know that? It's a nightmare for

me too!"

"Listen. I had Magnolia with me for years, and Gemma, too. I still do. We've made it work. I'm here to help you."

"Yes, we've been lucky. But knowing the risks—" Dust must have caught in his throat. "I'd never forgive myself…" His words fizzled out.

Olivia set the steaming tea on the mantel and covered her eyes with a hand, her flesh soothing and warm from the heat of the mug.

He spoke again. "I will never stop second-guessing myself about Sam's death. I still—"

"Stop. I'm going to say this one last time. We don't have crystal balls. You couldn't have known. He would be furious at you for blaming yourself. *Furious!*"

Zork paused. "I know, but—"

"But nothing."

He paused again. "I can't watch someone I love die in front of me again."

"Then don't. Right now you don't have to. Likely never will again."

No one spoke, but Olivia imagined he was nodding. The memory of Sam's death lay like an inconsolable stain on the fields between them.

"Maybe this is about missing Sam today," she offered. "I know I do."

"Maybe so." His tenor implied she was correct. "Missing my best man."

"That's right," Olivia said, determined to stay upbeat. "As soon as I'm dressed, I'll double check everything, including all the communications with the team."

"I know you will," Zork sighed. "But best man or

no best man, Bertie's safety comes first. And she's not safe living under my roof."

Olivia breathed in the citrus-sweet air over her mug. "I hate what we do. And I hate that we're still doing it." She paced across the living room. "And I absolutely don't agree that you should deny yourself this happiness. But if you're serious about calling things off, I know I can't convince you otherwise. And Bertie needs to know."

"I am serious."

"Then Bertie needs to know. *Now*."

Chapter Thirty-Five

A Spark of the Divine

The sky was holding something back. Maybe rain, maybe sleet, maybe hail the size of goose eggs. Olivia couldn't say for sure, only that a dark and heavy cold moved over her when she stepped outside. She scanned the marbled horizon. "Don't let loose," she told the weather gods. "Hold off till after the wedding." *Wait. There is no wedding...* She found her heavy rain gear in the barn and prepared to saddle up Buster. *Wait. There is no Buster...* She juddered when she passed his empty stall, trying to shake off his memory.

"Come on, Banjo, time for work." But before she could lead him out, she heard someone racking one into the tube. She dropped to the ground.

"Yoo-hoo! Anyone home?"

Why does everything sound like a gun?

"It's me, Bertie!"

Of course it was. She knew that voice anywhere.

She spotted Olivia squatting in the dirt behind the stall. "Here you are! What on earth are you doing down there? I thought you'd be getting ready."

Olivia eased up, one hand still on the pistol against her backside. "Well, why aren't you getting ready?" *As if I didn't know...* "You're the bride."

"I realize that," she said, misery in her voice. "I

thought I was. But now I'm not."

"What?" *This performance is worthy of an Oscar*… "Oh, Bertie, what is it?"

"Well, I guess I'm…" She rolled her eyes. "Please don't kill me."

"And why would I do that?"

"Because of all our planning. For my dream wedding."

"I didn't plan a thing," Olivia scoffed. She tied the lead to Banjo. "Have you spoken to Zork?"

"Of course not. Why?"

Olivia examined her face. "Well, maybe you should. About whatever this is."

"It would crush him like an eighteen-wheeler. I can't hurt him like that. I'm just so confused."

"Confused about what? You sound serious."

"I'm afraid I am. I think it's all a mistake."

"Wait…" Olivia squinted. "What's a mistake?"

"Marrying! Not him—but anyone."

"What?!" *I'm not acting anymore.*

"Seriously. I'm having second thoughts."

"You've gotta be kidding. *You're* having second thoughts? Getting married is all you've ever talked about since I've known you! What do you mean you're having second thoughts?"

"I mean, I'm not sure marriage is right for me. I realized what it would mean."

"Three hours before your wedding you realized what getting married would mean? Oh, Bertie."

"I know! It'd kill Zork if he heard me saying this. It would scar him for life."

"Well, I doubt that, but—"

"You doubt it?"

"I mean, he can take it. Whatever this is, he'll deal with it. What are you afraid of?"

Bertie's shoulders bowed. "Here's the thing." She plunked herself down on a bale of hay. "I love my home, and I simply can't bear to sell it. It's been in my family forever. And if I sell, I'll have to get rid of practically everything."

"Then live in yours and sell his."

Bertie sighed. "It's not that easy. Don't get me wrong—I love Zork. More than anything. I simply don't want to live with him. In either home."

"Oh..."

"We both have one-bath homes. Can you imagine? I have to have my own bathroom, Olivia. *Have to.*"

"I see." Olivia closed her eyes, nodding with empathy.

"It's not just that..." Bertie sloped forward, elbows resting on her knees. "The poor guy wants me around constantly. Every evening for dinner, then television, a round of cribbage, and then bedtime. Did you know he has to go to bed at the exact same time every night? *Every* night. With me. I'm a part of his whole routine now. Don't get me wrong. I love sleeping with him..."

"Bertie..." Olivia held up a hand. "Just say it. You want your own space."

"Exactly! The truth is I'm a little selfish. I didn't realize how much until I packed one box and couldn't bear to pack another. I love my home. With only me in it."

"There's nothing wrong with that."

"Well, of course you'd say that. I mean no offense, but you don't exactly have a man pining away for your company. You actually *like* being single."

"Yes, I—"

"Well, I don't. Except for this part."

"Then explain this part to Zork. He's an open-minded man."

"He'll be shattered! Did you know my home was built by my grandfather? I can't sell it to some stranger. I can't do it!"

"*Talk to Zork*. He can take it, Bertie. But you better act fast. Look at the time!"

The barn door creaked all the way open. "Did I hear my name?" Zork strolled in lifting his baseball cap. "You talking about me?" He ran the palm of his hand over his head and pulled his cap down tight again.

"No, Zork. We're talking about *Bertie*." Olivia tried to clue him in.

"Oh, Zork." Bertie dropped her head. "I've never been so sad in all my life."

"What the hell did you tell her, Olivia?"

"You know what?" Olivia grabbed her favorite hat off the post. "I'm out of here." She slapped it against her thigh, dust scattering down her leg.

"Oh, no, you don't." Zork blocked her exit with one arm.

"Yes, *please* stay, Olivia," Bertie begged. "For me."

Olivia closed Banjo's stall, ready to bear witness to who knows what.

"Oh, Zork," Bertie began. "I should've known it wouldn't work."

"What?"

"I've been in denial because I fell in love. I'm so sorry."

"Huh?" He rubbed the base of his neck. "Why are

you so sorry?"

"I'm going to be blunt as a post."

"I wish you would," he said.

"I love you, but I can't move in with you. I'm so sorry, but—"

"You can't move in with me? I don't get it."

"Of course you don't." Bertie glanced at Olivia, sitting on hay. "See?"

Zork's face twisted in befuddlement. "Huh?"

"Olivia told me you could take this. But I know you better than that. I know how much you need a woman around."

"I don't *need* a woman. I want *you*."

"Oh, sweetie, I know. That's what I mean! But I can't do it!"

"You can't do what?"

"I can't marry and live with another person. I know now I can't. That's all there is to it. What should we do?" Bertie swallowed hard. "We have a gaggle of people coming soon. We need to let them know."

"What are you saying, Boo? You want to call our wedding off?"

"I don't want to, believe me. But it's not fair to you. I know how I am, and—"

A loud crack made everyone turn. A sea of long bobbing waves, the ends dipped in hot pink, exploded through the barn door.

"So this is where everyone is!" Gemma bounded in and squeezed Zork like a teddy bear. "But why is everyone in here?" She took one look at Bertie and withered. "Are you okay, Bertie?"

"Yes, I'm fine, honey. It's okay."

"No, it's not," Gemma said gloomily. "I can see

it's not. It's not fine at all." She stood close to Bertie, her face in a knot. She started to hug her but stopped, as if Bertie might break if she tried.

"You're right, Gemma," Zork said. "It's not okay."

"Are you guys in a fight?"

"No darlin', nothin' like that," he said.

"Well, then, did someone die?" Her eyes glazed over with worry.

"No. Nothin' like that either."

Bertie forced a half smile. "We're discussing some things, honey. I'm not sure if the wedding..." She couldn't finish.

"Zorro!" Gemma faced him, hands on her hips. "I know what this means cuz I've seen it in the movies. Are you dumping her?"

"No, of course I'm not dumping her!"

Gemma swung around. "Are you breaking up with him, Bertie?"

"I don't want to, but—"

"But what? You think you aren't getting married? On your own *wedding* day?"

"Well..." Bertie stammered.

"Stop!" Gemma blurted, her neck red as a radish. "You guys can't break up. And you shouldn't. If you do it'll be the biggest mistake you ever made. And you're supposed to be River's godparents!"

"Oh, Gemma..." Bertie's words quivered. "Her godparents? What an honor."

"I know! So, listen to me," Gemma pleaded.

Zork and Bertie straightened to attention.

"You're meant to be together. You are! You're supposed to get married even if you don't live together at first. I'm telling you, it's meant to be! Don't ask me how I know. I just do."

My Tink does have a spark of the divine…

"Honey, what do you mean?" Bertie sniffled.

"I mean you're a perfect match and you'll always love each other—"

"No," Bertie intruded. "I mean the part where you said *even if you don't live together*. What did you mean by that?"

"Yeah, that part," Zork fired off.

Gemma recalculated her thoughts. "I mean—stay in your own homes. No one has to move. You'll be just as happy." Gemma gripped her hands together. "I promise."

"Were you out there listening in on our conversation?" Zork asked.

"No." She shrugged.

"Then, how did you know—"

"It doesn't matter, Zork." Bertie waved him off. "Go on, Gemma. What else do you think?"

"Oh, okay," she said. "Let me see." She tapped a finger over her mouth. "Well, I think you're not seeing the simple thing that's right in front of you. But don't feel bad. It happens to me all the time."

"What simple thing?" Bertie asked.

"Don't change anything. But get married. That's the simple thing to do."

"But Zork wants us *together*. He'd hate that. He needs—"

"Hang on!" Zork blurted. "Bertie, are you sayin' it's what you'd want? To keep separate places but still get hitched?"

"I know it sounds crazy, but yes. I would. I don't want to sell my home. And frankly, I don't want to sell

287

a darn thing in it. And as silly as it sounds—I need my own bathroom. I'm selfish, Zork. And I understand if that's a problem for you."

"Now wait just a minute," he ordered.

Olivia tilted to the left for a better view. A glint had returned to Zork's eyes, a flicker of relief. *He's practically whistling rainbows.*

"It's not crazy, and I don't hate this idea at all," he said. "Not if we still get married."

Gemma clapped her hands. "See? You guys can be together any way you want. Didn't you know that?" Her words had sway.

"She's right, Bertie. We can be together however the hell we want."

"You mean you'd actually agree to get married and not live together, Zork?"

"Well, yes! If that's what works. Sure I would!"

"It won't be forever, I can tell you that," Gemma added. Zork glanced at Olivia lounging back on the bale of hay, chewing on a piece of straw. "Did your nan coach you on any of this, Gemma?" Zork's inkling was palpable.

"No."

"You two talk about this idea at all?" He flashed an eye on Olivia again. She scowled back with sour lips.

"No, but if you like the idea, who cares? Sure as my baby is a girl, I'm sure about this."

"Okay, sweetheart." Zork squeezed her shoulder.

"Wait." Gemma glanced in a bunch of different directions. "I don't think it's a rule you have to live together when you get married, is it?"

"Nope. No rule at all," Zork said.

"No, but..." Bertie hesitated, giving it a careful

weighing. "Won't people talk?"

"Sure, Bertie!" Gemma scoffed. "Take it from me. They talk all the time when you're different. But who cares? Thumb your nose at the naysayers like I do! In your mind, of course. Or not."

"Well, I guess we can do whatever we want then." Bertie gave a toothy grin.

"Did we just solve our problem, Boo?" Zork stared at her waiting.

"No, we didn't. *Gemma* did." She leapt into Zork's arms. "You're sure about this?"

"More than sure. It's perfect."

"No feelings of rejection? Because I do love you, Zork. I love you more than ever."

"I don't care where we live, Boo."

Bertie took hold of Gemma's shoulders. "How *did* you know how to help us?"

Gemma stopped herself before trying to explain it. How her feelings told her. "Maybe I knew because it wasn't hard."

Zork's eyes expanded. "It was plenty hard for us." He put his arm around Gemma. "The truth is half the time we learn more from you than you learn from us."

"I'll say," Bertie said.

Gemma stood still, wide-eyed as an owl.

"Everything you bring to this world matters, Gem. Don't ever doubt it." Zork kissed the top of her head. "Let's get dressed. We have a wedding to attend."

"Some things are easy for me that are hard for regular thinkers," Gemma said, scampering out of the barn. "What I bring to this world matters."

Olivia knew she would hold on to those words forever. But she never imagined that one day, Gemma would stand and recite them to a room full of strangers.

Chapter Thirty-Six

A Country-Barn Wedding

A dozen hoary white wrought iron shepherd hooks flanked the aisle between two rows of hay bales. Large mason jars filled with raspberry-red roses, winter pink camellias, tipsy white snapdragons, and lush green ferns hung on each hook with gold ribbon bows glittering around the stems.

The air sparked with excitement when Zork and Bertie's song commenced. George Strait sang "I Cross My Heart," echoing deep and rich through the barn. The atmosphere, so imbued with loveliness, the lyrics, plus a soap bubble, would have been enough to knock every person off their feet had they not already been sitting. Magnolia led the procession of pink elegance down the aisle.

Next in line was Gemma. "Slow and easy," Olivia whispered in her ear. "Don't let your feet gallop."

"Slooow-ly," Gemma mouthed, staring at her pink satin ballet slippers. Her head popped up at the end of the aisle; Zork winked with a thumbs-up. She whirled around, leaned in, and beamed when she said, "You look handsome, Zorro. Your white sideburns match your shirt." She stepped away but spun back again. "You look just like a handsome cowboy."

"Over *here*." Magnolia motioned, her hand

flapping at high speed.

"I know!" Gemma giggled. "I didn't forget."

When Olivia took her place next to Gemma, she leaned in and whispered, "You look beautiful, Tink."

"You look like a movie star too, Graham Cracker. Just like Katharine Hepburn."

The audience stood and, like a wave of starlings, circled in unison to face the back. When Bertie appeared, a collective sigh sashayed through the air.

"Ooh," Gemma swooned. "Look at the queen! I mean the bride," she corrected.

Bertie clenched a large bouquet of pearly-white roses and 'Moonlight' hydrangeas aged to a pink blush, all wrapped in gold ribbon against her creamy all-lace, antique gown. She wore something blue from Gemma—a sparkling tiara made of rhinestone sapphires.

Reverend Samuel greeted the guests and recited poetry and scripture. Zork and Bertie read aloud the personal vows they composed. And when they did, there wasn't a dry eye in the barn. Zork went first. "Sometimes life plugs along, like an old dirt road that never changes. And sometimes God rains down rainbows on you all at once. Bertie, you are the brightest and most beautiful one I've ever been given…"

And Bertie ended, "…My life will never be the same because of you, Zork Canby. I was just another gal at the rodeo until you came along. From the first night we laughed until our stomachs hurt, you held my heart. You held it that night, and every night since. And you'll hold my heart for the rest of my days…"

Gemma's sniffling bucked into an unruly snort,

sending a chuckle whisking through the crowd. And then she sneezed. A glint of gold soared through the air. "The ring!" she pointed. "It rolled that-a-way!"

Heads swiveled right and left when Gemma chased after it. She scrambled through the chairs of guests and plunged to the ground. People leaned forward and backwards, Gemma on all fours skittering under legs until she reached beneath the gift table and hollered, "I found it!" But she forgot where she was and whacked herself on the temple when she bolted upward. The barn full of people cringed right along with her.

"That had to hurt," Zork said.

Gemma whipped back through the rows of chairs, smacked into people's knees, and skirted around their shoes before she hoisted herself up again.

Bertie scurried to her side. "Sweetie, are you okay?"

"I'm okay!" she hollered. "Here's the ring, Bertie. Is it time?"

"It's time," Reverend Samuel piped in. His broad smile met Gemma's.

"Let's get this done," Zork ordered. Laughter rippled around the room—the whole barn filled with happy noise.

But when Gemma took her place again, she stared down the aisle, star-struck. Heads started spinning. "Walter!" she cried. The jolt nearly knocked her over. "You came!" She loped across the barn, kicking up hay and wrapped her arms around him. "Look everyone, he's here!"

"Bravo!" Zork thundered. "Walter, come on up here and let's get this finished."

Walter pulled away from Gemma's vice-like grip,

and proceeded straight to Zork. "Yes, sir," he said. "Where would you like me?"

"Right next to me, buddy."

"Nani, Mama!" Gemma was breathless when she went back to her spot. "Did you see who's here?"

"Yes," Nani said.

"It's wonderful," Magnolia added. "Now let's all be quiet and let Zork and Bertie get married."

"Okay, Mama. Quiet, Walter!"

"I'm already quiet, Gemma."

"Dearly beloved," the reverend continued. "Now that everyone's quiet… The rings, please." He studied the rafters. "*Please*, let's get these rings on." A splash of mirth rained over the crowd.

****

The evening light washed over the landscape, the barn twinkling everywhere. Strands of white fairy lights glittered high up over the timber beams and swooped across the tables and dance floor. A single flame quivered inside each glass hurricane, a pillar of beeswax casting a warm, tallow light on all the tables—the scent like sweet honey baking in the air. Zork and Bertie were already swaying to the music, glowing like the candlelight.

Gemma held an ice pack to her temple when she came through the barn door and witnessed everything set alight for the first time. "Holy catfish," she said. "It's a princess castle! Holy catfish."

"Don't faint," Walter told her.

"I don't faint, Walter. Only you do. But I've never seen a room like this except in the movies."

Clumps of hay and sawdust scattered the floor, the rustic wood barn a perfect backdrop to the bluegrass band already singing "If You Ain't Lovin' (You Ain't Livin')."

"That's my favorite George Strait song," Walter announced.

"Don't forget 'Smokey Mountain Boogie,' " Zork reminded the band. He twirled Bertie under his arm and leaned in for a fiery kiss. "Give us a few fast jigs too."

The old barn roof rang with laughter, the walls bulging with children. Couples whisking across the dance floor whipped up the sawdust, their jolliness spilling out like champagne. The heat from dancing kept everyone warm. No one commented when Olivia moved to the rear, grabbed her coat, and slipped out. She'd taken the table closest to the back door for a reason.

The barn stood stoically beneath a dome of stars. Light poured out from the doors and vents and radiated for miles. The sound of a fiddle floated through the night air like balm, warming the frigid bite a little. Olivia heard singing until she didn't anymore. She traveled the perimeter on top of Banjo, making a long loop around the property. He whinnied and threw his tresses snappily when she checked her phone. *No reports from backup. Perfect.* She plodded on through sleety air when she discerned someone standing in the shadows on a small, treed hill.

She reached inside her fleece lined coat and took hold of her pistol.

"Olivia, is that you?" Frosty grass crackled beneath heavy boots. Reverend Samuel stepped into a square of moonlight.

Olivia's hand relaxed on the reins. "Yes, it is. I just came out for some air." She ambled closer in near the willow tree. "I enjoy the view of things from afar." She gazed at the barn. "Look at how beautiful everything looks from here."

The reverend sauntered over the small slope and joined her. He stood by Buster's side examining the view she was fixated on. "Changes the perspective, doesn't it?"

"Yes. Something Magnolia taught me to do. She took me outside my home one night and dragged me across the field. Then she turned and said, 'Observe, Mother. How do you like it from here? Doesn't the color and art on your walls look amazing?' And she was right. From the outside peering in, it was stunning."

"Getting distance is a good thing sometimes."

"Yes. You see the whole picture—like this barn tonight. All the lights and flowers and color. Bertie made it so beautiful." Olivia bunched up her satin gown, dismounted, and tied Banjo's lead to a post under an old, weather-beaten rusty tin cover.

A sudden surge in energy reverberated from the barn when the banjo and violin struck a saucy tune—"Smokey Mountain Boogie," bounced down the hill.

"Look at them go." Olivia brightened. "Zork and Bertie sure know how to swing."

"A shame everyone's having such a terrible time," he jested.

"Isn't it?" She folded both arms across her heavy russet riding coat. Her matching boot rested on an ancient branch married to the ground. "The ceremony was lovely."

"Well, thank you. Every wedding is original, but I think this one topped them all. You know the best part?"

"Let me guess. The run-away ring, Walter's jaw-dropping entrance, or the head injury?"

"All of it." He chuckled. "All of it was real. That was the best part. Laughter is just as important as tears. Especially at a wedding."

"So true. And, now you see what it's like to be part of the Porter family."

"Look what I've been missing! Glad I met all of you."

Olivia grinned. "We're fortunate to have you in Sugar Creek, Reverend."

"Call me Hap."

"Hap?"

"Nickname given to me as a child."

"Short for…" Olivia mulled.

"Short for *happy*," he said. "Friends and family call me Hap."

"A happy little boy." Olivia stared into the fire-gold speckles dancing in his eyes. "I'm not surprised. You seem content with life."

"I am. No complaints at all."

The music stopped, and a cowbell jangled raucously above the barn door, the sound ricocheting across the fields. "Cake cutting!" they heard Magnolia announce.

The reverend swept an arm out in front of Olivia. "Lead the way," he said.

Champagne bottles popped, toasts were bestowed, and children scampered through the barn with cake stuck to their faces. And throughout the night, Olivia heard how Bertie's birdhouses gathered the singing praises from the ladies of Sugar Creek—they were an outright hit.

After the break, the band took their places again, tuning their guitars, banjos and fiddles, sorting through sheets of music.

"This next song was made by special request," the scraggly, bearded musician announced. "Magnolia, will you please join the groom for this next dance, please?"

Magnolia turned and appeared as if she hadn't heard right.

"That's right, Mag-pie! You and me this dance," Zork hollered.

When they came together on the dance floor, the guests bellowed their approval. Zork and Magnolia graciously accepted the stormy applause.

And by the third note, Olivia recognized the song.

Magnolia glided gaily across the floor, one hand in Zork's, the other draped over his shoulder. She smiled adoringly, as if sharing her merriment with a much-loved father.

Outside, petals of snow floated on the air.

"Olivia," someone said from behind her.

The musicians sang the first line of the song and a flood of emotion overtook her. For a moment, she envisioned Sam there, dancing with Magnolia. *If only*, she thought. *If only he had been given the chance.*

Unprepared for small talk, she halfheartedly turned toward the voice behind her, the band singing about a harvest moon.

His hand touched her shoulder. "Would you like to dance?" Reverend Samuel waited.

"I… No. No thank you. Excuse me," she said, and zigzagged through the throng of dancers to reach the night air. The band's rendition of Neil Young's song, "Harvest Moon," was impeccable.

Is this a flashback? In that moment it was nearly impossible to separate the past from the present. Memories sat knotted in Olivia's throat. She breathed deeply, filling her lungs with the cold black of night and watched snowflakes the size of goose-feathers waltzing around her—everything floating in shades of gray. Not unlike the night she and Sam were married. January fourteenth remained a sacred date.

I never stop feeling you. She channeled Sam. *You're back again. God knows I wish you were here with me tonight.*

Olivia buttoned her coat, bunched up her dress, and climbed on top the roan's back. She took off for the river, looping the perimeter again.

"Shake it off," she heard Sam tell her. *"Shake this off and get your head back in the game."* It worked. Hearing his voice always did.

She rode back, afraid to be gone too long. She didn't want Zork to worry.

"Olivia?" Another voice was outside her head. For a moment she questioned her mental state.

"Who's there?"

Someone moved from the shadows, giving her a clear view. "It's Hap, again."

"Hi, Hap-again." She sounded silly, even to herself. "I needed a break from the noise. Guess I'm getting old." She meant to lighten the atmosphere but couldn't tell if she had. Olivia dismounted and led the horse to the barn.

"I'll walk with you," he offered, hands clasped behind his back. "My ears need a break too, but honestly..." He twisted his body her way. "Can we talk?"

Her spine tautened. "May I say something first? If you don't mind…"

"Of course," he said.

"I didn't mean to be rude when you asked me to dance. It wasn't intentional." She continued toward the horse stalls. "I'm sorry I overreacted. It was silly of me."

"No need to apologize," he said. "I came to make sure you were okay."

"Let me explain," she continued. "I lost my husband years ago."

"Yes, I'm aware—and I'm sorry. I heard it was a tragic accident."

"The song playing…" She stroked Banjo's nose in an effort to remain composed. "As much as I love dancing, that song is full of memories for me. And in that moment I was flooded with them. My husband and I danced to it the first time we met, at our wedding, and every anniversary thereafter. That song is only for him."

His face turned slack. "Olivia. I'm so sorry." The reverend helped lead Banjo into a stall.

"It's okay. Just one of those things. Reminders still pop up and always will."

"I understand more than you know," he said gently. "And I want to be up front with you about something too."

His tone took Olivia aback. "Please, say whatever you'd like."

"I enjoy your friendship, but friendship is the only thing I want anymore. I'm simply not interested in more than that. I won't marry again. I don't want my interest in you as a friend, or my asking you to dance to be misinterpreted."

"You were married?"

"Twenty-five years. She died of cancer."

"How painful for you. I'm sorry, Reverend."

"Hap," he corrected.

"Hap, I mean. How devastating for you both."

"Yes. And still is. One morning when we thought treatments were working well, she fell asleep and never woke up." He peered into Olivia's eyes. "Took the June sunshine right out of that day and for a long time filled my home with unbearable, aching loss. Saddest season of my life."

"I understand." Olivia gazed at the slushy mud covering the toes of her boots. "Sounds like it was a peaceful passing."

"Yes. For that I'll always be grateful."

"I bet," she said, thinking of Sam's last minutes.

He nodded. "But long story short, I'm not interested in anything beyond a friendship with anyone. Just so we're clear."

"Wow." Olivia's brows arched.

"I'm sorry. I know I'm blunt and I'm sure that seems a bit odd, but—"

"Odd?" She gasped. "*Odd*? Hardly!" she retorted. "It's a breath of fresh air! An absolute relief—because I feel the same way. The exact same way."

"Really?" he asked.

"Yes, really!"

"Well, that takes a load off, doesn't it?" He held the back of his neck. "And I want you to know it's not you."

"No, it's okay! And I want you to know it's not you, either."

"Clearly," he said, "we'll always be in love with other people."

"Yes. That's exactly it."

"Even though my wife died years ago, I won't ever leave her."

"Nor will I leave my husband. And I'm fine with that."

"Me too. I have true peace about it."

"I know what you mean." Olivia stroked Banjo's cheek. "It's the same for me."

"Well, I feel so much better. You know, you're the first person I've said this to who hasn't taken it all wrong. And if we ever do dance someday, we'll enjoy it without any strings attached."

"That sounds splendid, Hap. Let's shake on it."

So they did.

When their hands clasped, Olivia sensed something familiar about the warmth in his touch. For a fraction of a second she imagined the intimacy his wife had known with him, but swiftly dismissed the idea before she could think any more about it.

On their way back to the party, Olivia pondered the validity of someone's handshake. She was taught a handshake was as binding as an iron-clad legal document. In other words, something truly catastrophic would need to occur to void such an agreement. In her opinion only a miracle could break something as strong as that. But, as Olivia knew, miracles didn't happen often. Only now and then.

Both of them danced gaily the rest of the night, but not with each other. Still, the freedom on their faces, and the light that surrounded them was new. For Olivia, it was the joy in feeling deeply understood and of like mind with a friend—maybe she surmised, the same joy that makes friends into soul mates.

"If I didn't know better"—Zork leaned into Olivia's ear—"I'd think Sam was right here with you tonight."

"I'm having a great time." She smiled. "Such fun dancing with the girls."

"Yes, it is." Zork reflected. "And you know, while I was marrying Bertie, I imagined Sam right up there with me. He'll always be the best man."

Chapter Thirty-Seven

Two Strangers

The feathery snowflakes that had fallen over the valley the night of the wedding melted the next day. A dusty gray-blue sky with a purplish undertone shone as vibrant as a painting next to the lime green grass fields. Every time the light created this blend of colors, Olivia stopped and marveled. "Here you go, Banjo," she said. "Buster shared this view with me for years. It's your turn now."

A blustery wind knocked her hat off, whipping her hair into a frenzy. "Easy boy," she told him, bending to retrieve it from her boot. She repositioned it and grabbed for the phone buzzing in her pocket. "Yes?"

"Olivia, it's Hap. Thought you should know. I recognized those two fellas again. Not in the same place, but sure seemed like they were headed for Luper."

"Checking it out now." She nudged Banjo forward. "Thanks so much for letting me know."

"You know Gemma's there?"

"At Luper?"

"Yes. Just saw her. I think she's alone."

"Need to run. Thanks, Hap!" That's when she caught sight of the next message. A text that read: "Your lack of cooperation is getting on our nerves. But glad you and the kid have such an affinity for graveyards. She'll soon be in one if you ignore us. Send information ASAP. Clock is ticking."

Olivia dropped the phone in her breast pocket, pushed her hips forward, and gave Banjo a hard squeeze. "Go!" He broke, his hooves sliding on rock and dirt down the hill. He hit bottom, gained speed, and tore through the fields. As soon as Olivia reached Luper, she reined him back, glancing around.

"Nani!" she heard Gemma call out. Her voice was full of happiness like usual.

Olivia's spine softened, her drubbing heart did too. "Gemma? Where are you?"

"Hiding!"

Olivia scanned everything but didn't see her.

"In our tree!" she laughed.

The smell of good earth filled Olivia's lungs when she dismounted. "Everything okay?"

"Sure! And guess what? I get to babysit today."

"Gemma, you agreed not to come here alone. That was the rule." Olivia kept her tone steady, even as her fury swelled.

"Even to Luper? Besides, I wasn't alone!" Gemma scrambled out of the tree, her words racing. "Walter was here with me the whole time except for right now, because I have to drive home and babysit for my friend soon, but Walter and I walked to the river and guess what?"

"Slow your words, Gem." Olivia's lecture would have to wait.

"I told him River's name—and he loves it." She exhaled.

"Good. I was sure he would. Now about—"

305

"Zorro said we couldn't walk to the river during the party last night, so I didn't get to do what I planned, but it's okay. It was Zorro's wedding after all—he didn't want me to leave."

"Of course not. And if Zork hadn't forbid it, I would have. Because you know the rule—"

"That's why I asked! Plus I didn't want to miss the cake and dancing."

"No, of course not. But Gem—"

"At first Walter didn't like the name though. He thought only rivers should be called rivers. Not people."

"Ah. Well—"

"Then I told him lots of people have names like nature. You know, like Rainbow, and Rose, and Star, and things like that."

Olivia put the scolding on hold and peered through her binoculars, rotating until she had checked the landscape surrounding them.

"And now he likes it."

"Well, good." Olivia searched up the road. "Honey, where's your car?"

"At the church parking lot."

"I'll walk over with you. Have you noticed any strangers around today?" She plucked her field glasses back into her pocket.

"Yes. Oh wait. No. Only the reverend."

"No strangers on horses?"

"No…" Gemma searched the sky, thinking. "Wait. I did see those two weird guys again. I almost forgot they were strangers! They were at the river. And that was today."

"At the river?"

"Yeah. I think they could hear Walter and me."

"The same ones we saw before?"

"Yes. Pretty sure. But maybe not."

"Why?"

"They looked different up close."

Olivia's face must have blanched white. "How close were they?"

"Not that close, but sorta close. They were wading in the shallow rocks. Almost on the other side. But I kept my big fat eye nailed on them, Nani. And I heard them too."

"You heard them?"

"Hey!" Gemma's face lit up. "They *are* the same guys!"

"How do you know?"

"They talked funny."

"Like they were speaking Russian?"

"I don't know Russian, silly."

"You're right. But did they have strong accents? As if speaking a different language?"

"Yes. Choppy, hard sounding words. Not like ours."

Olivia waited for her eyes to meet Gemma's. "I'm saying this again. You must listen to me and do your best to remember this. I don't want you anywhere around here unless I'm with you. Not the river, not even Luper. We've been through this already. You broke the rule, Gemma. There cannot be any exceptions. *None*. Understood?"

"But I wasn't alone! I had Walter with me. He'll protect me. He promised he would."

"*No exceptions*. The rule is you don't come back alone with Walter, either. They aren't safe men to be around. Do you understand?"

"I understand. I don't like them either. But tell me again—why don't we like them?

"You have to trust me on this." Olivia held her hand over her gut. "You have to trust your feelings and trust *my words*. From here on, you only take outings with me. That's an order."

"Or with Zorro," Gemma added.

"No, Gemma. *Only* with me. Zork is gone. He's on his honeymoon, remember?"

"Oh, yeah!" A pained stare crossed Gemma's face. "Ohhh. Poor Bertie Lou. Poor, *poor* Bertie." Pain wrapped around every word. "I forgot to warn her about the honeymoon bladder attacks."

"No need, hon. They don't happen that often. She'll be fine."

"Well, one time's enough. I haven't forgotten it."

"I'm sure you haven't. But you handled it, didn't you?"

"Barely."

"Well, Bertie can too. She can take care of herself."

"Okay." Gemma fished for her keys and inadvertently pushed the panic button. The blaring horn caught the reverend's attention. He stepped outside and watched. "Oh, no." Gemma giggled. "Make it stop!"

Olivia waited for Gemma to figure it out.

"I gotta get going now," Gemma said. "The baby is being dropped off at my house soon."

"Who are you babysitting for?"

"A friend at my work. She has challenges too, but not many."

"So, it's okay with your caseworkers? They know, right?"

"They always know." Gemma scanned the road, her arms wiggling. "I have to hurry!"

"Who's supervising while you babysit?"

"I don't exactly know. But they'll be there like always."

"Okay, well, call if you need anything."

"I will, but I better get home fast." Gemma embraced Olivia with a firm grip. "Love you," she said.

"Love you more."

Gemma lit up when she dropped into the driver's seat and slammed the door. "More than what?" she grinned through the open window.

"More than the best gift *ever* under my Christmas tree."

Gemma's smile spread as wide as the McKenzie River.

"Drive safe," Olivia instructed. "Take your time, and watch your speed limit."

"I do, and I'm good at it. Sometimes I drive one mile an hour faster or slower, but usually not two."

"Okay. Good job. I do believe you're the safest driver I know. I mean it."

Gemma jammed down the accelerator and then abruptly hit the brakes. She jubilantly watched as a flock of wild turkeys strutted across the road in front of her, their rich bronze and copper plumage fanning out in full display.

After they passed, Olivia waved her off and Gemma laid on the horn in a long blast goodbye.

Hap turned after he finished locking up the church. "Everything okay?"

"For the moment, yes. But I don't like the way those two strangers keep showing up."

"I've tried to find out who those fellas are, but no one seems to know," he said.

"They aren't from around here."

"Oh? You seem more concerned." He stepped across the parking lot and stopped when he had a view of the hills.

"I am. I've warned Gemma about them. She's not to take any more trips here alone. And sometimes being with Walter is the same as being alone, I'm afraid."

"Well, they could be harmless. Maybe just a couple of fly-fisherman scoutin' around."

Sure. If they fly-fish with long-range sniper rifles.

"Let me know if I can do anything," the reverend added. "I'm usually close by."

"Thank you, Hap. Appreciate you watching out for her."

"Sure thing." He reached for the handle on a raggedy-ass '69 Ford Bronco convertible.

Olivia supposed at one time the two-tone paint shined like candy apple red and Wimbledon white. Not anymore. It was an old rusty clunker now. "That's *yours*?" she asked.

He nodded. "Running on prayers."

"Definitely has the cool factor," she said.

"It's a jumpy old banger." The reverend tossed his coat inside. "Somehow I've kept it going despite all logic and reason."

Olivia's eyebrows raised with pleasure. "I love it."

The reverend was halfway in but hesitated. "Hey, do you have a minute? Remember those photos I was telling you about?"

"The ones of the old schoolhouse on River Road? And of Luper?"

310

"Yes! I found them. And I was wrong about the year. They were taken even earlier."

"Wow!" Olivia moved toward him.

He checked his watch. "Have time now?"

"Let's go," she said.

He unlocked the sanctuary door, pushing it all the way back. A gust of old-church smell smacked her in the face. She stepped inside and breathed in. Waxed floors, dusty books, and ancient wood—the smell of history and religion.

"You think you'll ever give our church another try?"

"Oh, probably," she said.

"I hope you will. You should come back."

"I only attend when I feel inspired to. So maybe I will, maybe I won't. Nothing personal, Hap."

The reverend smiled. "Fair enough." He tossed the keys back in his pocket. "This way." He directed her to a library in the back of his office, switched on a light, and pulled a box off the bookshelf. One by one he lifted the fragile black and white photos out of the box and spread them across the table.

"This one was taken from the north end of River Road."

Olivia set her reading glasses on her nose. "All those orchards. How sad so many are gone."

"And here's a picture of the first railroad stop in our area. It's still standing."

"On Meadowview?"

"Yes, that's it."

"I love that building. And I love that it's been restored."

"My team worked on that one too."

"No kidding." Olivia perked up. "You give me an idea."

"What's that?"

"I'd like to volunteer on the next one you work on. Keep me informed—please. I love that you do this."

"I will indeed. Thank you." The reverend tapped his finger on a photo. "Now, here are the Luper descendants. Six of them anyway. In front of the original homestead. Little Harriet's relative is in this one. Bertie's too."

"Oh, my goodness. Those dresses," she said, angling it toward the light. "Did people ever smile in those days?"

The reverend tittered. "They do look like a gloomy bunch, don't they?"

"Yes. Dreadful."

"It wasn't considered proper smiling for photos back then," he said.

"No, I suppose not. They had reputations to uphold." She dragged a chair to the table and sat back surveying the windowsill. A gang of crippled daddy-long-legs lay belly-up on the windowsill, scorched, she assumed, by a beam of hot sun. "Ever notice how we disappear as we age, Reverend? I mean, Hap."

"Disappear?"

"It seems like aging is a bit of a vanishing act." Olivia scooted the chair closer scanning over the photos. "When I see pictures of myself as a teenager, I realize that young woman is gone forever."

The reverend turned and watched her speak.

"It's as if every year we lose another image of ourselves. Never that exact same person again. We simply disappear—left only with memories or pictures like these."

The reverend collected the photos, gently setting them in the box. "But your soul remains," he said. "It's your soul that carries your life, not your body. And the soul is ageless." He placed the box up on the shelf again. "It's the perfect argument for faith," he said. "We don't just disappear, Olivia."

Chapter Thirty-Eight

A Momentous Decision

Gemma was worn out. At twelve weeks pregnant, she still ate like a horse and could sleep all afternoon if she wanted. But the thought of the pint of chocolate mint ice cream in the freezer kept her upright and searching for a spoon.

Besides, she had a friend's napping four-month-old baby in her care. She wasn't allowed to sleep on the job.

The nurse at the prenatal clinic warned Gemma about eating too much sugar during pregnancy. But it sounded so good, she decided to forget. Just this once. She poured hot fudge, whipped cream, and chopped nuts over the whole pint and joined Walter in the living room.

"Whoa." Walter's eyes bugged out.

"I forgot. Did you want some?"

"No. Dairy gives me flatulence, remember?"

"Oh, yeah. You don't need a gassy chassis. The baby's mother might come back and think it's me."

Walter wrinkled his nose and nodded. "That would be a scream."

And then he shot to his feet, the remote and two pillows sailed through the air. "Touchdown! Yes!"

"Shhh!" Gemma ordered. "Be quiet! The baby,

Walter. You can't yell when babies are here."

"Sorry. But that was a touchdown."

"That does not mean you yell about it."

"Yes, it does, Gemma. Touchdowns mean it's time to yell." He sat again. "It's a game."

"Then you can't watch games here unless you cover your mouth with a pillow like I do when I want to scream and yell and bawl my eyes out."

"Okay."

"Do you want to hold the baby?" she asked. "For practice? It's easy when they're asleep."

"No," he said, eyes glued on the television.

Gemma set her casserole-sized bowl of heaven on the coffee table and scurried off. When she came back she had a flannel receiving blanket wrapped in her arms.

"Here," she offered. "Hold him, Walt."

His head jerked when he laid his peeps on it. "No, Gemma. I can't. Don't give him to me! And call me Walter. Remember?"

"Just try," she coaxed.

"I don't have to. I am not the babysitter. You are."

"Look, goofy." She pulled back the blanket.

Walter's eyes bugged out. "Potatoes?!"

"The real baby is asleep in the crib. Like this sack of potatoes."

"The potatoes are not asleep, Gemma."

"I know that! But when he's asleep this is how he feels. This is just practice."

"But he's not a sack of potatoes."

"Of course not, silly. It's pretend! You can't hurt potatoes. All you have to do is hold them. I'll help you."

"I don't want to, Gemma. That will make me sweat." Walter stood and paced across the floor.

"That's why you should practice. Babies won't bite you. Neither do potatoes."

"I know that." His pace quickened. "You're making me extremely nervous."

"What if I get sick and break a bone and you are the only one who can pick up my baby? I mean our baby. What then? It's half your baby, too, you know. You helped make her, remember?"

"I remember that, Gemma. I'll call for help."

"What if no one can get here in time and the baby might fall out a window?"

Walter spun around and searched. "What window?"

"I said, *what if*. I want to know if you'll save our baby if you have to."

"Oh." Walter's face turned pensive. His back straightened. "Yes. I will. I will save it and you too if you need help. I promised I would always protect you."

"I know. Okay."

"If I hold the sack of potatoes, is that all I have to do?"

"Yes. And pretend it's the baby. That's all you have to do. Just pretend."

Walter sat and leaned back into the sofa, arms outstretched and waiting.

Gemma gently set the flannel-wrapped sack in his arms. "There. Just like this."

Half the sack slid off the side of his elbow.

"Oh nooo," Gemma giggled. "You're losing the baby!"

"See?!" Walter blustered. "What do I do?"

Gemma was afraid he might cry.

"It's okay. Potatoes are much harder to hold than babies. Here…" She shoved the bag up over his arm and stood back. "There. See how easy it is?"

"Now what do I do?"

"Nothing. Well, you can talk to it and kiss it if you want."

Walter made a face. "I refuse to kiss a potato."

"Okay then, don't." She tiptoed into her bedroom to check on the baby. When the door squeaked open, his little arms and legs jerked. He sighed heavily, sound asleep in the new white crib—a gift to Gemma from the ladies of Sugar Creek. Hanging on the outside of the railing was a beaded wool baby bonnet covered in vibrantly stitched floral stars, a handmade gift from friends in the Cow Creek community. Displaying it made her baby feel real.

I can't wait to take her to a powwow. Gemma imagined River, scarcely out of the spirit world, twirling in a shawl—ribbons flying gracefully through the air, a heartbeat of drums beneath her feet.

She bent over the rail, leaning in. His new baby scent wafted in the air. *Is it sweet milkiness or buttermilk biscuits?* She only knew it was one of the most pleasing aromas she had ever come in contact with. In reality, Gemma knew a baby's fragrance smelled like nothing but itself. *It's a mystery,* she decided. *Like our old maple—you can't exactly describe it.*

The infant boy's puffy cheeks and tiny lips puckered a bit. Gemma peered closely at him, her hand planted on the fig-sized baby growing in her own belly. "Here's your friend, River," she whispered. "Someday you'll be in this same crib, and I'll stare at you and smell your baby scent too." A shiver of excitement made her spine tingle when she held the thought. *It's true. I'm having one of my own.*

The blanket rose and fell peacefully as the little boy breathed in and out. Gemma lifted the flannel sheet and stared at his chest to confirm it. *Yes, he's breathing.* She tenderly stoked the wild swatch of copper hair sprouted like a turnip at the top of his head.

Gemma reviewed in her mind what she would do if he stopped breathing. She opened the handbook from her class with pictures in it and tested herself. She made a quiet fist bump. *Yes! I got it right.* She lifted the light blanket over him again, poked around the edges of his diaper, and peered closely at his chest one more time. *Still dry and still breathing. Everything's good.* Gemma turned away feeling proud of herself.

Walter's nose appeared in the crack of the door. "Gemma," he said, his voice hushed but urgent. "*Gemma*," he said louder.

"Hang on," she snarled. "Don't say another thing until I come out." She tiptoed from the bedroom and nudged him toward the kitchen with a strong elbow. "Listen," she whispered, but not awfully well. "Don't come in there where the baby is and yell at me."

"I wasn't yelling. I lowered my voice like this, *Gemma,"* he repeated.

And this bothered Gemma, too. She shook her head. "You still sound too loud."

"But I have to go to work."

"Good! Because I want it quiet here, Walt. I mean, Walter."

"Okay. But you have to give me a ride,

remember?"

Gemma's face stiffened. "I do?"

"Yes! And fast. Or I'll be fired."

"*Today*?"

"Today," he repeated. "Now! Remember? I work at four o' clock in the afternoon."

"But the baby is here. Call someone else."

"There is no one else. I can't do that. I'll get fired. Take me like you said you would. You promised."

"I know I promised, but wait. I have an idea. We can take the baby with us."

"Okay," he said. "But hurry."

"Wait—" She halted again. "I can't. I don't have a car seat yet. It's against the law. And it's not safe holding a baby in a lap."

"Okay, well, you can drive me there and come right back. He won't know. He's asleep."

"Don't rush me," Gemma said, her voice on edge. "I have to think."

"Think fast. We have to go!"

"But what if he wakes up?" she asked.

"He's in a crib, right?"

"Yes."

"Are cribs safe?"

"Stop twisting me up like a pretzel!"

"A pretzel? How could I do that?"

"You're making me confused."

"Okay. But is the crib safe?"

"Yes. If the rails are up and locked. Maybe he would sleep the whole time. If I hurry. Wait," she said, arms wiggling. "I have to think."

"Keep thinking. But we're leaving!"

"I think it's okay because the crib rail can't come

down and I'll lock the front door. And he's still asleep. I'll hurry back super-fast before he wakes up. It'll be like I'm in the bathroom or something. Won't it?"

"Yes, it will. Now hurry. I can't get fired!"

"I know that!"

"Okay," Walter said. "We need to go." He stomped out the door and down the steps to her car.

"Everything's locked," Gemma said out loud on the porch. "He has a diaper on. And he's not crying. He already had a bottle so he's not hungry. And a fire protector is in his room. Okay, I'm hurrying, Walt. I mean Walter."

Something gnawed inside when she rushed after him. *Always trust your gut*, Nani had told her so many times. *Your feelings will tell you what to do.*

But Gemma ignored the gnawing in her gut and trusted the wrong thing. "My feelings are telling me to hurry," she told Walter. "I'm going to drive *three* miles an hour faster than usual. So, hold on."

****

On the way home, Gemma braked for a red light, remembering the sound of exploding glass and metal from the car crash. It was a violent, brutally cruel noise she hoped never to hear again. When the light switched green she inched slowly into the intersection, scanning for runaway vehicles the way she and Zorro scanned for air traffic. And then her gut wrenched. *I need to get home!* All her limbs, wiggling.

Only a quarter mile later, she had to stop again. *Nuts, another red one!* She braked, immediately distracted by a young couple strolling along the sidewalk. The man's fingers bumped against the woman's until their hands fully clasped; each finger entwined with the other so tight they became one hand. Gemma studied it in her mind. No one spoke, but something strange happened between them. *Like when we made River...*

A horn blasted from behind. "Oh my gosh. Sorry!" She waved at the driver in her rear view mirror and stepped on the gas. *The baby.* Her heart plunged again. *I left him!* Gemma knew she was in trouble even before she was. Even before she rounded the corner and spotted the police car.

Up the stairs, the door to her apartment stood wide open. And in front of it stood a uniformed police officer.

And that's when Gemma knew she had made a mistake so big that no matter how hard she tried, it could never be tinked away.

Chapter Thirty-Nine

The Turning Point

Please. Please, let him be okay, Gemma pleaded to whoever might be listening. *I'll do anything if you let him be okay.*

"Nani," she said, huddled over the phone. "I did a wrong, bad thing," she gasped. "Super bad." A spasm squeezed her abdomen.

"Gemma, where are you?"

"Inside my car." She blew air out like a horse. "At my apartment."

"Go upstairs, Gemma. The police are waiting for you."

"You know about the police?"

"Yes. They called me and…"

Gemma's brain did a somersault. She couldn't hear what she said.

"Gemma. Listen to me. Go tell them who you are. I'll be there in a few minutes."

"Is he okay, Nani? Is the baby alive?"

"The baby is alive, but—"

The phone tumbled out of her hands, her face pressed into the crook of her arm. *Thank you, thank you, thank you,* she silently mouthed. *It's all okay.*

Gemma climbed the stairs, knees buckling at the top step. A police officer and a familiar looking woman wearing a badge around her neck stood outside the door. Gemma's tongue tangled up when she tried to speak. She didn't know what else to do but freeze.

"Excuse me, may I help you?" The woman went up to her. "You're Gemma Porter, aren't you?"

"Yes. And I didn't mean to—" Air burst from her chest. The words had wheeled right out, but they didn't feel like her own. She pressed the palms of her hands against both cheeks, as if that would stop the waterworks.

"Come this way, Gemma." The woman introduced herself as a county social worker. "We met once before. Go ahead and take a seat in your living room."

"Where's the baby?" Gemma asked.

"He's been taken by a caseworker. His mother has been notified."

"Why, or how, I mean what…" Her words tripped over themselves. "How did you get inside?"

"You had inspections today."

I forgot! Gemma remembered that much.

"When no one answered the door, your manager let the housing inspector in. They found the baby alone and crying."

"Crying?" Gemma wanted to faint and never wake up.

"Yes. And he was here alone."

Gemma grabbed hold of her stomach and dropped her head. "I feel kinda sick. Can I go in my bathroom?"

"Of course," the woman told her.

Gemma sprang up too fast, her brain buzzing like a saw. She leaned against the wall.

"You okay?"

"Yes." She straightened and took a few steps.

The police officer went to her side. "Have you had any alcohol, or drugs today?" she asked.

"No. I never do that. Even when I'm not pregnant."

The officer glared at the social worker.

"Gemma *is* pregnant," she said.

"Oh." The officer glanced at Gemma's waist and cocked her head.

"She's still growing," Gemma offered. "See?" She pulled up her shirt and stood sideways.

"Go ahead to the bathroom, ma'am." The officer followed and stayed nearby until the bathroom door locked.

The sound of comfort soared through the air on wings when Gemma heard Nani's voice. "I'm Olivia Porter—Gemma's grandmother."

Thank Creator she's here.

"Your granddaughter's in the bathroom," the officer told her.

"Is she okay?"

"Looks a little woozy. I don't think she's feeling well."

When Gemma stepped out, Nani clenched her hand and lead her to the sofa. "I have the runs, Graham. It's my nerves again."

The social worker glanced up from her laptop. "There's a glass of water for you, Gemma." Her face crinkled noticing the sack of potatoes on the carpet.

"Oh—" Gemma offered. "That's our pretend baby."

All eyes skittered between the potatoes and Gemma and back to the potatoes again.

"See, I gave it to Walter so he could practice holding a baby. So he can feel braver about holding mine. I mean ours. He's the daddy, and he needs practice. That's all." Gemma searched the woman's face, waiting for approval. "And," she added proudly, "I've already been to a parenting class. Ten stars for all ten hours." She sipped the water, still not seeing her approval.

The woman fiddled with her badge. "I'm afraid this is more complicated than last time."

"Last time?" Nani asked, but everyone ignored her.

"I don't understand." Gemma gulped from the glass this time.

"Remember when we talked last year?"

"I think so. But maybe not."

"This is your third incident. And by far the worst."

Nani's eyes bulged. "*Third incident?*"

"But I never made this mistake before!" Gemma blurted.

The woman scrolled down her screen. "The first report involved an unrestrained child. You were the driver. The child sat in someone's lap," she read.

"But that was my friend's child!" Gemma's voice raised to a new level. "Not mine! That's what she told me to do. I remember that. The little baby was hungry! They needed their food stamps, and they *both* had to be there." She pivoted toward Nani. "I remember explaining this to them."

"Yes, you did explain this." The woman kept turning a pen over in her fingers while she spoke. "But you broke the law pertaining to child safety."

"I know that! That's why I didn't take the baby today. See? Because I don't have a car seat yet. I remembered not to sit a baby on someone's lap. I *remembered* that."

"But this time you left a baby alone." Her voice grew stern. "That's against the law too."

Gemma felt her eyes grow to the size of saucers. "But he couldn't fall out because the rails were up in the lock position and he was sleeping. And I locked the door, including the bolt. And I hurried as fast as I could."

"But Gemma," Nani said. "Fires happen—"

"I thought of that too! I did. See, my fire alarm works. It has a new battery in it so the fire trucks would be called."

Stony glances ping-ponged around the room. The whole apartment fell into a thick silence that pressed on Gemma's ears.

"Babies get sick," Nani said. "Things happen. Sometimes quickly."

"I know that. But he wasn't sick. Not even when I left. I touched his head. No fever. And the fire alarm is working!"

"But no one was here. Babies can never be left alone. Ever," Nani said gently. "There's a reason it's against the law."

Gemma's eyebrows gathered in, her peepers squeezed shut. "I know I messed up. I know I did. But Walter was right. He couldn't get fired. I thought of everything I could to make the right decision, but I knew driving home I did it wrong. I should have been with him every second."

"That's right," the woman said. "You made a serious mistake. You also broke the rules when you agreed to babysit without supervision."

Gemma's head dropped, shamefaced.

"Tink, you told me—"

"I know! But I wasn't alone," Gemma stuttered. "Walter was here. He *is* a supervisor."

"Yes. He works in auto parts," Nani clarified. "He doesn't supervise childcare. I think you know the difference."

Gemma crossed her arms and plunked her chin in a hand. "I thought it would be fun for us to practice by ourselves. That's all. With a real baby."

The woman blathered on as if nothing Gemma had said mattered at all. "So you made more than one mistake today. But leaving a child alone is a criminal charge. You'll need to go to court this time."

"I'm going to jail?" Gemma couldn't swallow, her throat as dry as Nani's homemade cornbread.

"I can't answer that. I don't make those decisions."

Gemma leaned back, squeezing her hands together. They were slippery wet.

"You said three incidents," Nani said. "What was the second one?"

The woman clicked through a file. "The second report involved an injury to this same child."

"What kind of injury?" Nani wore a bewildered expression.

"I drove him and his mom to the emergency room. That's all! She put his car seat in my car," Gemma said. "He hurt himself bad and needed help! Somebody needed to take him to the hospital, so I did."

Nani stared at the woman, waiting.

"It was suspected child abuse. Gemma went with the mother. She also had been in the home that day, so this was flagged on her record."

"And what did you find?"

"Inconclusive, but highly suspect for physical

abuse."

"Gemma?" Nani asked. "What happened?"

"Nothing. He fell and hit his face and broke his arm."

"You saw it happen?"

"No. His mom told me. She needed someone to drive them for help. I told them everything, Nani. Like I am now, and—"

"Yes, you did tell us," the woman interrupted. "And we also explained you were at risk of losing your license if there was a third incident. Which brings us to today. I'd like you to tell me everything you did from the time you…"

The woman talked and talked and talked. But Gemma couldn't catch her words. They spun around the room making her dizzy. She grimaced, leaning into her gut. "I have the trots again. I'm sorry."

"Okay." The woman stood. "Let's take a break. We'll talk more when you're ready."

Nani took Gemma's arm and led her to the bathroom. "You okay, Tink?"

"No. But yeah."

"Okay. I'm calling your mom. I'll be right outside your bathroom window. Holler if you need me."

Gemma locked the bathroom door and pushed the window up a crack. She wanted to air out the stink, but more importantly, she wanted to eavesdrop.

Nani's phone was on speaker when she stepped out on the front porch balcony. "You're hired, Maggie," Gemma heard her say.

"Mom? What are you talking about?"

"Gemma needs a good lawyer," Nani said. "And please… Don't tell me you told me so."

Chapter Forty

Judgment Day

The following week another ugly beast of a big, cold sky moved over the valley. Freezing rain soaked everything. But Gemma's usual zest for high-spirited talk hadn't been dampened by the weather—it had been dampened by her fears of what the judge might say. A sinking sensation hit as soon as she entered the courtroom, a sad, tired-looking place that smelled doggy.

Gemma sat in a blonde wooden chair, yellowed like an old tooth. She stared at her palms and tried to calm her breathing.

"Your Honor," Mama's attorney friend began, "as noted in Gemma Porter's evaluations, she is high functioning in all activities of daily living, and—"

The judge interrupted. Gemma didn't know why.

Mama's attorney friend straightened, turned a piece of paper over on the table in front of them and continued. "Furthermore," she added, "we would like to submit to the court our recommendations for a comprehensive parenting plan, which includes in-home assistance and—"

The judge stopped her again. Gemma couldn't listen anymore; the conversation was a bumpy one. Everyone speaking back and forth made her light-headed.

"Gemma," Mama said. "Do you understand what the judge asked you?"

"What?" The room funneled in, then whirled out again. *Who said what?*

"The judge is giving you the chance to speak right now."

"About anything?"

"Yes. If you want to."

"Should I stand?" She glanced between her attorney and Mama.

"Yes," her attorney said. "Stand and speak directly to the judge."

Gemma lifted gently off her seat, hands gripping the table's edge. "Your highness, I—"

Her attorney tapped her arm. "Your honor," she corrected.

Gemma heard the cracks of unkind laughter behind her. *I have to be brave.*

"Sorry, your highness, I mean honor! Your honor." She smiled, trying to be friendly, but the grin stuck to her face and didn't come off. The next words had to be elbowed off her tongue. "I just want to say that sometimes what's hard for regular thinkers is easy for me. Sometimes I even know things others don't."

For a few moments, maybe longer, Gemma made fish lips trying to relax her grin. Pulse pounding, she continued, "Sometimes people learn things from me. You can ask them. Because what I bring to this world matters." She gave her arms and fingers a quick wiggle.

Without warning, a perfect picture flashed in front of her. It was River, at five-years-old, swinging on the old maple. *Maybe it's a sign*. She closed her eyes to remember it. *A good sign.*

Moments later, Gemma's words rose up with newfound strength. "What I have to say is, I may not be able to do a lot of things. And some things I may never get right. But I *can* love. I can do that. And that's the most important thing. See, my baby needs me." Gemma lowered into her seat but shot back up again. "*Oh!* And she needs Mama, too. And Nani, for our rides to the bone orchard. I mean, Luper, the place for dead bodies where we have picnics. Thank you."

Gemma's cheeks must have pulsed ruby-red, flashing as bright as the ancient billboard off the freeway—the one ballyhooing the Go-Go Girls strip club.

The caseworker ushered Gemma to a private hall outside the courtroom, the attorney and Mama following. They all discussed one thing after another before the caseworker shifted and spoke directly to Gemma. "So here's the deal," she explained. But Gemma couldn't tune in. She only heard single words tossed in the air, such as, "charged," "criminal," guilty," "plea," "jail time," "Seattle…"

And some were phrases, like, "…your only option," and "…we need a plan or else."

But then she heard this: "You won't be going home from the hospital with your baby if you don't agree to a plan. That's the deal."

"Huh?" Gemma asked.

"The judge decided that you can't take care of a baby by yourself," her caseworker explained. "Which is why we were offered a plea deal. If you agree to live with your mother, you'll avoid the possibility of jail time and your baby won't be taken from you at birth."

"But Mama lives in Seattle. I don't live there."

"Gemma"—the caseworker steadied her eyes—"the only option you have is to move to Seattle and live with your mom. If you want to keep your baby."

"She's right," Mama said. "This is the best deal we could get. And it's a good one, considering."

Gemma swore the room rotated. She dropped on a bench and landed with a thunk. "I never want to be a jailbird."

Mama handed Gemma a small paper cup of water. She slugged it back the way Nani took a shot of Tennessee whiskey. "*Me?*" She hiccupped, sounding like a drunken seal. "Move to Seattle? That will change everything." She balled up the paper cup in her fist. "My baby needs to live near the river I named her for. We belong here, not in Seattle. I can't leave."

Gemma's lawyer was the first to speak. "There is one other option. One that would allow you and the baby to remain here."

"And not go to jail?"

"Correct. No jail time."

"Okay! I'll do that one!"

"Let her explain, first," Mama said.

"We could arrange for an open adoption if that's something you'd consider. I gathered some information in case you'd be interested. Locally, there's a family right now who might be a good fit. But of course, no one will ever be contacted without your permission."

"You mean, I'd give her away?"

"Yes, but with the ability to stay involved as her birth mother for the rest of her life. You'd be allowed regular contacts and visits. You'd have a relationship with her."

"Visits? I'm not *visiting* my baby. She's mine!"

"She *is* yours," her lawyer explained. "She'd always be yours. No matter who raised her that wouldn't change. It's simply another option."

"But I have to keep her." Terror clawed at Gemma's chest. "I'm her mama! No one else can be her mama, but me."

"I understand." Her lawyer nodded gently. "Then, can you agree to live with your mother in Seattle? Is that the option you'd like me to present to the court? We need to go in now. With a plan."

"I was supposed to get supervision before babysitting. That's all. Why can't the plan be to give me another chance?"

"It's not just about the babysitting," Mama said. "And there are no more chances. The judge made that clear."

Her words plunged Gemma deeper into despair, her forehead tight as a vice.

"You need my help, Gem. It means a move to Seattle."

Gemma nodded, even as everything inside herself told her she was dead. "Fine."

When they filed slowly back into the courtroom and sat, Gemma hardly felt a part of her surroundings. Even her own arms and legs didn't feel familiar.

The judge talked about police reports, caseworker notes, legal petitions, parenting plans, evaluations, and assessments. And in Gemma's mind, at least a thousand other documents, all of them rattling loose in her brain. She thought the words she had spoken to the judge would've settled everything. Because everyone said love was the most important thing for a child. *Why not mine?* But as the judge continued to speak, she knew his words spelled doom.

When he finished, he banged a hammer giving Gemma a jolt. Her mind disappeared and then came back again.

The crowd left the room like a herd of cows. Gemma followed Mama who led her through one door and then another. One more after that brought them outside and away from the downtown courtroom. A welcome blast of cold air cooled her face. It's all she felt plodding along the sidewalk.

Then it snowed. The streets turned white under a carpet of quarter-sized flakes as cars clattered all directions. When they crossed the street, an elderly woman slipped, knocking into Gemma. But Gemma's smile didn't break open free or easy as usual. She hardly noticed when the woman grabbed her arm to steady herself. She hardly noticed because that morning, her whole universe lost its balance.

Gemma blew her nose hard. "There's nothing else we can do?" she finally asked Mama. As soon as she stuffed the tissue in her pocket she plucked it out again, her nose raw from a steady drip.

Mama held Gemma's arm tight. "Let's talk when we get in the car." She shook off the layer of slush clinging to her hair, bleeped open the doors, and climbed in. "Here." She handed Gemma more tissue. "Allergies, or tears?"

"I think both."

"Let's get you home." She cranked the engine and blasted the heater.

Undigested fragments of information swirled in Gemma's mind.

"Sweetie," Mama said cautiously, "the judge asked you repeatedly if you understood everything. Was there anything you wanted to ask but didn't?"

"Sure. But I couldn't because then he would've *really* thought I wasn't smart enough. Like Walter's mom."

"Oh, Gemma—"

"Well, isn't that why he wanted to take my baby and throw me in jail?"

"No! It isn't. A lot of people with intellectual disabilities are excellent parents. *Anyone* can face consequences for making a dangerous choice, Gem— with or without a disability. And the choices you made were dangerous. The laws are meant to protect children. And this is about protecting your baby." Mama reeled the car around and nosed into traffic.

Gemma's prickly eyes closed, sorting through all she had heard. "I couldn't think straight half the time." Her eyelids blinked open, adjusting to the gray foggy light. "I've never been in a room like that with so many strangers watching me."

"I know it was hard." Mama glanced sideways at her. "You did extremely well. You did the best anyone could do in this situation."

"Even when I talked?"

"Yes, honey. You did great. You spoke from your heart, and that's exactly what you needed to do."

Gemma turned away and watched the railroad tracks whooshing by. "Then why didn't it help? And why do I feel so sick?"

Mama let air out like she had finished a marathon. "I'm so sorry."

"I know I can't drive for a while. I heard that part."

"Right. You need to retake the test before you get your license back, but that can happen fairly quickly. They warned you if there was another incident—"

"I know. I know." Gemma's eyes clamped shut again, holding tight to the image she had seen—the one of River swinging from the old maple.

"I understand this feels horrible. But remember, you *are* going to keep her. It'll just be in Seattle now. Hold on to that."

Our tree is here. Not in Seattle.

Gemma stared straight at the wind shield, her ribcage rising and falling in rapid succession. "I don't want to leave my home, Mama. Or Lolly, or Walter, or my job. I can't be away from Nani. We have to go on picnics to our tree. And Zork! We like to fly. How can I leave?" She pulled out tissue and buried her face. "But I won't let them take her from me. I can't."

Mama made a quick turn into a gas station and stopped at the side of it. "Honey, you did your best but—"

"I thought lawyers were supposed to help people! You didn't even want to be my lawyer."

"I told you, it wasn't allowed because I'm your mother. Remember? That's why my friend stepped in. She did everything I would have."

"I needed another chance."

"He wouldn't give it. The evidence against you was formidable. I mean it was substantial and compelling." Mama tried again. "There was too much evidence stacked against you. More than I knew."

And just like that, Mama's face dropped like a rock in both hands, her whole body quaking. In all her life Gemma had never seen Mama bawl like that. And she didn't know what to do.

"I'm sorry," Mama said, taking in air. "I don't mean to upset you more. But I want you to know we did everything we could. And the outcome was fair."

"*Fair*? That judge's voice didn't crack or bend at all!"

Mama waited.

"I mean he sounded like a robot. Not one bit friendly."

"It's not their job to be friendly. It's their job to be fair."

"He could've been nicer about it."

"Yes, he could have. You're right about that."

"Then, let's find another one. Can we?"

"It doesn't work that way. And let's hope you'll never go before a judge in Seattle either. You'll be on their radar now. You'll need to do everything right."

Gemma's insides stiffened. "If I don't, someone in *Seattle* will try and take her from me?"

A long line of Mama's words sailed around Gemma in the car. She didn't hear any of them, but thought she did. *Everyone wants to take your baby...No one believes you're smart enough...It's only a matter of time.* That's what Gemma heard.

The women in my class were right. They do want our babies. I'm not safe in Seattle either.

And that's when she knew what she had to do.

The rest of the ride home, Gemma stared at the chipped periwinkle polish on her thumb nails and reminded herself to keep breathing.

When Mama pulled into the apartment complex, Gemma clicked off the seatbelt and placed her hand on the door latch.

"Hang on. Let me park."

"No. Don't park. Let me out here. I want to be alone with my baby. No one else."

"Okay." Mama's hands gripped the wheel. "You can come home to Sugar Creek as often as possible. I promise."

Gemma couldn't speak.

"And we'll bring Walter up for visits too. Remember, you don't have to move right away—you can wait until after the baby's born." Mama dropped both hands in her lap. "You loved Seattle and the condo, Gem. In time it'll feel like home too."

It could never be the same...

Gemma stepped out of the car but paused at the bottom of the stairs. She gripped the rail, planting both boots on every rung before she climbed to the next. One calculated step at a time. For the first time ever, she reached the top without caring about the dizzy-making spaces between.

"You aren't leaving me, baby girl," she said out loud. "No one will ever take you from me. Not anyone here and not anyone in Seattle." Gemma stepped through the door with new strength of mind. "You're coming with me, daughter."

Nani says good ideas come slowly. But I say, sometimes they come fast.

Chapter Forty-One

Brave Star

She searched inside herself and found one brave spot.

Gemma hurriedly packed a small duffle bag and crammed the essentials into her backpack: prenatal vitamins, hairbrush, money, soap, deodorant, toothbrush, toothpaste, phone charger, bus pass, train schedule, and all her hope for a new life. On top of everything, she placed the beaded baby bonnet. On top of that she gently laid the floral head wreaths, the jeweled tiaras sparkling underneath the roses in front.

And then Nani called.

"Did Mama tell you to call me?" Gemma heard the anger in her own words and tried to hide it.

"No. But she told me about court. Zork and I flew north into bad weather and couldn't get back in time. I'm so sorry I wasn't there."

"I'm not mad at you. I'm mad at the judge because he's wrong."

"I see."

"He said I can't do it—because I'm not a safe mom. I can't do a lot of things, Nani, but I *can* love. I *can* do that."

"I know you can. I know that with all my heart. But it doesn't change what happened."

"I passed all the parenting classes with gold stars. I just need more time to learn and practice everything."

"That's true, but you can't undo what's been done. Your mother's right about that."

"What do you mean?"

"You did break the law. I know you didn't mean to, and I know it's a hard lesson, but this time you have to learn to live with the mistake. We all carry some regrets."

"You mean, I can't tink this mistake away."

"Right. You can't go back and fix it. Not this time."

"But I said I was sorry. And I learned from it!"

"That's the good part. You did learn from it and—"

"I can't live without River!"

"Honey, you don't have to. Don't you see? You'll have River with you in Seattle. And you'll have to trust me on this, but it's the safest place for you to be right now. I'm actually relieved you're moving."

Relieved I'm moving? Gemma couldn't remember a time she had felt so misunderstood by Nani.

"I know it feels awful right now, but it will get better. I promise. You'll grow to love Seattle as much as you love it here."

Gemma stopped listening. "I have to take a nap," she lied.

"Hang on, Gem. I need to say something. You know I'd do anything in my power to help you if I could."

"I know." *I thought I did anyway.*

"I would've offered to let you and River live with me, but it isn't possible right now. It wouldn't be safe."

"Safe? You're not *that* old, Nani."

"Well, old enough. I'll have to explain another time when I can. I'm only sorry I couldn't help."

"It's okay."

"Anyway, it will be a good thing to be with your mom. You'll see."

"I'm tired now and need to sleep. Love you, Graham Cracker."

"Love you more."

Gemma hung up without asking, "More than what?" *I hope she didn't notice.*

"We're running away, River," Gemma said. "No one wants us together and I won't risk losing you. It's time to be brave. I'll find us a new home, near a new river, and I'll get a new job, and we'll find a place far away where no one knows us. But don't worry, we'll find a way for your daddy to find us. And I will be a good mama. I won't make the same mistake again. I promise. I'll never let you go. I'll fight for you with everything I have. Even if it kills me."

Even if it kills me. Gemma shuddered. A niggle of fear crept into her thoughts and crawled up her spine.

The snowdust that covered the valley the night before had melted, but the wind and rain spread pollen from the orchards everywhere. It hung over the hills like a dusky smog—Gemma couldn't escape it. She tied her scarf over her nose when she stepped off the bus and took a different path to the river. A new sense of purpose nudged her courage forward, and yet, she couldn't help but feel something else too—the weight of dark secrets lurking behind the somber black ash trees draping the trail.

Nani's rule came to mind: *Do not go to the river without me.* But rules didn't matter anymore. None of them. She was about to embark on a new life—a life without rules or people telling her what she could and couldn't do, or who she could or couldn't be— including a mother.

"First, we have something special to do, River. I wish everyone were here, but you and I will have your baby blessing exactly where I planned."

The clouds separated and arrows of sun pierced the air reflecting flashes of gold on the river. *He's here again—in the tiny sparkles of light.* Gemma felt less alone knowing Grandpa Sam was near.

She scooted across the rocks to the edge of the river. When Nani's name flashed across her phone again, a tiny ache rolled through her insides. She shut the thing off, stuck it in her backpack, and pulled out the floral wreaths. Gemma tenderly positioned them on a small, calm pool of water in front of her. She recited something she heard the Cow Creek Tribe say: "Water is sacred. Water is life."

Gemma inched her way to a warm patch of sunshine. She adjusted her aquamarine tiara scattering dots of light over the terrain and closed her eyes.

"Creator, please hear my blessing. And you too, baby girl. I pray you will be a brave star—blessed with the *force* of Mama, the *sparkle* of Grandpa Sam, the *light* of Nani, the *strength* of Zorro, the *kindness* of Bertie, the *honesty* of your daddy, the *faith* of the reverend, the *spirit* that's in me, and the *love of all of us combined*. Amen."

Gemma opened her eyes, stunned to see the wreaths out of reach, both of them bouncing along the shiny ripples pulling away from shore—the baby's wreath cradled safely inside hers.

Every time they crested a wave, sparks of light flashed through the roses, the jewels clinging tight to the tiaras nestled inside them. After her wild ride downriver with Lolly, she didn't dare try and save them. This time there would be no Lolly to save her.

Lolly! Gemma's stomach lurched. *I didn't say goodbye to Lolly. I hope she'll understand.* She watched heartsick with loss as the vibrant garlands drifted bravely away on the swift current. "It's okay, River. They're in the arms of nature now. The water will guide them where they're supposed to go. They're brave and free now, like we'll be soon."

The wind hummed through the willows, full of song, as Gemma watched the bobbing rings of red roses vanish. It was a heart-wrenching moment. And yet she refused to hold it that way—her sorrow already too big.

When the sun faded again, a cold, black wind spooled up between the trees. With solemn resolve, Gemma grabbed her duffle bag, flung her backpack over her shoulder, and set out. A steady drizzle turned to seeds of rain and muddied the path back to River Road. "Next stop is the bus station," she announced. "After that we board the train."

She froze for a second when an army-green snake slithered across the path and disappeared under a stump. She ambled on until the rustle of cracking twigs made her flinch again. She spun around and thought she glimpsed something creeping through the brambles.

Bigfoot. Gemma's pace accelerated.

And then she broke into a dead sprint, just in case. *Good thing I'm a gold-medal runner.*

Toward the end of the trail, she broke off, panting. She scanned backward, eyeballing the bushes on either side. *All clear. Must've been seeing things.* She bent to the ground and tossed a few sharp rocks in her pocket. *Just in case.*

But when Gemma glanced up, the dark figure of a male appeared. This time in the middle of the trail—blocking her exit. And he wasn't moving. Another paralyzing shudder rippled up her spine and spread to her limbs. Even the trees shivered.

The stranger waved his arm at the bushes, as if to signal someone. He was far enough away to run from, but close enough to catch up. Even in the shadows, Gemma recognized evil in his eyes. She felt it too—an odd charge crackling around his being. There was something ugly rooted in him. Something straight out of hell.

"I don't like the looks of him," she heard Nani say. *"Always trust your gut. Your feelings will tell you what to do."*

Gemma dropped everything and ran.

Chapter Forty-Two

On the Lam

It was like racing under water. Gemma couldn't feel her limbs beneath her but didn't stop. The mud made her slip, and she had trouble catching air, but she slogged on. She had no choice—he was coming for her. *"Don't roll over for evil,"* Nani always said. *"Never submit to it."*

She didn't care about ditching the duffle bag, but her insides rolled like rocks when she remembered her backpack. *The beaded bonnet!* More sinking sadness washed over her. But the next thought shot pure terror through her soul. *My phone... I have no phone.*

The stranger was gaining speed. Gemma rounded a bend, out of his view, and darted off the trail into the dark woods. She crouched behind a large fallen log and steadied her mind. *Work one thought at a time.*

The stranger sprinted past. She rocked back on her haunches, listening for his steps until they faded. "It worked," she muttered.

Gemma moved with the stealth of a mountain lion, traveling farther into the trees toward the river. When the water came into view, she followed it, ready to cut over at the right time. "Lost him. Hang on, River— we're gonna run faster." She scuttled on.

A midwinter cerise sun appeared again and blinked

through the trees like flashing red lights. Every view she had signaled danger. A flock of geese trailed in formation and then scattered overhead, honking in all directions. *The geese are squeaking! Even they know I'm in trouble.* She heard a woodpecker jackhammering, beeping grouse, and the flapping wings of turkey vultures. *All the birds are shook up.* She trampled the needle-bedded ground, pulse pounding, her hair lank from sweat and the drizzle of rain. She knew her way to Luper; she would cut through the scrub and move inland at the right time.

The tree appeared with the wooden sign nailed to it: KNEEL DOWN oh TRAVELER ON YOUR KNEES, GOD IS WITH YOU IN THESE TREES. *I sure hope so. But I don't have time to kneel.* She kept moving in a fast-forward push.

Gemma squelched through a puddle, all her senses open. The stink of mud uncoiled in her chest when the orchards came into view. Suddenly tired, she thought she'd never get there. She stopped, bent over with both hands on her knees, catching her breath. And then she bolted, cutting across the field and into the hazelnut trees, the pollen settling in her eyes and chest. But that was the least of her worries.

I can hide at Luper... Wild tangles of blackberry bushes snagged her sleeves like barbed wire, but she surged on.

Gemma caught sight of them—not one stranger, but two. Both of them trailing her. *The same men at the river.* They were gaining speed as a hawk screeched above her, its wings beating against the heavy, darkened clouds.

Nani's right. Some people do have evil mixed in.

Gemma crested a small hill, splashed her way across the cold, rustling creek and headed to Luper. She unfastened the beefy rope on the gate and darted to the old maple, climbing into its safe, hollow bowl. She tucked herself into a shrinking ball, lungs pumping at high speed—her breath echoing like Hell's Canyon. *Wish you would find me now, Nani.*

Someone's footsteps approached. But they weren't Nani's.

"In here," a man with a hard, raspy voice said. "There's her boot prints." He spoke with a heavy accent around his words.

Gemma tried not to breathe, her face trembling. In the distance she heard the train hurtle across the valley, horn blaring in short blasts. It sounded two hundred years away.

"We got ourselves a queen."

Gemma didn't understand at first. And then she did. A thick hand swooped over her head, veins bulging on the beefy arm attached to it. With one dive, her tiara lifted, ripping strands of tangled hair with it. "Ow!" she shrieked. *So that's what they wanted.*

Gemma couldn't stay there like a bump on a tree trunk. She sprang upright. "It's a princess crown, and it's okay. You can have it." His steel-wool brows, big as caterpillars, waggled when he howled. They both spit out a nasty laugh.

Gemma stared into the deepest crevice of the old maple, searching for any sign of Grandpa Sam. *If only he could rise from the dead now.*

They were awful old to be bullies. The taller of the two wore the same knit hat she'd seen before. His head snagged the low branches of the apple tree when he lumbered over next to Wooly Brows. "Hey," he said, closing in. "She sure is a sweet young thing. Looky there." Gemma heard a whistle in his nose, like a tea kettle heating up. She was right—there was evil in his eyes. And something crazy too.

"Stop bullying me," Gemma said forcefully. She felt for the jagged rocks in her pocket.

"You think that's all we're gonna do? Bully you?" Crazy Eyes spat when he said it, his enormous nose wrinkling.

Gemma thought of River and her insides seized up.

Woolly Brows tossed the tiara over his shoulder, never taking his bone hard eyes off Gemma. "You're a little hellion like your old nanny-goat aren't you?"

"She's not a goat."

"No, she's much worse than that," he said roughly. "Hope you're not too attached to her."

A cold, piercing wind ruffled through the branches and Gemma caught a whiff of nose choking body odor. "Why?"

"She's not long for this world, that's why. But don't worry," he scowled. "She deserves everything she gets."

The bitter air snaked up Gemma's arms. She tugged at the sleeve of her sweatshirt from underneath her jacket.

Run, hide, fight, flooded Gemma's mind. She reviewed Nani's instructions. *Treat them like active shooters. If you can get away, run.* Without alarm, Gemma lowered herself slowly from the tree. *If I remain calm, I might find the chance to get away.* It had worked as a child.

Gemma knew the strength of the devil was alive in

her midst; these two yahoos were the opposite of love.

On your mark...

She stepped to the side, her eyes on the gate to freedom, preparing her limbs for the race of her life.

Get set...

Gemma detected the surge in her step, ready to spring, her heart charging.

But before she made it to *Go*, Crazy Eyes slammed her chest backward and pinned her against the tree with such force, her feet lifted off the ground.

Her brain started spinning. She checked his face to see if he was still human. His eyes swirled in his head like storm clouds, and she decided he wasn't. There was something wild there, as if some feral spirit had replaced the human one.

"Where's Granny, now?" he laughed. "Huh?" He spread his bony fingers around her neck and squeezed. The knit hat slithered down the back of his head, a mat of stringy hair glued to his scalp.

Gemma's pulse shot up. *Lie. Say whatever you can to survive.* Nani's words always came back when she needed them. She caught her breath. "I know," she choked out. "Let go of me, and I'll tell you."

He loosened his grip but kept her pressed against the tree.

"I always know where she is."

When he pinched her cheeks together, she got a peek of his stained, rotting choppers square on. Like a shot of raw onion to the eye, she almost couldn't take it.

"Don't worry. So do we, you little..." He finished his sentence with a poison word. It burned into her like buckshot. "...you're only the bait," he finished.

Gemma wriggled something fierce but he only

squeezed tighter, his breath hanging rancid over her face. She grit her teeth. "Your smell is enough to make a jay scream."

"Did you hear that?" he asked Woolly Brows. "She's got the same sass as the infamous Olivia Porter. Not the smarts though," he glowered.

"How do you know her name?" Gemma asked.

"Oh, we go way back... Friends for eons." He loosened his grip but kept his arms on either side of her.

"She'd *never* be friends with you," Gemma spat.

"Your I.Q. is better than I thought." He scanned his surroundings. "Hey." He motioned to Woolly Brows. "On the horse coming in. *Right on time.*"

Gemma squirmed, trying again to escape his grasp and scream, but he covered her mouth too fast.

With one hand he cinched her upper arm so tight she let out a muffled yelp. He yanked her out in front of him but concealed himself behind the tree. Something cold, like metal pressed into the back of her neck. Gemma pretended it was his knuckle so she wouldn't panic. *Panic is never useful*, she heard Nani say.

"Keep your mouth shut," he said. "One word and I take a slice."

Woolly Brows crouched behind a bulky grave marker.

"Don't you dare hurt her," Gemma mouthed into his smelly palm.

The "knuckle" burrowed deeper into her flesh until she flinched. "*Zat-kneess.* That's Russian for *shut up.*"

Nani bolted off Lolly and tore through the gate. "Gemma?" She slowed, inspecting the ground covered in boot prints. She stared at the dirty mitt covering Gemma's mouth. Her eyes shifted left and right when she leisurely reached to the back of her waist.

"Stop!" Crazy Eyes ordered. "Throw it over the gate. Now."

"Take your hands off her." Nani's eyes bared down on him.

"This won't feel so good across her throat," he threatened. "But as you know I slash without delay and I'm extremely efficient."

Crazy Eyes flicked the tip of a sharp blade under Gemma's chin, making it bleed. She squealed.

"I said throw it!" he blasted.

Nani tossed a gun over the gate. Lolly's ears pricked forward.

"Well done, Olivia. I'm proud of you. We'll go easy on her as long as you cooperate. I think you'll cooperate now, don't you agree?" Woolly Brows stepped out from behind the marker, his gun raised in her direction.

Nani cut a mean eye his way, calculating something. "You're looking old for your age, Donny," she said jovially. "You too, Marie."

"Stay where you are," Crazy Eyes threatened. "It'd be such a shame if you had to witness my culinary skills in person this time."

"I'll take my chances." She moved in closer.

Gemma tried to swallow, but it was tricky. His muscled arm cranked her neck so high it didn't move.

"You know, fellas, my memory isn't what it used to be," Nani said. "In fact, I can't remember a thing about what you need to know. Aging sucks, doesn't it?"

"Oh come now. We have ways to jog your memory. Or don't you remember that either?" He spit on the point of his knife. "You killed my brother."

"Sorry about that."

"We weren't close. But still…" He lay the blade flat against Gemma's inner thigh, slowly wiping it off. "Give us what we want, and I'll let that little sin of yours go."

"Of course you will."

"Make no mistake, Olivia. If you don't cooperate, I will make good on my brother's dying wish. And then some." He cast a long eye on Gemma.

"Well, I wish I were in the mood for games, boys. I really do." Nani's hands cinched her sassy hips. "But damn it, I'm not."

"You're crazy." He snaked an arm around Gemma's waist and glared at Nani. "Is it worth all this?" His tongue slithered into Gemma's ear.

"It is." Nani kicked up the dust in front of her, turning an unblinking gaze on him. "Because I won't let go of your sin, Donny. Not for anything."

"Oh, that's right…" Crazy Eyes crooned. "I do seem to recall that dreadful incident in the barn… Oh, wait. How insensitive of me. I meant your husband; not your horse. My apologies." He half bowed. "What a saint! I'll admit he made it a very difficult shot. But we digress…" He stabbed the air with the blade next to Gemma's neck. "Don't be foolish, Olivia."

"That's the last thing I'd be."

Gemma didn't understand what it all meant—but she understood enough. She booted Crazy Eyes in the leg. "Don't hurt her, you nasty nutrient!" The words came out wilder than she planned.

He lowered the knife and pushed Gemma back against the tree. "If we have to take your grandmother out, you're next. After we have some fun."

Nani's eyes flashed. "Pull in your horns, Donny. And don't get ahead of yourself." She spat like she had a mouth full of chew.

Gemma could see a wave of fury roll over her, but Nani smiled coolly. "I'm not afraid of these two, Gemma. They've been coming after me for a long time. Nice of you to finally make it, guys. Really. I've been anxiously awaiting your arrival." Nani wore the best poker face Gemma had ever seen.

"Why don't you tell your little princess about the things you've done, Olivia." Crazy Eyes ran a hand over Gemma's skull. "Tell her about the people you've killed. I'm sure she'd love to hear about it. And please. Give her all the grisly details."

Gemma's jaw slacked open. "Nani? This is scaring me."

"Gemma," she said, with weight. "It's time to be brave."

Nani's eyes shone angry points of light straight at Gemma—like booster shots of courage.

"Be." Nani nodded. "Brave."

A blast of rotting breath covered Gemma's face again; she blinked with surprise and then steadied her voice. "You know what, Nani?" She cast a cold eye over her captor. "His breath is so nasty it's enough to set a *squirrel's* teeth on edge." A picture of River swinging from the maple flashed in front of her. She turned to Crazy Eyes. "You might be sorry you found me."

With the strength of a lion, Gemma exploded—her boot like an axe to his groin as she dug both thumbs into his eyeballs. His knife wheeled into the air when he clutched his crotch in agony. And then her fist flew, meeting him in the cheekbone. *Keep fighting, keep resisting, don't stop calling evil out.*

Gemma sent him sprawling.

Meanwhile, Woolly Brows lost his grip and fired off a shot when Nani punted his gun into the blackberry brambles.

"Kick him in the cubes!" Gemma yelled, winding up for another thrust. She swung her boot into his man-lump again. Crazy Eyes made an "umpf "with the hit. He caught her by the ankle, but she slammed her other heel into his hand. He shriveled up in pain.

When Nani advanced on Woolly Brows, he pulled out his own long, shiny blade. She clambered backward, dodging the swipes he cut in the air around her. She reached for something in her boot when his knife brushed her chest and side; she twisted away, kicked the blade from his hand and fell backward. Blood sprayed the air.

Gemma grabbed for the rocks she had pocketed and hurled them at Crazy Eyes, trying to keep him pinned.

Nani pulled herself up, unsteady on her feet at first. She slowed her panting, ready for more combat. She lunged at Woolly Brows, flipped him on his back. They heard the crack of bone when she slammed his head against a granite marker. His body fell limp.

"*Whoa.*" Gemma covered her mouth with both hands. She didn't notice Crazy Eyes struggle to his feet.

But Nani did. She came up behind and wrapped both hands around his neck until he passed out.

"Sweet dreams..." Nani mumbled something else that wasn't very nice. But Gemma didn't care. Sometimes bad words slipped off her tongue too.

"*Whoa,*" Gemma said again, wiping drops of blood from the nick on her chin. "How did you..." She eyeballed everything around them in disbelief, her limbs wiggling. Nani had done everything with the speed of a superhero. "Do you have secret powers, Nani?"

In the distance, they heard the buzz of a high-pitched drone approaching. "And there's more," Nani said. The dull whine sharpened as it closed in. "They have eyes on us. It's not over yet."

Gemma couldn't believe it wasn't over. Whatever it was.

Nani prodded Gemma forward. "We have to ride. Stay with me." She dragged Gemma out the gate, reached for her pistol, and tucked it behind her waist again. Nani held her upper torso and cringed. But it didn't slow her. She sprang on top of Lolly with no trouble. "Mount up, Gemma."

"But the baby! I'm not supposed to ride!"

"No choice. Get up here, *now!*" She helped pull Gemma up over Lolly's glossy rump. "Hang on!"

Gemma wrapped both arms around her waist.

"She's about to go as fast as you've ever seen!" Nani wasn't kidding. Lolly lurched and broke forward—rocketing across the field. *Just like in my dream!* Gemma put her mouth to Nani's ear. "Who are we running from?"

Nani twisted a little to the right. "Them! Keep your head behind me. Hold tight!"

"More bad guys?"

"Yes! There's always more."

Chapter Forty-Three

The Voice of Light

Before Gemma could ask what she was doing with a gun, Nani shot at the black monster SUV chasing them. *Wish* this *was a dream...* She gripped Nani's waist like claws and curled her head low to one side, risking one peek from behind. "You hit their tire! They're slowing down!"

In zigzags, Nani charged Lolly through the grass. When they crested a hill and hurdled to the other side, gunshots rang across the field behind them.

We should call 9-1-1. Gemma didn't have time to suggest it.

Nani pulled Lolly to a sharp stop next to Zorro's plane and helped Gemma dismount. "Climb in fast."

"But—I don't know how without Zorro! I only know how to fly a little!"

"It's okay—I fly a lot."

"You do?" Gemma froze. "I didn't know that."

Nani turned ghostly-white, but ignored whatever swept over her. "Get your head in the game," she mumbled to herself. "I said climb in! Now!" she yelled to Gemma.

"But Lolly!"

"She's safer without us!"

Gemma trusted Nani—even when confused. But

the slack-jawed expression on herself was becoming permanent.

Nani switched the engine on and prepared for take-off. She taxied across the field, and in a shot they were up.

"Jeepers," Gemma uttered.

"I know what I'm doing," Nani said. "But hang on. This might feel scary."

She was right again. The nose of the plane shot straight up, climbing rapidly, straight for the moon.

Gemma gripped the sides of her seat, focused on the only thing she could—outer space. "It is a little scary, Nani. I thought only astronauts flew like this." She kept chattering, trying to calm herself. "By the way, who were those men?"

"Bad men."

"They know you?"

"Yes."

"But not like friends…"

"No. Like enemies."

"Why did he say you killed people?"

"Because I have. But only to protect innocent lives. And only when there was no other choice."

Gemma believed her. "That was *some* sales job. You weren't kidding—you really aren't safe to be with. I didn't know sales work could be so dangerous. Glad you quit that job… You definitely learned how to shoot, though." Gemma stopped her nervous babbling when she stared at the gun tucked halfway under Nani's seat. That's when she spotted trouble. "Something's wrong," she said. Her stomach iced over.

"No worries. I've been a pilot for years." Nani leveled the plane, scanning the sky around them. "Help me watch for traffic, Gem."

"I will, but it's not that."

"What's not that?"

"It's not your flying! You're doing great," she shouted. "As good as Zorro."

"Well, then what's wrong?"

"It's the blood I'm worried about."

Nani's head kangarooed, searching Gemma's torso. She lifted Gemma's chin. "Not bleeding. Are you hurt somewhere else?"

"I don't think so."

"What are you talking about then?"

"*You.* I'm talking about you, Nani. You're bleeding bad…" Gemma inspected the gore soaking through Nani's side. "Bleeding like a stuck pig."

Nani twisted. "So I am. Just a little flesh wound. Hand me your sweatshirt."

Gemma peeled off her jacket and wrangled her hoodie off underneath. Nani folded everything over and pressed it into her side.

"That's a lot of blood, Nani. We should land."

"Planning on it," she said, her face turning woozy. "This spinning will pass," she told Gemma. "No worries. Just a little turbulence."

"But we're not spinning. And the air is calm. Also… You don't look right."

Nani laid two fingers on her own wrist feeling for a pulse. "Still alive!" she heartily announced. And then she held up her pointer. "Maybe not," she corrected, her words barely a wisp. She moaned, slumping against the door, her head limp as a rag doll.

"Nani!" Gemma shrieked. "Come back!" She jostled her shoulder, but her eyes didn't open. "Graham

Cracker, you have to wake up. Please!"

Still nothing.

"This is a long ways up." Gemma peered at the valley floor, dots of white sheep peppered the hills. "What should I do?" she cried. "We're all going to die!" She laid a hand on Nani's hip and nudged. "Please sit up! We can't die!"

But Gemma pulled back her hand, wet with blood. She wiped it anxiously on her pants. *Is she dead already?* The question yanked at her. *No. She is not dead.* There was no other answer allowed but *no.*

Gemma took in more air when her breathing changed. A ten-pound hammer went to work inside her chest. She knew what it meant. *I can't focus on my palms up here…*

She wiped the sweat from her temples, clenched her fists, squeezing pretend lemons to stop the wiggling.

And then, like a miracle, she heard a voice. A voice so clear and bright, she hardly believed it came out of nowhere.

"No use in worrying," the voice said. *"Worrying never saved anyone. Be still and wait."*

Chapter Forty-Four

On Wings of Courage

"Be still and wait? How am I supposed to do that up here?"

And then the legendary words of Chief White Eagle of the Ponca Nation settled in Gemma's mind. Words she had learned as a child: "When you are in doubt, be still and wait...be still until the sunlight pours through...then act with courage."

She searched in her bucket for everything Zorro had taught her. Gemma grabbed the stick, checked the altitude, and relaxed into the plane the way she had with Zorro so many times before. *"Focus on the feel of the plane, Gemma,"* he had said. *"You have a sense for it now. Like riding a bike."*

The sky was radiant again, and the nose of the plane was practically reaching for the sun. A strange and beautiful courage poured over her in the light.

"I can do this," she said out loud. "And I will. I am bringing this plane down. That's all there is to it." She placed a sweaty hand on top of her baby bump. "I made you a promise, baby girl, and I mean to keep it."

Gemma searched for the landing strip she and Zorro used. "There's the water tower, so I know it's coming soon. It's time to fly this bird to the ground. *To* the ground, not *into* the ground," she clarified. "Be brave, River! This is part of your exciting life. Sometimes you have to learn to be brave."

The wings tipped and rocked when a powerful blast of wind thrust the nose up. "Whoa!" *Where did that come from?* "Hold 'er down," she said, the way Zorro had instructed more than once.

"It's not going to be pretty," she continued. "Sorry everyone—it won't be a greaser. But I can do this." She recognized the airstrip and a helicopter not far from it. "I better stay away from that thing." Gemma wiped a clammy hand on her pants, taking a long pull of air.

"I can do this," she repeated. "Look out, everyone. The Porter women are landing."

Gemma checked the instruments, only because it seemed like the right thing to do.

"Bring her down slow and easy." She pulled back the power. "I got this." She began descending. "Coming down…" *I can do this, I can do this, I can do this.* "And down some more…"

The ground drew near, rushing under the wheels. Faster and closer, until a jolt and then another. "I got this!" They hit the ground violently, bouncing eight times, maybe more, before the plane careened off the runway and slid into a grassy field. "Touchdown!" she cried.

How'd I get so close to the chopper without smacking into it? Gemma choked the engine off and rolled to a stop.

"It's okay, Nani! We made it. You can wake up now because we made it. Squirrels, Nani! Do you read me? I said, *squirrels*!"

Gemma waited. She grasped her hand, but Graham Cracker was cold, all the life wheeled out of her.

Gemma's heart collapsed.

Trucks swarmed around the airplane. *Bad guys... There's always more...* Lights flashed, sirens blared, and Gemma couldn't trust anyone. She reached for the gun on the floor and steadied it with both hands—aiming across Nani at the door behind her. When it swung open, she closed her eyes and pointed outward, her lungs out of air.

"Simmer down, Gemma."

She gasped. The hum of Zorro's voice loosened her spine, but her hands started to convulse.

"Put the gun down. Easy now…"

A vibration rippled through her arms and out her fingertips. It lowered when her eyes opened. "Zorro."

"I'm right here." Zorro handled the gun at top speed, removing something from the bottom. A brass bullet spluttered into the air before he handed it to an officer.

He took one look at Nani, and roared, "Medics!"

He held the sweatshirt firmly against her side, the blood soaking through everything. "*You* landed this?"

Gemma nodded.

His fingers pressed into Nani's neck. "I'll be damned."

"You have to help her," Gemma begged.

"Medics!" he bellowed again. "She's bleeding out!"

His words stopped Gemma's heart. She swore it did.

When the medics swooped in, Zorro hurried to Gemma. "They'll take care of her. You're coming with me."

Gemma latched on to Zorro's neck, her face

pressed deep into his shoulder. He lifted her from the plane and carried her away. "How did you get here?" she asked.

"By chopper."

"That's yours? It sorta got in my way. But how did you know we were here?"

"We have our ways. Too much to explain."

"You mean Nani pushed the emergency spot on her phone to signal you? So you could track her?"

Zorro did a double-take. "How'd you know that?"

"I see a lot of things people don't know I do. But how'd you get here before us?"

"The reverend called. He heard gunshots and my plane taking off. I had a good lead, was already in the air." He repositioned the arm cradling Gemma's legs. "Knew your nan would be headed here. Didn't know it'd be you flying though! Although that *was* quite a landing—"

"Good thing we practiced so much," Gemma said. Sometimes I remember things I didn't even know I remembered."

"Well, you did it, Ace. That's all that counts." He set her gently on the grass. "You hurt anywhere? In any pain?"

Yes or no, it didn't matter. Gemma didn't know how she felt. And then she burst out crying.

"It's okay, sweetheart. You're going to be fine." Two paramedics hovered over her. "Let them check you and the baby over."

"But..." Gemma's air caught. "Is Nani..." It hitched again. "Is she—"

"They'll do everything in their power to save her. Everything," he said.

"You have to be with her."

"I'm not leaving you."

"Yes, you have to! You need to be with her," Gemma pleaded. "It's what I want!"

"You sure?"

"Yes! Go."

"Okay." Zorro faced the ambulance. "You're taking me too!" They started loading the gurney, Nani's body still motionless.

"Go, Zorro."

"I'll stay right with her. I promise. Great flying, Gem," he said in a rush. "Bravest thing I've ever seen. You saved your lives."

"But what if I didn't save Nani?"

"You got her down. No matter what, you did exactly what she wanted you to do. You're the bravest woman I've ever known, next to your nan." He smiled. "You're a hero, Gemma Porter. So proud of you." He kissed her on both soggy cheeks, squeezed her tight, and darted for the ambulance.

Before they closed the door he called out, "The Reverend has Lolly! She's fine!"

Under a cascade of anguish, a shaky grin draped across Gemma's face. She waved to Zorro, breathing in relief for Lolly and exhaling unspeakable sorrow for Nani.

I learned how to be brave, Nani. But you have to come back. None of it matters if you don't.

Gemma watched as the flashing red lights vanished into the bleak gray expanse of sky.

I'm no hero, Zorro.

Chapter Forty-Five

Beams of Love

Pale golden sunlight brought a springtime aura into the hospital room. Gemma stepped in not knowing what to expect, but she knew Nani didn't hold the same light the room did. She had lost too much blood.

The reverend signed the cross and prayed over Nani, smudges of holy oil shimmering on her forehead.

Gemma pulled out four small royal-blue glass bottles, each labeled with a different name: White Sage, Yarrow, Sweetgrass, and Juniper. "Is it okay, reverend, if I put these oils on her too?"

"Of course."

With one trembling finger, she tenderly dabbed drops of each on Nani's face and palms. "She's not even moving."

"She's not in pain," he said.

"The Cow Creek community showed me how to use the oils. They can help her... But I'm not sure I'm doing it right—" Gemma felt her eyes fill with alarm. "What if I'm doing it all wrong?"

"It's your presence that matters most, Gemma. It's okay." The reverend kneeled next to her. "I know how hard this must be. You're not alone."

She nodded, her gaze pasted to Nani's face. "Tell me the truth," she said.

"Okay."

"I don't want you to say what you're supposed to. I want you to be honest."

"You have my word."

"I've never wanted anyone to tell me Creator was like Santa Claus. Even if it was the truth. But now I do—if it's the truth. Is Creator, who you call God, actually real? I mean for sure real?"

"I have no doubt about it."

"Why?"

"I've seen enough in this life to be convinced of it."

"Like what?"

The reverend's face strengthened in kindness. "Like you. And your grandmother, and the love I still feel for my late wife—so many people with love inside them. It comes from somewhere good, Gemma. I believe it's God."

"Can Creator save her?"

"I don't know. I can't begin to speak for God, or Creator. And I have no idea what's next for your grandmother. But at some point, we all say goodbye to life. We have to. Even the strongest human love can't stop it. I'm living proof of that."

"I can't lose her." Everything turned blurry.

"You haven't yet. She's still here. Talk to her. Don't grieve until you have to. If she leaves us, you'll have plenty of time to mourn then. But right now she's still with you… Do you want to be alone?"

"Yes," she said weakly, clearing her eyes with a sleeve.

"Your mother should be here soon."

"I know." She glanced at the reverend's face, his

eyes glistening. He still reminded her of Paul Newman.

"Okay." He placed a box of tissue on the tray table next to her, squeezed her shoulder and left.

Nani appeared as thin and cold as an icicle. Gemma reached for her hand. It was still limp, but warmer than the rest of her looked. She reached in her pocket for a string of pea-sized river pebbles, polished and strung together like a rosary. All of them gleaming in shades of blue, green, and amethyst against the crisp, linen sheet covering Nani. Then she pulled out tissue paper and unwrapped a broad leaf she had saved from the old maple—still glistening a light shade of autumn in the light. She gently placed both over Nani's still-beating heart.

"Graham Cracker..." She struggled to swallow down a neck bone relocating to her throat. "Guess what? I did it... I learned how to be brave." Gemma leaned in to Nani's ear and whispered, "Zorro said I'm a hero." She sat back again. "But I don't feel like one. Please... Please, don't leave me. I'm not brave enough to go on without you. I'll never be brave enough for that."

Gemma pulled a handful of tissue and sponged at her swollen eyes and then at the snot streaming from her nose. "I'm sorry I broke your rule again... But everyone wants to take my baby away. Even the judges in Seattle. That's the only reason I ran. Honest! I remembered the rule, but I never meant... I'm so, so sorry. I never thought it would kill you. Never!"

Gemma bowed over, rocking. "The judge is right. I don't deserve to have a baby." She drummed herself repeatedly in the side of the head. "I can't do anything right. I'll never be smart enough."

Watch out, Nani would've told her. *Look at the facts. You must speak truth to yourself.*

Gemma tried: *I deserve to love a child of my own. Sometimes I make mistakes, but plenty of times I don't. I'm smart enough about lots of things.*

But it only helped a little. *The truth is, I broke the rules. And it changed my whole life. Now I might lose Nani, too.* "And that's a fact," she said out loud.

Gemma cupped Nani's hand against her silky olive-brown cheek. "I won't run away again. I promise. But you have to be here." She squeezed her palm and summoned every ounce of energy inside her—channeling it straight into Nani's heart. "I'm sending you beams of love, Graham Cracker," she said. "Take in my spirit." She wove her fingers through Nani's. "Please—take it and live." Her head dropped in prayer, but her eyes lifted when she felt a stirring in the air. The leaf fluttered over Nani's chest. She swore it did. But Nani didn't wake up.

Give us a miracle, Creator. Her eyes pinched shut. *Just this once. Please.*

But nothing changed when she opened them.

She arranged the string of pebbles to lay like a necklace over Nani's chest.

"Remember what you said in our tree, Graham? You said you'd live forever if you could, just for the love of me. That's what you said. Please," she begged, "come back—just for the love of me." Dark spots splattered the clean, white bed sheet, as tears slipped off Gemma's face.

When the room turned to a velvety black, Gemma crawled cautiously into bed next to her Graham Cracker. She curled up delicately, hugging Nani's hand gently to her chest, gasping in short bursts as love continued pouring out.

****

When dawn painted the sky pink, a nurse led Gemma, staggering and dazed, out of Nani's room and into a waiting room. She curled up on a loveseat, closed her eyes, and drifted off to a string of constant bells dinging in the background.

She roused for an instant when someone covered her with a coat. "Thank God you're alive." It was Mama, her voice safe and warm. "Go back to sleep, honey. I'll keep checking on Nani. I'll let you know if anything changes. And Gem," she remembered hearing, "what you did took more courage than most people will ever have. I was wrong to think you couldn't make your own decision about having a baby. I should have told you this sooner. I know you're going to be a fabulous mother. I have no doubt." Some small part of Gemma tilted a little. Mama truly believed in her.

"I'll stay by her side," Gemma heard Walter whisper. "Don't you worry about Gemma," he said. "I'll protect our courageous hero."

Their words helped her surrender to sheer exhaustion. *But I'm no hero.* She slipped under into a deep sleep.

****

Gemma thought she was dreaming when a voice buoyed her to the surface. It was Grandpa Sam's voice. She knew because he introduced himself.

"You don't have to wake up, Gemma," he told her. "Your grandpop has some things to tell you while you're resting. Share as much of this as you can."

His slow, measured cadence surrounded her with a

369

peaceful affection.

"It was only twenty-two degrees on the railroad tracks. And they were caked in ice," he said, his voice deep-seated and solid. "Our train groaned as it struggled to inch its way through the pass—an old rusted-out freight train trying to outrun the devil. Even for a man like me with nerves of steel, the metallic grinding of the wheels set my teeth on edge. I hunkered low in the boxcar, peering through the slats and watched the world transform into white and gray—half a world away from the cloudbursts raining green on Oregon. Home was a verdant oasis compared to this place."

The tone of his voice wrapped Gemma in warmth.

" 'Here's your documents,' I told the man who was with us. I flipped open an American passport and showed him it was stamped for the next day, January 14. 'It's good luck,' I told him. 'It's my wedding anniversary tomorrow.'

"I cracked the freight car door, smelling diesel fuel and wood smoke, and peered out at the snow—a deep, soft powder surrounded the trees. Ideal for a jump, grueling for an escape.

" 'If anything happens, keep running,' I told him. 'You know the way. Someone else will come for you at the next checkpoint. A woman.'

" 'How will I know her?' he asked.

" 'She'll know you. And she'll tell you something interesting about squirrels.' I'm sure a smile tugged at my face when I said that...

"I told him her eyes were as blue as the river—eyes he'd never forget. And then I placed my revolver inside the man's backpack. 'Take it,' I said.

"The lyrics of a song about a harvest moon ran like a ghost serenading in my mind. I was too far from the woman in my soul—and the daughter who was the sweet topping on our lives. One day I imagined a grandchild or two. Someone exactly like you, Gemma. I imagined *you*.

"I checked my watch and waited, the cold leaching through my clothes.

"The train chugged to a near stop.

" 'It's almost time to jump and roll,' I told him. I pushed the rackety door back three more feet and the sting of air slapped my face, snow spitting in all directions. A split-second memory of the rising mist off the McKenzie River washed over me then. The cooling sensation over sultry flesh when summer was ablaze. 'Ready?' I asked him.

" 'Ready,' he said. 'Whoever you are, no words can express my thanks.' He gripped my hand and turned to Zork. '*Blagodaryu*. It means thank you,' he said. 'I thank you both.'

" 'Go!' I pushed the man out into whiteness.

"We only had seconds of silence before gunshots riddled the boxcar, splintering the air. We opened fire— our bullets blistering through the trees into the white isolation of winter. I went down, but I never felt the shot.

" 'Hang on, Porter!' I heard Zork yelling. He cradled my head.

"I knew it was too late. 'Remember what I told you…' I whispered as much as I could through strained breaths.

" 'Don't you dare leave me, Porter!' he yelled.

"But I was leaving. And I knew it. *You're too far*

away my friend. So sorry. I tried to speak those words but couldn't.

"I want your grandmother and your mother to know my last thoughts of them:

"*...They sit under our magnolia tree, smiling. The blue of the river and the gold of the earth shining in their eyes as bright as the harvest moon. Eyes I'll never forget. Their love warms like a lit ember inside my chest. It goes with me...*

"There's nothing to fear, Gemma. Never be afraid."

Grandpa Sam whispered one more thing in Gemma's ear. And then, like holy air descending, a kiss fell at the soft spot in the center of her cheek.

And he was gone.

Chapter Forty-Six

The Healing of Wounds

Magnolia gently pushed the door into her mother's room, leaned inside, and nearly plummeted to the floor.

Olivia was sitting perfectly upright watching television and drinking a carton of milk.

"Maggie!" Olivia chirped. "You made it!" She took a swig from one hand and waved with the other. "Come sit. Watching the morning news."

Magnolia stood awestruck.

"It's okay," Olivia told her. "I'm alive."

Magnolia lowered herself into a chair without comment.

"Yikes. You look awful, honey. Put your feet up. Gayle King's on. Love that woman."

"Mom, seriously?"

"Yes. She always says exactly what I'm thinking."

"I don't mean her. I mean *you*. You're okay? Just like that?"

"Yes, I think I am. Except for this." She pointed to her wound. "Otherwise I feel strong. You know, it was the funniest thing. As soon as Gemma sat with me, I felt myself coming back. I think she performed a healing…"

Magnolia's head tilted. "They prepared us, you know. Said you may not make it. Gemma was certain you were dying."

"I don't doubt that I was. But I've bounced back. I feel human again."

"I've never seen such a fast turnaround. Believe me, I sat with you last night and—"

"I told you—it was Gemma. Oh, and a nurse named Bob." She winked. "Gave me some good morphine." Olivia patted the IV bag hanging next to her.

"Whatever the reason, thank God you're okay." Magnolia lifted off her seat and gave her mother a delicate half embrace. She pulled back, studying her face. "You look so much better. Your eyes are clear and still the same young blue they've always been. A miracle you and Gemma survived." She sat again, her features chiseled with bewilderment. "When I heard what Gemma did—"

"I know! Zork emailed me this morning and filled me in. Not only did she land that plane—you should've seen her in the cemetery."

"It's truly unbelievable. I heard two men were trying to assault Gemma. Tell me what happened!"

"I will, Maggie. Because I can now."

"What do you mean?"

"I mean I'm free to talk. Not about everything, but I'll tell you as much as I can. I'm retired CIA—"

"What?" Magnolia didn't move.

"CIA. Central Intelligence—"

"I know what it is…"

"Never ran a business. Don't know the first thing about sales management."

"What?" Magnolia's eyebrows furrowed. "*Come on.* You're saying you lied about your job?"

"Yes, but not very well, I'm afraid. I've always been a lousy liar when it came to you. But I had no choice. We were all in danger. But thank God I'm the only one who ended up in a hospital bed."

"Yeah…" Magnolia straightened. "Okay, I think the morphine's making you a little loopy.

"I'm not loopy. I'm sensible again. And the throbbing dropped from a nine to a four on the pain scale. Thanks to Nurse Bob."

"Good. But you're sounding a little paranoid. CIA? Everyone's in danger? *Really*? You don't sound like yourself."

"It's true, Maggie."

"So, you're not in pain?"

"Not at the moment."

"Good. Then lay off that stuff. You're making things up."

Olivia repeatedly pushed the medication release button in a frenzy. "I'm *kidding*," she sneered.

Magnolia shifted in her seat. "Look, you don't have to pretend to be someone you're not. We don't care if you're not exciting or important. We love you the way you are."

"Well," Olivia huffed. "What a relief."

"Listen, morphine can do strange things to a person. Next you'll say you were being bugged."

"Well, of course we were. Our team confirmed it."

"Your team? Wait. Let me guess. Machine guns also come out of the taillights of your truck, and it turns into a submarine under water." Magnolia giggled the way she did when she was ten years old.

"Hey, that *would* be exciting. I can fly though."

"Right. And the spies were listening through the

microwave in your kitchen."

"Oh, Maggie, really. Not the microwave. But listen, I'm trying to tell you the truth. Our team put the FBI on us as a way to get eyes on our electronics. Being retired, we didn't have all the resources at our disposal anymore."

Magnolia's face glazed over. "You're saying the FBI raid was part of this?"

"Part of it, yeah."

"So now we're talking undercover espionage, FBI, CIA, and covert operations." Magnolia couldn't hold back her amusement. "And then two bad guys, oh, wait, *secret agents,* probably from Russia, came to little ol' Sugar Creek and chased you and Gemma around the pioneer boneyard."

"Yes. As a matter of fact, they did."

Magnolia burst out laughing. "Nurse Bob definitely overdid it. You need to sleep before Gem comes in. She'll believe this stuff!"

"Of course she will. She knows when I'm telling the truth. Zork and I had unfinished business—"

"Wait. Zork is CIA too?"

"Was. Technically we're retired again. As of today."

"Lordy." Magnolia shook her head. "I wonder if you'll remember anything you're saying right now. You—" A loud guitar playing a slow, sultry blues rendering of "The House of the Rising Sun," suspended her words.

"That's Zork." Olivia fumbled for her cell. "Hey there. Putting you on speaker. Maggie's here."

"Hi Mag-pie! Still feeling okay, Olivia?"

"Fine," she said. "And by the way, that was not the

way I planned to take them down. Should've had my backup pistol on me but left it in the saddle bag. Big mistake."

"They're down and that's all that matters. No mistake in that."

"True," she said.

Magnolia's eyes narrowed; she cocked her head at the sound of Zork's words.

"Sam is sitting proud up there, Olivia."

"Thought I'd be joining him there for a minute," she said.

The phone fell quiet.

"If they had done anything to Gemma," Olivia continued, "I—"

"Hey. If they had done anything to Gemma, you would've done exactly what you did."

Olivia took a deep breath. "Thanks for sending the full update this morning."

"Grateful you were alive to read it."

"Me too. And I do remember you being with me in the ambulance. You seemed far away, but I knew you were there."

"Good. It's finally over, Ollie. We got 'em."

"Yes, we did. Please thank the whole team for me."

"Will do. Fill Maggie in on all this? Must be a relief for her to finally know the truth."

"She's not buying any of it."

Zork howled. "Why doesn't that surprise me?"

"Give Bertie my love. Tell her I remember her being here last night too. Thanks again, Zork."

Olivia shut off the phone. "So. Where were we?"

Magnolia stared blankly. "You sound... Totally with it."

"I *am* totally with it."

"And Zork…" Magnolia's countenance changed. Her eyes laid steady on her mother's, her mouth somber. "You're *CIA*? For *real*?"

"Yes. For real. A sniper murdered your father because he helped someone defect. Someone extremely important to our country."

"So it wasn't a hunting accident, or a defective gun. I was right…"

"Yes, you were. On the right track anyway."

Magnolia reached for the extra blanket folded at the foot of the bed. "Wow. So my father was CIA too?" She slipped the thin white cover around her shoulders.

"Yes. Murdered in the middle of his mission. A mission I finished, not knowing yet that he was gone." Olivia glanced out the window and watched a million tiny stars of light, dancing wildly on the river. "I still hold information they desperately wanted. We did all we could, but even after all these years, they found me. And they knew Gemma was their ace in the hole."

Magnolia tilted forward. "This is scaring me. But go on."

"For a few blissful years, we thought we were free of them. Last year we had to come out of retirement and go back to work. Learned they were alive and well."

"Wow." Magnolia flopped backward. "Are there others who could still be after you? And Gemma?"

"No, hon. Not to worry. The defector they wanted recently died of natural causes. Our team took the rest of them down." Olivia lifted her knees, her side aching again. "My intel wasn't useful to anyone but them."

"Oh." Magnolia's face went limp. "Zork wasn't on his honeymoon?"

"Only long enough to get Bertie somewhere safe." Olivia adjusted her pillow and turned slowly toward Magnolia. "I never would have put a sales job over you. It killed me knowing that's what you thought. The birthday parties, amusement parks, your graduation. I never missed those things for a sales job. I missed them because people's lives depended on it. Sometimes the safety of the country did. It's been torture not to tell you."

"I had no idea it was something like this. I wish I would've known."

"Telling you wasn't an option."

"No, I'm sure it wasn't. It's just hard to wrap my head around. I've held so much resentment…"

"I know you have. You've sacrificed too. And not by choice."

"I'm not sure if that helps or makes it worse."

"Give it time, honey. And keep talking to me about it. You aren't wrong to feel any of the ways you do."

Magnolia's shoulders loosened as the tension seemed to ebb. "I'm okay. Just a little blindsided as you say." She tightened the blanket around her. "How did you know Gemma needed help at Luper?"

"I didn't. But she sounded so troubled when we last spoke I knew something was off. Had a gut feeling she might go there and hide."

"She feels tremendous guilt, you know. Blames herself for everything."

"I know. I remember a lot of what she said to me last night." She shifted her hips. "You'd think everything she did would count for something with the court."

"Well, it doesn't."

"She kicked-ass in the cemetery. She is one brave young woman."

"Heard you did the same. Lucky you weren't the one who killed those guys."

"Lucky? The truth is I thought I did. And I didn't care."

"Oh." Magnolia sat in silence for a moment. "I need to get Gem. She doesn't even know you're okay."

"Let her sleep. She and that baby need all the rest they can get after what they've been through." Olivia rested her cheek against the pillow. "She promised me she'd never try and run away again. I think she's accepted the idea of Seattle now."

"I hope so. The police found her duffle bag and backpack at the river. She was trying to leave the state. If she doesn't comply with this plea agreement, they'll take this baby." Shards of light reflected off the window and shone in Magnolia's eyes. "It would hurt all of us if they took this child."

"Well, what do you know," Olivia simpered. "You've already bonded with this baby and she's not even here yet."

Magnolia sneered in agreement. She poured ice in a cup and sprinkled a few chunks in her mouth. "Did you know Bertie offered to let Gemma and the baby live with her?"

"*No.*"

"I had to talk her out of it. Like I did you. The truth is, none of us is in the position to raise a child for Gemma."

"I suppose. But I am safe to be with now—"

"No, Mom. She needs to be with me. And I want to make it work. I really do."

"Then you will. And I think you're right. She does need to be with you. Sure sweet of Bertie to want to help, though."

Clouds settled over the sun, blanketing the room with a shadow. "You've truly been doing all this spy stuff since I was born?"

"Since before. Zork and your father worked together before we met. He was with your dad when he died. That part is true."

Magnolia's chest expanded with one deep breath. "This is so much to take in."

"I know it is. I'm sorry."

"Don't be. I want to know as much as you can tell me."

"Well, I did travel overseas a lot, but I was collecting intelligence, not meeting a sales quota. I worked as a medic too."

"A medic? So you *do* have medical training?"

Olivia snickered. "A lot."

"Holy smokes."

"I can't tell you everything we did, or why, but I can tell you I loved my job. You can be proud of your father, too. He earned the highest medal of honor there is in the CIA."

"Wow."

"We both did. The medals are locked in the bank vault. I can give them to you now. He'd want you to have them."

Magnolia reached for a tissue. "I hardly know you do I? I never appreciated what a powerful, brave mother I had. And still have. What a career…"

"Almost all of the clandestine operations we took part in were successful. Except for missing time with you, I don't regret a thing."

"It must have been hard juggling it all. How strange that you were basically a lie my whole life."

"You held the only part of me that wasn't. You and Gemma both held the one authentic part of myself that never changed—my love for you as a mother. That part was genuine."

"I never doubted that, Mom." Magnolia's face softened, her hands kneading the sides of her arms. "But I am surprised you wanted to be parents doing this kind of work."

"We wanted a family more than anything. Your dad was crazy about being a father, and I always dreamt of being a mother. Just like Gemma." She reached for Magnolia's hand and squeezed. "Your dad and I risked everything for this country and we were honored to do it. But we also longed for a normal life of balance between work and family. We didn't get that—but we did get you."

Magnolia tenderly adjusted the blankets over her mother's side. "You must know a lot of things we don't. No wonder you spout off so much about politics on social media."

"That was a lie too. It's not allowed. Can't post anything regarding what's happening in this country. But trust me, Zork and I know the truth about that too. All of it…"

"Oh, I wish you could tell me." Magnolia waited.

Olivia's facial expression didn't change.

"Okay, you won't. I get it." Magnolia stood and twisted her back until it popped. "Sorry I complained so much as a kid. It had to be tough on you."

"Don't apologize. You had every right to feel the"

way you did. It wasn't your fault. Or your doing."

Magnolia's features relaxed, her gaze weightless when it fell on Olivia.

"I swear I keep catching whiffs of your father's after-shave... Maybe telling you all this brought him back..." Olivia's nose lifted when she breathed in and sighed. "You will know the truth, and the truth will set you free... I can't tell you how many times I've recited that. I've waited so long for this day."

Magnolia whisked a tear off her cheekbone, nodding gently. She ambled to the door. "Your granddaughter needs to know you're alive." When she reached for the handle, it opened on its own.

In came Gemma.

"Hey!" Magnolia yelped. "Sweetie, look! She's okay."

"I know," Gemma said sure of herself.

"You know? You're not even the least bit surprised?"

"Nope. It was the last thing Grandpa Sam whispered in my ear. Sit back down, Mama. I have a bunch of things to tell you guys. And I promise—this is going to curl your toes and make your socks roll off."

Chapter Forty-Seven

Letting Go of a Dream

Spring came right on time. One last cold snap threatened the peaches and pears in March, but all the fruit trees blossomed by April. Yellow daffodils, full of splendor, opened across the fields. By May, everyone had tucked away their wool caps and gloves, and the air tasted fresh and new again.

A high canopy of leaves let creamy light fall over Nani's picnic table where Gemma sat in the gathering dusk. The pear-green fields of winter wheat swayed like silk in the gentle wind, pollen floating on eddies of air like cotton puffs.

Gemma blew her nose hard, her eyes raw from itching when she heard Mama's voice.

"I'm home," she announced. "Only for the weekend though."

Gemma didn't leap for joy. Not like she used to. At thirty-eight weeks along there was no leaping.

Mama approached Gemma sitting spread-eagle on the bench.

"I'd get up, but I'd rather not," Gemma told her.

"No need. Not so easy anymore is it?"

Gemma ignored her.

"I think your tummy has grown all it can."

"*She* has grown all she can," Gemma spat out,

shifting her bottom in search of a soft spot. "Why did you come home?" She didn't care how snarky she sounded.

"To see you. And have dinner together at Bertie's."

"I'm not in the mood."

"Why not?"

"I don't feel like talking to people. Or acting like I'm happy."

"Still seeing your counselor, hon?"

"I have no choice. Why?"

"Well—"

"Don't panic, Mama. Look at me. I can't run away. I can't run, period." She picked at a fingernail.

"Your Nani's worried about you too."

"Nani does not worry. She knows it doesn't help."

"Well, that's true except when it comes to you."

Gemma rubbed the inside corners of her eyes again. She couldn't satisfy the tickle.

"Your mom's right." They flinched when Nani set a tray of hot mugs on the table. "Okay if I join you?"

"Of course," Mama said. She shifted toward Gemma again. "Honey, I'm concerned you're depressed. All the changing hormones and—"

"It's not hormones!" Her jaw clenched. "And of course I'm depressed! Nothing worked out the way I wanted. No offense, Mama, but living in Seattle was not my dream. And it isn't River's either. So don't blame my hormones!"

Mama and Nani said zilch. They warmed their noses over tea and sipped.

"Everything that happened is all my fault, and everyone knows it." Gemma's head dropped when she said, "A precious baby boy could have died because of

385

me."

Nani set her tea down and spoke words that sang like a river of wisdom. "Forgive yourself, Tink."

"Why?"

"Because this will eat you up otherwise. The anger—the bitterness—the guilt. You did your best, but you made a mistake. One mistake," Nani said.

"And now my whole life is ruined because of it."

"Your whole life? One mistake is not your whole life. You're also the bravest woman I've ever known. You saved our lives. One mistake does not define all of who you are."

"How about two mistakes? Because it was me who almost got you killed."

"You're the only reason I wasn't. It was my responsibility to protect you from the evil in my world. But we have only those wicked, despicable men to blame. No one else."

"Well, losing River is my own fault. I'm trying not to blame anyone. Including the judge."

"But you aren't losing River," Mama corrected. "And there's no reason to believe you will."

"Yes, there is."

"Why?"

"Because I'm not moving to Seattle." Gemma cradled her belly. "Sorry, Mama."

Nani's eyes sparked. "Gemma, you *will* lose her if you don't."

"I know that. But she has to stay here. Even if she's not with me."

Mama's chin jutted back. "What are you saying?"

"I'm saying my caseworker said she would help. I want River to have a family who will keep her safe."

"But she does have a family who will keep her safe. She has *us.*" Mama's voice filled with alarm. "I want to help you, Gem. You don't have to think about giving her away."

"Yes, I do. It's what Creator wants for River."

"What do you mean?" Mama cautiously repositioned the spoon in her mug.

"I keep seeing it in my mind—River swinging from our tree. Now I know why. She's supposed to stay here where she belongs. My feelings are telling me it's a sign."

"A *sign*? Gemma, feelings are not facts. Don't—"

"Sometimes they are, Mama! I told you—I believe Creator wants her here. So yes, it was a sign." Gemma wondered if her eyes looked as dull as she felt. "It wouldn't be right to raise her anywhere else. She needs to be near the river, and Luper, and Lolly, and her daddy. This is her home. Even if she won't live in mine."

"Honey..." Mama said. "Not every thought that runs through your mind is some kind of sign. You can't let your imagination—"

"*Maggie.*" Nani's voice brought everyone to attention. "If Gemma believes she's been given a sign, then she's been given a sign. I believe her."

This time, Mama didn't argue. Instead, she tenderly brushed Gemma's locks off her face, smoothing her hair back.

"She's meant to be here," Gemma said again. "Don't ask me how I know. I just do. I have to give her the life she's supposed to have. River and I are *not* moving to Seattle. Nothing will change my mind."

Mama had a far-off look in her eyes. "Okay, then,"

she said. "It is your decision."

"I know." Like a lazy breeze, Gemma blew a stream of air over her tea, skimming the steam off the top. "Letting go of my dream is the hardest thing I've ever done, but I know it's Creator's plan, so it will all be okay. I believe that." Trinkets of sadness hung on Gemma's words. "I did my best. And I honestly tried."

"Oh, Tink." Nani cradled Gemma's hand and planted it on her own heart. "You only keep growing braver."

"I didn't know being brave would be so painful."

Nani's eyes told Gemma she understood.

"It's an unselfish act of love..." Mama said. She turned away blubbering. She stared off into space, but she was blubbering.

"This will be hard for all of us," Nani said. "But we'll focus on what we have. And what we have is a lifetime to spend with River—to help shape the way she grows up. You'll always be her mother, Gem. And you'll always be involved. That's how an open adoption works, right, Maggie?"

"Yes," Mama said wiping her face. "Have you spoken to anyone about this yet?"

"No. But your attorney friend said she knew a family... Right?"

"She does. They're lovely people who will—"

"No more." Gemma clapped her hands over her ears. "I can't hear this right now. Not yet." She bowed over her mug and inhaled the lavender scent steaming into nothingness. "Nani, will you and Zorro make sure they're not bad guys?"

"Of course we will."

"You'll have the final decision in all of this,"

Mama said.

"Okay." Gemma traced a finger around the rim of her mug.

"It may not be the exact dream you expected, Tink," Nani offered. "But your child will always be yours. Just in a different way."

"I'm sad you guys can't be a nani and great-nani the way you wanted. The way I wanted."

"We'll still be her grandparents," Mama assured. "Like Nani said, it'll just be in a different way. Once you get to know the family, you'll—"

"Mama, stop. If we talk about the family I won't feel like eating tonight. I don't want to talk about them or any of this at Bertie's either. Not one word."

"I'm sorry... I understand." Mama leaned back. "Whenever you're ready."

Nani checked her phone. "We need to get going."

Mama stepped over the bench and held out an arm for Gemma. She tucked in close under the protection of her Mama's wing as they tottered away from Nani's backyard.

A fat, blazing moon and one brave star appeared as the sun faded from the sky. It was just enough light to get them to where they needed to go.

****

When Bertie opened the door, she took Gemma in her arms first. "I'm thrilled you're here. I made your favorite tonight. Fractured tacos. Are you hungry?"

"I might be starving, but I'm not sure," she said. "I'm sorta down in the dumps, Bertie."

"Well then we'll do our best to cheer you up. Let me take your jacket."

Zorro stood at the counter shredding cheese. "Hey

389

there, Ace. Want a hug?" Gemma leaned in and felt a big bear of love embracing her.

"Do you guys like traveling back and forth between your houses?" Gemma asked.

"It's worked out great," Zorro said.

"Whose house do you like best?" Gemma kept glancing between them waiting for an answer.

"Mine!" he hollered.

Bertie laughed. "He's right. We love his house best."

Nani eyeballed new construction at the side of Bertie's living room. "I bet that's gonna be a second bathroom. Am I right, Bertie?" Nani winked.

"You sure are. Zork's adding a whole separate wing with it. I can't wait."

"Why do that if you like Zorro's house better?" Gemma asked.

"Because I'm selling this one," Bertie piped. "And I've never been happier about it."

"What?!" Nani's eyes nearly popped out of her head. "You can't be serious."

"Oh, but I am. I'm moving in with Zork as soon as I can. I'm getting my own bathroom there too," she grinned.

"I thought—"

"It's all good, Olivia. It's what I want now."

"What changed your mind?" Nani planted both hands on her hips.

"Gemma did."

"Huh?" they said in unison.

"What do you mean?" Nani asked.

"I mean, Gemma, River, and Maggie are the proud new owners of this home. That's what I mean. The new addition is for them."

"Wait." Gemma shook her head. "River isn't mine to keep. You don't understand, Bertie. And Mama lives in Seattle."

"Not for long," Bertie said.

"She's right, Gemma." Mama smiled. "I bought this house for you, for River, and—"

"How can River and I have a house together?"

"Because I'm moving back, and we're the family who will be raising her. The perfect one, I might add. She needs you, Gemma. She needs her mama."

"But... You said you knew the family who wanted River..."

"I do! It's us, sweetie. And hopefully Walter too, if he wants. You'll have your own entrance, and we'll both have privacy when we want it. Zork and I designed it together."

Gemma's mouth wouldn't shut. At first, either would Nani's.

"You're moving back to Sugar Creek, Mag?" Nani sounded like she didn't believe it either.

"Yes! It's a done deal. Already accepted a cash offer on the condo."

Gemma had to sit. "But the judge. I thought—"

"As long as you're with me, the agreement stands, whether we live in Seattle, Sugar Creek, or Timbuktu."

"But your job, Mama, and your cool new condo..."

"I'm opening an office here for the firm. It's the same job in a new location. And we'll make this home as cool as the condo. You'll see." Mama squeezed Gemma's hand. "This is what I want."

"What terrific news!" Nani enveloped Mama in a hug.

"Why didn't you tell me sooner?" Gemma asked.

"Or me?!" Nani flashed a snarly face at Zorro.

"I had to be sure about the job before I spilled the beans. Besides, I wanted Bertie to be the one to tell you. It was all her idea."

"Bertie's idea?" Nani's face glowed with excitement.

"This calls for a celebration!" Bertie bellowed.

Gemma frowned. "But I thought you wanted your house to stay in your family, Bertie?"

"Well, yes, of course I do. And it is! You and your mom *are* my family."

River swinging on our tree was *my sign.* Gemma closed her eyes, sending a silent prayer of thanks.

Zorro poured sparkling cider into five long-stemmed champagne glasses and handed them out. He raised his glass so high it barely missed the pendant light hanging over Bertie's kitchen counter. "To the Porter women. The whole gaggle of them," he toasted.

Right when Gemma had decided the entire universe had lost its balance, it straightened itself out again. *Another miracle.*

"To Bertie!" Nani cheered.

"For keeping us all together," Mama added, clinking everyone's glasses.

"And to Mama," Gemma chimed. "And to River, who is mine again. Mine to keep." She examined her belly. "You can come out anytime you want now, girl," she said. "Because I don't have to let you go anymore." As Gemma's hand splayed over her ribcage, smoothing out the wrinkles in her shirt, a powerful wave of emotion arose. Feelings with a message. She swore it came directly from the womb. She felt her eyes balloon.

"This crazy good news is enough to put me in labor."

The room froze. Everyone ogled Gemma.

"I don't mean now."

They loosened up and continued sipping.

"But I think I'll need a ride to the hospital tonight. Well, not tonight. More like three in the morning." Gemma was sure of herself when she said it. "Then things will *really* get exciting right before the sun comes up."

The kitchen came to a standstill again.

"Don't even ask," Nani told them. "*She knows*."

****

The next day was barely three hours old when Gemma's water broke. River made her entrance into the Porter family by sunrise, with hair black as a crow's wing and eyes as blue as the solitary pools in the river.

Inspired by Gemma's heroism in the air, Walter decided to be brave too. He insisted on being in the room with Gemma for the birth of their child.

Nani revived him with smelling salts as soon as he dropped.

"I knew we'd lose him," Gemma told Nani. "And by the way, it felt harder than cement."

But the best part of the labor and delivery? Gemma never had to say good-bye to her daughter. Only hello.

Chapter Forty-Eight

Love is Ageless

Time passed like twenty pages turning.

That year, friendships grew, a baby was born, bunco played on, the powwow returned, and Olivia safely retired. Fully retired at last. And so did Zork.

"Funny, isn't it?" Olivia asked the reverend. "I barely remember the snow and ice from a few months ago." They sat on their horses when a sudden, uplifting rush of silent birds circled above them. Olivia watched, filled with peace.

"And all that soggy rain in the spring." He snickered. The reverend gave his horse a little kick. "The dog days of summer are back, and I love it. But I have to wonder if we'd appreciate it as much if we had it year round." His eyes swept across the jewel-green countryside—the fields lush again, hazelnut trees billowing with leaves, and chickadees singing their hymns.

"True. You were right about another thing too." She gave Banjo kissing sounds, smooching him forward.

"What's that?"

"Something you said a while back. How the soul is ageless."

"Oh yeah?" He pulled a cowboy wild rag from his

back pocket and wiped his neck.

"Yeah. I decided love is ageless too."

The reverend reined his horse back long enough to give Olivia a look. "I agree. I'd say our marriages are proof of it. Hasn't grown old for either of us."

"No, it hasn't. My love for Sam hasn't aged a day."

"It never will then," he told her. "At least we both have that. And a whole lot more."

A clear, tender breeze soaked with sun, blew over the hills. Olivia brushed away the strand of hair dangling in her face. "I suppose loss is the cost of love, isn't it?"

The reverend drew in a long, deep breath as if freeing himself of something. "I guess it is."

"Most people never get what we had, Hap. Not even close."

"I don't take it for granted for a minute. I know you don't either."

Banjo slowed, stopping at the top of the hill. Olivia fumbled for her pocket. "I still do it. Still reach for my binoculars to check on things," she said.

"Leave them home this time?"

"Yes. Still trying to break the habit of searching for danger."

"I imagine it'll take a while. But I think it's a good idea. You deserve a rest."

"Zork and I both," she said.

The two horses met shoulder to shoulder, put their noses together and shared the air. "I'm proud to know you, Olivia Porter. I don't know why I haven't said that to you sooner. You're an amazing woman, you know that?"

When he said it, Olivia thought she heard

something different in his voice. Something new. *I love his face.* Something stirred inside her, like a massive iceberg beginning to melt. *I'd like to touch his hand again.* The thought made her spine tingle.

"Thank you, Hap." Olivia's cheeks betrayed her. She turned away.

"What's wrong?" he asked.

"I don't know. I guess I'm embarrassed."

"You? Embarrassed? Of what?"

"I'm used to hiding my life. Of never talking about a thing I've done."

"Wish you could tell me more, but I know you've done extraordinary things."

"I've never had anyone outside the agency compliment me for it." But Olivia knew it was more— the real reason for her flushing cheeks.

"Well, then. I thank both you and Zork for your service and sacrifice. And I thank Sam, too. Hope he hears me."

"Thanks, Hap."

The reverend nudged his horse along. "You know, I have to say it again. I'm so relieved we understand each other the way we do."

"Me too."

"It takes such a huge weight off. Not having to 'date,' no one getting hurt because you're not in love with them and never will be, never having to explain why the attraction isn't there. Know what I mean?"

Olivia's mood plunged and when it did, she recognized a familiar sense of loss. *This is what happened with Zork. What the hell is wrong with me?* She tried not to show the dive her heart took. She straightened in her saddle. "We are *so* lucky." Olivia hoped she sounded confident when she said it.

"Oh, I consider it more than luck," he said. "It's an act of God. Has to be."

"Wow." Olivia made a face. "Sounds serious." *These feelings are about Sam, not Hap. Let it go.*

"Of course," the reverend continued, "in the unlikely event you ever changed your mind, I'd trust you to let me know."

"Let you know?"

"Yes. Let me know if your feelings toward me ever changed. Because I'd consider that an act of God too, and in that case I think we'd have to be open to it."

"Open to it?"

"Yes. Open to being more than friends."

Her mood kicked up again. *What is going on?*

"Well," Olivia said judiciously, "I suppose we'd have to be open, yes. I suppose in that case you'd be right."

"If you ever changed your mind," he repeated.

"Right." She paused. "Only me?"

"Only you. My mind *has* changed." His words grew rich and steady.

"What?"

"I just this minute recognized it."

"Are you serious?" His words tapped her heart.

"And now I've thrown a huge monkey wrench into everything. Sorry, but I have to be honest."

"It's okay, Hap, but—"

"Now, please. Do not worry. Like I said, we'd both have to change our minds—not just me. I get it. And I'll never discuss it with you again unless you want to. You have my word."

"Thank you for understanding." Olivia said it even

as she felt a ping of joy. *This is not about Hap,* she reminded herself. *It's Sam I'm longing for.* The thought held back a gush of joy threatening to fill her. *Or is it?* Suddenly, nothing seemed sure.

"I don't want our friendship to end," he said. "I enjoy your companionship too much."

"I feel the same way, Reverend."

He raised a brow.

"I mean, Hap!"

"It's all good," he said. A quiet fortitude surrounded him even as he shifted in his saddle. "Let's see what this horse can do. I'd like to see how fast he can run right now." He dotted his last utterance with an awkward chuckle.

Me too... Without another word to the reverend, Olivia slapped Banjo's dusty-blue hindquarter and took off, his burnished mane like a shiny penny against thunderclouds. "Burn the breeze, boy!"

****

Olivia stepped into the darkened barn, leading Banjo through the dusky light into his stall. The sun had melted, leaving silky scarves of pink and amethyst draped across the horizon. "No need to turn on lights. We can bask in the natural light, boy. It's finally safe."

The quiet filled her with calm. Being alone was nothing to shun. *After all these years, I still cherish it.*

She nuzzled Banjo, closed her eyes and breathed in his horse scent—a relaxing, crisp smell, like a wild meadow of sweet clover. She spoke to him in quiet clipped phrases. "Such a pretty boy. You ran so fast tonight. Exactly like Buster would have. What a good boy." She left him and strolled into the field, the light of sunset nearly gone.

"Sam," she said. "Give me a sign. I won't move on without it. I need a sign, or…" Olivia swallowed, a tight knot expanding in her throat. She nudged the words out. "Or I'll never leave you. I can't without your help."

She couldn't deny the joy that had trickled in when she heard Hap's words. Not really.

Can't leave him, or won't?

"Won't," she replied.

Olivia hiked across the property, past the walnut tree, along the creek, and through the orchards. A sense of safety roosted in her soul. The freedom to be lost in her thoughts without worry of snipers, drones, or enemies lurking in the shadows was utterly thrilling. The freedom to be her true self, uncensored, even more relieving. She didn't expect she'd ever be able to sleep at night without a pistol near her, but at least she would sleep.

And then Olivia strolled past the plum tree. "The plum tree!" she yelled. She aimed her flashlight. "You're alive!" Olivia inspected the new growth budding from every branch. "You survived," she said, hardly believing it.

Is this the sign?

She crept through blackberry bushes to inspect the backside, still marveling at its will to live.

"If there's any doubt about it, it's not a sign," she said to no one. Olivia slipped out of her boots, peeled off her socks, and found the warmth of the days sun still trapped in the grass beneath her feet.

With every step closer to home, she grew more certain. *My life is absolutely fine the way it is. Sam already gave me everything I need to be entirely content. I don't need any sign to know that.*

Chapter Forty-Nine

The Mother-Daughter Circle

"The Indian needs no writings; words that are true sink deep into his heart where they remain in silence. He never forgets them."
~Chief Four Guns Oglala, Lakota

The morning unfolded in perfect stillness below the big blue bowl of sky over Oregon. The Porters had reclaimed their tree for summertime picnics, the branches of the old maple cooling the feverish August air. Baby River slept comfortably under its wings.

"Walter stayed awake all night, Mama."

"What happened?"

"I think River's teeth are busting in."

"Already? Did you give her the ice ring?"

"It helped, but only when Walter held it. He slept on the floor next to her crib all night. Every time she fussed, he bounced up and cuddled her with the ring. He can hold her real good now."

"Oh my goodness—such a helpful, loving daddy."

"He'd do anything for her."

"I see that. She's lucky to have you two."

"She wouldn't, if it weren't for you. You're the reason, Mama. Not just Bertie." Gemma's easy joy spilled into view when she said it.

"Next to having you," Mama said, "I've never been happier about a decision in all my life."

Gemma's face raised slowly, as if she had heard the most amazing message of all time. And maybe she had. She told Mama, "I guess that's what mothers do—we save each other."

Mama agreed. "A mother's love knows no bounds. And honestly, Gem, I've never seen a better mother than you. That's the truth." She kept a steady eye on Gemma when she said it, her pupils big and bright. "I get why you and Nani love this old tree so much. It's breathtaking here."

"See? We told you so!" Gemma clambered off the maple. "Can you hand River to me? If she wakes up, I want her to watch me put flowers on the graves."

Mama placed her grandbaby in Gemma's cradled arms. Strands of River's luxuriant raven-black hair wafted under her nose, the aroma as wild and sweet as the antique roses Nani grew.

Mama settled back against the bowl of the tree. "Will Walter be joining us?"

"No. He and Nani are painting River's room."

"Oh, that's right."

"I picked the color." Gemma latched the infant seat, readjusting River's flax-blue cotton sundress. "Did you see it yet?"

"No, what did you pick?"

"Vintage Periwinkle." Gemma reached in the bucket of apricot and red roses and arranged a little bouquet for Harriet's grave first. "We're painting it on all four walls. Isn't that perfect?"

"Sounds gorgeous. Maybe I'll try it somewhere in my half of the house too."

"You should! And her ceiling will be sky blue like my tiara today. Do you love the way I match my tiaras to River's outfits now? Oh, and did I tell you Bertie's making us new rose head wreaths? Which I think is *so* nice of her. But anyway, the name of the ceiling paint is Heavenly Mystery. Do you like it?"

Gemma waited.

"Do you like it?" she asked louder.

More silence.

Gemma turned. "Mama?"

"Gemma," Mama said, her voice quaking. "Come here—fast."

"Why?"

"Quickly." Mama motioned.

Gemma double checked the buckle on River's seat and darted to Mama. "What is it?"

"Here." Mama pointed to the soft spot at the center of her cheek. "I felt it right here. Like someone blew on me."

"What?"

"A strong puff of air hit my skin."

Gemma gasped.

"Like this." Mama blew on Gemma's cheek. "It's perfectly still today. There's no wind at all. I know it sounds crazy, but—"

"No! It's not crazy. I believe you. It happened to me too!" Gemma pointed to baby Harriet's grave. "Right over there."

"It came out of the crack of this tree," Mama marveled.

Gemma's mouth quivered. "From here?" She rested a hand over the deepest crevice.

"Yes," Mamma said. "Strangest thing. It felt like

403

someone's breath."

"It was." Gemma's eyes sprang around like pinballs, searching for ghosts. "Or maybe his spirit."

"Whose spirit?"

"Nani poured your dad's dead body into our tree."

"What?!" Mamma stiffened. "You mean his ashes?"

"Yes."

"Here in this tree?" Mama looked creeped out.

"Don't worry, Mama. You're not sitting on him. You're *surrounded* by him…" Gemma's head tilted, her eyes fixated on baby Harriet's grave.

"What is it?" Mama asked. "Gemma?"

She didn't answer—her gaze unmoving.

"Honey, what's wrong?"

When a swallowtail butterfly flittered black and gold around Gemma's face, her attention sprang back. She dashed to River and checked her diaper. "I have to tell Nani." She carried River back to Mama. "Can you take her again? Is that okay?"

"Of course, but—"

"I have to tell Nani right away. In person."

"Tell her what?"

Gemma kissed River's forehead and then gave her a smooch on each cheek. "I need to tell her what happened to you. And something else."

"Something else?" Mama scooted down the trunk and planted both feet on the baked earth, snuggling River to her breast. "What is it?"

"I'm not sure." Gemma lifted her face to the white-hot heat of the sun, and held it there, eyes squeezed shut. "Maybe it's the voice of light. I think it comes from Creator." Her face unrumpled. "It happens,

Mama. And this time it's only for Nani. She needs to know." Gemma sprinted to Lolly, the gate clanging hard behind her.

"Needs to know what?!" Mama yelled.

"I'll explain later! I have to hurry so I don't forget!" She jerked Lolly's reins, hedging back to say one last thing. "There's all natural, unscented, organic wet wipes and clean diapers in the bag," she said breathlessly. "Oh, and a full bottle I pumped this morning. Just in case. But I'll breast feed again when I get back." She reached down her bra, adjusting her nursing pads. Sometimes merely thinking about it made her milk squirt. "And the icy chew toy is in the thermal bag. In case you need that too." She whipped Lolly around again and took off, floating effortlessly above her, cantering across the field.

When Gemma glanced back, Mama waved. It was then she took in the full beauty of their tree. The leafy paradise stood stoic against the pale turquoise sky, sheltering the living and the dead with unequaled grace.

Before she lost sight of Luper entirely, Gemma turned for one last view. This time she had to squint. The old maple's massive boughs cradled the sun, glistening in green glory like a crown of jewels against the sky. She filled her chest, recalling its cheery aroma. *That's it! Baked apple...*

Soon she would find Nani and take her outside. First, she would describe what happened to Mama in their tree. And then she would take hold of Nani's hands, the silver drop necklace gleaming against her neck, and recite the words she had been given. The words meant only for her.

"This is your sign..." she told Nani. "Follow joy

wherever it takes you next." The words encircled them, grandmother and granddaughter, sparkling like diamonds. "Don't ask me how I know," Gemma said. "I just do."

Nani lowered gently to the ground—as if she had heard a miracle. A wild, awakened happiness streamed down her face with such strength, Gemma wept right along with her.

She crawled down next to Nani and cleared her crying. "I felt you in those words, Nani. There was so much love... This is your sign..." she recited again. "Follow joy wherever it takes you next."

And that's what Nani did.

The message was for Nani, but the words sank deep into Gemma's heart.

****

Excursions to the old maple never grew old. And Gemma never tired of chronicling for River the miracles that had taken place there. Both of them anticipated summer picnics at Luper with the same zeal Gemma had trumpeted at age five.

To start, they would tie satin ribbons around small bouquets and place them at the markers—always kneeling at baby Harriet's grave first. Then they climbed into their tree, breathing in the rose-sweetened air lifting from the nearby bushes. Once they settled into the craggy bowl of the trunk with a basket of apples and cheese, River would ask her mother to tell her the true-life stories she had witnessed there.

"First, there was perfect stillness," Gemma always began. "And then a stirring in the air... And you, River," she reminded, "you were the happiest miracle of all—better than the best gift *ever* under my

Christmas tree."

"Pass them down," Gemma told her. "Share my words the way the Cow Creek community has taught us to. Place them in a pocket in your heart so you'll never forget. Tell all the Porter women who follow us about the lessons we've learned—how sometimes you must take risks to learn to be brave. And especially remember Nani's words: *'Never forget what Creator showed us. Death is not the end and joy is for the living.'* Think of these stories, River, and you'll know that's the truth."

Her words encircled them, mother and daughter, in the perfect stillness of a midsummer day—glittering like the river in sunlight.

A word about the author...

Debra Whiting Alexander won multiple awards for her debut novel, *Zetty*, including the prestigious 2018 WILLA Literary Award in Contemporary Fiction. Prior to making the leap into Women's Fiction, she authored numerous nonfiction books for children and families recovering from trauma. With a Ph.D. in Psychology, Debra's career in mental health spans thirty years in California, New York, and Oregon. Her passion now is to write stories about the humor, strength, and spirit of unconventional women—matters of the heart and soul. Debra currently lives with her husband and two labs in Oregon, where she enjoys walks through the orchards and the pioneer cemetery with her granddaughter. This is her second novel. Learn more at:

https://www.debrawhitingalexander.com

~

https://www.facebook.com/
TheAuthorDebraWhitingAlexander

~

https://www.twitter.com/DebraWAlexander

~

https://www.instagram.com/DebraWhitingAlexander

CPSIA information can be obtained
at www.ICGtesting.com
Printed in the USA
BVHW051343070821
613846BV00009B/1055